Praise for *Her Darkes___*

"Gritty and terrifying, *Her Darke___*
story and I will never be able to l___
again. Ms. Patch masterfully we___
characters and a villain that won ___
what happens next."

—Natalie Walters, Carol Award finalist and author of *Living Lies*
and the Harbored Secrets series

"*Her Darkest Secret* takes the reader on an intense experience
with a superbly deviant serial killer. For readers who love all things
Criminal Minds and behavioral science, this story will play with your
senses and toy with your mind!"

—Jaime Jo Wright, author of the Christy Award–winning novel
The House on Foster Hill

"*Her Darkest Secret*…is a taut, psychological thriller with deeply
relatable characters. Patch's brilliantly created plot will keep readers
turning pages until they reach the shocking conclusion. I highly
recommend it!"

—Nancy Mehl, author of the Quantico Files series

"*Her Darkest Secret* keeps you on edge until the very end! Patch
knows how to masterfully weave a suspenseful tale. This is one book
you won't want to miss."

—Christy Barritt, *USA TODAY* bestselling author

"Read with all the lights on! The suspense increases with every page
until it twists into a deadly spiral that had me racing through the final
scenes to the satisfying and redemptive conclusion."

—Lynn H. Blackburn, author of the award-winning
Dive Team Investigations series

"*Her Darkest Secret* is a spellbinding thriller bursting with dynamic
walk-off-the-page characters, mind-bending plot twists and a
swoon-worthy unforgettable reunion romance. Hold on to the edge of
your seats, readers!"

—Elizabeth Goddard, bestselling author of *Present Danger*

"Beautifully flawed characters face off against a deadly serial killer with a
complex criminal psychology. This gritty thriller is one you won't want to
miss!"

—*USA TODAY* and *Publishers Weekly* bestselling author Lisa Phillips

"*Her Darkest Secret* is a gripping story of loss and redemption with many
twists and turns that kept me guessing until the very end."

—Terri Reed, *Publishers Weekly* bestselling author of *Alaskan Rescue*

Visit the Author Profile page at LoveInspired.com for more titles.

HER DARKEST SECRET

JESSICA R. PATCH

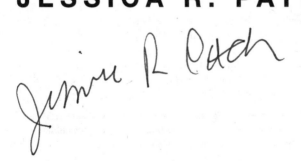

LOVE INSPIRED

Stories to uplift and inspire

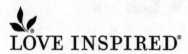

LOVE INSPIRED®

Stories to uplift and inspire

ISBN-13: 978-1-335-53002-8

Her Darkest Secret

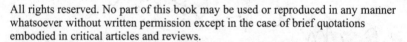
Love Inspired
22 Adelaide St. West, 41st Floor
Toronto, Ontario M5H 4E3, Canada
www.LoveInspired.com

Printed in U.S.A.

For Jesus, the lover of my soul. All that You've given me,
I give back to You. Always for Your honor and glory.

And God said, Let there be light: and there was light. And God saw the light, that it was good: and God divided the light from the darkness.
—*Genesis* 1:3–4

HER
DARKEST
SECRET

Prologue

"Here, kitty, kitty." His voice echoed through the forest.

Disoriented and unable to gauge distance, she pressed on, her brain pushing her feet faster than they could carry her. The bitter wind nipped through the thin, white gown he'd forced her to wear. Brittle twigs, pine cones and fallen tree limbs broke through the tender skin of her bare feet with sharp stings.

An owl hooted; a coyote howled.

Naked branches clawed her face, ripping skin from her cheeks and chin. Her lungs burned as she sucked in the frigid gales, but she couldn't slow down. The man in the white-feathered mask with the long beak would kill her if he caught her.

"I hear you, naughty kitty," he drawled in a singsong tone, his high-pitched voice like tiny shards of glass slicing through her flesh and penetrating her bones.

Her heart lurched into her throat and pulsed in her ears.

She couldn't die. Not at seventeen. She hadn't even experienced her first kiss. Hadn't chosen a college or gone to prom.

Tears sprung into the corners of her eyes, then raced across her skin into her hair.

Moonlight stabbed through the trees, teasing her with peeps of light. With hope that a road would be nearby.

"I smell you, kitty."

Her vision blurred. The crunching and cracking of footfalls hunting her halted.

She froze, struggling to hold her breath in case he could hear it. The tattered, lightweight gown fluttered in the wind, but she didn't dare move, blink, whimper.

Snap!

She darted ahead, but her hair tangled on a branch, wrenching her backward. Fire shot through her scalp, but she contained the scream rising in her throat. The quicker she worked to free herself, the more she fumbled.

"I'm close, kitty."

With a sharp pull, she broke away, leaving thick strands of hair hanging from the winter wood.

Crunching came louder, faster.

Nerve endings popped, muscles twitched and her blood raced hot.

She spied a huge tree, the bottom open to a dead, hollowed out middle. Bolting inside, she braced her arms and feet on each side; the smells of decaying carcasses and earth nailed her gag reflex with precision. She shimmied up as high as she could, concealing her bloody and broken feet from his view.

Wait him out. Tire him. Then go for help.

God, if You're at all for me, please don't let him find me. Keep me safe. Keep us all safe.

Arms shaking and legs trembling, she continued to hold

on. Hold out. But her muscles spasmed. Squeezing her eyes shut, she willed herself to stay strong.

Her breath plumed with every exhale.

"Hickory…"

She inhaled sharply and dug her fingers into the rotten, spongy wood.

Warmth flowed down her bare, filthy legs; she chomped her lower lip to keep it from quivering. The taste of iron coated her tongue, the smell of ammonia pierced her nose.

"Dickory…"

His voice reached out, its chilling tone wrapping around her heart like a vise.

Glancing up, she had nowhere to go.

She'd trapped herself. A burst of panic gripped her chest and wrung her breath away.

Something skittered across her hand, but she refused to react.

"Dock…"

No.

"The mouse…ran up…the clock."

Her heart hurt from the pounding force.

Quiet. So…quiet.

A small amount of pressure released in her lungs. Had he passed her by? Had she outsmarted him?

Suddenly, the white-feathered mask with the long nose splintered the darkness and he turned his sinister eyes upward; they bore into hers.

"Boo!"

Her blood-curdling cry rushed through the trees, startling a host of resting birds from their branches with a resounding flutter.

But nobody heard.

Not even God.

Chapter One

"'When this monster entered my brain, I will never know, but it is here to stay...'" Special Agent Fiona Kelly scanned the packed Loyola stadium-seating classroom. Every eye trained on her. Not a sound, not even a cell-phone interruption. "Most serial killers, like Dennis Radar, can't pinpoint the exact moment they craved to murder. But they all share a voracious appetite to inflict pain, exact control and take human life. Some killers are shaped by environment. Abuse, neglect, torture. Lack of love or a twisted falsehood called love. These killers are made. Not all fall into this category." She surveyed faces. One student covered her mouth. "Some serial killers are born that way."

Murmurs stirred the atmosphere, as if she was telling a ghost story around a campfire as they awaited the *boo* to scare them into laughter. If she didn't need the extra money, she wouldn't even be lecturing part-time at the university. These kids had no clue what was out there hunting, stalking and making campfire stories sound as terrorizing as a baby bunny.

"Your job won't be to determine which is which. It's to catch them. Whether born or made, they all have similar minds. And you'll have to learn to think like them." Fiona had spent eight years with the South Division of the Strange Crimes Unit before transferring two years ago here to Chicago with the Midwest Division.

But she'd been learning to think like a killer much longer than her career with the FBI.

"If you can't do that, then working in Violent Crimes—especially in the Strange Crimes Unit—probably isn't for you."

A girl that looked like she ought to be majoring in getting her "MRS degree" raised her hand. "Can you explain the difference between working for Violent or Strange Crimes since they both investigate serial killings?"

A decent question. "The Strange Crimes Unit only deals with the bizarre and unexplainable. Ninety-eight percent of these crimes will have warped religious undertones and ritualistic-type behavior. Sometimes we know that up front based on the nature of the crime or evidence, sometimes we don't know until after we apprehend the criminal. We do not handle mass shooters, serial rapists—unless it's considered strangely ritualistic or religious—or gangs and terrorists."

"Are there that many bizarre crimes?" she asked. "And how do you decide? Jeffrey Dahmer's crimes could be considered strange."

They'd be shocked to know how many bizarre crimes happened daily. "True, but cannibalism doesn't fall under strange, unless it has ritualistic undertones, or our caseloads are low and Violent Crimes needs a favor. On occasion, we will take a violent crime off their hands to aid in caseloads, such as cannibalism. We can and do assist other FBI divisions, as well as consult and profile for local law enforcement."

Another hand shot up. Fiona pointed to her. "The Funeral

Director was a Strange Crimes case. How does he differ from Dahmer?" the girl asked. "Did you work on that one—the Funeral Director?"

Fiona had transferred before that case came to the South Division. "No," she responded. "Florida falls into the South Division. We have four regions throughout the US—Northwest, North, Midwest and the South. We weren't called in to assist, but on occasion the regional divisions will aid and work in tandem."

If the South Division had needed help, Asa Kodiak wouldn't have called in the Midwest. The last person he'd want to see, let alone work with, was Fiona.

"As far as the differences, Dahmer was a cannibal and sex offender. The Funeral Director tortured women, then embalmed them alive. Which would have fallen under Violent Crimes. However—unlike Jeffrey Dahmer—Dorian Kosey Khan, aka the Funeral Director, murdered his victims as a sacrificial ritual to the god of death in hopes he'd give him reigning power in the underworld. That special brand of cuckoo landed him on the Strange Crimes doorstep."

"But how did they know that's why he was murdering the women?"

"Good question. At first local investigators led the charge, but when three victims were found, they enlisted the FBI, Violent Crimes. In their efforts, they discovered markings on each victim and called a member of the South Division's Strange Crimes Unit who is a religious behavioral analyst— he specializes in religions and religious behavior including rituals. When he concluded it was markings to the Egyptian god of death, Anubis, the case changed hands and the SCU took it from there." She missed Tiberius Granger's practical jokes and famous double burgers with fried eggs and bacon.

Her hips did not. "But sometimes it's not always that cut-and-dried."

"That's messed up," a young man in the back quipped and grinned.

"It is...*messed up.*" Criminal-justice majors pretty much all had the same notion.

Excitement. Anticipation. Intrigue.

Believing TV shows portrayed truth. Thirty to forty percent of these students were here because of *Criminal Minds* and *CSI.* Film made the occupation appear glamorous. Seductive. Where the good guys always won and fell in love with their therapists, if they were forced to visit one.

In reality, year one would be a wake-up call and many would toss in the towel over the mountains of paperwork alone. Year two, the nightmares would be in full swing. Insomnia. Paranoia. Agents rarely slept even when they had the opportunity.

By year five—if they hung on—they'd drink too much, likely have their first affair, and by years six to ten be divorced, cynical and maybe suicidal. But if they could survive all that and keep going, they might have the mettle it required to track down these monsters. And with each win it gave a sliver of hope that they could do it again and again. That maybe good would conquer evil in the bitter end.

Another hand shot up. A young man with hair hanging in his eyes. He'd have to cut that mop at some point. She automatically touched the back of her hair, lying at the nape of her neck. "What's the strangest crime you've ever encountered?"

Always the same questions. She bypassed the strangest crime she'd ever encountered and shared the strangest crime she'd ever solved.

A guy with a trendy man bun and eyes so blue they appeared photoshopped raised his hand. "Is it true that in your first year with the Violent Crimes Unit, you linked three murders to one man? The Nursery Rhyme Killer."

A burst of heat rose from her belly into her chest, tightening it.

Rhyme.

He'd been with her for almost twenty years, the driving force behind her career path. She woke up and fell asleep to him. "Yes." Since she'd linked the first three crimes with a death count of six people total, he'd strangled and staged his victims in different nursery rhyme scenes two more times. Two more lives snuffed out. The last four years had been silent.

"How did you do it?" someone else chimed in. "Figure out they linked and that they were nursery rhymes?"

Sheer luck. Fiona inhaled and exhaled. "The first victims were abducted seventeen years ago in the Memphis area. Four teenage girls. Forced into white gowns. Three of them murdered in the woods. One escaped. Her eyewitness testimony revealed he wore a Venetian plague doctor's mask, the beak covered with white feathers—"

"Do you always refer to yourself in third person, Agent Kelly?" The student with the man bun, who asked the original question, broke in. "It was you who escaped, right?"

Busted. Not that it was a secret, but seventeen years ago these kids were playing in the dirt and potty training. "Yes. I escaped." A harsh taste filled her mouth.

Another man—a little older with blond hair and a bushy beard—interjected. "Do you think being in the grasp of a killer has helped you think like one? What was that like?"

Being the sole survivor? Knowing that she'd lived, but her younger sister and two other girls had been strangled with ropes? Murdered at the hands of Rhyme? She felt their nooses choking her daily. Like balancing on the edge of a rickety chair that was about to fall out from underneath her, leaving her to asphyxiate. Not only the guilt slowly killing her, but also the secrets.

Secrets she'd never told a soul. Wouldn't. Couldn't. There was too much shame. Too much guilt. Too much fear.

What was it like being in the hands of a killer? She cleared her throat. "Well, it wasn't as exciting as Christmas morning, but to answer how I did it, I happened to be in the right place at the right time." Fiona came around the podium and crossed her arms.

SCU hadn't been organized yet. The cases were bizarre but appeared isolated, not connected.

A pastor and his wife.

A high school track coach.

And the very first murders were teenage girls, including her sister. Just a lone feather to connect crimes two and three. But there had been white feathers on Rhyme's mask when he'd abducted and hunted her in the woods that frigid night… before he'd become practiced and skilled, creating his signature and his MO.

"I was doing a summer workshop at the Collierville library. Talking to kids about the FBI. On my way out, I noticed the librarian dressed as Mother Goose. She happened to be reading the nursery rhyme 'Georgie Porgie,' which sounded eerily similar in description to the way the victim in the third killing had been staged. I borrowed a copy. That was that."

It was more than that, but some things couldn't be disclosed to the public—a few private things she wouldn't.

It had been when she stumbled across "Hickory Dickory Dock" and "Three Little Kittens" that there was no doubt he was staging his victims in scenes from nursery rhymes. She rubbed her arms at the cold memory.

It was that discovery that landed her in the Strange Crimes Unit in the Memphis field office and the nursery rhyme murders exchanged hands from Violent Crimes to Strange Crimes, with no apparent religious undertones, but it was bizarre. She hadn't moved office buildings, only floors. She was already acquainted with the task force. Though at that time, Asa wasn't the special agent in charge.

Their relationship went all the way back to Quantico training.

"Why does he do it?" Man Bun asked. Some were obsessed with Ted Bundy. Some the Night Stalker. In months to come, the Funeral Director would be someone's focus. But for this guy...the Nursery Rhyme Killer.

"There isn't always a why like on TV or in movies. Serial killers like Rhy—the Nursery Rhyme Killer—have no empathy. No remorse. No genuine emotion like love or compassion. Only need and drive to kill. I could speculate why he stages these scenes, but it would only be conjecture."

"But I thought you said you had to think like them," he countered, baiting her.

She wasn't seventeen anymore; her cards weren't on the table for the world to see. "The profile of this killer isn't public knowledge."

"Then you do know why he's doing it?" He smiled, entirely proud of his line of questioning, slightly reminding her of a young Asa Kodiak. Full of himself.

"I have a pretty solid clue. Now, any other questions? That's all I can discuss with you about the Nursery Rhyme Killer."

Thirty minutes later, she turned the lecture back over to Professor Lang and excused herself. Her feet ached; she hated heels but always wore them to speak. On a workday, she wore shoes for comfort. After shrugging out of her gray blazer, she draped it over her arm as she clip-clopped through the parking lot to her car. Chicago was hot in this late June heat. Not as hot as Memphis would be right now. Wouldn't be long before the Fourth of July. Crowds would gather on Mud Island to ooh and aah over the explosion of fireworks that would dance over the Mississippi River. Concessions. Picnics. Water activities for children.

The Fourth didn't hold quite the same meaning to her anymore. This year she'd celebrate independence with a red-white-and-blue Popsicle, a Christmas in July Hallmark movie and an early bedtime.

She turned into the Chicago field office, passed security and headed for her floor. Time to get to real work. Inside her small cubicle, she glanced at the three photos on her desk. A family portrait—Dad, Mom, Fiona and Colleen. One of her and Colleen from nearly twenty years ago.

And one photo she should have left packed away.

It sat as a glaring reminder that happy endings didn't exist. Even when killers were caught, they left a string of pain and grief in their wake.

If she could find a single way to repair the damage that had been done to her—to her family—she'd pay every dime she owned. But nothing assuaged the destruction. Nothing made turning off the lights at night okay. Nothing stopped the nightmares and cold sweats. Not yoga. Not boxing. Not shopping. Not chocolate. Not even a whiskey neat...though that would dull it for a minute.

Not even love. One more peek at the photo garnered a regretful sigh.

If she could track down Rhyme, she could bring justice to herself, the victims and the families. Then she might be free to move on from the pain and the grief. A normal life would await her.

Fiona studied the photo, feeling the weight of everything it had meant and everything she'd lost. She slid it inside a drawer then closed it, shutting out that chapter of her life—one that couldn't be rewritten.

And until Rhyme was behind bars, nothing new could be penned.

The moon had ascended into the dark sky like a lone eye watching over the night. No condemnation. Only a soft glow of approval coaxing and urging him like the voice that whispered to his soul. A familiar voice that had first called to him when he was only ten years old as he'd discovered his grandfather swinging back and forth from the rafters. Like the old grandfather's clock that chimed each hour in his study.

Tick tock. Tick tock.

Grandfather's body hung from a thick rope and lulled him into a trance as he studied the unusual but fascinating angle of his neck. Then it dawned that Grandfather's head had been jarred from his spine as if it was a fragile branch being snapped under a foot.

The sickening scent of vanilla clung to the air.

Tick. Tock.

Back and forth.

Grandfather's frightened dead eyes had peered down at him, jolting him with excitement. How would it feel to be this powerful? To put that kind of fear into someone's eyes?

In those thoughts, he heard the voice purr and scold eerily, like Grandmother's.

You're a naughty kitten. Naughty kittens do bad things and they shall have no pie.

Hairs rose on his arms and neck as the whispers swirled and enveloped him, enticing him into his mission. Naughty kittens deserved no pie…deserved to die.

Grandfather's corpse had slowed to a stop and he'd tiptoed over.

Do it.

With trembling hands and wild fascination, he'd reached out and pushed. Grandfather swayed again; the rhythmic rub of rope on wood soothed him as he stood in the dim moonlight peeking through the window.

Laughter interrupted his unholy moment. Outside a few girls strode by—too late for good kitties to be out.

As he'd peered from the window, a fleeting thought had paused then grown. What would they look like dangling from the rope? How would it feel to watch fear rise in their eyes before their life drained away?

Naughty kittens. All three of them.

A car horn in the distance interrupted the treasured memory and reminded him that right now, ten feet away in a brick two-story, another naughty little kitten had cut the lights and tucked herself into a bed with white Egyptian cotton sheets and a matching quilt.

The epitome of innocence. Cleanliness.

The streets were quiet minus the hum of traffic in the distance. The lingering smells of family barbeques and good times hovered in the muggy air.

Slipping through the shadows, he moved with purpose, easily scaling the wooden privacy fence. The sizzling air blanketed his body, producing sweat; it slicked down the chill bumps that had broken out on his arms in anticipation.

Under the purple-and-white crepe myrtles, he murmured this naughty kitten's personal rhyme—Rhyme. What *she* called him. He loved it. Loved that she'd given him a term of endearment. Excitement coiled in his gut as he thought of Fiona, about how often she thought of him. Daily.

Not one day had passed that she wasn't on his mind, too. He'd been with her throughout the years. Even when she'd left for Chicago. He'd been there.

But he was about to bring her back.

Even though Naughty Kitten insisted Rhyme was stupid and weak. Since he was four he'd had to hear this.

Easing upward, he peered into the window of Jenny Miller's bedroom. He'd had months to watch and discover truths and lies about her and to plan the perfect nursery rhyme scene. Could someone stupid and weak lurk in the shadows without being sensed or seen?

He'd allow her to fall into a good, deep sleep. It was much more thrilling when they woke from sound sleep, disoriented and unsure. He wrapped his hand around the thick hilt of his blade and trembled with intoxication. As the hours ticked by, lights dimmed, dogs stopped barking and TVs were silenced. He watched her chest rise and fall rhythmically, her delicate hand hanging off the bed. No leg twitches. No fear of something creeping out from under the bed to grab her hand.

She was exactly how he wanted her to be.

Under tree covering, he worked slowly but smoothly. Using his crowbar, he raised the window, allowing a blast of cool air into his face. The hum of the box fan tuned out any noise he might make. First he placed his duffel bag on the carpet and then he moved with agility as he entered her home, quietly unzipping the bag and sliding on his plague doctor's mask. Time to purify.

Flowery scents mixed with spices from dinner.

You shall have no pie.

Jenny's blond hair spilled over her pillow.

Slowly, he rested on the edge of her bed, listening to her even breathing. She stirred, then froze.

Ah, yes! The first stroke of elation—the moment her subconscious cautioned her. *You're not alone anymore. This presence and scent do not belong to your husband. To anyone familiar.*

Danger.

It's not a bad dream.

Warning.

Wake up. Wake up.

Alert.

Jenny's blue eyes flew open and she gasped, paralyzed with fear.

Covering her mouth, he muffled her scream. "Shh...hush now, kitty."

Rhyme had five seconds max before her flight-or-fight kicked in and she began clawing him, or thrashing to get free from her bed.

Neither would prevail.

He slipped his knife from his side belt—not his choice of death but a well-made instrument of submission. "You're going to be quiet or I'm going to gut you." He caressed the serrated knife down her torso to her abdomen and applied gentle pressure—enough to warn her to obey.

"You've been a naughty kitty. You shall have no pie." He laughed as confusion and horror dilated her eyes.

She glanced across the room to the doorway.

"No one is coming to your rescue, kitty." He lifted his hand from her mouth. The begging would come next.

"Don't kill me. Please," she cried. "Please. I'll—I'll do anything. Anything you say and I won't fight. I promise. You don't understand, I—"

"I do understand, though." He wouldn't be here if he didn't. "I know everything about you." He pulled a feather from his bag. "Here," he whispered, "hold this." He forced the goose feather into her clammy hand. "I said I wouldn't gut you. You've been very good, so I won't. I'm a man of my word."

A pop of relief settled in her eyes. She would live through this. Even now she was gearing up to deal with her worst fears, and survive them. "No, I'm not about the sensationalism of blood. I find it unnecessary and hard to clean up." He lifted the rope from his bag and fear seized her as she finally realized what he was saying.

"Please. Please!" she begged.

Her words and her scream fell on deaf ears.

She'd already sealed her fate.

There was nothing she could do.

But die.

Chapter Two

The shrill ringing roused Special Agent Asa Kodiak from the three hours of sleep riddled with nightmares. They always came on like a reckoning after he closed a case. Sometimes sporadic depending on his stress level. Once upon a time he'd have poured a Scotch to force him back into rest. Last night he'd read Psalm 23 instead.

Mouth like cotton, eyes scratchy and protesting light, he fumbled until he found his cell and checked the time—9:00 a.m. One day. He wanted one day to himself. Guess he should have chosen another line of work.

Swallowing and pawing at his unshaven face, he answered the phone with a grunt and said, "This better be good. I didn't get in until three, and I'm supposed to be taking the day off."

"I wouldn't say good," his administrative assistant, Cami, said with a heavy drawl, "but we got a call from the Memphis homicide unit."

That stole his attention and he sat straight up, covers in disarray around him. He must have clawed at them in the night. "Which detective?"

"Thought you'd ask that." Cami's know-it-all tone wasn't as amusing on next-to-no sleep.

"Cami..."

"Amanda Barnes."

"Why didn't she call me?" Possible she didn't know he was back in town. It was too early in their relationship to wake her up at 3:00 a.m. to let her know he was home and safe. His team had spent the past two weeks in New Orleans catching the "Alligator Man." But that sicko wasn't the star in his horror show last night, though torturing and feeding women to "demon" alligators made excellent material for nightmares.

Last night's fitful imagery had been reserved for one special psychopath.

"I don't know," she said. "Protocol? Either way, she wants someone to come out for a consult. I figured you'd want it to be you since you haven't seen her in two weeks. Besides only Violet is here and she seems like she doesn't want to be bothered."

"That's just her face." Violet Rainwater reminded him of a French model. Bored and hangry. "Where's Owen?"

"Said he'd be in at noon. Was I wrong, Asa? Do you want me to send Violet, or call in Tiberius or Owen?"

"No."

"I figure," Cami went on, "on a case is as good a time as any to see her, am I right?" Barely twenty-eight, she acted as their caregiver and unwanted matchmaker. He had a decade on her, but he let it go since she was right. Calling him had been the wise choice.

A crime scene as a backdrop to a date wasn't a good time. But it would be good to see Amanda. That alone proved he was moving forward, healing from the past. Baby steps.

"If it's all about protocol, call her back and tell her it'll be an hour before I can get to her, and to keep the scene intact and the body on site and untouched until I get there. And, Cami—"

"No prying. Your relationship is private, but, Asa, if she offers tidbits, I can't hang up on her. I'm a Southern girl, ya know. We're not anything if not polite." The smile in her voice put one on him. And after the last two weeks, there hadn't been much smiling. It had been a grueling investigation and manhunt. The team was exhausted. He was exhausted.

"I was going to say, I need an address."

"Right." She rattled it off and hung up.

He yawned and refrained from swearing—an ugly habit he was working to correct, more baby steps—then swung his legs over the bed, the light beige carpet wrapping around his feet as he puttered from his bedroom into the living room then into the kitchen, the tiles chilling his toes.

After scooping hefty amounts of coffee into the filter, he hit the button and the machine went to gurgling as if it was being strangled. He made it to the shower and skipped shaving. It was entirely too hot to wear a suit and tie, but it was what it was. Asa wasn't expecting July to show any mercy. In his line of work, not much mercy was shown on any given day, and that was from the good guys as well as the bad.

He opened the fridge for cream and a sea turtle magnet with Key West written under it clattered on the floor. The whole door was covered with the stupid things, but he hadn't been able to toss or leave them behind. So here they were slapped up on his new fridge. One day he would chuck them. After placing the magnet back in its place, he skimmed the others. Each one a memory he'd like to forget.

It was time to make new memories.

If work would cut him a break. He poured the coffee in

his Yeti and grabbed his wallet and keys as he rushed out the door. He lived about twenty-five minutes from the crime scene, which was located in an upscale Germantown home. As he arrived at the scene, the yellow crime tape withered in the heat and several marked and unmarked cars lined the street and drive.

He showed his creds to a uniformed officer and slipped under the tape. His feet sank in the thick Bermuda grass that led to perfectly landscaped flower beds full of bright, cheery colors. Like the other homes in the subdivision, this one was also a two-story McMansion with light-colored brick, French shutters and a small wrought-iron balcony.

Amanda graced the outdoors, latex gloves on her hands and paper booties on her feet. Her long blond hair was up in a sloppy knot on her head, and her blazer accented her trim but soft figure. She spotted him and approached. Her gloved finger touched his hand, a more personal greeting but so subtle it wouldn't be noticed by other colleagues. "Solid work on the Alligator Man case. I saw the news."

"Thanks. Completely ruined my love for alligator bites. You doing all right?" *You doing all right?* Could he be any rustier at relationships? It had been a long time since he'd ridden this road, and dating wasn't anything like hopping back on a bike.

Amanda flashed a girl-next-door grin. "I am, but you look exhausted. I know it's your day off. I didn't ask specifically for you. I only wanted a consult—this is the most bizarre thing I've ever seen up close."

He loosened his tie as the whirring and buzzing of various insects created a cacophony. Car doors slammed. People in vehicles rubbernecked as they passed the house. Neighbors stood in their equally perfect manicured yards, murmuring with one another. The sun baked his head. "Work for Strange Crimes one month. You'll think whatever is in there is child's play." He'd seen more than one man ever should—personally and professionally.

"Anyone else from your task force on the way?" Amanda asked and waved at a hefty detective who had sweat pouring from his brow.

"One woken bear on the scene ought to do it." He smirked and caught a whiff of her flowery perfume. Fresh-faced. Light in her eyes. No question she was pretty. He'd thought so the first time he'd met her during the St. Jude Marathon. It had taken him two months to get the gall to ask her out. Then almost another month to make their schedules work. But here they were.

"Give me the details." Time to get to work.

They walked under the front stoop, a sliver of reprieve from the Southern sun. "Our vic is Jenny Miller, twenty-eight. Schoolteacher at St. George's. Germantown location. When she didn't show up to lead summer cheer practice and oversee the practice for the fall school play, they called her husband. Thomas Miller—works the night shift at FedEx. Was out for breakfast with some coworkers, which he said isn't uncommon, when he received the call. Came home and found her. That image will forever be in his brain."

St. George's. Fiona had gone to St. George's.

"Forced entry to the back window leading into the master bedroom."

"House like this. No alarm?"

"Nope."

Security systems could be expensive. Big house. Could be living beyond their means and in debt.

Wonder what she was worth dead?

"Where is the husband? I don't want him leaving the crime scene."

Amanda's lips twitched. "How about you see the scene, and

then you can decide if you want to take over this case." She was equally used to being in charge and he certainly wasn't assuming she wasn't capable. She'd secured the crime scene and conducted the preliminary survey. Crime scene photos were being taken.

"Sorry." Asa accepted a pair of paper booties from a crime tech. "I don't want to take over your case." He hadn't even seen it. Bizarre to Amanda might be nothing to him. He smirked, hoping it would lighten the tension. "I come by it naturally." Asa had been the man of the house until Mom died and then again after Grandpa passed. He couldn't remember when he wasn't in charge.

Amanda responded with a shimmer in her bright blues, then led the way to the master bedroom.

"Where's the husband now, out of simple curiosity?"

"Kitchen with a uniformed officer. He knows not to leave. I'm not saying he didn't do it, but if he did…it's strange to say the least."

Photos of her and the husband lined the hallway. Jenny Miller was a looker. Blonde. Blue eyes the color of first place ribbons. A lot like Amanda. "Any kids?"

"No. But they were planning a family according to the husband." Amanda turned before going inside the master bedroom and shuddered. "I think whatever happened in here is going to happen again. I feel it."

Ignoring professionalism, he touched her cheek to give her some kind of reassurance that it would be okay. They'd find the guy, make the world safer—at least that's what he always told himself, but he never truly believed it. "Is it gruesome?" If he could only protect her from seeing heinous things. But she'd chosen this profession. Not for the same reasons as him, or any of his task force members—each one had been touched and changed by the evilest killers in a deeply personal way.

"Not gory, but she's posed. Creepy." She shuddered again. "The killer left something in the victim's hand, too."

Posed. Clutching something. Asa's pulse spiked. "What is it?"

"A white feather." She scrunched her nose. "Weird, huh?"

A goose feather.

Asa's stomach pinched.

The Nursery Rhyme Killer had returned.

Rhyme easily blended in with the rest of the onlooking crowd.

Asa Kodiak.

The name alone gave him a sour taste on his tongue, but things couldn't have panned out any better. Kodiak's new girlfriend was in charge of the crime scene. Not that it would have mattered who had been lead—Kodiak would have been called in once they saw Jenny's body. Saw the feather.

Asa was right now seeing it. A million thoughts flying through his thick skull—one in particular.

Before the day was out, Kodiak would call for Fiona. Tell her he needed her back in Memphis to work the case, but she'd know that it was Rhyme who had actually beckoned her.

It was time to come home.

To him.

To this newest rhyme. Fiona knew them as if she'd been forced to repeatedly listen to them as much as Rhyme had been.

Her study of him—to know him, to be near him—undid him in ways he couldn't even describe. He'd seen the evidence in the spare bedroom she'd used to piece his story—their story—together. Like it was their own private room, where they shared intimate details together. Photos. Scribbles.

Printed-out nursery rhymes. Whiteboards. Bulletin boards. All dedicated to him. To them.

Come back to me, Fiona.

Rhyme nearly did a victory pump with his fists.

If Kodiak so much as tried to stand between Rhyme and Fiona again, he'd unmask him for the world to see. He might just do it for the thrill regardless.

Chapter Three

Asa entered the master bedroom. Jenny Miller was propped on an array of pastel accent pillows and her lifeless eyes bored into him. Her honey-blond hair had been splayed across the pillows like a woman in a shampoo commercial. The white quilt had been carefully turned down to expose the entire scene.

Across the crisp white sheets, black rose petals had been scattered in place of red ones.

A vanilla jar candle had burned down to nothing but the scent lingered in the room, along with the presence of evil and darkness as if it refused to vacate until the victim it had swallowed up exited first.

Jenny Miller had on a black nightie. Not too wild, but alluring enough to drive home the message she had more than sleeping on her mind. Her slender arms rested out to her sides and were propped on pillows, as if she was awaiting a significant other, and her right knee was bent, placing her in a seductive pose.

Draped around her neck was a black feather boa.

Clutched in her right hand was a lone white goose feather.

The Nursery Rhyme Killer's calling card.

It had to be. A copycat killer wouldn't have unreleased knowledge…and the goose feather information had never been leaked to the public.

"Did you ask the husband if that was her lingerie?"

Amanda paused, a puzzled look creasing lines around her eyes. "No."

Asa inched closer to the vic. "Has she been photographed yet?"

"Yes."

He lifted the boa from the vic's neck, revealing wide shallow furrows and a faint braided pattern that matched all the other NRK's victims. His signature, a manila rope—the kind Grandpa had secured to a tree and tied to a tire for a young Asa's merriment.

Upon closer examination, he observed petechial hemorrhages, confirming strangulation. Asa winced as he imagined the horror Jenny Miller had endured. Pressure within her neck veins would have suddenly spiked when the rope was pulled taut, applying pressure to the veins in her eyes and forcing blood to leak into the whites, giving her this present haunting appearance.

If the NRK had been merciful it may have only lasted a few seconds before she lost consciousness and died, but Asa feared it had been far more terrifying for the young teacher. The sadist that he was, he would have forced her through several minutes of agonizing torture before she lost consciousness and he staged the scene. They'd assumed his grand displays were designed postmortem. Never any signs of struggle. But Asa couldn't be sure; it was possible he demanded their submission into the poses before he finished his twisted fantasy.

"What fresh...?" The dry, bored tone of the newest team member, Violet Rainwater, was unmistakable. She stood at the threshold wearing paper booties and snapping a latex glove against her wrist.

"What are you doing here?"

Entering the room with caution, she surveyed the sick scene. "I overheard Cami telling Selah you were on a consult. Thought I'd lend a hand. I couldn't sleep."

No evidence of exhaustion, but then Rainwater rarely complained and lacked dramatic flares or animated facial expressions. The woman was a hard read. Good thing she spoke her mind bluntly and without apology. Asa could appreciate that.

"You overheard them, did you?" Cami and their computer analyst, Selah Jones, loved the scuttlebutt. What Violet wasn't saying was that their gab session had more than likely been about Asa and Amanda, not the actual consult.

"Not here for the Asa is Dating Again show."

Amanda's cheeks reddened and she cleared her throat.

She hadn't been around Violet enough to know she meant nothing offensive. She was like bleach. Sterile and abrasive ninety-five percent of the time. The other five percent, she was sleeping...or trying to.

"Looks like she was gearing up for a good time and it went south fast. Sexual assault?" Violet asked.

If it was the NRK, there wouldn't be one.

Amanda stood at the foot of the king-size bed. "I don't think so but we'll know more once a death investigator gets here."

"No abrasions around her inner thighs. Doesn't mean there hasn't been one." Violet scanned the room then dropped on her knees. "Nothing under the bed. That's odd."

"Why is that odd?" Amanda asked.

Violet raised her head. "Everyone has junk under their bed.

I'm not saying it's pertinent to your case. I'm saying it's odd. An observation."

"You want to know what's under mine?" Tiberius Granger, with his cocky yet comical expression, disheveled hair and a tad more than five-o'clock shadow covering his face, filled the doorframe. He showed signs of exhaustion, but like the rest of the team, he likely hadn't been able to sleep.

Violet stood and brushed her black dress pants. "No. I can only handle one nightmare at a time."

Ty shrugged and bounced her a wicked grin. "Suit yourself."

Asa wondered how long it would take for him to stop acting like a hormonal sixteen-year-old boy.

Finally focusing on the victim, Ty grimaced when he saw the goose feather.

"I was waiting on you to notice that."

"The feather? Why?" Amanda pressed.

"I'll fill you in, just be patient a little longer." This was how they worked. Initial theories, bouncing ideas. "Violet, what do you see?" As a psychologist with a background in profiling and victimology—not to mention some otherworldly super power she seemed to have—she had the skill to move inside a killer's mind as if she was one. She'd only been wrong once in two years, since she'd transferred from the Violent Crimes Unit in Jackson, Mississippi. She'd taken *her* place.

It was practically impossible to think of Fiona without blinding pain and tsunami-size outrage. If she had any inkling the NRK had started up again, she'd want to be here in the thick of it. Right now, he couldn't even consider being in a room again with her. He needed Violet's take. She wouldn't have any background or knowledge of the Nursery Rhyme Killer, like Amanda, who had moved here from Texas three years ago.

Violet approached the king-size bed. "She's staged like a working girl waiting for a john. But black petals instead of red denote death." She lifted the black feather boa and squinted. "Black birds could be a raven or vulture. Both scavenger birds. He's posed her to reveal something. That she's a scavenger of some kind. Eating already dead prey. Leftovers? Is he trying to tell us she's been sleeping with someone's leftovers? An angry divorcée could have done this. If there's no sexual assault it could have been a woman." She stepped back, examining the pose from another angle, her head cocked. "Her positioning is key. It's how we see her when we enter a room. She's displayed like lust. Lust is one of the seven deadly sins. Both scenarios fit."

Naturally, she'd go to a religious theme first, since most of their cases had a twisted religious undertone driving the killer's motive to commit homicide. Violet inspected the abrasions and bruising as well as her eyes, coming to the same conclusion as Asa.

Folding her arms across her chest, she deliberately blinked as her lips pulled to the side. "Am I passing your test, Asa? It's clear you know who's doing this. It's all over your face—you should shave, by the way."

Asa rubbed his chin and agreed. "I suspect this is the work of the Nursery Rhyme Killer. Eight kills prior to this one going back at least seventeen years. He hits anytime between two and five years apart. Men. Women. Even teenagers—in what we believe to be his first murders. All in the Memphis area. This is his signature. Public has no knowledge of the feather being left and we'd like to keep it that way." They didn't need some moron with a wild hair committing copycat crimes.

Amanda asked, "Why is he doing it?"

"He's a serial killer. Why not?" Violet said dryly.

Just when things had been quiet, a sliver of hope that this killer was long gone, in prison, or even dead. When Asa had been determined to move on, he'd reentered his life, now forcing him to deal all over again. Because he couldn't not call Fiona. Yeah, he was over resenting her for the most part. But that didn't mean he wanted her in the room, filling it with her scent of tropical islands, shooting off her sarcastic mouth, pushing him to levels of red no human should be pushed to. And he sure didn't need her reckless behavior. He'd all but invested in antacids before things took a devastating turn. Asa was at war with himself. The inner good guys wanted peace and forgiveness. The bad guys wanted to be angry, resentful, bitter and, even to a degree, vindictive.

Come on, good guys. Fight the good fight. Muster some faith, Asa.

"Asa? You having an out-of-body experience or something?" Violet's cloudy blue-green eyes drilled into his.

Maybe. Quite possibly.

She raised her eyebrows and refrained from commenting on his inner turmoil, though most likely she'd pegged it. Shrinking him quietly like the psychologist she was. Instead, Violet's attention went back to their vic. "What rhyme is this? I hardly think she's dressed for a children's story."

Asa wasn't the expert on all things Mother Goose. That would be Fiona's department. His head spun as the truth set in, but he worked hard to deny he needed her help. "Ty, call Selah and have her set up a major case room. Tell Cami to pull all the files on the Nursery Rhyme Killer."

"Anyone else you want me to call?" Ty had remained unusually quiet until now. No doubt feeling the same pit in his gut and coming to terms with it in his own way. His pointed look said it all. Ty had been with the SCU as long as Asa, but Ty never wanted to lead the charge; that would mean more responsibility than he preferred.

Asa pinched the bridge of his nose. This was his decision and right now with the Fourth of July and all its meaning looming, he refused to deal with Fiona. "Just the two."

"Bad call, Kodiak. Bad call," Ty said.

Amanda heaved a sigh. "Who needs to be called? Will someone please explain what is going on?"

"What do you want me to do?" Violet asked.

All three fired off questions and remarks at one time. Asa needed to process, but his head pounded like giant angry fists.

He pointed to Violet. "Victimology. I want to know everything on Jenny Miller."

He softened his voice when he focused on Amanda. Her frustration was legit. "I'll explain everything. For now, work the case as normal and we'll compare notes."

Raking his hand through his hair, he avoided eye contact with Ty. "My call to make. I'm making it."

Ty threw up his hands and he and Violet strode from the scene, leaving him with Amanda.

"I'm sorry you're having a bad day on little-to-no sleep," Amanda said. "Tell me when you get some ducks in a row. Maybe over dinner on the Fourth. Picnic. Watch the fireworks on Mud Island. A date?"

Mud Island? Two years had trudged by since he last attended. Wasn't sure he could go now. It had been Fiona's favorite holiday and their thing. The holiday represented something neither of them had back then but desperately desired— freedom. The light show had been a beacon, proving liberty could be found out there in the darkness. They only had to make it through the choppy waters to reach it.

"Okay. Sure." He was moving on, which meant not letting the past prevent him from living fully in the present. "If the case allows. You know the job."

Amanda's face lit up. "I do. I hope you catch a break."

"Say a prayer." Something new he'd been doing of late.

"I always do." She winked and excused herself.

Ty reentered. "It's done. Death investigator is on her way. Apparently she's been busy this morning. You want me to come with to interview the husband? You know it's always the husband."

"How could it be this time? The feather in her hand."

Ty shrugged. "I just think you spend that much time with someone...you wanna kill 'em."

Asa snorted.

"Asa, you don't have to enlist Fiona's help, but you owe her a courtesy call."

Ty was right. But it would ignite a different set of fireworks. The kind that didn't light up the night sky, but set emotional fires and burned everything to ash. "It'll put her on a plane out here. Give me some time. It won't hurt anything." Asa could move past the Fourth of July, then call and inform her that he was handling things and would keep her updated.

Unfortunately, that wouldn't be enough for Fiona.

Asa was going to have to pin Scripture verses all over his town house, car and office to keep his temper in check and his heart guarded.

After slamming the rental car door, Fiona stalked across the Memphis field office parking lot. Last night, she'd had to hear through the grapevine that Rhyme had taken another victim. How could Asa have left her in the dark? Did he not want to hear her voice or have a real adult conversation? Well, too bad. She had high stakes involved here and that's what grated her nerves most. If anyone on this planet knew how much she needed to catch Rhyme—what it would mean to her and for her—it was Asa Riley Kodiak.

After she'd already booked a flight, she'd called her SAC.

While she couldn't impose on another region's case, she did have vacation time. If they invited her into the case she could keep said vacation days. If not, she had two weeks to work from Memphis without Asa's permission—after all, she was on vacay. The files and information were burned into her brain, and she had contacts in the field office who would lend her a hand and give case updates.

Asa might not want her on Memphis soil, but he didn't always get his way. If he wanted to rise up, show those bear teeth and claws, and roar his head off at her—for which he'd earned the nickname Kodiak Bear—then fine. *Rise up, ol' boy. Growl and snarl. I'm not going anywhere. This time.* She marched through security and briefly greeted old colleagues on the way to the elevator. No time for small talk. Rhyme was out there. Punching the elevator button with more force than necessary, she tapped her foot and tamped down her temper the best she could.

The door opened and a woman with sunshiny hair and twinkling blue eyes politely smiled as Fiona stepped inside. They were both going to the SCU floor. The woman had a gun and a badge, but she wasn't a federal agent. "Homicide?"

The woman nodded. "What about you?"

"SCU. Midwest Division."

A knowing look came over her and she extended her hand for an introductory handshake. "Detective Amanda Barnes. I'm the one who called in the SCU on the nursery rhyme murder yesterday."

"How do you know I have anything to do with that particular case?" Did she have Rhyme tattooed on her forehead? Felt like it at times. She was permanently carrying his mark for all to see, with no hope or way to rid herself of the feeling she belonged to him, and always would.

"I'm pretty sure you're the *her* who needed to be called."

Another syrupy but genuine grin. This woman hadn't once been stained by evil.

The elevator dinged.

"Do you hail from a long line of LEOs?" Fiona asked.

Surprise registered, then amusement stretched her mouth into grin, as if Fiona's deduction was a cool party trick. "Yes, actually. My great-grandfather, grandfather and my dad are in law enforcement in Texas. How did you know that?"

Fiona traced an air circle around Amanda's face with her index finger. "You still have innocence—nothing dark has touched you." She didn't have the feral, hungry look like those who had a score to settle with evil. Nothing in her springtime-sky eyes screamed broken, beaten or bruised by loss. "You're a daddy's girl who wants to live up to his standards and make him proud. But not even to prove something because he loves you whether you're a cop or a kindergarten teacher." Amanda Barnes bore the rainbow-and-roses gleam. Loved by all. Family. Teachers. Friends. The man in her life— which, with those good looks, she was bound to have—was devoted to her and doted on her.

"I envy you that." Fiona's parents had shattered into jagged shards with Colleen's murder. Mom—who hadn't wanted to move to Memphis in the first place—returned to Ocean Springs and Dad stayed in Memphis, where work had transferred him. Fiona had stayed behind for college and MPD, and to ultimately go to the FBI Academy and become an agent.

Mom hadn't understood. In her eyes Fiona had chosen Dad over her and she'd never forgiven Fiona. In reality, Fiona had chosen Rhyme over them both. She walked off the elevator before Detective Barnes had a rebuttal or asked for another parlor trick and strode into the SCU division.

Eight cubicles. A copier and coffee bar resided on the back

wall, and to the left was Asa's secretary's desk. Behind that door, the bear himself.

Cami looked up, stunned. "Fiona, hey…"

"Save it." Cami had taken sides that had never needed to be taken; stuck her nose in where it hadn't belonged. Fiona blew past her desk and busted through Asa's door, ready to throw down. Every word, expression and hand gesture had been rehearsed on the plane. With each scenario she'd played in her imagination, anger had bubbled up and boiled over. Asa glanced up from his mountain of paperwork, his tie loose, a pen in hand, and every heated word froze on her tongue.

Stone-gray eyes met hers without an ounce of surprise. Only weariness. The shade of skin below his eyes confirmed he hadn't been sleeping. Probably not eating much, either. In that instant her heart stretched out to offer comfort and embrace his, but she reined in the intense desire with Mach speed.

She no longer had that right and didn't think she had the ability, but the instinct had been there, which surprised her and brought a good dose of fear. Two years had aged Asa, adding more silver at his temples and throughout his dark hair. The trendier cut might be his fight against age. Not that thirty-eight was old, but the job sucked away youth like a vacuum ate up dust.

His appeal hadn't diminished since he'd strutted into Quantico like a gift from above. He'd grabbed her attention, but she was too focused on her mission to let it pass casual appreciation and a few dalliances. After graduation, they'd parted ways until he transferred into the new SCU here while she was still in Violent Crimes. At some point one of them was going to have to speak, but her insides had melted like goo.

"Ty call you?" he finally asked; his voice held a hint of a rasp, his expression unreadable on purpose. Asa's game face.

This was how he wanted to play it? Fine.

"No," she replied, trying not to choke on the sentiment swelling in her chest, making it hard to breathe. His understated cologne and fresh scent dryer sheets clung to the entire office, and with every inhale, memories surfaced she'd worked diligently to bury. Fiona forced herself to swallow personal feelings. "Why didn't you? You've had over twenty-four hours to at least give me a courtesy call. You'd rather cut me out than work with me?" She raised her hand to halt him. "Typical. You're the king of cutting." Personal feelings rebelled.

Asa's eyes darkened like thunderclouds as he raised slightly from his chair and leaned forward, his hands gripping the desk. "Cut you out?" he growled. "Are you delusional? Have you forgotten...?" Throwing up his hands, he inhaled sharply. "You know what? I'm not doing this. This is why I didn't call you. I don't have time to pick apart our past and argue. I have a case to solve!" he boomed, then collapsed on his leather throne. Pawing his face, he muttered under his breath. Couldn't possibly be a prayer but it sounded like one. In typical fashion, he'd shot off hot and fast, but quickly reeling in his temper was new.

"Well, I am here. Let's pick apart the case instead. You can use me and you know it. Swallow your pride and invite me in."

Asa studied her face until she squirmed inside—ugh, she hated the way he could arrest her with his eyes while reading her inner thoughts. Granite expression. Nostrils flaring and jaw working overtime. Nothing but the sound of his breathing. Hope sank. Asa was going to march her back to Chicago and if she violated his orders, he'd make it difficult for her. Asa's hammer struck hard if he intended damage. Thor had nothing on him.

Then she spotted it. The three staccato blinks and the release of his clenched jaw. Permission granted!

"Invite you in?" he mused. "Since when you do you ask permission?"

Fiona found she could actually smile at his insult. "It's just formality."

His right eyebrow rose and his mouth marginally slid to the same side—his signature smirk. Appealing as all get out without intent or effort.

"I won't come in like a rabid dog with teeth bared."

"Oh, I *know* you won't. If I have to personally muzzle you, I will."

And who would muzzle him? Had he forgotten he had a set of sharp teeth, too? Ones he'd plunged deep into her heart with four words.

"There are ground rules, Fiona. In case you've forgotten, I'm the alpha dog. This is my team. My calls. You don't run point because it's the Nursery Rhyme Killer. If I even get a whiff that you're being insubordinate, I'll have you on a plane so fast your head will spin. Clear?"

All work. Nothing personal. Hard-nosed. But Fiona knew what fueled his bravado—panic and fear. For Fiona. And because she was aware of that, she owed him compliance. "Crystal. Anything else?"

He tossed a hand frivolously in the air. "I guess not."

"Then I'm getting coffee and down to work." She marched out the door and smacked into the hard chest of Tiberius Granger, who'd clearly been eavesdropping, no doubt for entertainment value. Two years had added a few extra lines around his fall green eyes. His goofy, boyish charm tried to hide under the sandy brown scruff, but it peeped through regardless.

"Well, well. Look what the cat dragged in."

She bristled.

Here, kitty, kitty.

Forcing herself to relax, she ruffled his already messy-on-purpose do. His burnt sienna hair had a few streaks of gold highlights and his skin was sun-kissed. "You going to tanning beds now, too?"

"Ha. Ha," he stated dryly. "I spent a week in Barbados. Me and mai tais. Then I got stuck in NOLA catching the alligator guy. But, hey, thanks for calling me and keeping up." He clapped a hand to his chest. "Means a lot." The sarcasm was laced with good humor and a dash of disappointment.

They'd been a team. Family. She'd cut all ties when she'd moved.

"I am sorry for that, Tiberius." Ty didn't fit him like his given name did. "I needed a clean break." Yet here she was again. Leaving Memphis—the division—had done nothing to mend her. She was as broken as ever.

"I get it." He glanced at Asa's door. "How'd it go in there?"

"What—you didn't hear us, you giant eavesdropper?"

He smirked. "Nah, I did. But I've heard you louder. And longer."

They hadn't always fought. The good times—and there were far more than bad—had been the best times. Remembering the bad was easier. "Indeed." Fiona couldn't put her finger on the changes, but something was different about Asa.

"I'm glad he called you."

"He didn't."

"Who did?" he asked.

Asa swung open his office door, full-on scowl. "How did you know about the murder? If Ty didn't call. No way it made it to Chicago news, at least not this early."

Tiberius pointed to himself, feigning shock. "You thought I called? You told me not to."

"You never do what you're told," Asa responded.

Legit pride replaced his fake outrage and dismay. "That's fair."

Tiberius was the maverick of the team, yet he didn't get the third degree from Asa like Fiona did when she'd gone off half-cocked. But then Asa hadn't ever declared his love and devotion to Tiberius. Love changed the way a person behaved toward their object of affection when their life was at stake. She never liked it, but she understood.

"I heard through the grapevine." Fiona's cheeks heated. Asa was going to blow a gasket when he figured it out. The fact that he hadn't put it together revealed how frazzled he was at her arrival, even though he was expecting it. Or, who knew? He might be past caring about her source.

"What grapevine?" He shot Tiberius a glare and thrust a finger toward him. "Don't you dare start with that blasted song."

Blasted? That was a new word choice.

Tiberius pretended to zip his lips, lock the key and toss it. "Wouldn't dream of it, Bear." Tiberius's term of endearment for their fearless leader. Fiona had only used it when he was being surly. At work, it was often. Outside of work, he was more teddy bear than Kodiak.

Fiona didn't have time to enjoy Tiberius's antics or Asa's irritation.

"I asked a question, Fiona," Asa grouched.

Her insides flamed. Yep. Work. Kodiak Bear.

"I'll let you come to your own conclusion. You're a master detective and savvy at solving puzzles." Maybe she had a little maverick in her, too.

He growled under his breath and held her defiant gaze, although she dreaded where it was going to lead when he connected the dots. *Oh, boy.* The snarl guaranteed he'd done it. "Rathbone?" he spewed.

Luke Rathbone had been Fiona's SAC when she'd joined Violent Crimes, and though they hadn't had a romantic relationship there had been a bond between them. One Luke had wanted to explore further. When the position opened in the SCU, Luke hadn't wanted Fiona to transfer. Asa never denied Fiona was a skilled agent, but he assumed Luke's negative response was more due to Fiona working closely with Asa if she left Violent Crimes.

Not true but not worth the debate.

Disgust gnarled his features. The same look before he broke Rathbone's nose in a crushing blow one night in the FBI parking lot. "Rathbone! I should have known. He's quite the informer of information."

It had been Luke who had alerted Fiona of the open position in the Midwest SCU. He'd transferred to SAC of Violent Crimes in Chicago a couple of months prior, and with everything going down the tubes for her and Asa, she'd taken it. Fiona would never forget Asa's reaction to the transfer. Vitriol spewed. Nasty implications. And a final "good riddance" before the office door slammed in her face.

Fiona remained calm. "You know he's tight with Owen." They also played poker on Wednesday nights, now that he'd left the FBI altogether and was currently working private security here in Memphis. Apparently, Owen had purposely failed to mention this to Asa.

Asa's jaw convulsed. "And he just needed to call you immediately?"

More implications. Fiona's blood turned hot. So much for keeping calm. This behavior was why she had no plans to mention Luke had left Chicago six months ago. Asa would assume she had underlying motives to be in Memphis now. Not that it was his business, but they had to get along to work together. "Unlike someone staring me down this very second, he thought I had a right to know. He understands my need—"

"I'm quite sure he understands your needs."

"You—!"

"Let's not argue, children," Tiberius interrupted and stood in between them.

Tears burned the backs of her eyes and she willed herself to reclaim the power that refused to allow Asa to wound her with so few words.

He's angry. He has the right to still be angry with me. But he didn't have the right to hurl insults. Was this how it was going to be the entire case?

Asa rubbed his face and the fight in him drained. "I'm sorry for what I implied. It was out of line and childish. It won't happen again."

Reeling in his temper, not using colorful language once and now hurriedly apologizing? Was he chipped or something? Who was pulling his strings?

He rolled his head, stretching the tension from his neck. Signature Asa. "Everyone's in major case room one. Let's get to work." He gave a curt nod and strode toward the room.

Tiberius ran his tongue across his teeth. "I haven't seen him this keyed up in a while."

"It's Rhyme." He put Asa on edge with every strike.

"No—" Tiberius slung an arm around her shoulder as they made their way down the hall to the case room "—it's you, and the fact that the NRK is close enough to reach out and grab you. So give him some breathing room."

"I wasn't the one blowing up over wild imaginations about Luke Rathbone."

At the door, Tiberius paused. "I normally wouldn't say this, and while I have no intention of doing what I'm about to tell you to do, take heed, my friend. And toe the line this time. No need to go all lone hero."

"Thanks for the advice."

Inside the room, Owen Berkley stood next to a dark-haired agent. Must be the agent who filled Fiona's spot when she transferred. Tall. Lithe. Long, almost black hair parted down the middle. Dressed for the job, not style. Short bare nails. No jewelry. Flawless skin and long eyelashes that canopied blue eyes with flecks of green. Cleft in her chin. She was one of those women who wasn't initially pretty, but upon closer examination could be described as uniquely beautiful.

Owen cleared his throat as Asa made serious eye contact with him. There would be a conversation coming between those two later. One Fiona didn't want to be anywhere near. He simply gave her the two-fingered wave. They could catch up later.

The agent with the impassive facial expression held a red dry-erase marker and batted her glances between Asa and Fiona. She removed the lid with a squeak and gave them one more intense stare. "I'm a federal agent, not a babysitter. Do I make myself clear?"

"Yep," Asa said.

Perceptive. No-nonsense. She won Fiona's instant admiration and respect. She nodded her reply. The blonde detective—Amanda—sat at the table with a stack of file folders. Lead detectives usually sat in on cases, but they typically had one or two more local investigators sitting in with them.

Asa seemed to notice her for the first time and he paused midstep. "Oh, I, uh… I didn't know you'd be here."

Amanda blushed. "I'm sorry. I didn't mean to overstep. I thought I'd sit in on the case briefing, but I can go—"

"No—stay," he said with more inflection than Fiona

thought necessary. "Stay." That word. Repeated. Softer. Gently insistent.

The room freeze-framed. Tension climbed to its peak. Invisible hands punched through her chest and clutched her lungs. Amanda's gaze was set on Asa, unsure but secure. His neck had turned three shades of red and his cheek twitched.

"I forgot the coffee," Fiona choked out.

Air.

She needed air.

"Start without me." Forcing herself to calmly exit the room, she made it out and then rushed on wobbly legs to the coffeepot to try and get her bearings.

Asa was *seeing* her. The lovely blonde with a friendly smile and happy eyes. Petite, at maybe five feet five. Soprano voice. Polar opposite of Fiona.

He wanted everything she wasn't.

Fiona's hand shook as she poured a cup. If she'd had some time to digest the news, it wouldn't have hit as hard. But this was a shock. Not that he owed her a heads-up concerning his personal affairs; his life was his own. He'd moved on and Fiona admitted she was green-eyed over it. She couldn't move on until Rhyme was brought to justice. Then she would be free. Somewhere in the back of her mind she always assumed it would be with Asa. But he'd given up on them too soon and wasn't going to pine over her. She didn't want that—well, a little pining wouldn't have hurt.

"Fiona." Asa's tender tone traveled to her sore heart.

No. Go away. Don't talk to me like that. Don't see me. Asa would read her pain and she couldn't handle any more humiliation. She felt his presence, close enough that his breath brushed the back of her neck. He rested his strong but delicate hand on her shoulder—the warmth and familiarity seeped through her shirt to her fragile heart. How could one touch evoke this much emotion, tenderness and power?

She bit back regret and tears.

"I would have told you at some point," he murmured, "but I didn't know either of you would be here today."

She forced herself to regain composure, to pretend it didn't matter, didn't hurt. He needed to step back. Close—too close. Fiona crunched the inside of her bottom lip to hide the trembling, then closed her eyes, willing all of it to go away—back to the dark, locked places she didn't visit. When she opened them, she planted an impassive expression on her face and stirred her coffee. She lifted a shoulder to portray indifference, bumping his hand away, then faced him. "We don't owe each other rundowns of our relationships."

"Then you are seeing Rathbone?"

Admitting her ineptness to move forward embarrassed her, especially since it had been two years since their split. Felt like yesterday.

Those four words.

"Let's leave our personal lives out of this and work the case. The sooner we put this to bed, the sooner I can get out of your hair."

He opened his mouth to further the conversation but closed it. Guess it wasn't worth the words. "Okay, but you need to understand that Amanda is the lead detective and you'll have to interact with her."

"Is she why you didn't call me? Didn't want us working together *Three's Company* style?"

Asa ran his hand through his hair and massaged the back of his neck. "No. Although, I admit I'm not looking forward to extra awkward tension."

"I can't leave." She wanted to, though. "I've earned the right to be here. To put him away." She needed to peer into those shark eyes and slam the door on his life and her past. "It has to be me. You know this."

"Nobody knows it better," he said sadly. "Please play nice, Fiona. I—I really like her, okay?" He blinked rapidly and licked his lips.

"Does she know about me?"

Guilt stained his face. "No. We've only been dating a couple of months and talking about you, that would take...a lifetime."

Fiona couldn't get past "I really like her." Four more piercing words.

But she would get past the initial shock of being replaced. It was bound to happen. The jealousy wasn't due to a continued love for him. Love had been lost long ago, but they did share a deep history. Once she processed the situation, everything would be fine.

"Well, she deserves to know she's gonna be working closely with your wife."

"Ex-wife," Asa whispered.

Chapter Four

Ex-wife. The word that continually reminded Asa of one of his epic failures—that and the bare ring finger. He'd thought he had a few more days before her storm into the office, but seeing her blow in less than twenty minutes ago had sucked the air from his lungs.

Asa should have known Owen would tell Rathbone—they'd been buds for years. Had his brain not been buzzing and failing to fire on all pistons, he'd have done a better job of emotionally prepping. He'd had every intention of notifying her. After the Fourth. Now, when the anniversary of their first real date and his marriage proposal rolled around, she'd be here. Every year they'd celebrated on Mud Island. This year he'd be there again but with a brand-new woman. He wasn't sure how to feel about it, but he couldn't avoid every single place they'd been together because they weren't together now.

"Right," Fiona said, "that's what I meant." She waved it off as a mistaken slip of the tongue. "I'll play nice. I have no reason not to. But if she gets in my way…"

Fiona would mow her down. Had nothing to do with him dating Amanda and everything to do with her drive to find the Nursery Rhyme Killer. He hated the killer who had been the wedge between them. They'd never had a fighting chance. Between both of their baggage and her obsession.

It has to be me. Fiona's only way to freedom. A lie. It didn't have to be Fiona to catch Rhyme. This innate drive to be the one to find him, to never take breaks, rest, or slow down for a second, had been unhealthy from the beginning, and in the end, it had torn them apart. In the back of Asa's mind, he'd feared that very thing, but he'd overlooked it, hoped their love could be enough to carry them.

It hadn't been. Or it hadn't been the right kind of love.

"She won't be an issue."

It was Fiona who wanted to take over and direct this ship, and in doing so—at times—she'd been reckless. Her hazel eyes glared into his—one a little lazy but only noticeable if studied long enough, or if she were tired or stressed out, or on her third glass of wine. The things he still intimately knew of her slayed him but they were unforgettable. Like how she kept her rich brown hair short, resting on her neck and barely over her ears, because long hair was a distraction and in the way. No matter what length, it always smelled of tropical islands. And he'd loved it short because it showed the femininity of her delicate neck. He knew at the back of her head toward the scalp was a small scar where hair had been ripped away as she'd been running from a killer.

Hiding under tailored pants were legs that wouldn't quit with wildly toned calf muscles. Same with her arms, back and abs. She kept in top condition—not at all for vanity's sake—to stay strong, because once she'd been weak and it was her biggest fear even if she refused to admit it.

Asa related to that fear. His wasn't so much fear as the hovering truth. He'd been too weak to rescue his mother from a savage serial killer who had broken into their home in the middle of the night. He'd been forced to watch her death. It had changed the trajectory of his life. Of his sister Kacie's life.

"Why don't you bring me up to speed?" Fiona asked.

He blinked out of his stupor. "What?"

"Work. Bring me up to speed." She frowned but didn't comment on his zoning out.

"Right. Yes." Work was easier to focus on. They headed back toward the major case room.

"I noticed Wheezer isn't around," Fiona said.

"He left to work with a private security company in Atlanta six months after you transferred." Asa wasn't sure they'd ever find a computer genius as good as him, but then he'd interviewed Selah. "You'll like our new analyst, though. She's snarky like you, and a pain in the you-know-what half the time, but she's so good I overlook it."

Fiona smirked. "The *you-know-what*? What are you, six?"

This was going to be an interesting conversation. "I've, uh…toned down the language lately."

"Handiwork of the girlfriend?"

Heat filled Asa's neck and cheeks. Fiona was going to pounce on this. "I've actually been going to church."

Fiona laughed. Cackled actually in her deep buttery tone. But he didn't laugh with her. Her eyes grew wide and she sobered. "You're serious."

"I am." It had only been about eight months, but with some pastoral counseling, a few new friends from the men's ministry and joining a small group he was learning a lot and making strides to lead a new kind of life. Wasn't a cakewalk, though; it might be one of the hardest things he'd ever done. Just kicking out the four-letter words was a fiery trial.

"It's…" She gaped.

They'd never been the faith-filled kind of people. This job had a way of souring a person to believe there wasn't any good in the world. On earth or in heaven.

"I know. I get it. But, it changed me—not church but my faith." He wasn't sure how to explain the fact that one day he didn't believe in God and the next...he did. "It gives me hope. Soothes me."

Skepticism ruled in her eyes. "A hot shower and a Scotch on the rocks does, too."

Asa held the knob on the case room door. "You and I both know that isn't true." With that, he opened the door to the case room. Everyone was seated at the table including Amanda, who was tapping her pen nervously and shooting him wary eyes. She'd put two and two together. Or Ty had decided to unlock and unzip his mouth, and had given her the 411 on him and Fiona.

She had no idea that Fiona had been the greatest love he'd ever known, and she'd been the cause of some of the deepest pain he'd ever experienced. Like drowning but never dying—panic from the need to breathe, only to almost make it to the surface of the water before being pulled back into the depths by a current of grief so powerful there was no hope of breaking free.

"Agent Fiona Ko— Kelly." He cleared his throat at the embarrassment of almost slipping up. She'd gone back to her maiden name a year ago. Nothing said final like handing a man back his surname. Fiona stood stiff and stone-faced, not making it easy on him.

After Asa made the introductions, Owen swaggered to Fiona and embraced her, holding on a little tighter than necessary in Asa's opinion. "You lookin' extra special." He winked.

Owen was one of the best criminal-pattern-theory experts he'd ever worked with and an insatiable hound, but he kept his personal exploits outside the office. Asa and Fiona might have learned a lesson from him. He once told them, "Dogs don't dump where they eat. Just saying."

The mess had rained all over the office when they split. He was surprised the Bureau hadn't decided then and there to put an inner-office-relationship policy into place.

"It's the shower," she said, patting Owen's cheeks and flashing him a winning smile. Asa'd once loved that smile. But as the NRK continued to slip through their fingers, smiles had disappeared from her delicate face and been harder and harder to come by. "Sorry I got you in trouble," she whispered, but not softly enough.

"Woman, I love trouble," he murmured.

Ain't that the truth.

"Yeah? What's her name this time?" Fiona teased.

Asa cleared his throat again, this time to get down to business.

He gave Fiona the rundown from yesterday morning as she examined the crime scene photos. "ME confirms strangulation. Forensic analysis is being done on trace evidence. You know how that goes. TBI will do what it can and assist us in any way possible if we need them." The Tennessee Bureau of Investigation did all forensic analysis for every law agency in Tennessee. To say they were slammed was an understatement. "But I've had evidence sent to the lab at Quantico. Might get it faster."

"What about a copycat killer? I know the feather has never been made public that we know of. It's possible someone knew," Violet said.

"We can't rule out a copycat killer, but it's unlikely," Asa returned.

Fiona scrutinized the photo of Jenny Miller. "What naughty thing did you do?"

"Pardon me?" Amanda said.

Fiona passed her a stoic expression. "He kills them because they've been naughty. At least in his eyes."

"I've read the profile," Violet said, "and while I agree that he's probably a white male thirty-eight to forty-eight, how can you be so sure that he's suffering from dissociative identity disorder? I also read your witness statement."

Asa trained an eagle eye on Fiona. This is where she got uncomfortable talking about the NRK, and he was almost certain that she'd held back information about that night when she'd been abducted. A secret only she and the killer shared. Asa had never pressed her to reveal it; he had a secret of his own, but he couldn't deny the feeling of jealousy over a sick killer who had something of Fiona—even knowledge—that Asa wasn't allowed to have.

Fiona scanned the room. Everyone but Amanda, Selah and Violet knew her story. "If you've read my witness statement then you ought to clearly see why. He switched personalities on me twice in that one evening. In control and dominant—hunting me in the woods. Then meek and mild and confused—out of sorts. As a teenager I was baffled by it and assumed he'd been toying with me, but as I studied and matured, I realized what was actually transpiring. Personality shifts due to extreme circumstances. I didn't work up the initial profile. Behavioral Analyst Solomon Reigel with the BAU did, and once I joined the FBI, I agreed with his assessment."

Violet's eyebrows raised. "Okay. Go on."

"We believe he's a vigilante killer. A protector of children due to the fact that each victim allegedly harmed a child or teenager."

"Who did you allegedly harm?"

Fiona ran her tongue over her top teeth. "My sister, her two friends and I were taken early on, likely his first victims before he got a real taste and a signature. We can't be certain why us. I can't speak for all the girls, but me and Colleen never hurt or harmed anyone."

She was in her element now. Talking all things Nursery Rhyme Killer.

"You said Jenny Miller was a teacher? High school?" Fiona asked, moving away from Violet's questions. Didn't mean Violet was done yet, though.

"Yes," Asa said. "At St. George's."

Fiona met his eyes and like old times, they silently conversed. Yes, there could be a significant connection since Fiona, her sister and the other girls all attended St. George's. "Have you interviewed teachers and staff yet?"

"We interviewed faculty and students who were available at the school—it is summer, you know—and those who weren't, we have on the docket to call or canvass. Nothing but love for Jenny Miller so far."

"No one is squeaky clean," Violet offered. "There's someone who has dirt on this woman."

"We'll follow up. Compare notes," Asa added.

"I want to go. Today."

Asa gritted his teeth. There she went calling shots and making demands.

"Sorry," she said, reading his body language, instinctively knowing his feelings. Guess she'd done a poor job of forgetting, too. "If it's on your schedule, I'd like to accompany whoever goes."

An olive branch. He'd take it. "Okay."

Violet clasped her chin and tilted her head. "Finish your loose theory, Agent."

Fiona pointed to the victim board on the wall at the head of the table and to a photo of Robert Williams. Track coach and US history teacher. Germantown High. He'd been twenty-seven at the time. Married. No children. Youth leader at his church, Abundant Life. "We thought of pedophilia when we realized he'd been staged like 'Georgie Porgie'—he kissed the girls and made them cry in the rhyme."

Amanda scrunched her nose as she held his crime photo. "Found in the girls' locker room with lipstick smeared on his mouth and fake tears drawn on his cheeks. That's sick."

Taking advantage of young girls was sick, too. If it was true.

Fiona pursed her lips. "We never found concrete evidence that he had done anything illegal. Two girls admitted he flirted and 'sort of' came on to them. With Robert dead, it was hearsay. His wife, Tanya, swore he was the greatest guy that ever walked the planet besides Jesus."

"They might have been afraid to admit it. Shame. Unnecessary guilt. Fear of what their peers might think. High school can be vicious," Violet said. "Why nursery rhymes? Are they personal to him?"

This was her baby right here. She'd created a sick nursery in their home together, but instead of housing an infant, it cradled a twisted sicko who had his clutches so deep into her she didn't even realize they pierced and pained her. The few times Asa had mentioned starting a family, she'd reminded him they didn't have room until the NRK was caught. In hindsight, Asa should have known then that there would never be a real life or any normalcy for them.

Fiona commanded the murder board and everyone's attention. "I believe that Rhyme—"

"You're on a first-name basis with him?" Violet asked, one dark eyebrow raised.

Fiona bristled and refrained from meeting Asa's eye. "I believe Rhyme was abused from early childhood—old enough to have heard or read nursery rhymes. He may have used these rhymes to escape horror that was inflicted upon him, or it's possible these rhymes may have been used to punish him in some form, and now he's using them to punish others—to tell a story."

"What kind of story?" Amanda asked.

"Possibly the children's stories through the victims and their staged nursery rhymes. 'There was an Old Woman Who Lived in a Shoe.' That was his fifth staging and eighth homicide. Maria Windell. Age sixty-three. Appears he's outing her abuse of her grandchildren. Though only one said she hurt them. The others denied it. But we do think he's exacting punishment on his victims."

"How did he exact punishment on you?" Violet asked.

"That's where things get sticky. Again, we hadn't inflicted any pain on children." Fiona's chin raised as if she was physically rising above the tragedy. "But the theory of exacting punishment holds because when I was abducted, he called me 'kitty' and 'naughty.' Both come from the same rhyme. 'Three Little Kittens.' I assure you it was not said in an endearing manner."

Violet raised a skeptical eyebrow. "And what did you find running the DID trail?"

Ty stood and pressed his hands on the table, leaning his weight into them. "When the case was under the violent crimes unit, they hunted for possible suspects in the area with a dissociative identity disorder diagnosis. Prisons. Hospitals. Dead end."

"When did it change hands to the SCU?" Violet asked.

Fiona massaged her neck. "I connected the feathers while in Violent Crimes and a rookie. My sister and her friends, the Shetlands and Robert Williams, had already been murdered. Their cases had gone cold."

"But you never stopped tracking the man who abducted

you and killed your sister." Violet's eyebrows inched upward slightly as if she could appreciate the obsession.

"Once I transferred with the case to the SCU—" she glanced at Asa "—we began reinterviewing victims and trying to piece together new leads. The cases remained cold, but I never personally stopped. No."

"We were directly involved in the last two homicides, and we chased the same DID avenue," Ty said. "We had a few leads but they didn't pan out. Still, we believe the profile stands."

His protectiveness over Fiona was brotherly and fierce, but Fiona hadn't ever accused Ty of being overprotective. Asa, on the other hand... That had been an unending argument between them. Fiona could label it as possessive or controlling all day long. But Asa had been forced to choose if his mother or his sister would live or die at the hands of serial killer Raymond Vect. At his mother's insistent pleas to choose Kacie to live, he had. Both of them had then watched in horror as Raymond Vect slit their mother's throat. So Fiona's gripes about overprotectiveness had fallen on deaf ears and would continue to as long as she was under his charge, either personally or professionally.

Asa wouldn't ever go through something like that again.

Worn out and stomach rumbling, Fiona slumped in the chair at the conference room table. She'd spent the past hour meticulously briefing the newbies on the team of each nursery rhyme murder, and guiltily withholding information.

She'd had no choice. Fear and feelings of utter humiliation kept those moments locked down deep, where they festered and reached into her dreams at night, hissing dark truths with a forked tongue until she awakened in a full sweat and a panic attack. How many nights had Asa tried to coax her back to peaceful sleep with hopes she'd reveal the cause for such horrible nightmares? Too many.

And night after night she refused to open up to him. To unload the heavy secret and then be forced to see contempt and disgust in his eyes—not love and loyalty. So she'd held back. Because she couldn't bear for him to discover who she truly was. She could barely stand it herself.

It didn't affect the profile. Didn't change the fact Rhyme was a murderer. Beginning with Colleen and Colleen's two girlfriends, then moving onto the murders of Pastor Mark Shetland and his wife, Valerie. Staged to "Johnny Shall Have a New Bonnet."

The sixth victim but third to be staged was Robert Williams, the high school coach and youth leader who had been posed to "Georgie Porgie." Next came Alan Minton—a property law attorney—staged to "When I Was a Little Boy I Lived by Myself" and then Maria Windell, a widowed grandmother of eight grandchildren positioned to "There was an Old Woman Who Lived in a Shoe."

They'd been dramatic. Meticulous. Horrific. And some hard to place with the corresponding rhyme. It had taken Fiona memorizing each one in great detail to discover some of them, while others had been obvious from the beginning... at least to her.

"Who wants to grab food? I need a break." Tiberius didn't wait for an answer and strolled to the door. "Gus's fried chicken? Great. It's unanimous. I'll drive."

Some things never changed. "Asa, I'd like to go St. George's and talk to colleagues and administrators instead if that's okay with you." She hoped playing nice and recognizing him as the SAC would play in her favor. "Also, Detective Barnes, I'd like to read the statements concerning Jenny's Miller's homicide before I go."

"I'll get those immediately," she said and pulled her phone from her pocket as she exited the room.

Asa pressed his tongue to his cheek and rubbed his earlobe. "Fiona, you have to eat. Everyone is itchy to get rolling on the case, but it's fuel. And I know you ain't sleeping tonight, so get a bite and then we'll make a game plan."

She wanted to protest but Asa had always insisted his team eat and try to at least rest in order to be productive, and he was right; running on empty was a distraction. If she bucked him now, she wouldn't get anywhere later. "Okay."

Owen waited by the door and Violet continued to stand at her chair as if debating whether to eat or remain.

Asa's smile was appreciative and genuine. "Meet me back here after and we'll go to St. George's."

He wasn't planning to join them.

"Owen, after you're done, work on the geographic locations. One thing in common is churches or church people. Maybe we can develop something new."

"Do you want us to bring you anything?" Owen asked.

"No. We'll get something."

We'll. Him and Amanda—who was in the hall on the phone. Fiona opened the door and marched out. Tiberius was waiting by the elevators. "I'm thinking extra spicy. What say you, Fi Fi McGee?"

"I say you know I hate it when you call me that." She stepped into the elevator, refusing to look back at the happy couple.

After lunch, they exited Gus's and headed for the Suburban. A flash of white drew her attention, then stole her breath.

Tendrils of ice chilled her bones.

Swallowing the sharp ache growing in her throat, she scanned the parking lot. Nothing out of the ordinary. No one lurking, but the feel of watchful eyes kept her glued in place.

Tiberius stopped at her frozen state. "What's your deal, Fi?"

Fiona pointed to the side of the vehicle she'd been sitting on. Now next to the rear wheel was a small round bouquet of white roses and lilies. "Pocketful of posies," she murmured as she inched to them and kneeled.

Owen cursed and Tiberius grimaced at the flowers. "Those aren't posies. Those are lilies and roses."

"No," Fiona said, "the way they're put together is the posy. Small. Round in shape."

"Ty," Violet said, "get some gloves. Now."

Ty got the gloves and Fiona slipped them on and held up a small white envelope that contained a card. It hadn't been sealed, only tucked. No DNA. Probably not going to get prints, either. Rhyme was too smart for that.

The world tilted and her head buzzed. Blood whooshed in her ears.

Removing the card, she read the words.

Still so pure. So lovely. Welcome home, my love. I knew you'd come. I only had to call. I anticipate our reunion. To finish the dance we began. Ring-a-ring o' roses...

The old rhyme written originally, unlike the way kids sang it today: ring around the rosy. A rhyme most likely about the Great Plague, though many folklore scholars regarded the theory as baseless.

The doctor's plague mask Rhyme wore. Did he find his victims a plague to children? He was the remedy—the purifier.

"What dance did you begin?" Violet asked.

Round and round they'd been going for years. Her sister, her family and even her marriage had already fallen to ash. What more did he want?

He'd touched her face. In the woods. In the cabin. She could still feel the cool touch of his thumb caressing her cheek.

So pure. So lovely.

She squeezed her eyes closed at the memory and shuddered while willing herself not to cry. No tears.

"What's this mean?" Violet asked.

"I honestly don't know." This recent murder had been his beacon in the night. He was right. She'd picked up everything and come. She'd had no choice. Never had. But what was the endgame? Was there one? Asa was going to be livid. Use this message to rehash old arguments, make old points.

Rhyme knew he would, too. That was partially his intent—to keep them divided.

"Bag it," Tiberius said. "We'll send it off to the lab. Fi, you okay?"

No. Not even close.

Owen must have left because he jogged back to the vehicle. "No cameras. The Suburban wasn't in our view. No way to get any identification. Not even a logo for a floral shop. Could be out of his own backyard. Who knows?"

But Rhyme had followed them, been brazen enough to get this close. Fiona mechanically entered the vehicle and strapped on her seat belt, but the past played on repeat in her mind, creating a dizzy spell.

As the field office came into view, her stomach churned as she imagined Asa's reaction, his temper. The words that were coming. She was so tired of fighting.

Inside, they met Asa in the case room. Tiberius looked at Fiona, offered for her to take the lead with a head nod, but she waited a beat too long.

"The NRK decided to drop by for lunch," Tiberius said.

Asa's head snapped up. "What do you mean by that?"

Tiberius held up the flowers and handed him the card now inside a plastic evidence bag.

"What is this?" Asa barked.

"A gift," Fiona mumbled.

Asa's jaw hardened and he ate up the ground, reaching her and staring until she met his steely gaze.

"They're posies." She explained what posies were again.

He read the message, his nostrils flaring. He pursed his lips. "Well…he got what he wanted, didn't he?"

"Yes," she whispered.

"Like he always has." He heaved a sigh. "What's this line mean about purity and loveliness and dancing?" He tapped his foot, waiting impatiently.

"I don't know." She couldn't do it. Couldn't bring herself to confide. To explain this would be to reveal her own shortcomings. She could have stopped Rhyme years ago with one simple act. Instead Fiona had been cowardly. She shoved down the dark memories.

"I don't believe you, Fiona," he said softly and left the conference room.

"I'll make sure this gets sent to the lab," Tiberius said.

Owen went straight to his board and Violet leaned against the wall like a statue, studying Fiona. She pretended not to notice. Five minutes later, Asa returned with his suit coat hanging over one shoulder. Even he was feeling the summer heat, as his sleeves were rolled to his elbows. "Let's head to St. George's. Violet, you're with us." As a colleague or a buffer? Fiona hoped for both.

"Asa, is that all you're going to say?" Fiona asked, following him to the elevator. No yelling? No hurling accusations? No unending drilling of her?

"Is that all you're going to say?" he countered and pressed the elevator button. "And, I quote, 'a gift.'"

Touché.

Fiona said no more about it, but it was obviously eating at Asa, judging by his cheek twitching and thumb drumming the wheel as they sat in traffic. Fiona had jumped in the back before Violet had a chance to offer her the passenger seat. Traffic was bumper-to-bumper on Humphrey's. The air-conditioning worked overtime to do its job. The radio played a current pop song and the sky was cloudless and blue. It was hard to believe that death and destruction had rained down only a day ago and now this dark foreshadowing of impending doom. This was a Louis Armstrong's "What a Wonderful World" kind of day.

Asa maneuvered them to St. George's with little to no conversation, lost in thought or simply ignoring them. For summer, the parking lot wasn't too sparse. Camps, various athletic events and other extracurricular activities were taking place. Inside, the icy temps were a welcome reprieve. A redhead occupied the front desk with a venti coffee and a Julia Roberts grin. "Good afternoon. How can I help you?"

Asa introduced them and held out his creds. "We're investigating Jenny Miller's murder."

Tears sprung to her eyes. "That was so awful to hear. Jenny was the sweetest person. We all loved her."

"Your name?" he asked.

"Andi. Andi Fleming."

"How well did you know Jenny?" Fiona asked.

"We were friends. A few of us would go out on Friday nights twice a month. Dinner. Have a few drinks and unwind."

"Could we have the names of the ladies who attended these nights?" Fiona recorded the names. "Also, did you go to the same place each time?"

"Yes. Mollie Fontaine Lounge."

Fiona had never been but she was familiar with the place. Located on what once was called Millionaire's Row. Victorian mansions. Many were now businesses, museums and bed-and-breakfasts. "I hear Ricki's toasted brioche chocolate sandwich is divine," Fiona added as she jotted the information.

"Oh, it is. You should have one. Seriously." Andi paused then sniffled. "I feel so guilty talking about desserts when Jenny is gone. She lives in a good neighborhood. Lived. I don't know who would do this kind of thing. Do you?"

"We're working to find out," Asa offered.

"Andi, have you seen my glasses? I've lost them again. I feel like I can't keep anything straight these da—" A man with more pepper than salt in his hair appeared, dressed to the nines. Clean-shaven. Since when did teachers and administrators become this good-looking? Fiona had never once had a crush on a teacher when she attended. "Oh. Hello."

"Agents with the FBI Strange Crimes Unit," Asa said and revealed his creds.

"Oh. FBI?" The man's jet-black eyebrows pulled together. "Strange crimes..." Those same eyebrows rose as the homicide went from a random home invasion to something more sinister. "No," he breathed.

"I'm afraid so. You are?"

"Sorry." He thrust a powerful arm out and shook Asa's hand. "I'm the head of school. Daniel Osborn."

Fiona made note and glanced at Violet. Impassive. But a lingering gaze gave her away. Daniel Osborn was a treat to the eye—even eyes of a woman who didn't appear to have much personality. Possibly mid-to-late forties. A couple inches taller than Asa's six-foot-one frame. As if Asa felt her perusal of the head of school, he shot her a glare. She returned it with an innocent expression.

"What can you tell us about Jenny Miller?" Asa asked and

stepped in between Mr. Osborn and Fiona and Violet. Guess he was taking back the interview. She exchanged a glance with Violet and for the first time since she'd been introduced to the hard-to-read agent, Violet graced her with a close-lipped smile.

"She's been with us...had been with us for about eight years. She taught American literature and helped with the fine arts program and was assistant cheerleading coach. We knew when she didn't show and didn't call that something was wrong. She's never late to work and rarely calls in." His line of sight went over Asa's shoulder and met Fiona with a lady-killer grin. She debated if it was flattering or in poor taste when his teacher had recently been brutally murdered. "We will cooperate fully like we told the police."

Asa's glance was disapproving, but no one but Fiona would notice. "Thank you," Asa said. "We, too, will need full access to the school, her classroom and available colleagues for our own investigation."

"That can be done. Is there anything else we can do?"

The door opened and a man of average height and weight entered. Sandy blond hair. Short beard. Early-to-mid forties. Not dressed as stylish as Mr. Osborn but in a light blue dress shirt, a navy vest over it. Khaki pants. Shockingly blue eyes impaled Fiona's gaze. "Hello," he murmured. Soft voice. Fiona noticed smooth hands.

"This is James Furman, associate head of school. My right hand." Mr. Osborn grinned but Mr. Furman dipped his head. Legit modesty. "These are agents from the FBI's Strange Crimes Unit."

He perked up at that and made a quick perusal of the three of them. "I didn't realize..." Verbally revealing that Jenny's death was beyond the scope of a shooting or stabbing was too hard to articulate. Those kinds of crimes were seen daily on

TV and online. While tragic in and of themselves, people had become desensitized. Oh, they were shot. Oh, they were stabbed to death. Beaten to death. Day in and day out, humans wiped out other humans' lives this way. But something like this—the kind of crime that hid in dark corners and generally was only revealed in Netflix documentaries when it touched a person's own backyard—was all too ghastly. Fiona witnessed this on an almost daily basis. Murder, in any form, should always be abominable. Always be hard to express in words.

"How well did you know Jenny?" Asa asked.

"I suppose as well as any of us in administration. She was a good teacher. Jenny always took an express interest in her students and their lives." If Fiona hadn't been paying close attention she wouldn't have registered the hint of disdain in his voice, the small flare of his nostrils.

"What was it about Jenny Miller taking interest in the lives of her students that was so distasteful, Mr. Furman?" she asked.

The question clearly startled him and he licked his lips, looked to his supervisor. Mr. Osborn stood patiently, awaiting the answer along with the rest of them.

"I, uh, I think she was a little too personal. There have to be boundaries between faculty and students regardless of how much we might care for them and their situations."

"Any particular student or situation come to mind?" Fiona inquired. And was he talking about Jenny Miller or himself?

"No. Just in general. Now, if you'll excuse me." Mr. Furman slipped past Mr. Osborn.

Andi held out a folder of papers. "List of the names you wanted with addresses. Two are here today working. One tutors, the other helps with our summer camp. If you need anything else let me know."

Mr. Osborn rested a hand on her shoulder. "Thank you, Andi. If you need a few moments to yourself, take them." He then placed his attention on Fiona. "My office is down the hall." He motioned behind him. "If you need anything and Andi isn't available, come on back. You're more than welcome." His smile was kind but Fiona still couldn't shake the impression he was expressing interest in her.

Maybe it had just been so long since anyone had.

"We'll do that." Asa swiftly exited the office.

Fiona and Violet followed him into the foyer, and Asa spun on them. "Is it at all possible for you two to not ogle potential suspects?"

"He's a suspect?" Fiona asked.

"We were ogling?" Violet also asked at the same time. "I wasn't ogling. Were you?"

"No, not me."

"I was admiring. He's admirable," Violet stated dryly.

Fiona snickered under her breath. "He was."

Asa huffed and folded his arms over his chest. "Whenever you're done and want to act like professionals, let me know. Just because you're in a school doesn't make you schoolgirls." After a few beats, he added, "And he was not that much to admire."

Fiona held in snarky commentary on that statement. "We're ready to do our job now, Bear."

The tic near the corner of his right eye let her know the nonendearment wasn't lost on him. "Let's divide and conquer," Asa said, then split the list between the three of them. "We'll have to door-to-door the others."

Fiona headed for the theater to talk to Lindsey Monroe, who was working on props for fall. If she was close enough to Jenny to hang out twice a month for drinks and dinner, she surely had to know something. Rhyme had a reason— unhinged as it was and other than getting Fiona's attention— to kill her. Now to find out what naughty thing she'd done and to assign the proper rhyme to her. She hated to admit she was stumped on which one he'd used to stage her.

He couldn't slip through her fingers this time. She wouldn't let him.

Chapter Five

This day was not even over and was past the point of stressful. Asa pinched the bridge of his nose, hoping to stave off the headache coming, and stood from the chair in the major case room, stretching his aching back and wishing he'd eaten lunch earlier. He'd ordered in but didn't touch it due to relaying the news to Amanda about his former relationship—marriage—to Fiona and how the Nursey Rhyme Killer fit into the sordid details.

Personally, Amanda didn't love it and point-blank asked if there was any chance of reconciliation between the two of them. He'd given her an emphatic no. Besides, the only man in Fiona's life was her precious Rhyme. Even now she wasn't owning up to every detail, but Asa couldn't force her hand. No, only the NRK got to do that. Never had been space for anyone else—though Fiona had genuinely attempted to try to make room for Asa. But the NRK knew how to crowd every corner, and even if they finally caught him, Asa was no one's leftovers or someone's second choice.

So, no. Amanda didn't need to worry about even a slim chance of romantic reconciliation.

Asa wouldn't be so stupid to deny that their shared history left a few old feelings clinging to his heart, but that's all they were. Old memories. But today, for an instant, those feelings had surfaced and popped bright green when Daniel Osborn had shown unabashed interest in Fiona; her teasing in the hall was nothing more than jesting and somehow bonding with Violet in a small way, as well as trying not to fixate on the posies she'd received. Fiona had zero interest in the head of school; her focus was on one man, as it always had been.

Amanda seemed wary but satisfied with his answer, and let him know she wouldn't be back to the field office today due to a load of work from other cases, which he believed was true, but he had to wonder if she was slipping into the background to make things easier for him with Fiona. And that he appreciated because nothing about Fiona and this case was easy.

Their earlier interviews with staff and students hadn't given them any strong leads and after a few hours of going nowhere, they'd returned here to look over the cases with fresh eyes. Fiona sat opposite him at the end of the table with her nose in a Mother Goose book, working to decipher which rhyme the NRK had attached to Jenny Miller. Ty rocked in his chair, antsy—he'd never been one to enjoy long bouts of silence. He broke through the quiet. "I want a birthday party this year."

Violet, who stood at the back of the room staring at the board, slowly turned her attention to him along with Owen, who was tacking pins on the board to pinpoint locations— Mollie Fontaine Lounge, where they had girls' nights out, and the residences of the teachers who had attended those evenings.

Fiona paused from reading the book. "You want what?"

"I want a birthday party this year."

"Let me get this straight. Instead of working on the case,

you're thinking about party hats and balloons?" Fiona asked with a scowl.

"It's been two years since you've thrown me one and the gang is back together again. Y'all's house hasn't sold so we have a venue."

Asa's stomach roiled. Last he'd talked to Fiona was about nine months ago and it had been all business. No longer could he live in the house they'd purchased together, dreamed in, hoped in. He'd called to notify her he was putting it on the market. While it was being shown, he and Fiona were splitting the mortgage and the utilities since the Realtor felt keeping them on would help, especially in summer. Once it was sold they'd divvy the money.

"And don't say you'll celebrate it on the Fourth—that's like a kid whose birthday is the day after Christmas."

Asa glanced at Fiona. They'd always thrown a party for team members; it brought unity and some downtime from their grueling jobs. After Asa and Fiona divorced, the celebrations stopped and Ty had never once mentioned it until now.

He leaned back in the chair, a smug expression mixed with mischief. "I also want fireworks purchased prior to the Fourth. I'm worth more than the after-holiday sale price."

Fiona grunted. "That's debatable."

"I mean it." He thrummed his fingers on the table, awaiting the verdict.

Violet capped her Expo marker. "Celebrate your birthday on your own time. We have a killer to catch. Besides, birthdays are just another day. Get over yourself."

Ty didn't seem to take offense. He clucked his tongue against his teeth. "You're rude, Violet. Anyone ever tell you that?"

She ignored him and busied herself with a file.

A birthday party wasn't a bad idea. This would be a bru-

tal investigation and after coming off two weeks in New Orleans on a rigorous case, the downtime would be healthy. Not
to mention Ty was clearly trying to bring the team together
in camaraderie, lighten tension. Tension on the team meant
they'd miss things. They needed to be relaxed and focused.

"Okay. You can have a party."

Fiona raised her eyebrows.

Ty fist-pumped the air. "Like old times."

Owen high-fived Ty. Already the idea of a celebration had
breathed some life into the team, except Violet. Asa explained
their tradition. "All the team shows up. No work talk." He
cut an eye at Fiona. "Just fun."

"I don't do birthdays," Violet retorted.

"Kill. Joy!" Ty groaned and collapsed in his seat. "It's one
night, Violet. Pretend to have a personality that enjoys parties."

Again, she ignored him. Asa raised a hand to signal Ty to
back off. "Okay, let's focus on the case."

"In Thomas Miller's interview, he said his wife was a God-
fearing woman. She'd never cheat on him and was faithful.
Where did they go to church?" Owen asked. "I'll get a pin
in place."

Asa blew a sigh of frustration. They hadn't asked. What
they knew was the lingerie wasn't Jenny's—or if it was Mr.
Miller had never seen it before. Most likely she was dressed in
it after the murder. He hit the intercom button and put Selah
on finding out where they'd attended church. The Shetlands
had pastored Hope Community. The Williamses had attended
Abundant Life. Both churches were within ten miles of each
other.

"Fi? Any idea what nursery rhyme Jenny Miller is staged
in?" he asked. She'd been at that book for over an hour. He
wondered if she was searching or pondering on that vague
threat wrapped in a romantic notion. His blood raced hot. The

NRK was not going to lay one finger on Fiona. Asa would make sure of that.

Fiona studied the crime scene photo. "The black rose petals had me thrown off and centered on rhymes with the words *black* and *flowers* or *death* and *flowers*. But she's dressed scantily and the boa is made of feathers. Also, look at this photo." She held it up. "That's a lot of used perfume on her vanity. Nearly forty bottles."

"I noticed that at the scene, too," Violet said. "She either didn't know the word *subtle* or they were placed there by the killer. I also think the candle on the vanity was staged—it was vanilla-scented. Mr. Miller should be able to confirm the perfume bottles and the candle."

Asa hit the intercom again and requested Selah to join them.

"Where did he get this many bottles of empty vintage Shalimar? What's Shalimar smell like?" Fiona huffed.

Selah fired her fingers across her computer keyboard. "A vanilla-and-musk scent."

The NRK seemed to have an affinity for the scent of vanilla. "Why these bottles and this brand? Is it relevant? Does someone he knows wear it? Someone from his past? Of significance? Maybe he has a sister, a mother, a wife. A lot of serial killers carry out perfectly normal lives and jobs. Upstanding citizens and even church deacons have been serial killers. But even so. Forty bottles. That's odd. Why so many?"

"One or two wouldn't stand out. Forty makes a statement." Violet tapped a pen on the table. "Overkill. Indulgence. It sets the stage for what she's dressed to do. He might be trying to convey she indulged in extramarital affairs." She shrugged. "Maybe we'll get a print off one of them."

"That would be fantastic." Asa crashed back into his chair. "Rhymes?"

Fiona held open the Mother Goose book and pointed to

a nursery rhyme. "'Higgledy Piggledy, My Black Hen.' Fits even though the meaning is a bit skewed." She read the rhyme to the team.

"'She lays eggs for the gentlemen,'" Fiona said. "'Sometimes nine. Sometimes ten.'"

Violet grunted. "Black feathers. Hens. She's had multiple lovers though she's married. I'm tracking. How does that play into your theory on being a vigilante for kids?"

Fiona frowned. "It doesn't. The word here is *gentlemen*, which implies adults."

"Eggs are almost baby chicks," Ty said. "What if she's giving children to gentlemen? Pimping out students? That would fit the profile."

This entire case was getting worse by the second. "Before we get on that path, let's work the case based on the facts we do have, not the theory we might lean toward. Follow the victimology and see where it leads. If it directs us to an underage prostitution ring, then we go from there."

Fiona tossed the photos on the table. "It makes sense this would have to do with adolescents. We need to reinterview old witnesses and people surrounding prior murders. Levi Shetland, for one. He was eighteen when his parents were murdered and in his early twenties when we personally interviewed him. He might know and be willing to divulge more now that he's a more mature adult. I'm aware his father was a pastor, but we've discovered pastors aren't perfect and hide secrets. These victims are all too perfect and that's wherein the problem lies."

"If his parents abused him, he might be willing to talk now that they've been dead a while, and that's only if our theory is correct. We've got some holes," Ty admitted. "But I agree with Fiona."

Fiona's abduction and the murder of three teenage girls

threw a wrench in their entire theory. But she stood by her initial statement that neither she nor the other girls had behaved in a way that was damaging to a child or other teenager. But Fiona was also hiding something. Surely it wouldn't be something that skewed the profile. "Let's pretend we haven't looked in to these cases before and treat them as if they're new, including your case, Fiona."

She acquiesced with a stiff nod. "We need Levi Shetland's address."

Selah piped up. "Hey, boss. The Millers attended Full Life Christian. It's off Poplar." She recited the exact address for Owen to add a pushpin in the wall-sized map of Memphis and the surrounding areas.

"Thanks. And Levi Shetland's current address?"

Keys clacked and a few seconds later Selah rattled off the apartment address Levi now lived at and his job location.

Owen pressed a pin into the map. "Full Life is also within ten miles of the other two churches associated with our vics."

This could be important, a solid lead. Hope took flight.

Violet perched on the edge of the table. "You said you thought Levi Shetland had been abused. Nothing I've read in his or others' statements lead to that conclusion."

"He'd recently turned eighteen when his parents were murdered and staged to 'Johnny Shall Have a New Bonnet,'" Fiona said. "They were sitting at the table dressed in bonnets and stockings and they held *belts* in their hands. Which was bizarre because that has nothing to do with the rhyme."

"Maybe you got the rhyme wrong," Violet replied.

"I don't think so," Fiona said. "When we personally talked to Levi, he said he left at eighteen and he hadn't seen his parents in four months. Legal age. Got out of Dodge. Who does that? A lot of kids. But no communication? I felt he was hiding something."

Levi Shetland's possible confession wouldn't catch the NRK, but it was a piece of the puzzle and every piece they slipped into place would eventually reveal the full picture, and that would aid them in finally putting an end to this sick jerk.

"What about Jenny Miller and the possibility she was turning out students in a rich kid school?" Violet pointed at him. "That's gonna stir some stink."

"We'll be discreet in our questions." No need tarnishing a reputation if it was unwarranted. They'd tread lightly. They had no other choice since the team was technically grasping at straws.

With about thirty minutes left until Mollie Fontaine Lounge opened at 5:00 p.m., Asa had chosen to go by Levi Shetland's place first.

The air swirling in the vehicle held a dose of awkward tension between Asa and Fiona. No buffer this time. Violet was working her way from most recent to oldest cases, doing victimology. Owen was with her, and Ty had visited Full Life Christian, where the Millers had attended, to garner possible information on Jenny Miller. Was she involved in any ministries or programs? Who were her friends? Had she ever been to counseling? Hopefully, something would pop.

Fiona broke the weird silence. "I guess you told her about us when we went to lunch earlier. She good with the situation?"

Discussing his new girlfriend with his ex-wife wasn't exactly the kind of conversation Asa would like to be having. "She knows our past and that you're only here to work the case before you return to your life in Chicago…and I guess to Rathbone." If they were going to poke around in each other's personal lives his wasn't the only one on the table…but, gah, he detested that smug jerk and always had—Fiona aside.

Fiona had been blind to what an arrogant manipulator Luke

Rathbone was. Now she was seeing him romantically. Not that Asa had a say in whom she dated—or even cared—but she could do better than Rathbone. Guess after all these years, Luke hadn't been able to get over her.

Asa had barely survived it. Scars littered his heart and soul.

She released a weighty sigh. "I'm not and have never been romantically involved with Luke. He helped me transfer—which I needed to do at the time. And, yes, he had hopes it would lead into something more, but the truth is I don't have any more to give. If I had, I'd have given it to you. So maybe it sets your mind at ease. Maybe you don't care. Either way, you know."

Admittedly, it gave him some relief. The guy sat wrong with him. Period. "I appreciate the honesty. And you can do better than him."

A throaty laugh escaped her lips. "Yeah? Can I do better than you?" she asked with ease, a hint of the once playful and even flirty Fiona.

"Me? Not hardly."

"Then I'm doomed." She laughed again and he laughed with her. Maybe if they played their cards right they could come out of this as friends.

"So about this ridiculous birthday," Fiona said. "Has it been two years? You stopped throwing them birthday parties because I left? No wonder they're so glad to see me."

There was no question that Owen and Ty were stoked to have her back, like the old days, and Selah had noted she liked Fiona. Cami, however, had kept a cool distance—bad blood and all with Fi. And Violet was another matter altogether; rarely did Asa have an inkling what she was thinking unless she voiced it.

"You were the party thrower. I was just the grill master. I tried one after—they weren't the same without you. So…"

He couldn't bring himself to keep trying. Not alone. Not without her.

She looked away then huffed. "I'm not buying fireworks full price. That's all I'm saying about that."

Asa chuckled. "I'm with you. I'll handle it." They talked party ideas, purchases and dates, which were flexible depending on the turn of the investigation. Nothing was ever written in stone in the SCU.

"Levi Shetland lives on Poplar Avenue now. Midtown Place Apartments."

"Which set?"

"Stratford." Asa cranked the air higher and loosened his tie. "Reasonable rent but small. Works at the Zebra Lounge. Trimble Place. Bartends. Not married. No kids. Selah says there's nothing exciting to tell or that she can dig up. No social media."

"Hmm." She flicked the edge of her index finger with her thumb, a sure sign she was thinking. "Works at a bar. His parents were religious. His dad a pastor. Doesn't religion frown on drinking?"

"Some. I'm not the religion expert. I am learning stuff, though, when I read my Bible."

"Yeah? Like what?"

"Well, today I read that we have to stop living the way we did before we put our faith in Christ. And then it gave a few of those ways and one was putting away anger. To say I nearly threw the book across the room was an understatement." He laughed but he was serious. His temper was his archenemy. "I am trying, though."

"I can tell. I noticed it first thing. You reeling in that bear-like temper. Your prayers or whatever you're doing…it's working."

He glanced over at her and saw the sincerity, the encouragement. It meant everything to him. "Thank you. I needed to hear that. I sometimes feel I'm losing the battle with it."

"Once you'd have never even engaged in the fight. You'll get there. Have some faith," she teased.

He grinned but she wasn't dogging him. She was spurring him on to do better even if she didn't embrace the same faith. He parallel-parked, and they stepped out into the Southern sauna.

A couple of young men on bikes rode by, backpacks jiggling. Cars zoomed up and down, the smell of grilled beef and exhaust clung to the sticky July air.

Fiona rubbed her palms on her thighs as Asa knocked on Levi Shetland's door. Scuffling sounded inside and then the door opened and a rail-thin man with bleached spiky hair and a Dunder Mifflin T-shirt peered at them with sleepy hazel eyes. He looked like the pictures of his mother. Soft, feminine features. High cheekbones. Full lips. Long lashes.

At first he smiled. "Agents Kodiak. Times two."

Back then when they'd talked with him, they'd been married and he'd gotten a kick out them having the same last name. Not anymore, but Asa didn't correct him and he didn't laugh either.

"How can I help you?" Levi asked, wariness narrowing his eyes.

Fiona showed her creds. "Been awhile, but we need to talk to you again about your parents."

Levi shook out of his deep stupor. He rubbed his sandy stubbled chin. "Do you have new information?"

"There's been a murder similar to theirs. Maybe you heard of Jenny Miller—teacher at St. George's?"

He shook his head. "I don't watch much TV unless it's *Grey's Anatomy* or *Amazing Race*." He welcomed them inside.

"Pardon the mess. You want coffee or something? I'm gonna make it, anyway. I work nights."

That explained him being asleep this late in the afternoon.

The almost seven hundred square feet of living space had new stainless-steel appliances, laminate floors. Fresh paint. "They do some remodeling recently?"

"Yeah. A few weeks ago."

"I just had a house I'm trying to sell repainted. I like the smell of new paint," Asa said. "There's something about 'new' that makes you feel like you can start over fresh, too." Break in with friendly. Subtly tell him that he can have another chance and tell what he may have held back before.

"Yeah, I guess that's true. I'm used to it now, though. I don't smell it." Levi motioned them to have a seat in the tiny kitchen and he proceeded to the coffeepot. "I like it strong. That okay?"

"Yeah, sure," Fiona said.

"Another married couple died?" Levi asked as he scooped heaps of grounds into the filter.

"No, just Mrs. Miller. But the manner of death was the same."

Asa surveyed the apartment as Fiona led the interview. A large rainbow flag hung over the black leather couch and on the floor sat two pair of men's tennis shoes but different sizes. Coconut wafted in the air and he spotted a partly burned-down candle. A bottle of wine sat on the counter opposite the coffeepot, two empty glasses. Not only did he work late, but it also appeared he'd had a guest late last night or in the early hours this morning. Might even be here now. A male guest. Had Levi's parents known about Levi's sexual orientation?

"He left it like a nursery rhyme," Fiona continued. "Not the same one he staged your parents in. Again, I'm sorry to be opening old wounds but we hoped now that time has passed—"

"Fifteen years," Levi muttered. The coffeepot gurgled as it began the rich brew. Smelled expensive. "Fifteen years and I hardly ever think of them. Sometimes on Sundays when I wake up and it's noon. I think no one forced me up. I can be who I am and not have to hide it. Live my truth."

Fiona nodded and Asa motioned her with his eyes to look around. She caught the flag in the living room. "It's hard to pretend to be someone you're not."

Asa cleared his throat. "You were asked if your parents ever mistreated you. Both times you said never. Other than forcing you to church, did they ever hurt you? Abuse you? Did they pretend to be people they weren't?"

Levi sat at the faux-mahogany barstool near the small island and his eyes watered. "You have to understand. I grew up in a strict home. My parents expected me to obey all the rules and never voice my opinion or ask questions. When I made mistakes…when I questioned my faith, my father dished out tough love."

Asa hadn't had the chance to grow up with his father. He'd died when Asa was only four and Kacie barely two months old. Car accident.

"He said a good father disciplined his children. Discipline, of course, at the time is painful but it would pay off in the end and reap a righteous man. He was quoting the Bible." A tear dripped from his cheek onto the island. "I don't think God displays tough love in the same way as my dad. At least not the God I believed in. Not to say He didn't set rules and stuff. I know the garden story… I know the Sodom and Gomorrah story. I know that one well."

The coffeepot beeped and he mechanically rose and poured three cups, then set out cream and sugar.

"When I was fifteen my father asked me if I was gay. I told him I didn't know. So that's how it began. From fifteen to their death, on a regular basis, he would quote Scripture to me while whipping me with a belt. Beat the gay out. No son of his was going to be a sodomite. I was going straight to hell." He wiped his eyes again and apologized. "I never said I was gay. I said I didn't know. I was confused and afraid. I figured if my dad was working so hard to beat it out of me, then I definitely must be." He sipped his coffee. "At eighteen, I swore to live my life how I wanted. I never stepped foot in church again, but the crazy thing is sometimes I miss it."

What an evil monster. Beating and humiliating a child regardless of why was vile. Heartless. Merciless. None of which God would be pleased with—that much Asa did know. No wonder Levi had been confused and stopped everything to do with the Christian faith. Asa might have, too.

Fiona waited a beat. "I'm so sorry, Levi. Did anyone else know your secret? Would your dad or mom have confided to anyone? Did they take you to any kind of program or counselor?"

Levi shook his head. "If they told anyone, I don't know about it. But my dad was close with one of the deacons. Kirk Loren. I don't know where he lives or even if he's alive. If Dad would have told—and I doubt he would because of the shame—it would have been him."

The nursery rhyme hadn't made complete sense until now. But it had been obvious that the Shetlands were staged in "Johnny Shall Have a New Bonnet." Both in bonnets. And both with a blue ribbon tied in their hair.

And why may not Johnny love me? And why may not I love Johnny as well as another body?

The belts in their hands. They knew their son was gay. And they, or at least his father, had physically and mentally abused him. And the NRK knew it somehow. Mark or Valerie had to have confided in someone.

"Did you ever tell anyone, like a teacher or church member, what your dad was doing to you?" Asa asked.

Levi shook his head. "No, I was ashamed."

Asa thanked him for his time.

"Did that help? I didn't know how it could back then, and you have to understand I was afraid of them. And angry."

"You helped tremendously," Asa said. "If you think of anything else, please call." He handed him a business card and they left.

In the Suburban, Fiona turned in her seat, clicking her belt in place. "'And Johnny shall have a blue ribbon to tie up his bonny brown hair.' The question is who else knew about this family secret? Rhyme knew. How? Church? People feel safe and open at church. Do you?"

"Do I what?" Asa asked.

"Feel open and safe at church. Everyone loves God and is happy to be there. A family of people. No one expects darkness to lurk in the halls of God's house. And yet, it becomes more and more obvious that it does indeed exist. Pastors abusing and taking advantage of women. Youth pastors grooming and molesting young girls and boys. You've been hearing it for decades. People let their guard down at church, and I suppose it's the place you should feel safe and able to let your dirty laundry out. But maybe Rhyme used churches to collect secrets. They're all within a ten-mile radius. That smells like hunting ground to me."

Fiona was on to something. "I thought you didn't believe in God." Fiona had gone to church a handful of times growing up. But they'd never talked about faith much during their time together; it hadn't been relevant.

"I never said I didn't believe in God. I said it's hard to believe God is good. I don't want to be a part of an organization where a people's god can't or won't protect them from bad things." She rummaged in her purse and pulled out a mint. "You know, I prayed that night running through the woods. When Rhyme was chasing me down. I prayed he wouldn't find me. That God would protect me and Colleen. But he found me. And we weren't protected. Either God didn't hear me, or He didn't care to get off His holy throne and help me. I'm okay protecting myself now." Her tone was harsh. Her words bitter.

Asa understood. He'd said basically all the same things and wrestled with his past. "I don't know why Colleen had to die or why you were abducted. What I do know is you'd never be here. Doing what you do. And you're good at it, Fi. The best. You help people every day. Good things did come from bad." And she would have never crossed paths with Asa. Granted, it had ended badly, but he didn't regret knowing her. Loving her. The good memories were worth it. "Maybe He allowed those things to happen to set a course for your future. I don't know. I don't have all the answers. I have very few answers if I'm being honest. I'm not sure there truly is a reason for everything."

They headed toward Mollie Fontaine Lounge. After interviewing the workers, they realized they'd have been better off returning tomorrow, when the other manager and employees who regularly worked Friday nights would be there. They might be of more help. No one tonight had been. Asa and Fiona had passed on dinner, though the food smelled divine and Asa was starving.

Instead they ran through a fast-food joint and ate on the way back to the office without much chitchat, the interviews of the day turning over in their minds. Asa had called Selah and discovered Kirk Loren had died three years ago. If Pastor Shetland had confided in him, they'd never know.

Fiona wadded up the bags and carried them inside the field office.

"Well?" Ty asked as they entered.

Fiona chucked the bag in the trash and told him the news on Levi Shetland. "Mollie Fontaine Lounge was a bust. We're going back tomorrow. What did you get from the church?"

Ty yawned and stretched. "Jenny Miller was in a small group for teachers. I got a list of names. She also helped with church dramas—I got more names. No go for any kind of counseling. The pastor didn't actually know her personally. Big churches and all—they push small groups so there's tiny communities of believers to support one another." Leave it to Ty to take interest in the religious behavior since that was his expertise. "I guess the preacher gets to get up on Sunday, teach the lesson and call it a day the rest of the week." His tone was clearly lacking in positivity.

"I wouldn't say that," Asa said. How could one man know hundreds or thousands of people intimately? Ty was being unfair, but after all his research and studies on religions, he'd resigned himself to the fact that none of them were of much value, but were a way to manipulate and control people. Of course, that was his personal experience talking, too. "What I would say is that your interview didn't go well."

"No. But there's always tomorrow."

They batted around theories and finally Asa called them off for the night. Fiona opened her mouth to protest but he raised his hand. "My team. My call. No one works well without rest and, mind you, we've all been exhausted from our two weeks in New Orleans. We need sleep."

"And food," Owen added. "I didn't hear my phone ringing with a request for my order." He winked and rubbed his stomach. "I need sustenance, woman."

As they made their way to the elevators, Asa held back Fiona. "Hey, I think it would be smart to tell me which hotel you're staying in. Safety precautions. The NRK not only knows you're here, but has been within feet of you. If he's blatant enough to put flowers by the car of a team of agents then he's wily enough to follow you to a hotel."

"I'm not staying at a hotel."

No way she was staying with her dad. "Where, then?"

"The house." She licked her lips and gave him a defiant stare. "I travel all the time and I'm sick of hotels. I pay half the house payment and utilities since we have to keep it staged for walk-throughs." The real estate agent said it would sell faster if they could envision it as a home, not a house. And possible buyers wanted to see the water pressure, make sure the plumbing worked, and if she had to show after dark, there needed to be light. But the bills were killing them both.

"Why would you do that? It's way out in the middle of nowhere. I can't get to you if something happens—"

"Nothing will happen I can't handle," she snapped. "You asked where I was staying and now you know. I have a rental. And I don't need major amenities. Anything else?"

Conversation over. What else was there to say? Fiona was going to do what she wanted and Asa could get over it. "Fine. Call if you need me." He'd be the one wide-awake with stomach-acid buildup.

"I won't need you." She spun and entered the elevator.

No. She never had.

Chapter Six

Fiona had sounded braver than she felt last night about staying at the house alone. She'd been fine until the posies. Every single pop and crack had kept her awake. She'd closed every blind, but the thought of Rhyme watching her sleep kept her eyes open, though they grew heavy around 2:00 a.m. Now she pounded the pavement, one long stride after another. Pushing. Harder. She'd set out at sunrise, when she knew sleep wasn't going to come but she needed energy. She was still racing through her old routine at twenty after seven. She'd taken up long-distance running at eighteen. Never again would she not be able to outrun someone.

The sun had peeped over the horizon in soft hues of pink, blue and orange. How could something so marvelous, so glorious and full of wonder, rise like this only to be chased away by utter darkness, chaos and terror?

The sunrise evoked hope and a fresh slate.

But sunset trashed everything the sunrise promised. At night, darkness crept on its belly, slithering into peaceful places—places of hope and joy—to destroy everything that had been built in the beauty of light. Was there an ultimate win to this never-ending battle?

In between trying to catch Rhyme, there were thousands of other maniacal predators hunting unsuspecting victims. It was Fiona's job to expose the darkness. Bring light back to families—that's what they hoped for. Some kind of good to come from the surrounding evil.

But when the darkness had touched Fiona, it was obvious that light would never dawn again. Not on the inside. The veil had been dropped. She never shared that with families of tragedy, though. She lied and told them as time progressed, it would get easier. Never back to the same, but easier. Some days she supposed that might be true. Most days it wasn't. Not for her.

Her playlist clicked and went back on repeat as she pushed the last mile toward home.

Home.

Not anymore.

The modest farmhouse on four acres of land with pastures framing it had once been a dream—a pipe dream of hers and Asa's. They would remodel and during their short stays home from hunting darkness, they'd cocoon themselves in this little piece of paradise off Fogg Road in northwest Mississippi. Thirty-five minutes from the field office on a good day. It had been worth the drive.

Now it was simply a house for sale in the middle of nowhere that no one wanted. She should have come clean during their party planning for Tiberius's birthday that she was staying at the house, but she and Asa were getting along and it was as if they were old friends again. Bringing it up would only have made him angry earlier. Would benefit the party-planning aspect, though.

Last hill. She paced her speed and breathing. The temperature was already climbing and the humidity was sticking to her like a hot, wet bath towel. Her hair had wilted to her head in a damp cap and her sunglasses kept slipping off her nose. The run felt good, though—the old routine. She'd missed this. Running on a blank path in Chicago wasn't the same as the hilly pastureland of the quiet country.

Up ahead, the white farmhouse with the wraparound porch beckoned her. Behind the house a sagging red barn sat as a glaring reminder of what had once been. Asa working out in the mornings and striding toward the house, muscled abs and pecs glistening in the morning sun. Some men sweated. Asa Kodiak... Asa glistened. Her stomach pulled at the memories.

Now the barn was as empty as Fiona. It had become a monument to their failure. Pulling up last night had been emotional. Perhaps a mistake on her part, but she'd...needed to be here. She'd brought all her toiletries and a pillow—she always traveled with her own pillow. However, her own pillow hadn't helped her drift off last night. Not when all she saw were their lives crumbling to ash and the creepy posies Rhyme had left for her.

She slowed near the driveway, evening out her breathing until it leveled, then she headed inside through the small entryway that opened to a staircase. She padded down the hardwood hallway to the galley kitchen with an open breakfast area—the wobbly table she hated still there.

She went to grab her Yeti to fill with water, but it wasn't on the counter by the sink. She scratched the back of her head and glanced around the kitchen. "Where is that stupid thing?" she muttered. Hadn't she swallowed down two Tylenol last night and left it right here? The Tylenol bottle was still by the sink.

Hairs on the back of her neck rose and a chill blanketed her perspiring body. She listened, but nothing sounded out of place. "I'm losing it." She turned on the faucet, cupped her hand and used it like a glass, then padded down the hall, turning left into the master bedroom.

On her nightstand was her Yeti cup. She snorted. "Yep. I'm losing it."

After peeling off her running gear, she grabbed a towel they'd used for staging, snapped it a few times for dust and hung it on the towel bar, then stepped into a cold and glorious shower. As her body temp dropped, goose bumps broke out over her skin and she turned the nozzle to hot, letting the spray of water beat and massage her tired muscles. Steam filled the bathroom and fogged the frosted shower door as her skin turned red from the scalding water.

A prickly awareness tickled her scalp, and she froze, chill bumps returning to her skin, then swiped the shower door of steam with trembling hands, but it was too misty. She cut the water and inched open the shower door, her heart beating wildly and her mouth cotton-dry.

She reached for the sunshiny towel but her hand met nothing but the metal bar. Adrenaline kicked in, raced through her veins, and she darted out and grabbed her gray terry-cloth robe off the counter.

The towel she'd hung was lying on the floor by the tub.

She snatched it and held it to her, catching the faintest hint of vanilla. Legs and feet still damp, Fiona crept into the carpeted bedroom. A shadow caught her attention; her heart lurched into her throat. She immediately went for her Glock.

The house was eerily quiet.

Gripping her gun and allowing her training to kick in, she kept close to the walls as she inched down the hall toward the kitchen.

A floor joist squeaked in the living room and her breath caught.

Slowly, keeping careful not to hit the areas that creaked, she tiptoed her way toward the living room.

She rounded the stairs to a gun in her face.

"Asa!" she hollered, keeping her own gun aimed.

"Get that muzzle outta my nose," he growled.

"Likewise." She frowned and lowered her gun. "What are you doing here? In the house?"

"I tried to call you six times. Maybe answer your phone and I wouldn't have to come inside to check and see if you're still alive. I drove your running route. Checked the barn—"

"Why would I be in the barn?"

His jaw ticked, his hair messy from his hand tearing it up in frustration. "Well, for all I know a sadistic killer knocked you out and hauled you out there. I was worried. Sue me. It's my house, too. I have every right to be in here."

He was going overboard again. "Well, I think it's obvious I've not been in a serial killer's grip." Though she thought for a few seconds she had been. That Rhyme had been in the house while she was on her run, had moved her cup and been in the bathroom while she was at her most vulnerable and taken her towel from the holder on the wall. Fiona pointed to her attire. "Last I checked, my phone wasn't waterproof." She huffed and held his glare, angry at herself for feeling afraid. "Furthermore, I can take care of myself. I almost rearranged your face with a slug."

A glint flashed in his stony eyes. "I'm well aware you can take care of yourself."

She had the urge to stomp for effect, but she gripped her gun tighter. "Clearly you're not, as you're standing in my foyer."

"Our foyer."

"Whatever, Asa." Five seconds and here they went again. No point arguing. She was being childish and argumentative because he'd scared her. She hated feeling afraid. He hadn't done anything wrong. He was well within his senses to be concerned. Sighing, she asked, "Is the reason you're here an emergency or can I finish getting ready?"

Asa cleared his throat. "Oh. No. No, go ahead." He slid past her, his arm brushing her shoulder.

"It may be a few minutes, so don't go getting paranoid and rush in to rescue me from the closet monster." She refrained from the eye roll but the sarcasm couldn't be contained.

He muttered under his breath and stalked toward the kitchen.

She hurried and changed into charcoal-gray high-waisted slacks, a sleeveless white blouse from Ann Taylor and comfortable shoes. After drying her hair and using mascara, blush and some pale pink gloss, she waltzed into the kitchen.

Asa sipped his coffee and scowled. "It's cold now and I took the microwave." His accusing tone mixed with a slight pout only amused her. He'd brought coffee. She'd only now noticed.

She accepted her lukewarm coffee without whining. "Thanks." She sipped. Blech. "How was I to know you'd step foot on the property this morning? It's not even eight. Why are you here?" She sat across from him at the wobbly kitchen table and drilled him with her gaze. "Well?"

"I figured… I guess…"

Asa wasn't a man often at a loss for words. "Did something happen?"

"No… I mean possibly, who knows?" He pushed aside his coffee. "I don't like you out here alone. I was worried. And I thought I'd come by and check on you. Pick you up for work. Bring a coffee as a peace offering."

"This coffee is cold. Pretty pitiful peace offering," she teased and tried to tune out the warmth his words brought.

He chuckled. "Say that five times fast." He toyed with the green stopper he'd removed from the lid opening. "You sleep okay?"

Did she sleep okay? What in the world? He leaned forward and the table tipped, nearly knocking over their drinks. "I hate this table."

"I know," he said with resignation and a hint of regret. "I should have bought a new one."

As if the argument over the table was what had ripped them apart. "Nah. This adds character."

"And cussing."

She laughed. "Yeah, it does add that." One too many spills. They'd tried putting something under the table to stabilize it, but it was the actual tabletop that wobbled. Asa never got around to fixing it. So much they never got around to doing.

They sat in silence. Birds singing. A dog barked in the distance.

"Asa, please don't worry. You have enough on your plate without adding me. I'm fine." To prove it, she patted his large, rough hand. "Okay?"

"I worry, Fi. It's my thing. And you're my responsibility if you're here working on my team." He rubbed his hand where she'd touched him, as if trying to brush away the feeling her contact had brought.

"I understand."

Don't argue. Don't touch. Got it.

He stood and threw away his coffee. "I see you're not only back into your running routine, but cutting fresh hydrangeas from the side of the house, too." He snorted. "You could have at least put them in some water."

Bones shivering, she came around the side of the table, and where her Yeti had been last night, a fresh cutting of pink hydrangeas rested on the counter—but they hadn't been there before her shower.

The cup. The towel. The flowers.

She wasn't losing it. Rhyme had been in her home.

"Great news!" Tiberius said. "Robert Williams's wife re-married three years ago. She has a baby girl. A *girl!*" His victory air-pump, excited eyes and mile-wide grin fell flat with Fiona. Especially after finding the hydrangeas, which she'd played off for Asa as putting them there herself. He was already worried sick and she feared he'd make her go back to Chicago under the guise of protecting her if he knew how close Rhyme had been—closer than when he dropped the posies. As close as her shower door.

She wasn't running from a killer again—Rhyme or his alter ego. Fear had held her captive—fear had caused irrational behavior. Fiona was done with letting fear make the calls on her life. Yeah, guilt nipped at her heels, but she wasn't leaving or backing down because Asa said she had to. He could call it reckless or stupid or empty-headed—or anything else—but he hadn't been there that night. Asa didn't know that Fiona had wrongs to make right.

"Did you hear me, Fi? A girl!" Tiberius hooted again.

"Yay for all things pink." Fiona set a bag of muffins on the counter by the carafe in the major case room.

His expression deflated. "You've lost your edge and I blame Chicago. Let me connect the dots for you." He leaned on the conference room table. "Robert Williams's wife stood by his side and proclaimed him the straight arrow after he was murdered. 'He would never stray and these rumors are trumped up by school girls who had a crush on him.' But now—"

Ah, it was jelling. "Now she has no reason to stand by his side." Fiona grinned. "Now she has a daughter. She's a mama bear and protector. Would she want someone doing to her little angel what her deceased husband might have done to others? She might have a new tale to tell."

Tiberius sprung his hands forward as if to say "finally!" "Way to connect the dots. I fed them to you, but you did connect them. You might still be salvageable, Fi Fi McGee." His eyebrow wiggle didn't hold the same amusement for her as it normally did.

"Ha. Ha. Quit calling me that."

Violet stalked into the room. She probably did yoga or Pilates. Her hair hung loose past her shoulders—that strategic windblown look. Same impassive symmetrical face. "Well? Did we catch him?"

If it wasn't so ridiculous of a question, Fiona wouldn't have known Violet was joking. "We did," she jested back. "Everything was wrapped up in a pretty bow."

"Blue or pink?"

Definitely not pink. "Red." She winked and Violet gave a semblance of a smirk.

"I was up most of the night working the victimology based on statements given by our victims' families, friends, coworkers. Trying to figure out what would make these victims, who are so different in gender, age and pretty much everything, targets for this killer. Going through nine victims' complete histories is going to take time, and since I'm unfamiliar with the case—"

"You'll have fresh eyes," Asa interjected as he strode into the room and tossed his suit coat on one of the leather chairs. "How far have you gotten?"

"I'm working backward. Jenny Miller could have been targeted at the bar. But based on what I've read in the case files, no other victims visited that bar. However, we haven't actually asked anyone. Probably should. The only common denominator—except for Alan Minton, the victim in our fourth staged scene—is religion or church. I didn't find anything that would corroborate Alan as a man of the Christian faith. However, his sister's husband is a pastor in California, which makes me believe he may have been raised in a Christian home, but that's a stretch."

Owen pointed to the board. "The churches our victims attended are all within ten miles of one another and fifteen miles of each of their residences. Workplaces vary. The only victim that didn't live within the fifteen-mile radius—the blue pin—is our 'Old Woman in a Shoe.' Maria Windell. She lived in the Hickory Hill area."

"But she collected groceries from a food bank at Hope Community every Thursday morning, which is in the Germantown area." Fiona tried to puzzle it out. There had to be something significant. "Rhyme has to have some kind of access to these people. Would he work within this fifteen-mile radius? Live? Both?"

"Work, yes. Live, highly unlikely," Owen stated. "He clearly knows and is comfortable in the area. Blends in easily. Germantown is upscale. He looks upper middle class to rich with ease. Probably drives a nice car, not super flashy. He doesn't want to be noticed. But most killers—not all—won't hunt where they live." He tossed a knowing look between Fiona and Asa. "Killers don't dump where they eat."

Even serial killers had been smarter than the two of them. No wonder they couldn't catch him.

Violet's natural frown deepened. "If he has DID, then he may not be able to hold down a job. Could be on disability. Not that every person who suffers from this disorder can't work and keep jobs—even good ones and long-term. We need to remember he might be targeting his victims from churches because he belongs to a support group at one of them."

Not a bad line of thinking at all. Though DID was extremely rare.

"I can get lists, see if anyone with DID might attend—if they'll give us this information. It falls under confidential, but if we can determine one of these churches has a mental illness program that would narrow it down. I'd be willing to go to church and to one of these groups undercover to see what I can discover," Violet said.

"I can go, too," Tiberius added.

"You've been around too long. Rhyme—" Violet looked at Fiona "—if I may call him that, too, has watched the news over the years. He'd be familiar with you and it's possible the alter ego can pull from the primary's memory bank."

"But the main dude can't pull from the alter ego's?" Owen asked.

"Not in the same way typically," Violet continued. "Rhyme—because we don't actually know this man's name—has created this alter ego to block out trauma. It's like a memory bank with a name. Everything bad goes into that memory bank and it's locked tight. He'll experience blackouts, lapses of time, when the alter takes over. The alter ego steps in to handle tough or stressful situations. He's created a monster that likes to kill."

"Well, that sounds just delightful," Tiberius said.

"It may have started as a protector alter ego. Someone who could fight and outsmart Rhyme's abuser. Take control. Be fierce. Everything Rhyme is not. The primary personality probably suffers from anxiety and panic disorder. He's a weak man and aware of this alter ego, but he can't control him. The more the alter ego fights his way out of the mind, the easier it becomes for him to come out at will and stay out longer."

It hadn't been the alter ego at her home this morning. It had been Rhyme. The primary personality—not the one who hunted her like a naughty kitty in the woods. The one who believed they were bonded, and in a sick way, they were.

"The primary won't have a clue the alter ego is killing?" Tiberius asked.

"That's a bit tricky. The main personality may suspect the alter ego of doing bad things, but he doesn't know exactly what, and he'll become frustrated when he tries to remember, which could trigger the alter ego erupting."

"We should feel sorry for him, then?" Tiberius asked. "He's murdered several human beings regardless if he knows it or not."

Violet shrugged. "I'm not telling you to feel anything for him. I'm saying an abused child created another personality to protect him when no one else did, and in doing so he created a killer who is acting as a vigilante to avenge children and adolescents who have been allegedly abused or harmed by adults...in theory."

Fiona didn't know how to feel, either. Rhyme had traumatized her, murdered her sister, broken her family, and yet he'd been traumatized and may not even know he was doing these things as a whole other personality. While DID couldn't be cured, long-term treatment could help. That might be why his kills were sporadic, some being five years apart. He may have been in treatment or able to contain the alter ego for long periods of time.

Asa stood. "I'll get Selah on contacting churches that have treatment programs for mental illness. Fiona, see Williams's widow. Violet, I hate to pull you from victimology, but if she's bitter, then having a man there to ask questions might not be as effective."

Violet nodded. "And if she's bitter then who better to bash men with than a couple of other women who she thinks hates men?"

"Exactly."

"Well, we have plenty of fodder," Violet quipped.

Asa quirked an eyebrow. "I feel somehow that's a barb at me."

Violet slid her charcoal-gray blazer over her lavender blouse. "Guilty people are usually paranoid." She pulled her hair from inside her blazer and looked to Fiona. "Ready?"

"Meet back here and we'll trade info." Asa gave a half-hearted wave and Fiona trailed after Violet to the Suburban. After thirty-two minutes, they arrived in Hernando, Mississippi, where Robert Williams's widow now lived with her new husband. They turned left off of 51 into a newer subdivision. Middle class.

"I'd like to talk to those old high-school girls who allegedly spread the rumors. How old would they be now?" Violet asked.

"Late twenties." She pulled up the digital files on her phone. "Twenty-eight and twenty-seven. We can chat with them after we talk to the former Mrs. Williams."

"What's her first name and new last name?" Violet asked. "Tanya Heathcliff."

Violet parked behind a newer model Altima. "Tanya. You think she was named after the country music singer?"

Fiona slid from the Suburban and smirked. "I have no idea." Violet was implicitly random.

They knocked on the front door and waited until a disheveled Tanya appeared, toddler hanging on her hip. She talked through the glass. "Agent Kelly?"

Yes, she was back. Again. "We'd like to talk to you about Robert. Can we come in for a few minutes? We won't keep you long." The towheaded toddler looked sleepy and a wee bit cranky, but her sweet face and chubby legs tugged on Fiona's maternal strings. Guess she still had some.

Tanya allowed them inside. "Excuse the mess."

Standard procedure from most homes she entered. Come in. Excuse the mess.

The house was lived-in, but not dirty. Toys, shoes, diapers and children's books littered the living room, which opened to the kitchen. Sippy cups, papers and a few dishes cluttered the counters.

"Have a seat, please."

Violet and Fiona perched on the faux-leather love seat. Tanya sat across from them in the rocking chair. After snuggling the babe close to her, she began to rock. "It's naptime. Sorry."

"You denied the former allegations about your husband," Violet said. "Do you still hold to your original statement that those girls were lying?" She pointed to the adorable child she held. "I would hate for someone to get off scot-free if it were my daughter. You know that feeling now, don't you?"

Tanya averted eye contact.

"Moms protect daughters. Be a good mom, Tanya. Protect other daughters from monsters like your dead husband." Violet's tone didn't change, but the urgency was tangible. Was she a mom? Fiona knew nothing about her other than what Asa had supplied—which was little—and what she'd professionally gleaned.

Tanya kissed her baby's head and when she glanced up her eyes held a sheen of moisture. "I wanted to believe him," she muttered. "I wanted to trust him but..." She shook her head as if she could erase the past, the truth.

"But what?" Fiona gently prodded. Excitement bubbled in her chest. Tanya was going to tell the truth and it was going to give them a more solid profile and a possible lead.

"I should have known. When allegations started about him acting inappropriately with some of the girls at Houston High School. I mean I was sixteen when he started flirting. He was my youth leader. Twenty-four. I thought I was mature for that age—what teenager doesn't?"

Fiona had thought herself invincible at sixteen and seventeen. Until Rhyme proved her wrong.

"Not long after that allegation, Robert resigned his position at the school and started coaching at Germantown High, and we changed churches."

Dread filled Fiona's gut.

"Robert was never happy. We constantly changed churches, anyway. Someone always offended him. We moved three churches in less than five years. It was taxing. I'd made friends. Joined groups. We were heavily involved in youth programs..." Fresh tears streamed down her cheeks. She kissed her toddler's head again. "We joined Abundant Life Church over on Poplar Pike."

Germantown area. A common denominator.

"We got involved with the youth department. After about a year in, we had a sleepover at the house for the youth—you could do that then and not worry. I caught him..." She pursed her lips, taking a moment, and looked to the heavens as if praying. "I caught him outside with one of the girls. They weren't engaged in anything, but the way he rubbed her back... I knew. It was the same way he'd rubbed mine. I wondered if we moved churches so much because he'd been doing it at each one and was afraid of being caught."

Violet leaned forward on her chair. "You confront him?"

Tanya nodded. "Not in front of the girl. I did make my presence known and he jerked his hand away. She went inside. But she had a guilty look. Robert was all kinds of good-looking and charming. Students had crushes on him. Women always came on to him. I was always in awe that he was mine. Except he never was."

"Did he admit to inappropriate behavior with the girl?

Also, I need her name." Violet put her pen to her pad, await-ing answers.

"No, he got angry. Turned it on me. Jealous because a girl was giving him attention. If I'd still kept myself looking young, I might not be so envious. I wasn't even out of my twenties! But that was the downward spiral. I approached her. She denied any inappropriateness. She was defending him, of course. Thought there might be a relationship with him. Girls have no sense at that age. Don't see the big picture."

Violet scribbled her notes. "How long was this before he was killed?"

"Six months maybe."

"What was the girl's name?" Fiona asked.

"Lexi." She frowned. "Mc-something. I can't remember."

They thanked her for her time and let themselves out so she wouldn't have to disturb her baby girl.

"Whatcha thinkin'?" Violet asked as they stepped into the blinding sun.

"We have proof and a tighter profile. Maria Windell—"

"The Old Woman in the Shoe?"

"Yeah." Fiona pulled her sunglasses from her blazer pocket and shielded her eyes. "One grandchild said she hit her and put her in the closet sometimes. Now we have three murder victims that we can concretely say hurt children or teens. If we find that Jenny Miller was a predator, too, all we have left to confirm is Alan Minton, the fourth victim, and our first victims—children themselves." Could Colleen, Josie and Si-erra have done something hurtful to another girl? She didn't want to believe it, but she had no choice but to go down this road again and look with an agent's eye, not a sister's. "Fits the DID profile. The alter ego protecting. Vigilantism." Fiona opened the door and climbed into the scorching vehicle.

"None of that gets us any closer to finding him, though." Violet cranked the engine.

True. "Wait. How many times did she say she moved churches?" Fiona asked.

Violet reversed down the driveway. "Three."

"Stop the car." She jumped out and raced up the drive, knocking on the door again. If the baby woke, so be it.

Tanya hurriedly opened the door.

"What churches did you attend in those moves with Robert?" Fiona asked.

"Um… Abundant Life, First Christian and Hope Community."

Hope Community!

"Who was the pastor at the time? Do you remember?" Reverend Shetland and his wife had led that church when they'd been murdered.

"Pastor Tony Reeves." She squinted and cocked her head. "Why?"

Tony Reeves must have come after the Shetlands. "Did you know Mark and Valerie Shetland?"

"No. Why?"

How did Tanya not know what happened to them? It was no secret to the public that Rhyme staged his victims in rhymes. Would she not have connected her husband to the Shetlands?

"They were murdered by the same man who killed your late husband. How did you not know that? Did no one at the church mention it during a conversation when you attended? Did you not watch the news?"

"The news was slandering my husband. I didn't want to watch it. No one at church said anything to me." Tanya shook her head and covered her mouth. "You think Pastor Shetland abused girls, too?"

"I don't know." She doubted it. No allegations. But someone at Hope Community might be the killer. "Thanks." Fiona rushed back to the Suburban. "One of the churches they attended was Hope Community. After the Shetlands had been murdered. We need a list of membership and attendance records if they keep them. Could be Rhyme's hunting ground. And we need to check and see if they operate mental-illness programs. Look there first."

"We also need to see if other victims had attended Hope. Did you?"

"No. We didn't attend church often. Christmas. Easter. And when we did it was at Life Church." Fiona called Selah at the field office. "Selah, call Hope Community Church and see if they'll give you a record of members, and if they keep up with attendance, ask them to pull attendance from the time of the Shetlands' murder to one year prior. Pull men in our profile and then have Owen give you a perimeter to search as far as residences. Then from that pool, see if you can find anyone who might have DID, be in therapy or have been hospitalized for mental illness. Petty charges. Support groups. Anything. We may have a lead on Rhyme."

"You got it. Anything else?"

"Yes. Go back twelve years and see if you can pull a sixteen-year-old girl named Lexi Mc-something from Abundant Life Church. She'd be twenty-eight now."

She hung up. If Robert Williams had secrets, then it was possible this Lexi person might know a few. Maybe she saw him with someone that his wife wouldn't have. Maybe she knew Rhyme and never even realized it.

Chapter Seven

Asa opened the shiny gold door for Fiona and they entered the noisy Mollie Fontaine Lounge, which was located across the street from the elegant Woodruff-Fontaine House. Everyone knew Mrs. Fontaine-Winslow—an heir to the Fontaine fortune. She was up in age, but she was on TV often giving to charities like St. Jude and Feed the Homeless, and she still resided in her mansion, unlike other mansions that had been turned into museums, businesses and B and Bs. What in the world did it cost that old broad to air-condition the place?

"You're wondering what the upkeep costs on that mansion, aren't you?" Fiona asked.

"Possibly."

Piano music, conversation and laughter filled the air, along with scents of grilled meats, onions, garlic and something sweet. Victorian architecture mixed with modern deco gave it a unique vibe.

"You hungry?" Asa asked. It had been a stretch since lunch in the major case room, and it was nearly eight o'clock. They hadn't wanted to come too early for fear the regulars wouldn't be in yet. "Might as well kill two birds with one stone."

They sat at the small bar under fancy chandeliers. The bartender, in his late thirties with cocky eyes and a player's grin, handed them menus. He gave them the drink specials and winked at Fiona.

"He's eager for tips," Asa muttered and perused the menu. "This is a pretty intimate place. Easy enough for a killer to blend in. I hear four different conversations right now. It only takes decent eavesdropping skills to pick up on a person's sins."

Fiona casually scanned the establishment while periodically glancing at her menu. "The last novel I read had an author note that her idea developed from a conversation overheard at a Starbucks. I thought to myself, see if I ever speak in that place again." She laughed. "It was a great book, though."

"It's nice to hear you're taking downtime." At home—when they'd been married—her downtime consisted of Rhyme, running and working out. Not much reading before bed. A few times she took a book to the beach. "I heard you were in Iowa going after the Paper Doll Killer. Great arrest."

Fiona laid down her menu. "That was exhausting. Turned out he was trying to create angelic figures to worship. He had an entire room piled with dead women who'd been sewn together like paper dolls. All the same height, figure, hair color. When they decayed, he started again. The whole town knew him from the car dealership he owned." She told him how she'd created the profile that eventually led to Roger De-Marco.

Asa turned up his nose. "Wonder who eavesdropped on that little number?"

Fiona snorted. "Well, it's book fodder for sure."

The bartender returned. "Now, what can I get you tonight?"

Asa ordered the sliders and Fiona ordered the ravioli.

"Drinks?" he asked.

"We're on duty," Asa said and held up his creds. "We'd like to ask you a few questions."

"Oh, wow. Okay. Sure." The cocky air disappeared as quickly as it had come. "What's this about?"

"Do you recognize this woman?" He held out Jenny Miller's staff photo from the yearbook. "Her name is Jenny Miller."

He checked out the photo. "Yeah. Yeah, I remember her. She came in a few times a month with some friends. They never sat at the bar, though. Always upstairs." He craned his neck over the bar. "Hey, Donna, come here," he called. "She's our manager so she might know more."

Donna arrived. "What's up?"

"You recognize the lady in the photo?" The bartender pointed to the picture. "She came in with a few other women. Upstairs."

Donna took one glance and her eyes teared up. "Yeah. Jenny the big spender, I called her. I saw on the news she'd been murdered. A serial killer." She turned to the bartender. "Trent, do you never watch TV?"

"Not the news. Whoa. She's dead?"

"Afraid so," Asa said.

Donna sniffed. "She came in every other Friday with some teacher friends from St. George's. Ordered several rounds of drinks and tipped well."

"Do you know anything about her other than her coming in to blow off steam with her girls?" Fiona asked. "She ever come in with a man? Anyone seem more interested in her than he should? Even a group of men here hanging out. Might seem harmless. Any information at all."

Donna sighed. "A few times a group of men bought a round of drinks for all the ladies and they may have chatted, but it was harmless. And never the same group of men. She never left with anyone."

The bartender frowned.

"Something wrong?" Asa asked.

"I don't know. A month or so ago. Last of the month? A guy came in...well, a kid really. Looked, maybe, I don't know, seventeen? Anyway, he comes in and stands at the front door. Next thing, she's stalking toward him, pushes him outside and it looked like they were into it about something. I remember thinking she didn't look old enough to have a teenager, but whatever."

"What were they fighting about? Did you hear anything?" Fiona asked.

He shook his head. "Kid seemed real upset. She seemed miffed when she came back inside. I assume she went back upstairs. I had customers."

Why would a high-school boy come looking for sweet Jenny Miller at a lounge while she was with other teachers? Could she have been exploiting teens at St. George's? "Can you describe the boy?"

He groaned. "Maybe six feet. Dark hair. Real preppy. Khakis. Dress shirt tucked in. I thought that was weird. You would have never found me dressed like that at his age. Or now." He smirked.

His T-shirt hugged his muscles and a tattoo peeped out from one of the sleeves. When he wasn't here, he was clearly at the gym.

"Was that the only time a boy came in here?"

"Only time I ever saw." He shrugged. "You think he killed her?"

"No, but he might know something." She turned her attention to Donna, who was still shaking her head, hand over her mouth. "Did you see this? Hear anything?"

"No," she croaked, "but I do remember that night. She left the table. And when she returned she seemed distracted and agitated. I thought she had a bad phone call."

"You didn't overhear anything?"

"No. This place is busy and it's our job to know our regulars and interact, but we can't get behind on our service."

A server brought their food. Asa's stomach rumbled. "If you think of anything else, let us know." He handed the bartender his card, took his name. Trent Barton. Then he handed one to Donna and got her last name. Carston. "Thanks for your time."

"Meals are on the house," Trent said, and moseyed down the bar to take orders again.

"What do you think?" Asa asked as he removed the pickles from his slider and tossed them onto Fiona's plate. She mechanically reached out and plucked one up, popping it in her mouth.

"If she'd been pimping out kids, it could have been a dispute over that. Either way, he knew she was at the bar. He knew about her private comings and goings. Miller didn't want the other teachers to see her meet him so she came outside and they argued. She went back inside, agitated. Naturally, her friends would have asked what happened."

"Probably said a fight with the husband. Women would have been all sympathetic as they shared stories of how their men made them furious on a regular basis and it ended in laughing and more drinks."

Fiona snorted and forked a ravioli in her mouth. "You nailed it. And by the way, this is so good." Asa stole one and nodded. His cell rang. Kacie. "I gotta take this." He answered. "Hey, baby sis, I've been trying to get in touch with you." He listened as Kacie rattled on about her job, her breakup with the latest what's-his-face and her subtle request for rent money.

"Come by and have dinner with me next week and I'll take care of it. How much?"

After she gave him the number and repeated how great he was, she hung up.

Fiona had the look.

"She's low on cash. She started a new job and hasn't gotten a paycheck yet." Kacie had a hard life and he didn't mind forking over some dough for her. It was the least he could do for letting their mother die.

"I didn't say a word."

She didn't have to. They'd had this conversation a million times. Maybe it was guilt that kept him at Kacie's beck and call. He was guilty. He should have protected his family better.

"Let's go back to the school in the morning and talk to the teachers," Fiona suggested.

"Tomorrow's a holiday." The Fourth of July. Why had he brought it up? The night had been tension-free up until now.

"Right." She refused to make eye contact and shoved another bite in her mouth. "You got plans?" she asked in between chewing.

His insides wilted. "Do you?"

"Question with a question when you don't want to answer. I imagine you'll be watching fireworks somewhere with the girlfriend. Tell her she doesn't have to keep her distance because of me. I know she's lead on the case and detectives are in and out more than she's been."

"She's been overloaded. But... I'll tell her." He didn't answer her on where they'd be watching fireworks. Fiona would assume he'd never take another woman to Mud Island. And he wouldn't have if Amanda hadn't asked first.

Fiona's phone rang. She pulled it from her purse, blushed then cleared her throat. "Hello?...hey...it's going. Can I call you back? I'm in the middle of an investigation...yes. Yes. Okay." She hung up.

"What's up?"

"Nothing. Personal's all."

And her personal life was no longer Asa's business.

Fiona had done everything she could think of to keep busy today. Nine years ago, Asa had proposed underneath bursts of fireworks and then they'd had drinks on the Peabody roof. It was a breath of hope. She could marry. Have a family and a career. Be normal in her book. Light had exploded in her soul. Asa had proposed his love, his plans to spend his life with her. Slid a round solitaire on her ring finger.

She hadn't made his plans easy.

Now she sat cross-legged on the living room floor with case files and notes, a glass of store-bought lemonade sweating on the coffee table and her gun at her side—no taking a chance. It was too hot to be outside, anyway. The sun would set in a couple of hours and the real beauty would begin. Luke had called her last night while she was with Asa. Wanted updates on the case—concerned for her. And to ask her to a BBQ today. She'd declined when she called him back later and held firm through his protests and attempts to persuade her to change her mind.

Besides, it didn't feel right taking a day off when families had been destroyed and a killer was on the loose. Her grandmother's voice permeated her sullen heart with an old conversation. She'd been about twenty-one. Grandma Kelly lying in her bed, hospice care there tending to her. Her gnarled fingers with yellowed nails had gingerly caressed Fiona's forearm.

"You can't stop living, child," she'd said. "Colleen wouldn't want that. No one wants that. God has a plan for your life."

"Did He not have one for Colleen? Did He forget to plan

out year sixteen through years old-and-gray? That doesn't seem fair, Grandma." She'd laid her head on Grandma's chest, shallow breathing blowing her bangs.

"There's evil in this world, Fiona. Our family has felt its touch. But God has touched us, too. We've felt the warmth of His faithfulness. If you'd let the bad out, you'd remember. And you'd let the bad work itself out for the good."

They were almost the same words Asa had said about God using the bad to bring about good. It was difficult for her to reason out. She wished Grandma was here now. She needed a soft touch. A hand to hold. A shoulder—even if bony—to cry on. A bang startled her, so she snatched her gun from the floor and stalked to the front door. She groaned and opened it to find Tiberius. "Why are you here?"

"Hello, Fiona," he said in a singsong voice. "How are you? Can I offer you something to drink? A smile?" He frowned then tweaked her nose. "Me and you. Owen and Selah. Cami bailed when she heard I was coming to get you. Watching fireworks. Eating lots of barbeque and food that isn't good for us. Celebrate freedom."

How did one celebrate what they didn't have? "I was going to watch a Hallmark movie—"

"I'm gonna stop you right there, Fi Fi McGee. No one is going to watch a Hallmark movie tonight. And you aren't the fluffy romance type."

"I like a little happily-ever-after in my life," she protested. And she'd have him know that before her life was disrupted she adored romance books and movies and even played Barbie dolls!

Tiberius sighed and draped his arm around her. "No, Fiona," he whispered. "You don't. Or you'd have some."

Ouch—truth stung.

"Fine." Better to succumb than argue. "Let me change.

I'd offer to bring a dish but I have nothing but store-bought chicken salad and lemonade."

"We're eating at food trucks."

"Food trucks? Where?"

"You know where. It's the best place to see fireworks, and don't balk." He gave her an I'm-not-taking-no-for-an-answer look.

"Fine. But you might as well call Cami and tell her I won't kill her and dump her in the river even though she's loyal to Asa to a fault." In fact, Fiona was fairly certain the young admin assistant was head-over-heels for him, and part of her snip with Fiona was due to the fact she'd been married to him. Their office was like an on-the-bubble nighttime soap. They might get a renewed season. Might not.

"Yeah, she wouldn't believe me. Anyway, she's gonna go out with some friends from her D and D club."

"She would play Dungeons and Dragons." She laughed and went to change clothes. She'd go to Mud Island. Take Grandma's advice. Try to live a little. They hopped into Tiberius's truck and headed for downtown.

The crowds of people and mosquitoes were massive. She borrowed Selah's bug spray and coated herself. Selah seemed like a pretty decent human being. Fiona hadn't determined if she was joining the party because of nothing better to do, or if she was here for Tiberius or Owen. More soapy action. Live music and the smells of barbecued pork and beer filled the hot, sticky air. They pitched blankets on the south lawn and dropped the cooler full of a variety of drinks. Tiberius and Owen chose beer, but Fiona wanted crystal-clear faculties so she selected an iced tea.

Selah grabbed a Perrier and leaned back. "Fiona, do you miss Chicago?"

"I miss less humidity." Chicago wasn't Memphis. Or the

South. She'd been raised Southern. Loved every part of it. "You from here?"

"Born and raised. I love Southern summers." She closed her eyes and her head bobbed to the beat of the music. Owen plopped next to her and cracked open his cold one. "We gonna watch the fireworks from canoes, kayaks or Peabody rooftop?"

"Definitely not the rooftop," Fiona insisted. That's where they'd gone after Asa proposed. "I'm going to go buy a funnel cake." She stood and wiped the condensation from her bottled ice tea on her denim shorts. "Anybody want anything?"

"Extra powdered sugar on your cake, Fi, and I'll share it with you. Way to live a little." Tiberius took a deep drink and Fiona frowned.

"I never said I wanted to share." But she would. She slung her purse strap across her chest and maneuvered through the throngs of people to the food trucks that had set up on the pavement. The lines were long but a funnel cake was worth it and what else did she have going on? She scanned her surroundings, keeping a keen eye on everything. She'd been blindsided by Rhyme once—by his alter ego, that is. One minute she was putting her bags in the car, the next minute a searing pain and blackness. When she woke up, she was in a small cabin. A flowy white nightgown on a cot beside her and Rhyme's alter ego in his plague doctor mask before her. Demanding she wear the gown.

Plus, Rhyme himself was sneaky. He'd managed to place flowers by their government vehicle and get into her home while she'd been running. She'd never found a point of entry, though.

"Agent Kelly?"

She blinked away the memory, and Daniel Osborn, the head of school at St. George's, was standing beside her, dressed in khaki shorts and a red Ralph Lauren polo. Complemented his tanned skin and toned arms.

"Mr. Osborn—"

"Daniel, please." His winning smile forced one from her.

"All right. Daniel. You here with friends?" she asked and moved up in the line.

"Yes. A few small groups from our church are having a picnic." He moved up when she did. "What about you?"

"Colleagues. Well...friends. We're over on the south lawn." Church. "What church do you attend?"

"Abundant Life. Germantown area." His gaze was intense and he cocked his head. "You?"

"I live in Chicago, actually. I'm here consulting on a case."

"Jenny's?"

"Yes." She leaned in and he met her in the middle, as if she was about to share a delicious secret. "How long have you attended Abundant Life?"

"Thirteen years. Before that I attended Hope Community. But sometimes you need a change. I guess you know that, though." His knowing look unsettled her and he must have registered it. "I mean you're here—a change from Chicago."

"Uh-huh." Daniel Osborn attended two churches that connected to the murders and he was connected to Jenny Miller. Coincidence? "Did you attend Hope Community when Mark Shetland pastored there?"

Another bump in the line.

"I did, but I was visiting other churches to decide if I wanted to make the move or not. What happened to them was tragic." He shook his head, his face downcast. "Good people."

Were they?

"People are quite adept at hiding behind masks, Mr.—Daniel."

He seemed pleased at her response. "Yes, they are. What

mask do you hide behind?" he asked as they scooched up. "I'd love to take you to dinner and hear all about it."

"That's very kind of you to offer dinner and a listening ear." She wiped the sweat from the back of neck. "I'm afraid I'd be boring. What you see is what you get." Lies. She'd been hiding behind a mask of unspoken truth.

Daniel threw back his head and laughed. Deep. Rich. "Oh, Agent Kelly. No one is ever that transparent. But I applaud your attempt at a gentle rejection to my offer."

As she stepped up to order, he backed away. "Enjoy your evening. If you change your mind, you know where to find me."

He disappeared in the crowd. Flustered and her mind buzzing, Fiona ordered two funnel cakes—one with extra powdered sugar. She'd changed her mind about sharing. She tucked napkins in her pocket and balanced the plates until a woman holding a beer rammed into her, sending her toppling into a man holding a glass of homemade lemonade, which hit the pavement along with one of her funnel cakes. He grabbed her arm and kept her from losing the other one and biting it herself. Hallmark had never looked better.

"I'm so sorry," she pleaded.

"No worries," the man said and righted her. "Other than you're one less funnel cake. Can I buy you another?"

"I should be buying you another lemonade."

"I'd let you but the line is ridiculous and I kind of want to watch the fireworks."

He had a point. "True. I guess I'm stuck having to share this one now."

He chuckled. "Nobody likes to share."

"Especially funnel cakes."

That won her another grin. She raised her funnel cake in salute. "Again, I'm really sorry."

"Don't be. It's not every day I get to rescue a pretty lady." Brushing his hands on his cargo shorts, he stepped out of the way. "Enjoy the show."

"Thank you. You do the same." She did a juggling act to keep her only dessert from falling as she weaved and bobbed through people awaiting the fireworks. As she approached the team, Asa stood and beside him was…Amanda Barnes.

He caught her eye and guilt colored his face.

Fiona froze.

"Hey, I said extra powdered sugar!" Tiberius frowned, but snagged the funnel cake and shoved a huge bite in his mouth, powdered sugar covering him from chin to chest.

Fiona could act immature and bolt. Or she could muster up some maturity and pretend she didn't want to die right this second. This was their thing. And he was doing it with the new girlfriend? "Hi again," she said to Amanda. Maturity. "Nice to see you."

Daniel Osborn was right. No one was that transparent. Everyone hid something. If not a dark secret, an emotion, an angry thought or a snide comment.

"You, too," she said and extended her hand for a shake. Fiona put her hand in Amanda's. Civility at its finest. She was fresh and perky and festive in her red-white-and-blue flag tank top and red denim shorts.

"I didn't know you'd be here," Asa said, a hint of shame in his gravelly voice.

"I didn't know Daniel Osborn would be here." Subject change. Always easy. "But he is and I found out that he's attended two of the churches we have on our list." She relayed their conversation, omitting the invitation to dinner.

Owen perked up but Tiberius groaned and finished off her funnel cake. Whatever. She wasn't even hungry anymore.

"He also knows our newest vic." Owen opened another drink.

"True," Asa said.

"He meets the profile," Selah added and lifted her hair from her neck. Owen blew on it. What happened to not eating and dumping in the same place?

"He could have DID?" Owen asked. "Pretty important job. Stress."

If Fiona could go back and make a different choice that night she'd been abducted, she'd know if Daniel was Rhyme. But she had screwed up. And people were continuing to die because of her own selfishness.

"We'll talk to Violet about it tomorrow," Asa said. "See if a head of school could suffer from DID."

"I read about a social worker who had a successful career and she suffered with it." She'd read a lot of case scenarios.

"Again," Asa said, "we'll talk with Violet tomorrow. Where is she?"

"You know she don't do holidays," Tiberius offered. "She don't even do her own birthday." He glanced at Fiona. "I guarantee she's not watching a Hallmark movie, though."

Selah laughed. "She's probably at the gun range or something."

Amanda slipped her fingers through Asa's and a sharp pain stabbed at Fiona's ribs. "We should go, Asa. If we're gonna beat the line to get a canoe."

Hope it turns over. "Enjoy."

Amanda tugged on Asa and he started to follow, then paused, catching Fiona's eye. Apology. The question of whether she was okay or not. And an inkling of anguish for everything they'd broken.

She forced a tight-lipped smile and gave a slight nod. When they disappeared through the crowd, she exhaled.

No one said a word.

No one had to.

With the first explosion of red, Fiona couldn't fight it anymore, and in the darkness with quick successions of light, she bled her pain in tears.

From a distance, Rhyme watched. Had seen it all. From their dinner the night before at Mollie Fontaine Lounge to this moment when Fiona rested her head on her knees. She had no reason to be sad, to cry. Not over Asa Kodiak. Anger raced through his veins. Asa wasn't worth the pain.

"Shh," he whispered and rubbed his temple. Naughty Kitten was angry at him. He'd been angry at him since he was four. Too weak to stand up for himself. Too afraid to fight. Naughty Kitten knew Fiona was back. Rhyme had tried hard to hide her from him, but he hadn't been able to resist welcoming her back with the flowers or slipping into her home to let her know he was with her. Close. He'd been in their home before—when it reeked of Asa's scent.

But Naughty Kitten didn't know he'd been that close. *He* wanted to kill Fiona.

Wanted to feel the rope around her neck. Hear her beg for her life.

Rhyme would never let that happen. Not his Fiona. He'd been fighting Naughty Kitten since that first night and he'd proven he was strong enough to protect her. But Naughty Kitten continued to hound him over his ineptness and remind him that things were best when Naughty Kitten was in charge. Rhyme couldn't ever let that happen.

Bad, bad things would transpire.

To Fiona.

He wouldn't let her get too close to Naughty Kitten. Rhyme was keeping watch. Waiting to reveal his true identity.

She'd know it was him when he kissed her.

How could she ever forget the first kiss they shared?

Chapter Eight

Asa fidgeted in his office chair as he tried to play catch-up on an ocean's worth of paperwork from the holiday and the weekend and what had already been mounting on his desk. His mind wasn't cooperating. The Fourth of July event replayed on a loop, distracting him. With no heads-up from Ty or Owen, he'd been blindsided by Fiona's presence. The whole night had been off, even though he'd pretended that nothing was wrong so Amanda would enjoy the evening. Unfortunately, she was a rather good detective and finally asked him to come clean.

So he had.

It had rained on any fireworks between them and he'd driven home feeling like a bigger imposter than ever. Asa ran a task force but had no real power. He'd divorced Fiona but still felt married to her in many ways. Having her here had tilted his world, his moving forward. And it wasn't fair to Amanda. Asa wasn't a jerk. Had never been a player. He was no Owen.

His door was ajar, and Violet pushed it open, poking her

nose inside. "I have news from the ME's report. Everyone should hear it." She closed the door and Asa scooted aside his pile of paperwork, grabbed his coffee cup, which he'd emptied hours ago, and closed his laptop. He headed for the major case room. Everyone was inside, including Amanda.

"I called her," Violet softly said as he moved past her to his seat at the head of the table. "Jenny Miller was pregnant. About eleven weeks."

Faces fell. Curses were muttered.

"There's more. Based on our theory and how Jenny was staged, I asked the ME to send someone out to do a cheek swab on Thomas Miller. He now knows she was pregnant." She shook her head. "He doesn't know the results—that he's not the father."

Ty's hand shot up. "Not it!"

"Not it!" Owen said simultaneously.

Asa's temples thumped. As if he'd enlist either of them to inform Miller of that kind of information. "Who do we think the father is?"

Fiona leaned her head against the thick leather chair and closed her eyes. "What about the teenager from Mollie's? They may have been arguing about that. Happened about a month ago. She would have been a little less than eight weeks so she'd probably just found out. The question is, did Rhyme know she was pregnant?"

Violet took a chair three seats down from Amanda and across from Fiona. "I think you called the right nursery rhyme, but I don't believe she was running a prostitution ring. She may have been having an affair with a student. Likely the one she argued with, and if I had to guess, our killer was well aware."

Fiona muttered under her breath. Suddenly, her eyes flew open. "Ben!"

"Been what? Use your words," Ty encouraged.

"No." She waved away his buffoonery. "Ben. A man's name. A boy's name. There's another version where the hen is red and she lays eggs for 'Farmer Ben' instead of 'gentlemen.' The father may be named *Ben*. Perhaps a student—the one she was seen arguing with. We need that bartender...what was his name?"

"Trent Barton," Asa offered.

"We need him to talk with a sketch artist so we can take the drawing to the school. See if anyone recognizes him."

Violet frowned. "Hold on. That name seems familiar." She shuffled papers, a pen in her mouth. "Got it." She removed her pen and pointed it at the paper. "Assistant Head of School Benjamin James Furman. Goes by James, but his first name hits the mark."

"Looks like Farmer Ben's been plowing in the wrong field." Ty snorted.

Could be.

"I can go back," Fiona said. "Talk to him. Also grab a list of students named Ben. Work on finding the boy she argued with."

"Violet, Ty and I will go with you," Asa said. "We can cover more ground."

Selah stood, laptop under her arm. "I'll call ahead and have the school give us a roster of Bens."

"No, don't do that until after we talk to Furman. If he's guilty and gets wind we're sniffing at that name in regards to Jenny, he'll trump up a story. I want to see his face when we spring it on him initially." Asa stood as well. "I'll have them pull a roster after."

Amanda slipped on her blazer. "I'll notify Thomas Miller about the results. I won't mention anything other than it wasn't his DNA. If he's hiding anything, maybe this will give him motive to come clean. I'll have a sketch artist visit Trent Barton at Mollie Fontaine Lounge. Fax it over."

"Good. Good," Asa said. "Keep us posted." Should he walk her out? Touch her in any way? She didn't give him a chance to do either. She slipped out of the room behind Selah and Violet.

"If you get a solid name, text me and I'll see where his residence fits in my geo location board." Owen picked up his coffee cup and left the room.

Fifteen minutes later, they were walking back into St. George's. Andi, the redheaded assistant, welcomed them. "How can we assist you today?" she asked.

"We'd like to talk with the assistant head of school, Mr. Furman," Asa said.

"Oh." Pouty lips turned down. "He's not in. Migraine. Poor guy. They come on out of nowhere and he gets all confused and fuzzy. He's resting at home." She hit a button. "Mr. Osborn could help, though."

Asa and Fiona exchanged glances. Confused. Fuzzy. Like time lapses? "How often does he miss?"

"Depends. Last week twice. One day it was so bad he forgot to call in."

Mr. Osborn entered the office dressed like a Wall Street tycoon again. His attention on Fiona. "Well, we meet again. I guess you're not here to accept my offer?"

Fiona shifted her weight from one foot to another. "'Fraid not today."

"That gives me hope for another day, then." After a winning smile he looked at Asa. "How can I help you? Any new information on Jenny's killer? I hope you find him. I know this guy's got to be getting under your skin."

Asa's body temperature raised several degrees. "I'll need Mr. Furman's home address as well as every male student from ninth to twelfth grade with Ben or Benjamin in his name.

Could be first, middle or last. If any are present in the building today for various extracurricular activities, I need to know."

"May I ask why?"

"No." Asa didn't even try to keep the smugness from his voice. Daniel Osborn didn't need to remind him how powerless he was to catch the NRK. And what offer did he make Fiona? Not that it was his business, but Fiona knew better than to dally with suspects and Daniel had connections to a couple of churches. That counted.

"I don't have to tell you if you're interviewing a child who might be on campus, you'll need a parent or guardian present."

Asa's jaw twitched. "Incorrect. If we feel they were a witness to a crime, we can interview them like adults and they can decide if they want to talk to us without a parent or legal guardian. No one is under arrest or being questioned in regards to her murder." Take that, jerk. He pointed to the secretary. "Can you highlight or mark which students had direct interaction with Jenny Miller? Also we need all faculty and employees with that name as well." Chances were higher that if Jenny was having an affair with a student, it would be one she had contact with often.

She printed out the roster and handed it to him. "You think one of them witnessed Jenny's murder? How?"

"Yes, one of them could have witnessed a crime." When Jenny Miller had sex with a minor, this kid was there and witnessing it, so he wasn't lying per se.

Outside the office, Asa divvied up the sheets. "Forty students with Ben in their names. Ten are on campus today for various camps and activities. No employees except Furman." He handed one section to Fiona and one to Ty. "Violet and I will head to Furman's before he gets a call warning him we were looking for him. You two interview the ten Bens.

If they're a bust, we'll have to visit homes. Parents are gonna love us."

"I'd prefer to go with you to Furman's." Fiona folded her arms.

"No. Stay here. You'll get access to things you want better than I will. Daniel has a sweet tooth for you and a sour stomach for me. Violet has a degree in psychology. She goes with me. End of story, Fiona. My team. My call." Hopefully, she wouldn't push.

"Fine." She snatched the last sheet from his hand. "Guess I'll be heading to the theater in the fine arts department. I hope these kids can't act."

Asa chuckled, then sobered and pointed to Ty. "No calling 'liar, liar pants on fire.' Be the adult here."

"No fun in that," he mumbled and headed down the hall.

Asa motioned for Violet to follow him out.

"She's angry," she said.

"Story of my life."

Violet grunted as they climbed inside the Suburban, cranked the air full blast.

Furman lived in an older subdivision outside Germantown city limits. Modest home. A little on the run-down side. Siding needed painted. Grass needed mowing and the weed eater needed running. "What do you think his salary is?"

"Enough he doesn't need to live here. He's been at St. George's for five years. Prior to that he jumped schools. Mostly administration," Violet said and rang the doorbell. "This could fit a DID sufferer. Live below means. Stockpile money in case you lose your job, or the alter is spending it and he's confused or knows it. All kinds of scenarios in play here." She rang it again then rapped on the black wooden door.

Finally the door opened to a rough-looking James Furman. He hadn't shaved in a few days and his hair was flattened to one side of his head. He was wearing glasses, a stained Reebok

T-shirt and basketball shorts. Squinting and a hand shielding his eyes, he said, "Can I help...agents?"

"We'd like to come in and ask you a few questions. I'm afraid we can't be more courteous due to your headache, but it's important." Asa didn't give him time to decide; he placed a foot on the threshold and James Furman allowed him access.

The brown carpet was old and splotched with a myriad of stains. Something stale hid beneath the faint scent of cupcakes and old BBQ. The tables were littered with self-help books, sudoku, a bag from a BBQ joint and a chessboard set for two players. "Been playing chess?"

"Yes. No. I don't know." He rubbed his temples and winced.

Violet stepped into his personal space. "You have migraines often?"

"Yes."

"Do you take meds for them? Get an aura or signs one is coming on?" She cocked her head, held eye contact.

"No. And yes. I see spots. Sometimes it's so intense I black out." He backed away. Her strong presence intimidated him. And she knew it. She stepped forward.

"But no meds?"

"No."

"You been in bed all morning?"

"Yes."

"You eat breakfast? Maybe some leftover barbeque you picked up."

"No. I'm nauseous. I don't even eat barbeque."

"Why do you have a take-out bag from a barbeque joint?"

He shook his head. "I—I don't know. I eat chicken."

"You like chicken?" she asked.

"I just said I did."

"You like your job?"

"Yes."

"You happy there?"

"Yes."

"You sleep with Jenny Miller?"

"I—what? Did I what? No!"

Violet retreated and batted Asa an expression that said Furman appeared to be telling the truth. But if he suffered from DID maybe the alter ego had an affair, not Furman. "Jenny Miller was pregnant by a man who wasn't her husband."

"Well, it was not me!" he roared and grabbed his head. "I'd be asking a student. I told you on day one she took too much of an interest in her students."

"You suspect her of crossing lines with male students?" Violet asked.

"I just said I did."

That wasn't exactly what he said.

Violet didn't let up. "Would you be willing to take a DNA test to prove you aren't the father?" she asked.

"Absolutely."

"How often do you lose time?"

"I don't know. Wait. What do you mean?" He folded his arms over his chest as if that would shield him from Violet's blunt rapid-fire questioning.

"I mean how often do you black out and how much time lapses between blanking and waking?" She looked at the chessboard, considered it, then moved a player.

"Don't touch those! It's not my move!"

"Whose move is it?" she asked again and moved another piece, purposefully agitating him.

"I don't know."

"No?" His body began to shake and his hands balled tightly, then he proceeded to puke on the carpet. Violet covered her nose and mouth. "Go back to bed, Mr. Furman. We'll have someone come out and swab you. Brush your teeth, too."

She shook her head and Asa didn't question her as he followed her outside.

"You are ruthless," he said once they were in the vehicle. "What was that? And why didn't you ask him if he had DID? Were you trying to release a personality or something?"

Violet's probing stare unnerved him. "No. He wouldn't have told us if he did, especially if he suspects an alter ego of doing malicious crimes. I'm not certain he even realizes he has it—if he does—but he recognizes he has a health problem he doesn't want diagnosed. No meds for the migraines. Why? It's more than that. Could be DID. Could be something else. Something that might cause him to lose his job or something or someone he cares about. He's eating barbeque that he doesn't like and playing chess with someone."

"Maybe his alter ego."

Violet laughed.

"What do I know of DID?"

"Not much."

"But what if his alter ego plays chess and knows if Furman moves a piece, and it angers him and he does bad things?"

"You're going a little too M. Night Shyamalan on me right now, Kodiak."

Right now? It all felt M. Night Shyamalan to him. But this was Strange Crimes. Bizarre. Way out in left field. Made no logical sense to healthy-minded human beings. "Do you think he's lying about Jenny Miller?"

After a moment, she shook her head. "No. I think he's genuinely distressed and angry over her involvement with the students—he suspected, possibly knew. Maybe he even said something and was ignored. Let's talk to the head of school again. The one you don't like because he's attracted to your ex-wife."

Asa wasn't touching that subject with Violet. "What about

his blackouts and lapses in time? What if he's faking a migraine to cover up the blacking out and killing people? And that's why he doesn't have meds."

"Then I'm afraid of what we'll find in a day or two. He missed work today. I'm not ruling him out of being the NRK. I am ruling him out of sleeping with our vic. Still swabbing him, though."

As they turned into the drive at St. George's, Asa geared up to move another chess piece.

Fiona had blown through almost every name on her list that was available at the school today. She had two students left. Tiberius must not have been making any headway, either, or he'd have texted something other than birthday party texts. Those she'd gotten plenty of in the past hour. Was he even interviewing at all?

The air smelled like industrial cleaner and mulberry. Back in her day, it had been industrial cleaner only. The six months she attended before Rhyme abducted her hadn't felt like home. After the abduction, Mom had homeschooled her.

She walked to the boys' locker room. All she needed was to waltz in on teenage boys and parents would be charging *her* with something. "Hello?" she called over the raucous laughter and hooting. "Lady approaching!" That would drop pants and towels like gravity. "Federal agent! I'm coming in!"

"Would you like me to run interference for you?" An average-size guy with a navy blue uniform shirt and khakis approached, brushing his hands on the sides of his pants. He nodded toward the locker room. "They can't hear you in there. Not with those levels of nonsense."

Fiona agreed. "Yes, please." She'd barely noticed the maintenance man working on the ballasts. No one would pay him much attention, but that didn't mean *he* didn't pay attention. "Could I ask you a few questions first?" She held out her creds. "I'm Agent Kelly with the SCU. I'm investigating Jenny Miller's murder."

"In the locker room?" A skeptical eyebrow raised.

"Actually, yes." She shrugged. "Takes me everywhere. Locker rooms. Bathroom stalls."

"My job takes me those places, too." He reached for her hand. "Finley Lamm."

She shook it then wrote down his name. "Mr. Lamm, what can you tell me about Mrs. Miller?"

"Not a lot. Sometimes she tutored kids in the library after school. She shared her sandwich once with a girl who forgot hers. Good Samaritan, I suppose." The fluorescent light flickered and he frowned.

"You ever notice her around a student named Ben?"

He stuck his finger in the small cleft in his chin and puckered his lips. "She was around a lot of kids and I'm just trying to get to Friday every week, you know what I mean?"

Did she ever.

"Let me go make sure those boys are decent for you."

She sighed inwardly as Mr. Lamm raided the locker room for indecent exposure. He returned quickly. "Ben, you say? Ben Chambers is in there. He helps with stage lighting for plays. I know because he's broken more than a few lights," he stated dryly.

Fiona could relate to people making messes she had to clean up. Mostly killers, but she still had to do cleanup. Jenny Miller oversaw the theater program. That might be a connection. "Thanks so much. This was helpful."

"No problem." He climbed back up the ladder to the flickering light and Fiona entered the locker room.

"Ben Chambers?"

A tall muscular guy stepped up. He looked more like a

grown man than boy. The black-hen rhyme fit at least his body type. But he was seventeen. Still a child. "I'm Ben."

She introduced herself and asked if they could talk in private. She led him to the bleachers. He sat, wringing his hands. Time to play the game. "How well did you know Mrs. Miller?"

He flicked at one thumbnail with his other thumb. "I mean...she tutored me a couple times and we worked in the drama department together."

This was the first fidgety student she'd interviewed and the red flag raised high.

"Did you know she was pregnant? Whoever killed her also killed the baby."

His head whipped in her direction. "She was still pregnant? I—I mean she was...she was pregnant?"

Gotcha.

"We know you and Mrs. Miller had a fight outside Mollie Fontaine Lounge. I suspect it was about the baby. You want to tell me what happened? Because I'm going to find out either way. We have enough to get a DNA swab from you—" lies "—and you and I both know it's going to match the baby's DNA."

He remained silent and rubbed his hands together.

She waited silently.

Finally, he let it fly. "She told me she was getting rid of it. I thought she did." His eyes grew wide and then the waterworks flowed like a river. "I told her we could raise it together. I loved her." He sniffed. "But she called me a fool. A child. I made a baby with her. I'd say I'm a man."

She laid a hand on his shoulder. "Making a baby doesn't make you a man, Ben." Had Jenny Miller planned to make Ben think she'd aborted the baby and that she was now pregnant with her husband's baby, or had she changed her mind? "Do your parents know?"

"No way. I haven't told anyone, I swear. And I know she didn't." He hung his head and cried. "I loved her."

Poor kid had been taken advantage of and was confused. "How long had the affair been going on?"

"It started spring break of this past year. My mom had me get some extra tutoring for the ACT. She ended it after our fight at the bar about the baby. But I didn't kill her!"

"I know. The man who killed her has been doing this since before you were born."

"I hope you charge him for two murders. He killed my baby." Falling into her, he continued to bawl. She put her arms around him, unsure what else to do. "You need to tell your parents, Ben. And you need to get some counseling." Where was Violet? She was the psychologist for crying out loud.

"What do you do when you lose someone you love?" he asked.

One, he only thought he loved her, but he'd never see himself as a victim. Two, what good suggestion did she have? Go into the FBI? That's what she did after Colleen died. Get drunk? That's what she did when Asa served her divorce papers. "You do what you're doing right now and let it all out. Then you talk to someone who can help you work through your feelings and everything that happened." She'd had plenty of therapists over the years. Talking did help. But not everything could be told.

Ben sat up and wiped his eyes. "My mom is going to kill me."

Not if Thomas Miller caught wind first.

As Fiona walked Ben to the office to call his parents, she had to wonder if this was Jenny Miller's first offense. Who could have known if she hadn't told anyone—which was more likely than Ben not telling anyone. He had something to brag about. Jenny had something to hide.

Or maybe… "Ben, you promise you never told a living, breathing person about you and Mrs. Miller?"

"I promise. I knew if I did she would end things."

"Tell me this, and be honest, because it could help us catch who did this to her…and to the baby. Did you and Mrs. Miller ever fool around or talk about your affair here at the school or on a trip?" Someone might have seen or overheard, so they could be the killer, or they'd inadvertently confided in the killer, or the rumor mill turned until Rhyme had found out. Furman himself suspected. He couldn't be the only one.

He blushed. "Once in the library we kissed, but the place was empty. It was after school. I promise. No one saw."

Somebody saw. Student. Teacher. Staff member. Parent.

"What about flirting or touching hands inappropriately but secretly at school?"

"Maybe. I don't know."

"Did you ever meet her in a public place? Even if it seemed secluded?"

"Overton Park a couple of times. Once we ate barbeque at this little place on Raines Road. Tom's. It's a shack, really. Nothing over there but distribution and trucking. We didn't see anyone we knew."

Maybe not. But someone may have seen them.

Fiona pulled the watermelon from the fridge. The workday had ended before five. It was almost six now and she was prepping for the birthday party. Seemed crazy but she and Asa had instituted these parties five years ago. They waded in blood and death too often. Celebrating life was important and needed.

As much as she wanted to talk shop, especially after her

interviews today, it would have to hold until the morning. Earlier, she'd run to the party store for decorations and then Target to grab utensils, bowls and platters for the shindig. She sliced into the watermelon and the fruity fragrance sent her back in time, when summers with Asa were fun and steeped in love.

Using the melon baller, she began scooping and placing them on the platter along with cantaloupe, honeydew, grapes and strawberries. She'd ignored Tiberius's request for a watermelon soaked in vodka. A perfect way to ruin such a delicious fruit.

The party started in an hour and a half. No suits and ties. No blazers and dress shirts. Fiona had changed into her favorite worn cutoffs and a tank top with a sun wearing shades. The tile cooled her bare feet and her iPhone blared her Lee Brice playlist. She was a sucker for that guy. The monotony of scooping melon balls relaxed her and she sang along to "Hard to Love." Wasn't that the truth. She identified well. She wasn't easy to love. And, in the end, she'd lost it.

The front door's lock clicked and the door opened. Rattling plastic bags preceded Asa's voice. "Hey, I'm here!"

"In the kitchen."

Asa entered wearing gray basketball shorts and a Grizzlies T-shirt. His arms were loaded down with groceries. He laid them on the counter and grinned.

"What?"

"You still jonesing after Lee Brice?" He sang along to the chorus until it hit too close to home and then stopped. He always had a pretty tone to his voice.

"Lee Brice is a talented songwriter and singer."

"Sure," he drawled, "has nothing to do with him being easy on the eyes." He snagged a melon ball and popped it in his mouth, catching the juice before it dripped from his scruffy chin. "I remember you falling over like a lovesick puppy that time we went to see him."

"I did no such thing." She held back a grin. She might have. It was nice getting along with Asa, but even with the comfort between them, a stabbing pain refused to let up. They hadn't reminisced about good things in a long time.

"I got premade patties and charcoal." He'd brought his grill in the back of his truck. "Owen's bringing horseshoes." He grabbed one of the Kroger bags. "Ice cream's gonna melt." Shoving it in the freezer, he then stuck his head inside. "It's so hot."

Fiona laughed and stole a melon ball.

The next thirty minutes they hung a birthday banner, set the table with party plates, hats—at Tiberius's request—and utensils, and then Asa lit the grill. The party theme was mustaches and Fiona had grabbed some photo-booth props with a variety. Tiberius would love it.

Asa iced down the cooler and added a mix of drinks. "I forgot what a nifty party planner you were."

"I forgot you used words like *nifty*." She laughed and sliced tomatoes for the hamburgers.

"I'm nifty and thrifty." He winked and her heart fluttered. Asa was all natural charm and flirt. He meant nothing by it but it still had an effect on her and anyone else with a pulse.

Owen and Selah arrived first with drinks, chips and dips. Owen, in his bright purple shirt and dark denim shorts that looked more like pants, grabbed a curly mustache prop and Selah clicked a picture on her phone. "I'm digging the theme, y'all." He cracked open a cold one and snagged a pretzel.

"Glad you approve," Asa said and carried the cooler to the back screened-in porch.

"Do we have to listen to Lee Brice all night, Fi?" Owen scrunched his nose as if the music was a bad odor.

"We might."

Owen clasped her hands and twirled her, dancing her across the kitchen. Owen had moves and that's why the ladies loved him. She laughed and got into it as she sang "I Don't Dance." Man, she'd missed this. Round and round he spun her in circles, until she was nearly dizzy. Selah clicking pictures and encouraging it.

"I love this idea. Mine's in August and I want one," she squealed. "Retro-themed."

"Then a party you shall have, princess," he crooned and dipped Fiona as Violet entered the kitchen. "You want a turn?"

Violet raised an eyebrow and scanned the party decor, clearly put out with being here, though no one had forced her. "Fitting." She meandered to the table and plucked a strawberry from the tray. "Kind of a big deal for a grown man. I take that back. He's only a man in height and weight."

"I concur." Tiberius was a man-child but nobody knew religions and cults like he did. He was a secret brainiac.

Violet shrugged. "I didn't peg you for country music."

"No? What did you peg me for, soft rock?" Fiona asked and helped herself to a handful of cheese cubes.

Violet's mouth twitched. Almost a smile. "Emo indie music."

Selah giggled. "My turn! Take my picture." She held up a twisty mustache prop and Fiona grabbed her phone and took her picture as Owen photobombed it. "Send that to me right quick. I want to post it on my Instagram."

Fiona rolled her eyes. Selah ought to know better than anyone that social media was an evolved predator's hunting ground. She didn't have a single social media profile. She entered her camera roll to send Selah the photo and froze.

"What's wrong? Is it blurry? Let me see." Selah moved to take a peek, but Fiona couldn't allow it.

"No," she said with more inflection than intended. "It's fine." She hurried and sent it, then rushed into her bedroom and closed and locked the door to study the photo taken before the one of Selah and Owen.

Standing at the shower door was Rhyme in his plague doctor's mask, her shadowy silhouette behind the frosty door, the towel from the bar in his gloved hand. Her skin felt like bugs had crawled beneath it and were skittering all over. Heat flushed her body then it turned arctic.

Rhyme hadn't only been in her house, messing with her, but he'd also used her phone to take a selfie with her! Not on his own phone...but hers. She had a password but the camera icon was available for use without the password, which happened to be her and Asa's wedding day.

Why? Did he want her to have a memento of them? Was it to terrify her? It had worked.

A knock startled her. "Hey, you okay?" Asa asked.

She swallowed the knot in her throat and shoved the phone in her back pocket. "Uh, yeah. Just got dizzy from Owen spinning me. I'm getting too old to go in circles."

"Is that a metaphor?" he asked with humor in his voice.

"No." Maybe. She had to pull it together or he'd know something was up, that she'd been rattled to the core. After taking several deep breaths, she opened the door and pasted on a happy face. He squinted and cocked his head but remained silent.

"What time is it?"

"Time to finish up anything last-minute," he said as he entered the kitchen, Fiona following. He knew. He knew something was up but he wasn't pressing. That was new, too. "Burgers are on. Ty should be here soon. Where's Cami?"

"With Ty," Owen said and refrained from inquiring about her freak-out a few moments ago.

Asa tossed Fiona a play-nice face. Fiona could get along with Cami. She had bigger fish to fry.

"I told Fi that we are not listening to Lee Brice all night." Owen finished his drink and tossed it in the trash.

"Fat chance she'll listen." Asa clapped his hands. "They're here!"

"Get a mustache!" Fiona hollered and they all plucked one except Violet, who looked bored and unamused.

"Shh!" Asa hissed and they turned off the playlist and ducked behind the counters and table.

"He knows he's having a party. He suggested it. Demanded it actually," Violet stated, but had the common courtesy to conceal herself from view.

"Stop being a wet blanket, Rainwater," Owen growled.

The front door opened.

"Hello? Anyone here?" Tiberius dramatically called.

They tiptoed into the kitchen and the team jumped out and yelled surprise. He feigned shock and hooted at the mustache decor. "Sweet." He took one and Selah clicked his picture. "I smell burgers." He stopped and pointed to Fiona. "No Lee Brice. I know you."

Asa hooted. "Too late."

Fiona fake pouted and they headed out back, country pop hits playing. "If he makes it onto the station it ain't my fault." She forced a grin and put on a party personality, then waved at Cami. Tinker Bell in the flesh. It was kind of uncanny. Cami half smiled.

Okay. Good enough.

The next hour they ate food, talked about movies, new restaurants and the hot chick in the Violent Crimes Division that Tiberius and Owen wanted to ask out on a date. They were debating whom she would choose between the two.

Violet guessed neither.

Fiona did, too.

The sun set and cicadas sang. A light breeze blew in and Asa scooted his sports chair next to her. "We needed this."

The two of them or the team? "Yeah. We did." Would have been more enjoyable had a serial killer not taken a selfie with her in the background, vulnerable. She shivered and her nervous stomach jumped in the driver's seat. "Burgers were good," she said.

"As if I'd cook inedible food."

She snorted. "I was there for the turducken."

Asa sipped his drink. "That was the year we had a delicious Cracker Barrel feast."

"With a wait time of two hours. Well done, Chef Kodiak." She raised her drink and clinked it with his. He held her gaze a beat and then one more.

The crack of fireworks interrupted the connection. Green, purple and blue blasts of light hit the night sky as Tiberius whooped and hollered and obnoxiously sung "Happy Birthday" to himself.

Fiona shook her head and watched the display Owen set off. They were glorious. Beautiful. There, then gone. "You know when I was a little girl I never wished to be a princess. I wanted to be a firework. Did I ever tell you that?" she asked.

Asa's shoulder brushed against hers as the sky lit up again in red, blue and white. "I don't think you did. Why? 'Cause you burn hot?" He chuckled.

"No, that's you."

"'Fraid it is." He shifted and held her gaze. "Why did you want to be a firework, Fi?"

"I wanted to light up the world. Be bright and brilliant." She wasn't sure how, but she felt there had to be a way; it burned within her—that deep desire to shine.

Asa's smile was tender. "I always thought you were a star.

Guess we both know you can burn bright." He carefully tucked a strand of hair behind her ear, then rose and strode away.

The moment had been too intimate. And he had a girlfriend. A new life, and it didn't include her.

The sad thing about fireworks—they only lit up for a brief moment before everything went dark and empty again.

Chapter Nine

The conference table was littered with soda cans, bottles of water, pages of notes and crushed deli bags from lunch. Last night had been a work-free zone and much needed. Everyone had a great time, including Asa. Maybe too much. He'd almost forgotten what good times with Fiona had been like, though something had unsettled her. And while the others might not recognize her good show at being relaxed, Asa had observed it but felt he needed to give her space and refrain from prying, though that had been excruciating. During the fireworks, their conversation had taken a more intimate turn and when it started to make a mark on his heart he'd pulled away.

He was in a new relationship.

Fiona finished briefing them on Ben Chambers. Daniel Osborn was no doubt still getting an earful from Ben's parents. Once the media got wind of Jenny Miller's illegal behavior, and if it broke she had been pregnant, the school would be a news camera circus. Asa didn't envy the school that.

None of the teachers they interviewed that had gone to

girls' night out at the Mollie Fontaine Lounge had seen Ben outside the establishment, but they had noticed Jenny's irritation upon returning inside that night. She'd blown it off as a marital spat and the women had given it no other thought. No one had suspected her of inappropriate behavior with a minor and all of them had been appalled.

Thomas Miller would find out soon enough and no telling what he might do. Amanda had the privilege of dealing with that train wreck. In the meantime, there had been no prints at the scene that shouldn't have been there. But Asa wasn't surprised. The NRK was skilled and well-practiced at leaving no trace evidence.

Fiona hadn't said much about their interview with James Furman. While he wasn't the one having an affair with Jenny Miller, he was at the top of their list of suspects. Asa had Violet and Owen working his history and trying to connect him to all the murders if possible. He was hiding something.

"Did you ever come up with Lexi's last name?" Fiona asked. "The girl that Robert Williams's wife saw him with at the sleepover? I'd really like to talk to her."

"No," Selah said. "No one kept records digitally then. And they didn't keep their youth attendance cards from that far back. I'm afraid unless I have a last name, I can't track her. But I did put a call in to the youth pastor at that time. He's on a mission trip to Africa right now, so we'll have to wait for him to return in a few days."

"Contact Tanya again and see who the other youth sponsors were. Maybe they'll remember a name. I'd like to move faster than a few days," Fiona responded and rubbed her left shoulder blade. Telltale sign of tension. "Alan Minton, the property lawyer. He's a hole in this thing. We can't connect him to any of the churches. Only his sister and her husband are religious. And his rhyme makes little sense."

"Knock, knock." Amanda stood with two trays of Starbucks coffees in hand. "Thought I'd bring the good stuff." She set them on the table. "They're all black, but it's better than what's in that pot."

"Hey—" Asa stood "—thanks. You talk to Thomas Miller?"

Amanda snatched a venti coffee and sipped it. "Yeah. He claims he had no idea about the affair or pregnancy. I don't see how he could be a copycat unless he knows someone in law enforcement who has direct access to the case files."

Asa snorted then paused. "He told me he had friends in law enforcement right after I offended him by asking if his wife had an affair. Let's be safe and run down who he knows and if they'd have any kind of direct information involving the NRK's files."

"In the meantime," Fiona said, declining a cup of coffee, "Alan Minton."

"Maybe we got the rhyme wrong," Ty offered.

"No, we didn't," she said. "We may have been distracted on that one, but we didn't get it wrong."

"Why were you distracted?" Amanda sat beside Asa.

"He was killed on Christmas Eve. We were out of town and had to fly back in," he muttered.

They had been in St. Thomas on their honeymoon. The NRK had gone silent and the cases had officially gone cold with every lead exhausted, but Fiona had never stopped working off the clock. She'd promised to for the wedding and honeymoon and she'd lived up to it.

Until the NRK struck that night. Asa had never believed for a minute it hadn't been strategic. To bring back Fiona and keep her fixed on him. The NRK had always been watching. Keeping up with their press releases and lives. That had grinded Asa's nerves. Fiona lived as if he'd never touch or hurt her. Was even adamant at times he wasn't a direct threat to her, but never backed up her ridiculous thought with a concrete reason. Asa knew better.

Some day he would hurt her. They always did.

He'd been especially afraid after their wedding. They'd angered the NRK big-time. They got back the next morning on Christmas and, of course, Fiona went straight to work.

Honeymoon over.

It had been a dark foreshadowing.

"I agree with Fiona," Asa said. "I think that staging was on the money." "When I Was a Little Boy I Lived By Myself." Alan Minton lived alone. Traveled often overseas. The British flag and a teacup with *London* written on it, along with British tea, had been set on the table for staging. The rhyme said he was forced to go to London to buy a wife. The key phrase: buy a wife. He had to bring the wife home in a wheelbarrow, which broke and killed the wife.

The wheelbarrow broke and my wife had a fall, and down came the wheelbarrow, wife and all. At the bottom of Minton's stairs was a broken wheelbarrow covered with bread, cheese and dead rats. All from the rhyme.

But Minton had no wife.

They'd looked into his financials and found nothing indicating he'd purchased a child bride or any bride overseas or online, though if he'd used a dark web browser they wouldn't have any search history to browse.

Fiona held up his file. "We have better technology now. I'd like to give his case a go again. I hate to admit I may have been preoccupied but—"

"Getting a case on your wedding night'll do that." Ty tossed an apple in the air and then it must have dawned on him what he'd said aloud. He had the decency to flush red, then crunched into the apple.

Another wave of tightness pulled at the air.

"Right," Fiona mumbled.

Between loud chews, Ty went on. "He didn't have any religious affiliations but he was a big giver of charity. St. Jude Hospital, Boys and Girls Club, Memphis Child Advocacy Center—"

"All for children." Fiona pursed her lips and chewed the tip of her thumbnail. "We're missing a piece here. We're always two steps behind Rhyme. He's careful. Meticulous. He tells the story he wants to tell but we never know how to find him! If he wants to show these people as the monsters they might be, why not make their crime easier to know? Leave us more clues into who they were."

"His goal might not be to out them to the world, but put them on display. Degrade and humiliate them. We have no idea what he says, if anything, to them before he kills them. Maybe the satisfaction of knowing he ended their charade and torment of young people was enough." Asa had no idea why he didn't drop more obvious clues of the victims' secrets. Maybe he expected the police to do their jobs and figure it out. These people had gone to great lengths to bury their secrets. "Buried."

"What?" Fiona asked.

"Give me Alan Minton's file."

She slid it across the table and he flipped through it. "Neighbor across the street said she was always complaining because Alan continually remodeled or did repair work to the house and it was noisy. Didn't raise a red flag—his father owns Minton Construction. But what if we didn't find a bride because he buried her where we couldn't find her?"

"We searched the house meticulously and found zip."

"We were looking for evidence of a child bride, not an actual child bride." If they could peek through the house again... "Let's take fresh eyes this time." Asa picked up the phone in the room. "Selah, see who owns Alan Minton's old home in Germantown. Call them on our behalf. We need to come in and look around again."

"On it." A few moments later, she said, "It's still vacant. Guess no one wants to buy a house a serial killer murdered someone in. I can call the Realtor to meet you out there. Get you in."

"That would be great."

Another moment later she buzzed him and let him know that the Realtor would be there in forty minutes.

Amanda, Violet, Asa and Fiona loaded up. It wasn't long after they pulled into the drive of the large Spanish-style home that the Realtor showed up and let them inside.

"Have you been the Realtor since the house came available?" Asa asked.

"No. There was a year contract on it and then I took it. When you tell people about the grisly murder—and by law you have to—they don't seem nearly as interested. It's a real shame, too. All the work he did to it before he died. Fresh paint, new flooring, shelves added to the entertainment system in the master. The master bath has heated floors, by the way. If any of you are in the market." She gave a sheepish grin.

They already knew that from working the financials.

"Just because we see grisly crimes doesn't mean we want to live in houses that endured it." Amanda gave her a big smile and turned to Asa. "Where do you want me?"

"You take downstairs with Violet and Fiona and I will take the upstairs."

Amanda's eyebrows raised and she slowly nodded. "All right."

His mistake smacked him upside the head and he caught Fiona's eye and her pity smile. Picking her over Amanda to team up with had nothing to do with personal feelings. They'd worked together for years, knew each other. That was all.

He couldn't take it back now, though. That would be even worse.

Violet tossed him an eye roll and a headshake.

Asa and Fiona reached the loft area with an open balcony to the first floor. "I didn't even think."

Fiona twisted her lips to the side. "And that's what probably bothered her most." She gave him a slap on the shoulder. "Lucy, you have some 'splaining to do."

"You're enjoying my misery, aren't you?"

She pinched her fingers almost together. "Little bit."

"Let's get to the case." He made a grand display of the house with his hand. "We already know he entertained often, thus the large house, wet bar and billiard room downstairs. I'll take the guest rooms and theater room. You take the office and master suite." Asa strode toward the north end of the upstairs.

"What are we looking for?"

"A place to hide a secret bride." Asa entered the old theater room. Now it was bare. Deep red walls. White trim. Not a single neighbor had seen anything out of the ordinary. But if the vic shuffled guests in and out while entertaining, then strangers coming and going would have been common.

He remodeled a lot. But not in here, although... Asa knocked on the walls. Theater rooms typically had soundproofing for loud movies. Did any of the other rooms? He hurried into the master, where Fiona stood staring at the entertainment center.

"Do you think this room is soundproofed?" Asa asked.

"How would I know?"

Asa tapped the walls, then pulled a knife from his pocket and dug into the wall. "Double layer of drywall. It is." Chills crept up his spine. "Why are you staring at that entertainment shelf?" Two large shelves on either side of an electric fireplace.

"Why would anyone need to soundproof a bedroom or need an entertainment center this big when a private theater with surround sound is just down the hall? Also, why didn't we notice any of this before?"

"It was our honeymoon, Fi. I know I wasn't on my A game. Were you?"

She sighed. "No," she murmured. "And because of that we missed things. I knew we should have put it on hold."

Yes, because letting a serial killer dictate their lives sounded way more normal to Fiona than living a real life with him.

"Back to the wall here." Talking about their wasted honeymoon in the same house they had actually thrown it away in wasn't something he wanted to expound on. "The soundproofing isn't for blocking out TV noise, Fi."

"That's what I'm afraid of." Fiona pushed on the shelves, feeling underneath them. "What if it's a front?"

Asa joined her. Nothing under the shelves or above. He studied the fireplace. At the bottom was a small button, like the kind to light gas fireplaces. He bent down and pressed the igniter button.

A creak sounded and the right-side shelving cracked open. Asa pulled it the rest of the way and a wave of stale heat smacked him in the face as a secret room came into view. He used his cell phone for a light and stepped inside, batting cobwebs.

Fiona followed.

"Oh, my…" Fiona shone her camera light on the small furnished room. Neutral color walls. Tiled flooring. A queen-size bed. Dresser. No bathroom. No closet. Two racks with female clothing hung in the corner, covered in dust. A chest rested at the foot of the bed.

"What size are the clothes?" Asa asked as Fiona browsed through them.

"Two. We can safely say he wasn't cross-dressing." Alan Minton had been six foot three and the size of a linebacker. "Shoes are size five. We're looking at a petite female. I wear a seven. That's average."

"Child?"

"Possibly. But I know several women that size and who wear shoes that little. So I can't say for sure." She held up a few risqué pieces of clothing.

Asa opened the chest at the foot of the bed. "Oh, boy."

Fiona peeked over his shoulder at video equipment and a collection of DVDs. "I really don't want to watch those."

A sick feeling spread all through Asa's gut. "I can't say he bought a bride, but he was doing things up here that might be illegal. We're gonna have to see the DVDs to tell." He didn't want to watch them, either. This was part of the job he hated most. To catch killers, they had to see what killers were capable of and that meant through victim interviews, face-to-face interviews with killers and watching DVDs and videos that made his skin crawl. Strange Crimes took them into the underbelly of humanity on a daily basis. Asa had spent most of his early professional years unable to remove the grime from his skin or cleanse his eyes from what he'd seen even after several whiskey neats. But since he'd given his life to Christ, trudging through these kinds of gruesome things didn't always shove his spirit into a deep muddy funk.

He could pray away the filth he'd had to see and endure and gain some hope and light from the Word, though it was still hard to bear and scrape away. He'd do that tonight for sure. Fiona would wrestle in her sleep and fight the images, probably have a few stiff drinks. There would be no comfort like the comfort he was going to experience.

He called in the TBI for forensics, hoping they'd secure a set of prints that might point them to who wore those clothes and slept in this room. Then he went downstairs and found Amanda in the pantry. A wall had come loose, revealing a crawl space. She was on her hands and knees, flashlight in hand, peering into the opening.

"Amanda."

She shrieked and pulled her head out of the dark hole. "Something is back there. And it reeks."

"How'd you find it?" Asa asked.

"No baseboard on this section. That's odd."

Asa grinned at her savvy.

"My uncle flips houses on the side and I've helped." She shrugged and swiped at her hair. "I hate spiders."

He told her what they found upstairs. "TBI should be here to process. How far back did you get?"

"Not far. I'm not real keen on going in there." She stood and brushed her knees.

"I'll go." Asa took her flashlight and peered into the opening. No bigger than his guest bathroom. Dark. Dank. Something had rotted back here. Could be an animal but his gut said it was human.

Fiona had showered off the grime from the day—not only from the humidity, but also from the mind of a depraved human being—and finished it off with some cheap Scotch. Watching those DVDs had been one of the worst things she'd ever experienced, and she'd fought back tears the entire time. Once she'd glanced over and caught Asa and Tiberius wiping away moisture, and Owen's fists had been so tight it was a wonder his skin hadn't cracked.

But they now had a face that likely matched the body they'd found in the back of the pantry. Sealed in concrete. She'd been about thirteen or fourteen. They'd had to call out experts to break it up and remove the remains. It was now in evidence and being analyzed. They might retrieve DNA from the remaining hair.

But there was no doubt now. Rhyme was killing predators of children and adolescents. Fiona had been replaying the six months her family had lived in Memphis. Colleen had made friends quickly with popular girls in the sophomore class and most high school girls gossiped about other girls regardless of popularity. It wasn't a reason to kill her.

Fiona had caught her a few times with weed and threatened to tell. Could she have gotten into trouble with it or other drugs? Right before they were taken, Colleen and her friends had hung around with a girl who had an older guy friend, and Fiona suspected that's how they got their pot. The girl didn't really seem a part of Colleen's clique. The girl hadn't been at the cabin that night that she recalled. Fiona also wondered if that older friend had been Rhyme.

Questions whirled as she poured herself another drink and headed for the bedroom. She plopped down with photos and papers, a notebook and a pen. She scratched a few thoughts and questions. How does Rhyme know these secrets? That ate at her most. There had to be a connection. If it wasn't a church directly, then a friend-of-a-friend kind of thing. They had called all the churches with mental illness support groups and it hadn't panned out like they hoped. The few possible suspects that would meet the profile had been a dead end.

Fiona leaned back, resting her head on the wall, the smell of new paint clinging to it. Like Asa had painted over their lives. Everything looked new and pretty. But behind the walls was old paint. Their old life.

And behind the freshly painted walls of Alan Minton's

home was a dark secret. All the charities he gave to. The life he led. A lie.

Fresh paint.

Paint!

Painters would have access to schools, churches, homes. Places people carried on their lives and forgot ears were listening in. Had the churches in question or the homes of the vics been painted at some point prior to their murders? If so, what company or subcontractors did the work?

This might be the break she needed. An urge to call Asa overtook her and she grabbed her phone, then caught herself.

It could wait. He was probably trying to smooth over today's debacle when he'd instinctively chosen Fiona over Amanda professionally, though Amanda had certainly taken it personally. The insecurity was unnecessary. Asa's personal choice was obviously Amanda. But had Fiona been in Amanda's shoes, she'd be equally miffed, too. And hurt. She shoved aside her papers, slipped under the covers and cut the light. Nothing but moonlight drifted through the window. She lay on her back listening to cicadas and an owl, pushing out the images of the day and what she'd had to watch until she finally fell asleep.

Someone was in the house.

Close.

She smelled him. Grease from fast food. Old Spice. Smoke. Vanilla and lemon.

Fiona's eyes opened as a gloved hand slid around her throat. A stark white vintage venetian plague doctor's mask plunged her into the past. She grabbed his hand and kicked at the covers to free herself. Her heart hurtled into her throat.

"Naughty kitty. You've gone too far. You shall have no pie," he growled in a Batmanesque voice. "I know what you've been doing. Trying to hunt me down. Like I hunted you. You weak, stupid kitty."

His grip was like a vise. She snatched the leftover drink and tossed it into the eyeholes of his mask, giving her a quick window of time to roll to the other side of the bed. She grabbed for the Glock she kept under her pillow.

No!

She'd been deep in thought, and a few drinks in, and had left it in the kitchen. Fiona tumbled out of bed, hitting the floor with a thud. "You don't want to do this."

"I'm here, aren't I?" A knife glittered in his hand. She swiped a vase on the dresser and chucked it at him, then bolted for the hallway and to the kitchen.

He tackled her. Pain burst in bright white light through her vision, exploding in her head. She managed to elbow him in the sternum, scrambling out from under him and sprinting for her gun. Her pulse beat in her temples, nearly sending her heart through her chest. Fiona snatched her gun and pivoted, but he was gone. He must have seen her go for it. The front door slammed and she raced to the porch. Too dark to see. Not even a flash of his stark white mask.

She'd let down her guard.

All her training. All her hard work. And she'd panicked. It had all gone out the window, proving that when it came to him, she was powerless.

Now she had to call Asa.

Rhyme's alter ego hadn't had the chance to kill her. Asa was going to take a shot and get the job done for him. She hit his name in her phone. He answered on the second ring.

"What's the matter?" His gritty tone was laced with concern.

Fiona couldn't manage the words. "I'm…he—"

"Fiona. Fiona. Are you hurt?" Urgency blared through his voice.

"No," she whispered, though her body ached and her head pounded.

"Are you at the house?"

"Yes."

"I'm on my way." The line clicked and she closed the front door, locked it. How did he get in? She checked the house and found a window jimmied in the breakfast area. Was that how he'd gotten in when he'd left her flowers and messed with her head the first time? Hands shaking, she collapsed at the stupid wobbly kitchen table. She never expected Rhyme to come for her, but she should have known his alter ego might—the one that had murdered her sister. Wanted to murder her. Hunted her in the woods.

But Rhyme hadn't wanted her dead. And that was only a sliver of that night she'd never revealed.

Fifteen minutes later, Asa's car revved in the driveway and she jumped up and ran for the front door, unlocking it and throwing it open.

"Fiona!"

Before thinking better of it, she raced onto the porch and collapsed into his arms. A place she'd always felt safe, secure and loved. She could never deny that Asa Kodiak had loved her from the beginning. But their love hadn't been able to anchor them soundly when things fell apart.

"It's okay," he whispered and stroked her hair. "I'm here. I'm here."

"I didn't think he'd—"

"I know," he murmured against her hair. "Shh, now." He continued to whisper comfort into her soul. Words that sounded a lot like prayers, and at this moment she wouldn't object—wouldn't tell him that prayers fell on deaf ears. Because she needed the hope. The words slid somewhere deep within her—words she'd heard Grandma pray.

Words like "though I walk through the valley of the shadow of death, I will fear no evil: for thou art with me." Words like "he leadeth me beside the still waters." Asa's embrace felt familiar and yet foreign and new. Stronger. More secure. All she did know was that she wanted to stay here.

But she couldn't.

She pulled away from his chest, from listening to his heartbeat, and peered into eyes.

No conversation.

No voices.

He cupped her cheek, caressed it with his thumb, wiped a stray tear. Most of them had leaked onto his dress shirt. They stood that way for what felt like eternity, speaking in the silence—apologies, regrets, sorrows. Finally, she couldn't stand it one second longer. To be touched by him but not belong to him. She broke free, the chilly distance that swept through her bones reminding her of the hollowness inside. It ached and screamed to be filled, to be safe. To not be alone.

"I'll—" she cleared the emotion from her throat "—show you the point of entry."

He followed her inside and locked the door, then trailed behind her to the kitchen. She pointed to the window. Good. Yes. Focus on the case. "Didn't hear him break and enter. Woke me in my sleep. No rope. Knife." The horror of that mask scraped down her spine, leaving chills in its wake. "I'd left my gun in the kitchen." Stupid. Stupid. Stupid.

Asa examined the kitchen window, then flipped on the hallway light to search for footprints. "I don't want to walk on it, compromise anything. What happened after he woke you? He say anything?"

She licked her bottom lip and restrained her tears. So weak.

"He said, 'Kitty. You've gone too far. You shall have no pie.' Then he said, 'I know what you've been doing. Trying to hunt me down. Like I hunted you. You weak, stupid kitty.'"

Asa's nostrils flared and his lips went taut. "Did he hurt you?"

"I fell out of bed on my ribs. But I'm okay."

"Let me see." Before she had time to protest, he lifted the side of her oversize T-shirt and gently pressed along the already bruised area. She winced, not so much from pain but having his fingertips on her skin. It had been a long, long time since he'd touched her. He swallowed hard and let down her T-shirt. "You need to have that checked. Make sure nothing is fractured."

"I can breathe easy enough. It's bruised is all."

His look was disapproving, but he didn't argue. "I knew this would eventually happen. You don't listen."

"Rhyme doesn't want to hurt me. This was his alter ego. I know it."

"And how do you know it?"

He was going to come unglued.

"Because Rhyme's been here already. Not as the alter ego." She told him what happened last week, including the photo she'd noticed at Tiberius's birthday party.

"I want to see it. Now." His voice was quiet, fury simmering beneath.

She unlocked her phone, scrolled to the photo and held her breath as she handed it over.

Asa studied it and the vein in his temple protruded, his jaw clenched. She waited for the barrage of insults and anger to explode.

Instead, he inhaled deeply and took one last look at the photo. "You have three choices here, Fiona. And you're going to choose one of them. It's not up for debate."

She couldn't throw a fit. He'd been right. She'd underestimated the alter ego. She was in direct danger now; maybe she always had been. Maybe she'd lived on the false sense of security based on what had happened that night in the woods. "Okay."

"One, I can move in here until you go back to Chicago. Two, you can pack up and move in with me until you go back to Chicago. Or, three, you can pack up now and go back to Chicago." The grit in his voice, the seriousness in his expression. There was zero wiggle room.

She didn't want to do any of those things. But it was necessary. The guest room here only had a twin bed. They didn't have enough toiletries, and if he came here that meant packing up clothing and the headache that came with it. "I'll come to you."

"Yeah?" Surprise erupted from his one question.

"No point in you uprooting when I only have two rolling bags and a carton of yogurt in the fridge. I don't want to impose, though."

His jaw twitched again. "Your safety is more important than imposition."

But she was imposing. "I'm sorry."

"Don't be." He called in the crime scene techs and then the team to inform them and to meet extra early in the morning. When he hung up, he led her to the couch and sat beside her. "Go over it again. Every detail. From what he said to how he smelled. What was he wearing? Build? Voice?"

"Bulkier than he once was. Mature. Fit. Voice was low and raspy. Familiar." She told him how he smelled. "I didn't see a bag. Nothing to indicate he was going to stage me. Only the knife. His footfalls sounded heavy, as if he were possibly wearing construction boots. He wore the mask. But no feathers on it. It was dark and it happened fast. When I went for my gun, he bolted."

"I've got the county forensic guys going over the woods and road. He had to have parked somewhere. Maybe we can get something off the tire tracks. It's pretty dry, though. I don't know. It's a slim chance."

She dropped her head between her knees. "It was like being back in the woods. Same fear. You'd think I was seventeen and not thirty-four. What's the point of all this training and punishing myself at the gym if I'm going to revert into a gangly, scared girl who pees herself?"

"You peed yourself?"

Her head flew up. "No!"

"Well, then seems to me you're a step in the right direction." A lopsided smirk creased the dimple in his scruffy cheek.

She laughed. "I guess so. You always could make me laugh."

He sighed. "Not always." He rested his hand on her bare knee. "Not always. I'm sorry for that. For the things I said to hurt you. For the way things ended and my part. Can you forgive me for that? Because one thing I'm learning is that forgiveness is freeing. And I know you need to be free, Fiona. As much as I do. From our past—before we were a couple—and when we were. I've forgiven you."

"I didn't ask you to," she choked out. She didn't deserve it. "But thank you." Could she forgive him? For the hurt he caused? She'd caused even more. She didn't want to stay bottled up and angry all the time. But if she forgave him, she might have to deal with feelings she worked overtime to keep under control. "I'll try."

"Good enough. For now." He slapped his thigh, a sign this conversation was over. "Now, how are you getting too close to the NRK? Why is he upset you're hunting him down when you've been doing that for years and he knows it?"

"I wasn't dealing with the primary personality—Rhyme—but the alter ego. He's wanted me dead all along. He's the one who abducted me, chased me in the woods, forced me to wear that horrible nightgown. I think it was the alter ego who killed Colleen and the other girls, not Rhyme."

"You think this alter ego is doing all the killing and Rhyme—the actual man or primary personality—is completely innocent in everything?"

She was iffy on that. It was possible. "I don't know. We didn't fit the mold. I can't make our abduction and their murders fit what is happening now. I don't even understand why we were forced to wear those old white nightgowns. Part of me thinks Rhyme knows what his alter ego is doing and can't stop it but maybe wants to."

But she wouldn't reveal why she suspected that. The shame and her actions that night were too much to bear. There was too much blood on her hands as it was.

Chapter Ten

Asa slumped in his kitchen chair drinking his third cup of coffee and it wasn't even 7:00 a.m. Their house had been processed. They'd searched a mile in both directions and collected paper and litter that might have fallen from the NRK's vehicle. Slim chance, but Asa was willing to do anything at this point.

It had only been a matter of time before he came after Fiona. Asa couldn't be certain why now. Other than her notion it wasn't "Rhyme," but the alter ego. He'd land on that theory more fully once he had Violet's professional opinion.

It had been almost three this morning before they'd made it back to his town house. Fiona had never been here before. She was spent, so he'd shown her to the guest room and pointed out the bathroom, then he'd set the coffeepot and gone to bed. But he hadn't slept. Not a wink.

He'd never been so scared…except for once.

When serial killer Raymond Vect had broken into his home when he was fourteen and assaulted his mother. Asa had heard cries and entered Mom's room, and unknowingly walked into

Raymond Vect's sick world. He squeezed his eyes shut, re-membering his mother's screams and cries for him to choose Kacie.

Kacie has her whole life to live. Take care of Kacie. Do the right thing, Asa. Please choose Kacie.

So he had.

And then he'd watched Vect slice open his mother's throat, and before he left he'd whispered a question that had haunted Asa his entire life.

Why didn't you ask me to spare them both? You must have wanted your mother to die. Sleep tight, kiddo.

The media had plastered his face on TV and in the papers. The boy who had to choose.

He'd never breathed a word of what Vect had asked.

Vect had moseyed out the front door and Asa had done nothing. Never run after him. Never tried to fight him. He'd stood in a complete stupor. Blood everywhere. Kacie wailing. Sirens blared. He hadn't even alerted the police. A neighbor coming home from the night shift saw the door wide open and called.

Six months later they'd caught Vect. He'd been assaulting and slicing women open up and down Louisiana. But Asa had been the only one to interrupt him. The only one forced to make a choice. He'd seen his face and Vect had let him live. He would have let his mother live, too.

If Asa had only asked.

Asa promised to take care of Kacie, but he'd failed miser-ably at that. She had a possession charge, a hard time keeping a job and moved from place to place probably owing rent to landlords all over the Memphis area. He kept forking out the dough. She kept falling back into old ways. He tried to get her to live with him. Most calls she never returned.

Things had fallen apart when Grandpa died. Asa had been

sixteen. Then it was him, Kacie and Grandma. He had done his best to hold everyone and everything together.

It wasn't enough.

His coffee had gone cold and Fiona stood in the hallway, leaning against the wall, studying him. "Hey," she said. "You were lost in thought. Kacie?"

She knew him so well, and yet she didn't know the words Raymond Vect had spoken to him all those years ago. She didn't know how absolutely inadequate and unqualified to protect her he felt. But she knew his faces. The subject of his thoughts.

"Yeah."

"She come by for that money the other night?" She slowly moved into the space as if to give him time to readjust his thoughts and feelings.

"Yeah. I told her to be extra careful since we have the Nursery Rhyme Killer on our hands again."

"You enable her, Asa. I know it comes from what happened to you as children, but you're not helping her and deep down you know it. It's the exact advice you'd give someone else."

"I know you're right, Fi. I—I don't know. When it comes to her, I already feel like I've failed."

Fiona ruffled his hair. "Asa, you have not failed that girl. You have been everything she needs when she needs it. Except for a disciplinarian. She needs to know she has to be a productive member of society." She made her way to the coffeepot, paused at the fridge. At their magnets, which reminded them of all the places they'd been together. "I wondered what happened to these."

He simply shrugged. He had no answers. She scanned the cabinets.

"Cups are in the skinny cabinet above the coffeepot."

She opened the cabinet and retrieved a cup.

"Cream is in the door of the fridge. I don't have fake sugar. I can pick some up."

Fiona fixed her cup and used real sugar to sweeten it then joined him at the kitchen island. She was still wearing the clothes she'd changed into last night after she could get back in her bedroom. "I don't need you to go out of your way. Sugar is fine." To make her point, she took a sip of her coffee. "It's good."

"Ty brought it back from his vacation. I haven't had time to even brew a pot because we got sent to New Orleans on the Alligator Man case."

She took another drink of the rich brew. Full-bodied. Ty had done good. Last trip he brought Asa back a tropical shirt with multicolored toucans on it. Asa wasn't sure if it had been a joke or if Ty was serious. He'd thanked him regardless and hung it in the back of his closet right next to the one he'd bought Fiona.

"You thinking of the tropical shirts?" She laughed over her steaming mug. "Man, he's an idiot."

Asa laughed for the first time in hours. "Yeah, but we love him."

"We do. I'm glad I was here for his birthday party."

"Me, too. On a serious note, I may have made a mistake." He was second-guessing himself. Again.

"About Tiberius's party?"

"The Nursery Rhyme Killer. This is crazy bringing you here to my home. It'll set him off. I don't know how and I won't be able to stop it. But a hotel alone is out. I don't trust him. Dark hallways. Elevators. Stairwells. No way to know if it's a waiter with room service or a killer. Too risky. This is our only choice."

"I could stay with Violet."

"Violet won't offer. Not like she's insensitive but she's very private and…" And he wanted to do it even if he felt inept.

"We'll figure it out." She looked around the kitchen. "Where do you keep your pans? I owe you at the very least eggs."

He grinned. "With cheese?"

"Are you really even eating eggs if there's no cheese in them?" A pointed look had him laughing and digging out a pan from under the island. That was the one thing Fiona had brought to the culinary table. Scrambled eggs with cheese. She'd pretty much lived off of them when he'd met her.

"I have some sliced ham."

"Well, now we have a party." She went to work with the ingredients he set out. Ham fried, infusing the air with a familiar scent of lazy Saturday mornings. Fiona whisked the eggs and sharp cheddar together, added salt and pepper. Simple. But they were the best eggs he'd ever eaten.

Asa took down a couple of plates and Fiona flipped a slice of ham on his plate, along with a generous portion of eggs. "I have missed these."

She scooped some for herself. "Yeah? Maybe you should have asked for them in the divorce. Every other Saturday I make you eggs." She laughed and he realized she was making light. Teasing. Granted, it was over their divorce, which was the furthest thing from humorous, but he didn't kill the mood.

"Instead I kept the wobbly table. I don't really do divorce well." He forked a huge bite and drifted into glory.

Fiona pointed a fork at him. "I don't think anyone does divorce well. I know my parents didn't."

Asa's dad had died when he was only four. He'd like to think they'd have lived happily ever after. Mom wouldn't have been single or a target for Raymond Vect. "How is your dad?"

"I guess fine. I haven't called him yet. I know he's had to

have seen the news. But he's not called me, either." She cut into her ham. "I'll get around to it before I go back."

"When will that be?"

"Have I worn out my welcome already?" she teased.

"Make me eggs every day and you can stay forever." He smiled then caught his words. Forever. He'd said that once before. *Stay with me forever. Be my wife.*

Fiona didn't allow the moment to fall somber. "Well, keep me in ingredients and maybe I will. But seriously, I don't know. I guess until we feel the case goes cold again. Or—or if he's after me now. He might want to finish what he started. If I'm bait—"

"Not a chance in— Not a chance! Bad idea."

"It might be the only way to catch him. Nothing else is working." She let her fork clatter to her plate.

"We're closer than we've been before. We have new leads to work."

Fiona opened her mouth and seemed to have a light bulb moment. "Paint!"

He paused from eating. "Come again?"

"Paint. Before I went to bed last night it hit me that Alan Minton had fresh paint on his walls before he died. You had fresh paint. Even Levi Shetland said his apartment had recently been painted. Crews go in every public and private place. We both know people forget they're there. They talk on the phone, argue with spouses, gossip with girlfriends nearby. Let's see if anyone had their homes painted or even worked on. Flooring. Plumbing."

"That's good. That's real good, Fi." He grabbed his cell phone to call Selah and get her on it as a knock came on his front door. "If it's Ty, he's gonna want the rest of those eggs."

"You don't have to open the door." Fiona held up her hands. "Just saying. Your house. Your eggs."

Ty had a nose like a bloodhound. The minute he opened the door, he'd sniff it out. But it wasn't Ty at the door and Asa's stomach dropped. Amanda stood there with a box of Gibson's donuts and a fresh-faced grin. "Morning. Can I say I happened to be in the neighborhood? Would you buy that?"

He returned her smile. Oh, this was all too complicated. He glanced back at Fiona and she gave him the uh-oh face. He stepped out onto the stoop and closed the door behind him. "We need to talk."

"You don't like donuts?" She playfully shook the box. "Maple bacon." She sighed. "She's in there. I know. I heard about what happened last night and I was coming to check on you and see how she was…though I didn't expect her to be here to tell me herself. Besides, when you close the door on your girlfriend without inviting her in to the smells of breakfast, it's obvious another woman is inside. Clearly she slept over."

"She did, but nothing happened."

"I believe you."

"She's gonna be staying with me until—until I don't know when, and I know that puts us in a weird place. But Fiona and I are over romantically. We might be friends if that's possible, and we're definitely colleagues, but that's it."

She gave him a dubious smile. "Well, a better woman might say it wasn't a problem and she had no worries. I'm not that woman. I do worry. Asa, I think we have something and I want to see it progress. Sue me for being honest."

He laid his hand on her shoulder. He wanted to move forward, too. Amanda was a great person and detective, and even attended church with him. Fiona, on the other hand, laughed at his newfound faith, made him crazy and he didn't even know what else. "It'll be okay."

"We'll see. I should go."

"No, you shouldn't." Sending her away would give her reason to doubt him. Asking her in put everyone in an awkward position.

The door opened and Fiona stepped out with a cup of coffee. She handed it to Amanda. "Hey, Amanda. Come inside. Eat some eggs. Share those donuts. You got a maple bacon in there?"

Just like Fiona to take the acid out of a situation. Make Amanda welcome. And she knew if Amanda knew Asa well at all there would be his favorite donut in the box. It would say more to Fiona than Amanda.

"Yes!" She laughed.

Fiona motioned Amanda inside then patted Asa's shoulder and whispered, "I'll be eating your maple bacon. I earned it."

"You want to talk about last night?" Amanda asked her as they took up homestead in his kitchen, eating donuts and eggs as if they were old friends and not rivals.

"Right after I inhale this donut. I want to savor the sweetness before last night's story sours my tongue."

"Fair enough."

Asa wasn't sure if he wanted to go inside and close the door or stay out here and shut them in.

God, help me. I'm in a sticky place.

How dare he? How dare Naughty Kitten ignore his express wishes for Fiona to be left alone! And what had it done? Sent her right into Asa Kodiak's arms. Rhyme had less and less control of Naughty Kitten. But he had to do something to protect her; he had his own plans for him and Fiona. There had to be a way.

He wasn't weak.

He could outsmart Naughty Kitten. Keep his thoughts and actions to himself. There had to be a way to keep him away from her. He punched his temples with his fists. Think. Think of a way.

As for Asa, of course, he'd take advantage. Sweep her up in his arms as if he was some great hero to be worshipped and adored. Rhyme had no choice but to show Fiona the truth. Make her see how absolutely useless Asa Kodiak was. His were not arms she should be running into, but away from.

He would protect Fiona himself.

Then finish what they started.

Chapter Eleven

Asa sat at his desk. He needed time to think without interruption. There was no way they were going to catch the NRK if they didn't use Fiona as bait unless God divinely intervened. Asa had already been worried. Seen the posies and the hydrangea on her counter...but the photo. That had been the clincher. The horrific mask—he'd only seen them on the internet and heard Fiona talk of it. He'd never actually seen the monster in his mask. It went beyond unsettling.

He couldn't imagine Fiona running from that thing. And the photo. The NRK had been clear, but Fiona was blurred in the background, just a figure unaware of what had slipped into her most private moment. Asa'd had no choice but to give her an ultimatum. It was the only way to keep her safe. And he feared he might not be able to do that regardless, but he was going to give it everything he had in him.

She hadn't balked, which revealed how fearful she truly was, though masking it. Thankfully, this morning had been easier than it should have been since Fiona decided to play nice with Amanda and they'd worked together all morning before Amanda got called away.

The painting company Alan Minton had hired wasn't hard to track. He'd used his credit card and it was in his old financials. He'd used All Star painting. They'd put calls in to Abundant Life Church and Hope Community to see if they'd had any painting or remodeling done six months prior to the Shetlands' and Robert Williams's murders.

Since the eighth victim, Maria Windell, only picked up groceries from the food bank at Hope Community on Thursday mornings, they could narrow down a timeline. If Fiona was right, then one of the painters had to have been around on those days to either overhear or see something that would cause him to go after the grandmother who had been raising her eight grandchildren…and allegedly beating them.

Violet had contacted Robert Williams's widow again and asked if they'd had any painting or remodeling done before the time of Robert's death. She told them they hadn't.

Selah had contacted Houston High School and Germantown High, where Robert had worked and allegedly behaved inappropriately with girls, and St. George's to see if they'd had any painting or remodeling done. St. George's hadn't but Germantown High had. All Star painting.

Ty and Owen had taken a trip over there to retrieve employee records for the time matching Robert Williams's murder and Alan Minton's.

Robert could also be connected to Abundant Life. And that connected him possibly to Daniel Osborn, who had been comfortable giving Fiona info at the Fourth of July celebration.

The way he'd looked at Fiona… It had incited emotions in Asa that he'd placed as jealousy, but could it be something else? Did Daniel Osborn fit the DID profile? Furman did and he carried out the responsibilities of an assistant head of school. It was plausible. Either of the men would fit into a more upper-crust society. Both would blend into surroundings. Knew the area well. They had access to children's files. Which meant they'd have access to private conversations with counselors. Easy to eavesdrop. See things others wouldn't because of their status. Furman was forgetful and clearly hiding something. Confused. Frustrated. Both knew Fiona was investigating. Getting close, if either was the killer.

A knock sounded and Ty poked his head in. "We got records and something popped."

"I'm on your six." He followed Ty to the major case room. Everyone had congregated around the table, leaving the head of the table open for Asa. "Whatcha got?"

"Okay," Ty said and grabbed a dry-erase marker. "All Star painting did some work at Abundant Life during the time before Robert Williams's murder and they also did some work at Hope Community about nine months prior to the Shetlands' murder, but we couldn't get a timeline to fit for Maria Windell's murder."

"Good. What popped?" They were making headway. Finally.

"A name you'll recognize." He held up the employee record sheet. "Trent Barton."

Asa frowned, then it dawned. "The bartender from Mollie Fontaine Lounge."

"Yep," Ty said. "He was on the crew that painted both churches. He's got a rap sheet. Drug charge. Battery. Damage to property. He's never done any time."

"Get a more detailed background on him. Where was he for all the murders? Employment. Residences." He knew Jenny Miller had fought with a student. He might have only offered up enough to appear cooperative.

"How old is he?" Fiona asked.

"Forty."

Fiona's mouth wiggled as she thought. "That would make him twenty-three at the time of my abduction. Young enough to have worked up the nerve to kill. Not old enough to have practiced a signature, or found what worked best for him. It fits. Get a background on his mental health. Parents."

Selah clicked her tongue and made the "okay" sign. "On it."

This could be it. This could be the guy. "I want the background info before we question him. See if we can catch him in a lie."

"What do you want me to do?" Ty asked.

"Continue to study the cases and see if there's any evidence of a religious twist here we aren't seeing." Asa finished his coffee and chucked it in the trash. "It may simply be strange and bizarre without one, but if there's a hint of some strange religious behavior, it'll aid us in a more solid profile."

"Well, I was thinking about that and if he's punishing child abusers then he might be acting on the verse in the Bible where Jesus said, 'But whoso shall offend one of these little ones which believe in me, it were better for him that a millstone were hanged about his neck, and that he were drowned in the depth of the sea.' Clearly it's out of context, but most of our religious sickos twist some kind of belief. That could be our angle if there is one."

Made sense. They'd caught many killers who believed they were working for God. Or Satan. Or any other number of deities.

"Got it!" Selah chirped. "Trent Barton. Raised in Germantown. Only child of Trent Senior and Andrea Barton. Jobs include Logan's Steakhouse. All Star painting. Mollie Fontaine Lounge the last five years. But you'll love this. Minton Construction crew for two years—one year prior to and the year of Alan Minton's death. Nothing to indicate mental health issues, but I can check his school files for behavioral records."

Fiona slapped her hand on the table. "We got him connected to four of the six murders. Where was he for my sister's death and my abduction?"

"Earnestine and Hazel's. Downtown. Bartender."

"Would any of the girls have tried to go in the bar? Fake IDs?" Violet asked. "How would any of you have caught his attention?"

Fiona shook her head. "We were only here about six months before it happened, but who knows about the other girls. We'd been downtown, though. Hung out down there."

"I told you I was working my way backward on the victimology. It's time to work it on you and the girls," Violet said. "I'm going to want to question you."

"Fine," Fiona said in a clipped tone. "First let's talk to Trent Barton. See if he can alibi himself out of these murders."

"Who's going to remember where they were seventeen years ago on a certain night?" Owen asked. "I barely know what I did yesterday."

"He won't. Unless he was murdering people. But it might shake him up."

Time to shake.

Asa followed Fiona into the office and froze. Standing at Cami's desk was Luke Rathbone.

Fiona's eyes widened and she glanced at Asa before turning back to Rathbone. "Luke. What are you doing here?"

"I heard about what happened last night. Couldn't get ahold of you so I went by the house. No go. Thought I'd swing by here and check on you."

Rathbone had flown out within the last twelve hours to check on Fiona and nothing was going on between them?

No way.

His blood raced hot and a streak of jealousy followed. He had been to their home?

"I got your messages. I would have called you eventually," she said.

Rathbone slowly looked at Asa, a smug expression on his tanned face and a glint in his shark eyes. He looked more like he'd been on vacation than working violent crimes. "Well, I admit it was twofold. Want to grab lunch? Get you out of this place awhile, help you clear your head."

Asa clenched his teeth. "She's working. Why don't you get on back to Chicago and do the same."

Rathbone's daring smile itched to be punched off his face. "Fiona didn't tell you?"

"I was gonna," Fiona interjected. "I was."

"Tell. Me. What?" He was boiling over and his temper was getting the best of him. He should pray right now, but he didn't want to pray. He wanted to punch. To blow a gasket. Put a beatdown on Rathbone. This guy was nauseating. Never had liked Asa. He'd goaded him the entire time he'd worked in Memphis, just like now.

Luke slung his arm around Fiona's shoulder and nestled her against him. As if to remind Asa he'd failed with her. Failed at marriage. Lost to Rathbone—as if Fiona was a prize to be won and could be batted back and forth. It was sickening.

Fiona slipped from his grasp.

"I left the midwest division this past January. Moved back to Memphis. Got a place over in Harbor Town near the water. Quiet. Working the private security sector. Pay's way better. More free time."

"Is that right?" Asa asked.

"Yeah." He ignored Asa and cast those arrogant eyes on Fiona. "Come stay with me. I actually can protect you. State-of-the-art security. We can walk by the river at night. Sit on the balcony with a glass of wine and you won't have to worry about being attacked or unprotected."

Fiona's cheeks had turned bright pink. "Can we—we talk privately?"

The audacity! But the truth was, Asa wasn't sure he could protect her. He'd do everything in his power but that's where it fell apart.

He didn't have any power.

"She's fine right where she's at."

"Based on what happened last night, I beg to differ. Or does she have to be half-dead or deceased for you to realize you're doing a terrible job of keeping her safe?" Luke stalked toward him. "In fact, you left her out in the middle of nowhere alone, vulnerable. I have to wonder if you wanted her to die."

Maybe you wanted your mom dead.

His insides shuddered, hairs on the back of his neck stood and a white-hot fury blinded him. Asa pushed past Fiona and shoved Rathbone into the copy machine, knocking it and the trash can over.

Rathbone came up swinging. Asa ducked and knocked him into Ty's desk; papers skittered across the floor along with personal effects, pencils and pens.

"Stop! Stop it right now!" Fiona hollered.

Ty ripped Asa away from Rathbone and Owen held a seething Rathbone from going at Asa again. "Watch your back, Kodiak."

"You threatening me?"

"You better believe I am." He spit a wad of blood on the floor, wiped his mouth and straightened his golf shirt. "I'll call you later, Fiona. We can decide. Don't go back to that house."

"She's staying with me!" Asa growled.

"Not if I have anything to say about it!" He tried to wrench free from Owen, but Owen contained him.

"Stop talking about me like I'm not here. Like I'm property or a pet." Fiona pressed the heels of her hands to her eyes. "I have the same training as both of you. I have a brain and I get to choose where I stay and whom I stay with. I don't belong to anyone." She held up her left hand and shook it. "I have no ring anymore! And I've never dated you, Luke! Coming here was a mistake." She spun around and stormed for the door. "You're both horses' behinds!" Then she was practically running for the elevator.

Amanda stood in her wake, and the frown on her mouth and hurt in her eyes said she'd been there the entire time. "I see you're...preoccupied," she softly said. "I'm gonna go."

Before he could stop her, she turned and calmly left the office. Ty released him. Owen continued his grip on Rathbone.

Asa had made a mess. Of the office, the situation, his life. He owed everyone in the office, including Rathbone, an apology. Especially Amanda and Fiona. He'd embarrassed them both. Acted like a complete Neanderthal and disappointed himself. Taking out his fury on Rathbone hadn't given him any solace. It had made things far worse. Now he had to eat humble pie. "I'm sorry. I had no right to lose my cool. You can file a report against me if you want."

Rathbone ripped his arm from Owen's hold. "Give me a break, Asa. Don't pretend to be honorable. It's insulting." He stalked from the office, leaving Asa alone with Violet, Ty and Owen.

"I'm sorry," he apologized to Ty.

"Sorry means cleaning up the stuff you knocked off my desk and buying me a new mug. I got it in Barbados." He huffed and left.

"Owen—"

"I told Rathbone about the attack. Yell at me if you want. But I'd be more worried about the damage you done did with that sweet little blonde you been dating. You don't behave this way over a woman you don't love." He threw up deuces, grabbed his laptop and disappeared. Everyone was walking away from him, and he deserved it.

Violet sat on the edge of her desk, hands neatly folded in her lap, silent. Waiting.

"I don't love her anymore. He grates my skin. Antagonizes me. You heard him. It's him. Not her." It was as if Luke knew the secret he'd buried. Like some unforeseen enemy had whispered what to say in his ear to push him over the edge and into a heap of mess he might not be able to dig his way out of.

Violet finally spoke. "I could talk with you about this behavior clinically. Tell you you're in denial, so forth and so on. I won't. As a team member and colleague, I'll tell you to get a grip on your personal life and keep it personal. This was juvenile and misogynistic."

Ouch.

She was right. This would tear the team apart. Divide and distract them. No different than what the Nursery Rhyme Killer did. Killing on their wedding night. Getting in the way of their marriage making strides. Showing up at the best times and creating chaos.

Asa scrubbed his face. "You're right."

"I'll go with Fiona to Mollie Fontaine Lounge later when they open. I doubt she wants to be anywhere near you."

Asa didn't even want to be around himself.

"Clean yourself up after you tidy this office." She made her way to the door and swung around. "You're a good SAC, Asa. Keep your head in the game. Keep your heart out of it."

Asa had let his emotions run the show. Powerful emotions he didn't even realize he was carrying. Feelings that needed to be explored. And if he could miss his own emotional state, then what had he missed involving this case?

★ ★ ★

Streets were littered with people out for a good time. Mollie Fontaine Lounge had opened thirty minutes ago and Fiona was antsy thanks to Asa and Luke going off half-cocked. The jerk that Asa had acted like earlier was the Asa she'd been married to once, not the man she'd been getting to know this recently. She liked the new Asa much more.

After that debacle, she'd found Luke in the parking lot and lit into him. He'd come with ulterior motives to get under Asa's skin and accomplished his goal. Naturally, Luke hadn't admitted that was his intention and he'd tried to persuade her to come stay with him in Harbor Town. Not happening. But she could no longer stay with Asa, either. It had been a rotten idea to begin with.

"You good, Agent?" Violet asked. Her long hair hung in messy waves. Not a single one sticking to her neck. The humidity was out of control.

"Do you have some kind of condition that keeps you from perspiring?"

Violet paused on the sidewalk and narrowed her eyes. "No."

"You never sweat. I'm dying out here." Fiona fanned herself to no avail.

"Oh. I run cold."

"Nice. You must have good genes."

Violet's cheek pulsed and her eyes fell flatter than usual. "Those run cold, too."

What did that mean? As Fiona opened the door to air-conditioned bliss, Violet added, "Take lead. If he is Rhyme, he'll only give you attention, anyway."

Trent Barton stood in all his six-foot-two glory. Built. Attractive. Ladies' man. The last thing he'd be pegged for was a serial killer. He made eye contact with her—dark eyes. Rhyme had dark eyes, but nothing alerted her to his presence. No chills. No gut punch that she was standing before the man who had abducted her, killed her sister or attacked her last night.

A smooth-as-butter smile was smeared across his face, warming his eyes like espresso. "Agent." He nodded once. "What can I do for you this evening? You eating?"

"No, not tonight. Is there somewhere we can talk more privately?" she asked.

"Sure." He tossed his bar rag to a blonde working the far end of the bar and motioned for them to follow. Glancing back, he said, "Is this about that teacher that got killed?"

"Maybe." Could this be Rhyme? Fiona was sure she'd know him upon approach, but she could be wrong.

They entered a small break room with a couple of sofas, a table and a TV in the corner. He grabbed a chair, turned it and straddled it. She noticed heavy boots. Like the heavy footfalls on her hardwoods. A sweat broke out on her forehead. She chose to stand. Violet sat in the chair beside him, crossed her legs and threw her arm around the chair as if comfy with the situation.

"Did you ever work for All Star painting?" Fiona asked.

"Yeah. I'm not great at painting, though. I wouldn't label it a calling." He smirked and lit a cigarette. "You mind?"

"No." Except she did. Rhyme had smelled faintly of smoke. She swallowed hard and studied him. Surely something would give her an indication of his identity. But she came up blank except for a gut feeling. And she had no one to blame but herself for not being able to identify him.

"Do you remember painting Hope Community and Abundant Life Church?"

"I painted a lot of places. It's possible. Why?" He took in a heavy drag, the end of his cigarette glowing like an evil eye.

"Do you recall the murders of a Pastor Mark Shetland and his wife, Valerie? He pastored Hope Community."

"I'm not religious."

"Me, neither," she said. Go down another road. The sympathetic one. "Seems a little controlling."

"Right?" He exhaled through his nose and sized her up; she refused to shudder.

"Did you know Robert Williams or Alan Minton?" Fiona asked and he took another puff, gawked into space with squinted eyes, then a sense of knowing suddenly gleamed in them. Something clicked. Then he grinned and it vanished.

"I didn't know either of them, but I worked for a while for Minton Construction. Construction wasn't my calling either."

That was twice he'd used that word. A calling was something one felt compelled to do. It was born out of something much deeper than a hobby or liking.

"No?" She took the chair across from him and leaned into his personal space, inwardly gagging on the cigarette smoke. "What is your calling?"

He had the nerve to lean in, too, his nose only a few inches from hers. "I guess I'm still looking for it, Agent Kelly. Why? You interested in helping me find it?"

"Have you heard of the Nursery Rhyme Killer?"

His jaw twitched.

"He's been leaving bodies in the Memphis area for years. He's infamous. Students I teach ask about him. Surely you've heard of him. Unless you're living under a rock. Are you living under a rock, Trent?"

One more jaw twitch and he raised her a nostril flare. She'd struck a chord. All she had to offer was herself. Bait.

"Have you been a naughty kitty, Trent?" He crushed his cigarette on the table, licked his bottom lip and held her stare. "Well, have you? Naughty kitties get no pie," she whispered.

He blew back the chair, sending it sailing, and a vein in

his neck protruded. Oh, yes. She'd rung his bell. "Do I need a lawyer?"

"I don't know. Only if you've been naughty." She leaned back, felt some power come into her bones. This was him. What else could have him so rattled? At this point, they'd be denied a warrant. No probable cause and what they did have was circumstantial. Asa would be furious at her tactics, but after his tantrum today, so be it. Had she managed to pull out the alter ego? He'd seemed at ease and then a switch had been flipped. It had all gone down in his now hollow eyes.

Was this Naughty Kitten? The name Rhyme called his alter ego.

"You're crazy. I want a lawyer if we're going to keep playing this game." He moved to the far wall, away from her.

"Where were you June thirtieth, from about eleven to one thirty a.m.?"

"I was here until three a.m. Then I went home and I went to bed." He all but dared her to call him on it.

Violet stood. "Thank you. If we need anything else, we'll be in touch."

"You do that," he said, keeping his glower locked on Fiona. "If I do something naughty, you'll know it." He left them alone in the break room.

"It's him."

Violet shook her head. "He was agitated. Angry. Confused."

"Something clicked. He knows more than he's saying. I'm telling you it's him."

"I agree he was calculating something, probably how you plan to pin this on him, and it set him off."

"That's my point. I used all the words he used to me. That's when he was most provoked."

Violet pushed her chair under the table. "No. It wasn't the words, Fiona. It was getting up in his face, controlling the conversation, dominating him. Trent hates women. He likes control. That defines a host of men in the world, but it doesn't make them serial killers. This is too personal for you to be objective. And if that's not enough, he has an airtight alibi for the night of Jenny Miller's death."

"He could have left and come back."

"And we can ask all those questions and find out. We know he's a criminal with capacity to do harm and he has connections to some of our vics. That doesn't make him Rhyme. You want him to be because you want this to be over."

She did want this to be over. To move on with her life. To close the book on this horror story. Fiona trudged from the break room. Violet had been right. She needed to be objective. But Rhyme was personal to her and had been for seventeen years.

They found the bar manager and asked about Trent's alibi the night of Jenny Miller's murder. She vouched for Trent and they had no camera footage to prove or disprove it. Fiona couldn't concentrate. She went through the mechanical motions of getting in the Suburban and heading back to the field office.

Asa sat at the head of the table in the major case room. Head in his hand, staring at photos and case files. Owen, Tiberius and Selah all had similar poses. The room was quiet. "Well?" he asked as they made their presence known.

"It's him."

"It's not," Violet said. "He alibied out for Jenny Miller's murder. Solid."

"If it's him, the alter ego will come for me."

Asa drew his lips taut. "Why? What did you do?"

"Fiona baited herself. She all but dared him to come kill her." Violet sighed. "And if you start another yelling match, I'm resigning. This is asinine." She casually left the case room.

"Everybody, please leave me and Fiona for few minutes." Asa's voice was low and simmering. Once they filtered out, the lid would be opened and the pot would boil over. Fiona braced herself.

The team closed the door behind them.

Asa practiced a repetition of calm breathing. "Fiona, you may not care about your life—"

His phone rang and he held up a finger. He answered. "Hey, Kacie Sunshine. Glad to hear your voice." He listened a few moments. "Come by the house tonight. I'll cook." He hung up. "If Trent Barton is our killer, daring him to come for you is stupid. You are purposely putting your life and others at risk."

"He wants me. No one else. I'm not talking about the primary personality. I'm talking about the Nursery Rhyme Killer—the alter ego."

"I want word for word. Now."

She relayed the interview from start to finish. Asa sat stoic, then stood, walked out and went into his office without so much as a peep.

Fiona knew what she was doing.

This would work.

It had to.

Chapter Twelve

Asa had spent most of the evening hitting dead ends then he'd come home without Fiona. No opportunity to apologize for his caveman-like behavior, because after her reckless mistake, she'd avoided him and he didn't want to apologize—he wanted to ream her all over again—so he'd let her keep her distance. After cooking dinner—a simple chicken Caesar salad and garlic toast—he waited for Kacie, but she'd texted to say she was picking up a shift at work. He'd eaten alone and gone over the day's progress.

Owen and Ty had interviewed the manager and owner of All Star painting, Joe Pendergrass, and were working their way through the list of men who would have been on their jobs prior to the victims' deaths. But All Star admitted to hiring guys and paying cash off the books, so the possibility of an employee being on the crew but not accounted for was likely. They'd find the same with every trade. Cheaper labor to pay cash and keep it off the books. No records.

He padded to the kitchen. Made a pot of decaf and dropped

on the couch. Fiona hadn't called or texted. But Violet had. Fiona was with her and she would bring her back later. He was a little shocked Fiona hadn't ditched him altogether, but maybe after the bait plan, she realized staying here would bring him a measure of peace and she sure as Sherlock owed him that.

It was almost midnight now. He poured a cup of coffee and examined the last week's interviews and photos once again as if something new might appear. While on his third cup, he heard a soft knock on the door. Fiona.

"You want coffee?" he asked. "It's decaf." He locked the door after she entered.

"No. Kacie come by?" She set her purse and gun on the table by the door.

"No. She picked up a shift."

Fiona raised an eyebrow, but she didn't comment. Instead, she stood by the door as if she hadn't decided if she might bolt or stick around.

"I'm sorry." He raked a hand through his hair. "I acted like a fool today."

Fiona licked her lips and tucked a strand of hair behind her ear. "You both humiliated me today, Asa. I let Luke know as much. It was a circus in there. And I felt like the clown. What happened to God changing you? He drop the ball today?"

"I dropped the ball. Let my anger get the best of me. I should have acted better. But I'm not perfect and when it comes to Rathbone, I don't know. I lose my mind." He sank on the couch. "Why didn't you tell me he was back in Memphis?"

"Why does it matter?"

"I guess it shouldn't."

"I honestly never expected him to show up."

"I believe you." He'd always jumped to conclusions concerning Rathbone. "I'm surprised he didn't offer you a job in the private sector to keep you with him." He'd been quick to offer her a way out of Memphis and she'd taken it. First flight to Chicago. With him. It had been more of an escape route from Asa than a ticket to Rathbone. Lot easier to blame Rathbone than himself, which is where the blame rested.

Fiona rubbed her lips together "He did, actually, if we're being honest."

Had they ever been one-hundred-percent honest with one another? He snorted. "Pay would be better."

"I know. But…"

Her precious Rhyme was more important than money. Accolades. Anything. He swallowed the bitterness with his last gulp of coffee. "He's never once stepped foot in the field office in the six months he's been back."

"I'm sorry. I am." She sat beside him on the couch. "You talk to Amanda? I can't imagine what she was thinking."

He threw his aching head back on the sofa and groaned. "I'll tell you what she's thinking because she's pretty direct." Which he admired. "She's thinking that I'm not over you. I chose you without thinking in our investigation—though she gave me a pass earlier because we were partners so long and she gets that. But today—today… I didn't get a pass, Fiona."

"I'm sorry. I didn't want this."

"You didn't do anything. I did. She said we're taking a step back for now."

"Meaning until I leave."

"Or until I can look her dead in the eye and tell her I'm completely without a doubt over you." He squeezed his eyes shut and when he opened them, Fiona was intently staring.

"Did you not tell her that already?"

He swallowed the mass in his throat, his gut wound like a cord. "I told her, but I couldn't look her in the eye when I did. So, no, she doesn't believe it."

"Joke's on her then." Her attempt at laughter fell flat.

Was it? "We are over each other, right?" he murmured and felt his body shifting toward hers.

Her reply came in a strangled whisper. "Yeah. We have the papers to—" she choked up and moisture filled her eyes "—to prove it."

Those papers signifying death. Finality. "I didn't know what else to do." Lame. But true. Over and over the NRK came between them and Fiona broke his heart as often. Her obsession had been bleeding him dry. He'd tried everything he knew at the time, and the last straw—divorce papers. Clean break, but it was far from clean. It had been muddied and messy.

She gravitated to him and he met her in the middle. Their breath mingling. Noses almost touching, a confined space of intimacy and wanting. The air crackled with it, grew heavier by the second. He inhaled her tropical island shampoo, a hint of cinnamon on her breath from those candies she kept on her 24/7.

"And I didn't know what else to do but sign them."

"I'm so sorry." He nuzzled her nose, his blood racing and sizzling at her delicate fingers resting on his cheek.

"I'm sorry, too." She rested her brow against his. "I never wanted to hurt you. I tried to stay away from you."

She had turned him down on several occasions when he wanted more than something physical. Until finally, she didn't fight how she felt anymore. He cupped the nape of her neck, tears burning the backs of his eyes. This woman, larger than life, had waltzed into his and had made him feel for the first time since he'd been fourteen that everything could be okay again. She'd held him in the darkest of night when he'd awoken in a sweat from the nightmare of his past and rocked him in her arms back to sleep. She'd been the sunrise of his mornings, the sunset of his nights.

For a while.

"But I couldn't do it in the end. Stay away."

He was thankful for that—that she hadn't stayed away. Even if at the end it had been sheer agony. He'd die a thousand deaths for the few good years she'd made him feel alive and strong and safe.

"Fiona," he murmured and his lips met hers. Soft. Full. He gently kissed her, as if testing the waters to see if it was warm enough to immerse himself. She pressed into his kiss with more force, her arms snaking around his neck, and she granted him permission to get lost in her.

Familiar and yet somehow brand-new, which ratcheted his pulse. The feel of her in his arms, toned and firm, but soft in the right places... Suddenly the heady haze lifted and he wrenched himself free from her and put distance between them. He paced the floor and shoved his hands through hair only seconds ago she'd been clutching.

"What's the matter?"

"Nothing," he said breathlessly. "We can't."

She rubbed her swollen lips, but nodded. "No, you're right. We're a mess and this is only going to complicate things further."

Oh, so complicated. Kissing her, having her in his arms, wouldn't do anything but make a few hours feel livable and free, but there would be no real freedom. They'd still have a chasm of hopelessness between them. A killer in the middle, keeping them apart. And a new tangle of emotions.

"I'm gonna try and get some sleep." Fiona patted his shoulder and started toward the guestroom when his phone rang.

Kacie. He answered and watched Fiona amble down the hall, rubbing her neck. He felt the same frustration. Kacie's insistent voice jolted him out of the moment. Concentrating right now wasn't easy. "Sorry, Kace. Say that again."

"Asa? Are you hearing me?" He instantly recognized the timbre in her voice. Fear.

Laser focus set in and he gripped his phone. "Kace, what's wrong, baby? Where are you?"

"Home." A strangled sob broke through, reaching his ears and flooding him with ice-cold dread. "I love you—"

His chest constricted, his head buzzed and the room slanted. "Kace—"

"He said to tell you— T-to tell you—" She shrieked in pain.

"Kacie!" He snatched his gun, his fingers fumbling and body shaking, then he blew through the front door. Fiona was hot on his heels, hollering for him to wait.

"I'm coming. You just hold on, baby girl." Threatening the NRK wasn't going to do him any good. But he was there. Now with his baby sister! And Asa wasn't sure he would make it in time. "It's going to be okay." He knew as soberly as Kacie that it wasn't. Nothing was going to be okay.

She wailed again. "He says to tell you—you failed again." She cried out again and everything in Asa trembled; she sounded so much like Mom before Vect cut her carotid. "No. Please! No. Please don't! A-sa-a-a-a-a-a!" Kacie's scream grabbed him by the throat and squeezed; it broke through the speaker, stopping both him and Fiona dead in their tracks.

Nothing but the sound of a strangled, garbled cry.

"Kacie! Kacie! Sunshine?" The edges of his sight darkened and he lost his balance. Fiona righted him, grabbed his keys and forced him toward the Suburban.

"Hold on, Asa. You don't know what's happened. Let's get to her."

But he did know and so did Fi.

He'd witnessed it all over again. Those cries were unmistakable.

Fiona threw on the light bar and Rumbler siren, then punched the gas, flying down the street.

He had to get to Kacie. To his baby sister.

"He's killed her, Fi. The Nursery Rhyme Killer just murdered my sister."

Rhyme wiped the blood from the blade. Asa Kodiak would not take what rightfully belonged to him. He'd known her longer. And he hadn't worked this hard to bring her back only for her to be seduced once more by Kodiak. This was as much for Fiona as it was for Kodiak. She needed to see that he couldn't protect her.

But Rhyme could.

He was already working to make sure Naughty Kitten couldn't reach out and take her. He wasn't weak. Rhyme wasn't stupid and useless.

He'd show them. He'd show them all.

And Fiona would be his.

Fiona's pulse was off the charts but she concentrated on the road, gripping the wheel and refusing to imagine the worst. She was pushing 100 miles an hour on the interstate and it didn't feel fast enough.

Like the flashing light bar, everything that had transpired these last few days pulsed through her mind, and for the first time since she'd been abducted at seventeen, she whispered a prayer to God. Hopefully, tonight, He wouldn't ignore her.

Please don't let Kacie die. Please don't let her die.

Asa's fists were balled tight and his jaw was clenched as his knees nervously bobbed. Under his breath, his prayers were slurred, as if he was drunk.

She flew off the I-55 ramp onto Goodman Road and raced through the red lights. One after another—time wasn't on their side. They crossed 51, but this was where she was unsure of Kacie's location. "I need directions, Asa. Help me."

"Left on Dunbarton," he rasped.

She made a hard left, tires squealing, her insides mimicking the noise. He rattled off lefts, rights, a left. Fiona hadn't even stopped the vehicle before Asa jumped out into the yard, racing like a life depended on it.

Because it did.

Fiona sprang from the vehicle, drew her weapon and stopped short on the porch when the wail came, sending a frigid shudder through her bones.

Guttural.

Agonizing.

The kind that burned the lungs and seared the throat. Reached deep into the recesses of the soul and suffocated it.

Over and over.

Fiona's body froze, unable to move indoors. To witness the only man she'd ever loved in a helpless and broken state. Tears slipped over the edge of her lids as the one-two punch of realization hit her gut, leaving her breathless and nauseous.

This was all her fault.

She ripped her phone from her back pocket and called Tiberius.

"Fi, what's going on?"

She couldn't speak. Destruction had snuffed out every word.

"Fi?" Fear rattled through her name. "Talk to me!"

Through a strangled voice, she proceeded to tell him what had happened. "Get the team out. Get everyone out here and find out where Trent Barton is tonight. You bring him in, I don't care if he's dead or alive, do you hear me?"

Asa's raucous cries pierced the phone line and Tiberius desperately called out to a God he didn't believe in. "I'll do it. I'll do it right now."

She pocketed her phone, slid her gun into her waistband and mustered the courage to enter. Fiona stood like a statue inside the door, helpless. Responsible. Grief-stricken and appalled.

Blood. So much blood.

Asa was soaked in it as he cradled his limp sister in his arms. Rocking back and forth, stroking her blood-matted hair and profusely apologizing for failing her. For failing their family. For not being enough. Doing enough. Saying enough.

A noise sounded and Fiona pulled her gun, pivoted. An older man and two others stood at the porch with their hands up. "FBI. Stay back."

"We heard a man screaming."

"Please stand back. There's been a crime." She sniffed and waved them back. House lights peeped on all around. Asa had woken the neighborhood.

Her brain wouldn't allow her to see reality. This wasn't happening, hadn't happened. "Asa," she said and inched forward.

He shook his head and continued to rock Kacie, her lifeless eyes frozen in terror staring up at him. As Fiona approached, cause of death was obvious. Rhyme had killed Kacie in the same way Asa's mother had died. Slit throat. No mercy. Torment intended and it had hit the bull's-eye.

At the foot of Kacie's body lay one single goose feather.

"I'm gonna kill him," Asa growled. "I'm gonna kill him."

Fiona closed her eyes. If she hadn't provoked him, hadn't baited him. Hadn't dared him to do something naughty, this wouldn't have happened. "Asa..." There were no words. No apology deep or wide enough to make this right.

Suddenly, he flashed his attention on her with a scowl that sent a new wave of chills down her back. "You did this. I told you time and again how reckless you could be when it came to him. And now look. You all but begged him to come for you!"

"For me…to come for *me*." Why hadn't he just come and done this to her? It should have been her.

"But he didn't come for you, Fiona! He came for the only thing I have left in this world! I've lost every single person I love. You did this!" he bellowed.

The mountain lodged in her throat kept her from swallowing. Tears blurred her vision. He couldn't be more right. "I know." She had no words that would convey how remorseful and beside herself she was. "I'm sorry," she whispered. "I'm so sorry."

"Shut up!" he raged and she startled. "Sorry won't bring back my sister," he mumbled and rested his head on Kacie's blood-covered brow.

No. Nothing would do that.

God had proven once again that Fiona wasn't worth listening to. That He didn't care what evils happened in this world. They were all alone. To cope and maneuver with no hope or help. It was cruel. And it was lonely. Why did Asa place his faith in a God who wouldn't answer prayer or save loved ones? What drew him to believe? To change?

She had no comfort to give; Asa didn't want her comfort or her words.

Or her.

All she had left to offer was what she knew how to do best. Work the scene. Autopilot kicked in and she left Asa to his grief. His fury. His hatred.

An hour ago, they had almost admitted they still loved one another. An hour ago, she'd felt an ember of hope. Now there was nothing left. Not even a scrap. Asa would never forgive her for this and she would never forgive herself.

She stumbled out to the vehicle, grabbed a crime scene kit and put on gloves and booties. Before long the local police would arrive. On cue, several cars with lights flashing turned onto the street. Fiona had left her light bar on. She approached the officers, gave them the rundown. They secured the area while she returned inside to do her job. To try and bring justice to her sister-in-law.

DeSoto County CSU arrived to process the scene.

"We're going to need the body," the tech said.

Fiona nodded and carefully approached Asa. She squatted to his eye level. "Asa, you have to let them take her now. They have a job to do. He's deviated from his MO and he's angry so he may have made some mistakes, left evidence. You're compromising it if he did. They'll be good to her. You know they will."

Asa slowly faced Fiona, his face twisted in pain. "I couldn't save her. I couldn't save Mama. What he did to her..." A vein pulsed in his forehead; Kacie's blood streaked his face and his eyes were wet with tears. "I couldn't save you or our marriage. He's right. I'm a failure."

Fiona's heart crumbled into tiny shards, aching everywhere. "No. No, baby. You're not a failure."

"But I am," he whispered. Vacant eyes bore into hers. Asa was no longer in the present moment. He'd traveled into the past, where Fiona couldn't reach him. "I could have saved Mama. He told me so. He asked me why I didn't ask to spare them both. He said I must have wanted Mama dead...but I didn't. I could have saved her. I—I didn't ask. I failed her. I didn't ask the Nursery Rhyme Killer to spare her. I should have asked."

"That's not true." Fiona clutched his bloody hand, reeling from information she'd never heard before and wasn't sure she understood the meaning. "You don't know—"

"Agent Kelly," the CSU tech said, respect and reverence in his tone, but also urgency.

"We have to give her to them now."

"Asa!" Tiberius's voice boomed and he rushed into the house and halted when he saw Asa, eyes wide. "I'm so sorry."

Asa gently laid Kacie's head on the floor and reluctantly stood, but said nothing.

"Get him home and cleaned up," Fiona said.

"No," Asa protested. "I'm not leaving."

Violet and Owen rushed through the door, Selah and Cami in tow. All disheveled from being woken from sleep, but this team had come for their leader. Their Kodiak Bear. The man who held them together with his skill, his love and a strong hand that desired justice. The team rallied around their alpha, offering support and comfort. Not as agents, but family. When one fell, they lifted the fallen. Fiona looked on from the outside. A place she'd put herself.

Violet met her line of sight with understanding and left the huddle, then led Fiona outside. "Trent Barton worked until eleven and he lives with his grandmother, who verified he was home by ten after and never left. Ty sent MPD over immediately. Soon as he hung up with you. He was home. It wasn't him. He's not Rhyme."

She may not have directly dared Rhyme to do something naughty, but she'd willingly waltzed into Asa's home for protection, knowing that Rhyme would retaliate—even Asa had feared that—but neither expected Kacie as a casualty. Rhyme had proven once again that Fiona would never be allowed into Asa's arms. He'd pulled a similar stunt on their wedding night.

And she'd gone running back.

Her selfishness had gotten Kacie killed. Taunting Trent Barton—she was unconvinced it wasn't him. Challenging Rhyme by staying with Asa knowing full well it could go south. Ignoring Asa's reservations. The same selfishness that led her out of the woods while three other girls perished.

Rhyme was calling the shots, imprisoning her to him, and

she had no choice but to comply. The next life could be Asa's. She'd brought enough bloodshed. "Can I stay with you?" Private or not, she needed to leave Asa. He wouldn't want her there now, anyway.

"Sure." Violet patted her shoulder—more empathy than Fiona had ever seen. While huddled with the team, she hadn't exactly embraced anyone.

"Thank you. I know I'm imposing."

"I know why you have to go. I'm gonna do my job now."

Tiberius tossed her a compassionate glance as he led Asa from the house. At least someone could talk some sense into him.

Asa was done with her. But she couldn't leave. She owed him justice. And besides, Rhyme wouldn't let her.

Rhyme stood in the distance, blending in with the crowd of onlookers that had congregated to watch the horror show. But he'd been there much earlier. Heard Asa's screams at his helplessness, danced inside at his panic and fear. That had been even more satisfying than the horror on Kacie Kodiak's face when she realized she wasn't alone when she came home.

Finally, Asa would realize who had all the power.

And Rhyme would wield it however he chose.

Chapter Thirteen

Asa had been out of the office for three days, arranging the funeral service and trying to make sense of everything, but he simply couldn't.

Kacie was gone.

He'd been too late. He should have forced her to live with him the second the Nursery Rhyme Killer had struck again. So many regrets.

The hours he'd spent with his pastor had been comforting and helpful to his grieving heart. His new church family had flooded his home with more food than one person would ever be able to consume. The love they showed overwhelmed and awed him. People he didn't even know were bringing cards and casseroles and offering to pray for him, to simply hug him or sit for a cup of coffee. His job only revealed disturbed individuals twisting religion and many times Scripture to justify their heinous and often ritualistic murders. No wonder most of his team had been soured, but they'd never seen truth in action. Never seen the light, felt the hope. Experienced what it was supposed to be and could be.

And that brought a reminder that he'd hurled heated words at Fiona the night of Kacie's death—it was hazy but he remembered a portion—so it didn't surprise him when Violet swung by and retrieved Fiona's belongings. Watching her carry them out felt like the first time Fiona left him. Devastating. He hadn't laid eyes on her since that night and once again he should apologize. He was on a horrible cycle of getting angry, saying things that hurt her, then apologizing. When would this struggle with his temper end? Would it be a battle until he died?

Let every man be swift to hear, slow to speak, slow to wrath... James 1:19 had been on a continuous loop in his brain.

Now it was time to say goodbye to Kacie and lay her in the ground. Ty had driven him to the cemetery while the rest of the team and Fiona followed. Ty said she'd been working around the clock, no sleep and no eating, to find the NRK. The former youth pastor from Abundant Life was now back from Africa and they hoped to get the name of the girl Robert Williams had been involved with.

The heat was unbearable and the tent they crammed under did little to offer a reprieve. A few of Kacie's friends, coworkers and neighbors had come to pay respects, but it was mostly Asa's team, colleagues and church family in attendance. He spotted Fiona's father making his way to the grave site. Guess she'd sucked it up and called him. Asa had never had a strong relationship with Quinn Kelly, but it meant a lot to have him here today. Asa eased into the uncomfortable wooden chair in the front row. Ty was next to him, then the rest of the team— his family—occupied the remaining seats. He didn't see Fiona.

A hand touched his shoulder and he startled.

Amanda.

She squeezed it and leaned down to kiss his cheek. He thanked her for coming and she slipped into a seat three rows behind him. Even though she'd put a stop to their relationship, she'd cared enough to come, to stop by the house with a cake and stay for an hour last night. She deserved a man far better than him, anyway. Glancing to the other side, he noticed Fiona sitting beside her father in the fourth row on the end. Dark black tailored suit and large black sunglasses concealing her eyes.

No. She was family—the closest thing to a womanly figure Kacie had after Grandma passed. She may not have agreed with Asa's parenting, but she loved Kacie like a sister. Asa had his team scoot down a chair, then shuffled over to Fiona.

"She was your family, Fi. Come sit by me. We can talk later." Mostly him talking and hoping for forgiveness.

Her father patted her knee and nodded. Fi slipped her trembling hand in Asa's and took the seat beside him. When she attempted to release her hand from his, he held on tighter until she realized he needed the connection and then she held it firm and confidently. His anger had been misplaced. Trent Barton couldn't have killed Kacie. But Fiona didn't know that. Her actions had been reckless. Regardless, he needed her. His pastor delivered a short but comforting message about hope. Out of the corner of his eye, a man arrested his attention. Fiona tensed, must have noticed, too. His stomach coiled. The NRK surely wouldn't desecrate this memorial or have the nerve to show up with this many federal agents in attendance.

The man kneeled and laid flowers on a grave.

Paranoia was the name of the game. Everyone was a killer. Fiona continued to study the man, but Asa bowed his head as his pastor prayed, then invited guests back to New Hope Church for a meal. Several friends from his small group at church gave condolences, prayed with him and offered support. He rallied the team. "Come back to the church with me. Eat. Cindy Walters makes the best baked beans you'll ever taste and I know she made some."

Owen laughed. "Ain't gotta tell me twice. Church knows how to do up a potluck right."

"You go to church?" Ty asked.

"Nah, not much anymore. My mama's on her knees every day, though, so I guess those prayers are gonna work at some point."

"Doubtful," Fiona said and slipped through the crowd to the car.

"I'll go but if they invite me to some kind of baptism or ask me to handle a snake, I'm out." Ty clicked his tongue against his cheek. "But I could eat." He slapped Asa on the back in a brotherly fashion.

"I'm pretty sure you'll be safe. Maybe you'll get there in time to sample sausage balls by Jan Kerley. Make you wanna slap yo' mama."

"My mama makes me wanna slap my mama." Ty snorted. "You know she called me yesterday to remind me I haven't given her any grandchildren *that she knows of.* What's she think I am? Like I need a reminder that I am not a parent."

Asa laughed. Man, it felt good to laugh. No doubt Ty's intention.

Fiona was leaning against the car, fanning herself. "Give me a minute." He jogged through the cemetery and met up with her. "Hey," he said.

"Hey."

"Can we talk?"

"Sure." Her arms were folded over her chest and her glasses were still on.

"Can you take those off so I can see your eyes?" He pointed to her shades.

She complied. Soft hazel eyes rimmed in red. It broke his heart all over again. "I keep saying I'm sorry. I mean it every time."

"I know."

"It's not fair to you."

"I know," she whispered.

"I'm working on controlling my tongue when I'm angry." Battle of his life. "It's a slow process." Slower than he wanted. "Wish I was perfect. I'm not."

"You didn't say anything that wasn't true, Asa." She sniffed and kicked at a small piece of gravel on the road. She was wearing heels. Rare occasion. "I knew better than to come and stay with you. He dictates my life and when I veer from the path he wants me on...someone dies."

He was to blame for Fiona coming into his home for protection. He'd pressed and not given her much of an option. Asa had wanted her there and if anyone was to have partial blame for the fallout it was him. "You can't live your life in fear of his attacks. I don't want that and I never have."

"I guess I didn't think he'd go after Kacie—he's made it personal. More than ever. No one close to you—or me—is safe."

That's what he feared. And what if he couldn't protect the next person, either?

Asa guided her into his embrace and kissed the top of her head. "We'll get through this. Somehow. Come with me."

"To the funeral meal?"

"Yes. Meet some of my friends. And Sunday. Come with me to service. No pressure."

"Asa," she said as he opened the passenger door for her, "I prayed for the first time in seventeen years. I prayed we'd find her alive."

He had, too.

"But she wasn't. I get God never listening to me. But He

didn't listen to you, either. Aren't you mad? Isn't that proof God doesn't care or doesn't have the power to help?"

Asa had talked at length about this with his pastor over the last two days. "Yeah, I'm mad. I'm mad and I let Him know it, too. But I can't not believe. Not when I know how real He is. So, I'll work through it and I have people who will help me. But, yes, Fiona. I'm mad."

God had been first on Asa's list to apologize to as he'd said some mean things to Him, too. He had no answers. No written reason why God hadn't intervened and spared Kacie.

But that didn't make Him any less good or faithful.

Fiona touched his face. "I still see something real in you—even on the days you lose your cool. You're quick to apologize and you're sincere. And so I will come with you to church."

He placed his hand over the one she had resting on his cheek. "Thank you. If you want change, Fiona. If you want breathing room, it's yours."

"No promises on that end." She graced him with a tender smile. "But you are right. We will get through this."

"And then you'll go back to Chicago." The reality crushed him, but there was no future between them. Bringing Rhyme to justice wouldn't bring Fiona the freedom she hoped for. Raymond Vect's incarceration and sentencing to death row had brought justice, but not freedom. Asa still battled the pain and the guilt.

At least now, he had some help from above.

Fiona had nothing.

No! No! This wasn't supposed to happen. Rhyme seethed from the far side of the cemetery. Fiona had seen him, but he'd been well disguised once again as he brought flowers to a random grave. Killing Kacie should have proven that Asa had no power to protect Fiona and he wasn't the man for her.

It had somehow backfired.

His blood boiled and pulsed hard in his temples. He ground his teeth, disgust eating away at his insides as he had to witness her looking up at Kodiak with a lovesick expression.

Fiona, you've been a naughty kitten.

He'd miscalculated, now recognizing where he'd gone wrong. Time to change tactics.

Move earlier than he'd anticipated. Like the day she'd married Asa Kodiak. He'd had to move up his plans then, too.

Desperate times called for desperate measures.

You will come back to me, Fiona. You'll think about me first! Only me! Your first love.

Asa's phone buzzed in his shirt pocket during the middle of the sermon on Sunday. Pastor was preaching on Jesus coming to set captives free and Fiona seemed to be hanging on every word. If anyone was brokenhearted and needed healing it was Fiona. And him. And everyone.

Amanda.

"Excuse me," he whispered and slipped from the aisle seat. He dashed into the hall down by the church conference room and ducked inside. "Hey, Amanda."

"Hey. I'm sorry. I know you're at church. I got called in. Homicide. He's killed again."

Asa's stomach dropped and he sank into the thick leather conference-room chair. "Posed?"

"Goose feather and all. Our vic is male. Early thirties." She gave him the Germantown address. "I'll keep everything as is. Death investigator is on the way. TBI is working forensics."

"We're on our way."

"She at church with you?"

He pinched the bridge of his nose. "Yeah. She came. It's—"

"It's great. I only wish I hadn't interrupted. Church is a

great place to gain some faith. I hope she does. I'm certainly not implying God orchestrated this evil—He didn't. But maybe He's taking what was meant for evil and doing something good. If you need me on a personal level, I'm here for you, Asa."

"Thank you." He ended the call and sent a group text to the team, including Fiona. He was waiting outside the side sanctuary doors for her. She emerged and had been crying. "You okay?"

"Yeah. All good. What do you know?" They beelined it to the SUV as he relayed the sliver of information.

"He's never struck this soon. Something's off. It takes time to select, stalk and gather incriminating evidence on the perfect target. He'd have to purchase staging supplies, most likely online. Pick the night. He's rushed."

Asa had been thinking the same thing. "Killing—killing Kacie—" he choked on the words "—was meant to teach me a lesson that I fail at protecting people I love." How true it was. "He thought you'd see that." How had she not? "And you'd leave. Which you did." She'd left him twice. He may have served her the papers, but she'd left him long before that.

"Asa, you don't fail at protecting people. You do it every day. There was nothing you could have done to save Kacie. And as far as your mom... Do you remember telling me the night Kacie died what Raymond Vect asked you?"

A few things he didn't remember, but that he did. "I do."

"You don't really think he would have let her live, do you... if you'd asked?"

"He let me and Kacie live."

"True, but you were kids. He was banking on no one believing your testimony if he got caught—which he doubtfully thought he would."

Still.

"Anyway, I'm glad you told me."

He stopped at the red light and shifted toward her. "Fiona, that's the only secret I've ever kept from you. Secrets hurt people. I think not being absolutely honest from the start hurt our marriage. I was afraid to tell you. I didn't want you to think less of me."

"I don't. I wouldn't have. Asa, he was an evil monster toying with you. It makes me sick to think of it." Fiona closed her eyes and fisted her hands, then opened them and started to say something, but clammed up. What was she debating about saying? Her secret? She had one. Finally she tucked a hair behind her ear and shifted an air vent more in her direction. "Asa, speaking of evil monsters, Rhyme was at the cemetery. I sensed him and then I saw that man. You saw him, too."

Asa didn't want to believe that sicko would be there intruding on his grief, and had ignored the man laying flowers, but Fiona was right. It had to have been him. "I should have done something."

"I should have, too. But we didn't. And he saw us by the car. The moment was intimate between us, and without hearing us, no telling what he imagined."

Asa mulled over Fiona's implication. She'd nailed it. "He rushed this crime because he felt he had to. Killing Kacie didn't do what he had hoped—not in the end. You moved out but then returned to me, in his mind."

She nodded. "Killing and staging brings me back to him. My time. My focus. Solely on Rhyme."

"Like his killing on our honeymoon." Asa had wanted the team to run point; they were skilled agents, but Fiona had refused. It had to be her on the case, tracking him, arresting him.

Fiona's lips turned south. "I made a lot of mistakes, Asa. That's one of the biggest."

Asa entered an upscale neighborhood, similar to Jenny Miller's subdivision. Fiona was admitting mistakes, which was huge. Unlike her. "Thank you for saying that."

"And—" she blew a heavy breath "—since we're being open and honest, I have to tell you something I haven't shared with anyone in my life."

Asa parked behind a MPD patrol car.

"But it'll have to wait." She opened her door and hopped out. Fiona had made a good call. Now wasn't the time.

MPD. TBI.

Amanda.

All on the scene. Neighbors hung around lawns, gawking.

Another large brick home. Perfect yard. A woman walking two little dogs had stopped and they barked incessantly.

Amanda approached them with professionalism. "We got a call about two hours ago. Vic is Clay Weinstein. He was supposed to meet a friend for brunch and he never showed. Never answered his phone. Wasn't like him so his friend came by. Found him."

Asa slipped on booties and gloves. Sweat trickled down his back.

"Get one of the crime scene guys to discreetly take photos of the crowd. If he's out here, I want his ugly mug."

"I'm on it."

He turned to Fiona. "Ready?"

"Let's get this guy. For Kacie. For Colleen."

This wicked killer had taken both their sisters. "For all of us."

The killer had declared war.

Asa would give him the fight of his life and hope it was enough.

Chapter Fourteen

Clay Weinstein's home was large, open and airy. The smell of lemon hung in the air. Fiona observed her surroundings. Earth tones from walls to furniture. Pristine. Orderly.

"You said he's a bachelor. No kids?"

"No," Amanda said and paused at the winding staircase. Ornate iron railing. "Not according to his friend who found him." She glanced at her notes. "A Brice Forlan. They work together. Ryker's Realty."

Probably explained why a single man lived in a home ranging between four to five thousand square feet in a family-oriented subdivision. She'd noticed the community playground, bicycles and toys scattered in yards. What she didn't notice was personal effects. Pictures. "Can you find out if he decorated this place himself or if he had a decorator? Also check to see if he's had it painted recently." She didn't smell fresh paint, but she wasn't letting one of her five senses rule out a possible connection. Hopefully, a decorator would be able to shed light on the impersonal state of the home. "One more thing…a cleaning person. Someone keeps this place immaculate and has been here within the last twenty-four to forty-eight hours. I can smell faint scents of lemon and bleach."

Amanda scribbled notes.

Asa followed Amanda the rest of the way up the stairs, Fiona trailing behind. "Forced entry?" Asa asked.

"No. Mr. Forlan said the front door was unlocked when he arrived. But he had a spare key."

They turned left at the top of the stairs. Hardwood floors. A long hallway leading to the master bedroom at the end of the hall. "We need to find out who else might have a spare. Either the killer let himself in or he was allowed inside," Asa said.

The vic may have personally known Rhyme. This could be huge. Every other crime had been with forced entry. Why was this different?

TBI forensic investigators milled about, processing the scene. The death investigator stood inside by the bed. "Hey, Karen," Asa said.

"Asa. Fiona. Nice to see you again. I guess."

"Likewise. What can you tell us?" Fiona eased into the room. Kneeling at the east window, Clay Weinstein was wearing an old man's nightshirt and cap from the 1800s. A white half-burned tapered candle was perched on the window in a brass candleholder—vanilla-scented.

"Asphyxiation. Markings consistent with the other Nursery Rhyme victims." Fiona frowned. *What naughty thing have you done, Mr. Weinstein?*

Violet entered the room, in gloves and booties.

Tiberius stood beside her and low whistled then swore under his breath.

"Exactly," Asa said and caught them up to speed.

"I'll go talk with Mr. Forlan. He's downstairs." Violet left the bedroom.

Tiberius studied the staging.

"He's looking out the window. Clearly at night because of the candle." He kneeled beside him and peered out. "I see a house past the privacy fence. Backyard. Nothing particular. Posed because it was convenient placing?"

"Nothing is about convenience for Rhyme." Everything had meaning. He would have had to kill him, pose him and make sure he didn't slump until rigor mortis set in if he wanted him to be found this way. He knew he'd have time and he had patience. "He either wants us or the victim to see something."

"What's the rhyme?" Tiberius asked, the subtle scent of cologne reaching her nostrils. Five-o'clock shadow. He could wear light cologne but not shave?

"I don't know yet. You have a date last night?" Fiona kneeled as well and stared into the backyard of the house behind him. Family home. Doghouse. Swing set. In-ground pool. Grill area. Nice little setup.

"I did. With the new agent in Violent Crimes." His smug smile was too much. Owen had lost to Tiberius. Wonder if he knew yet.

"What did Rhyme want us or you to see?" She spoke to the vic, thinking out loud. "A family. Something you didn't have, Mr. Weinstein. Did you covet what they had?" Rhyme was a vigilante killer. Protecting children. Fiona jumped up. He'd been forced to stare at a home with children; kid cases sent her stomach roiling.

On the bedside table sat an antique clock shaped like a lantern. Didn't fit with the decor. Must have been brought by Rhyme. The time was set at eight o'clock.

"There's something in his pocket," Asa said. He plucked out an old-fashioned brass key. "Do you think this goes to something or is it part of the staging?"

"'Are your children in bed? It's now eight o'clock,'" Fiona

mumbled. "'Wee Willie Winkie.' He rides through the town in his nightgown. Rapping windows." She pointed to the key. "Crying or peeping through locks depending on the version. He wants to know if the children are in bed."

"Because it's eight o'clock," Asa offered.

She nodded. "It's a prop for the rhyme."

"Can I say what we're all thinking?" Tiberius asked. "Eww. He's a kiddie peeper?"

"Or worse," Amanda added. "I'll see if he has any criminal charges."

Asa didn't watch Amanda leave the room. "I need to know if he bought that clock around here. Ty, put Selah on speaker."

Once Selah was on the line, Fiona brought her up to speed. "It's unique. If he purchased it at a local shop, they'll remember and have a record. The gown doesn't look vintage. He could have purchased it online or anywhere. Work that angle as well."

Asa took his turn kneeling.

"Maybe he works at or owns a junk shop. An antique store or slot at a boutique. Cross-reference our suspects with antique/junk shops and let's see if anything pops."

"He doesn't even ruffle his sheets." The right side had been turned down, and a soft impression had been left. He'd been asleep or in bed before he allowed Rhyme inside. She switched on the TV. CNN. She walked to the DVD player and opened it. Empty. In fact, she didn't see any DVDs.

Computer keys clacked as Selah worked her mojo. "Right now he's looking squeaky clean, y'all. He donates to a host of charities and sits on several boards. He's heavily involved in crime prevention and community efforts in that regard. He's won an award with us."

"Us? The SCU?" Asa asked and frowned.

"The FBI. Public recognition for his achievements to make

extraordinary contributions to education and the prevention of crime and violence in the Memphis community."

Asa opened his mouth to speak, then clamped it shut, freezing in place. In thought. He had something.

"What is it, Asa?"

He shook out of the stupor. "Nothing important." What wasn't he telling her? "Selah, when was he recognized? Recently?"

"Last month."

"Public event or private?"

"Community event. Businesses. The mayor. Organizations. It was a swanky dinner. We got invites."

"I guess I was busy actually catching bad guys and unable to attend," Asa said.

"Or forgot to check your mail," she muttered.

"Did anyone from our team go?" he asked.

Why the big concern? Unless Asa was thinking what she was. Catering. Another place to eavesdrop, stalk, watch. Churches catered events. Schools. Businesses. And even law enforcement. Brilliant!

"I don't know," Selah replied. "Why? Owen, maybe, but I assure you he wasn't paying attention to awards unless someone voluptuous and single was winning it."

"It's the catering." Fiona gave Asa the thumbs-up. "Perfect way to prowl. Check who catered the event and see if they've catered anything our prior victims might have attended or overseen."

"Got it. Asa? Anything else?"

Asa rubbed his chin and returned a weak thumbs-up to Fiona. "No. No, that's all for now."

Asa pocketed his phone. "Let's search the house. If this guy is Wee Willie Winkie and it means what we think it does, then he'll have paraphernalia stashed somewhere. I'll get the

MPD to help. We need to tear this place apart. I'll send Violet to his place of business with you. Most real estate companies have model homes open on Sundays. If not, start knocking on doors."

"Peeping through the locks?" Ty added, humor dancing in his eyes.

"Not funny, Ty. Interview the people who live behind him."

"Okay. We're close, Asa. I can feel it."

They'd thought that earlier, before Trent Barton's alibi checked out. The manager said he'd been at work until 11 p.m. and his grandmother verified him coming home at 11:10 p.m. He couldn't have made it to Horn Lake, Mississippi, to murder Kacie and then get back home by the time Ty had the MPD knock on the door.

Amanda popped her head in. "Hey, to let you know, I'll have to step out of this investigation."

"I understand," Asa murmured.

Her cheeks turned pink and she glanced at Fiona. "No, it's a new homicide. Twentysomething woman went missing three days ago. They found her. She was holding a human bone—not her own. I may need another consult. That's bizarre, right?"

Definitely strange. Didn't mean it would fall to them, though. "I can come take a peek if you need me to."

Amanda passed him a look Fiona knew all too well. Regret and hope things might go in her favor. Amanda had pulled the reins on her and Asa's relationship, but she obviously hadn't stopped caring about him. Fiona understood that feeling. But Amanda had something Fiona didn't.

Something to offer Asa.

Fiona had come between them. Old feelings had gotten in the way. But there were new feelings, too. Didn't matter.

The situation hadn't changed. Rhyme was still on the loose and holding her hostage. Fiona didn't want to hold back Asa. It was unfair.

"Did you hear me?" Asa asked.

Fiona blinked from her thoughts. "What? No. Sorry."

Amanda was already gone.

"I'll be right back." She jetted from the room, bypassing techs processing the scene and uniforms doing a search for incriminating evidence to prove Clay Weinstein was a child predator. She ran out the front door into the blinding sun and scorching heat.

"Amanda!"

Amanda paused and shielded her eyes with her hand. "Agent Kelly."

Fiona caught up to her. "Can I have a second?"

"Sure."

She heaved a sigh. "I actually like you, Amanda. You're a great human being and detective. Asa really likes you. He asked me not to mess things up for that exact reason. Things have been off, I know, but don't give up on him." Like she had. "I'll be gone—"

She held her hand up. "Fiona, Asa's feelings have nothing to do with seeing you face-to-face. His choice to have you investigate with him, I could let slide, but it holds merit. The fight between the other agent and him—"

"Luke pressed his buttons." Looking back now, it had brought up his insecurity and guilt about not begging for his mom's life, too. "It wasn't about me."

Amanda lightly laid a hand on her upper arm. "Fiona, maybe he did press some buttons. But Asa does have feelings for you. This isn't about you being here in Memphis. It's about you being here." She pointed to her heart. "I can't compete with that. And I'm not going to. If things change, it'll be a different story."

"I only want Asa to be happy. I couldn't do that."

Amanda cocked her head. "You know, when you first met me you told me nothing dark had touched me." She shook her head. "That's not true—not even close. I refused to let it rob me of joy and peace, which I find through my faith." Her eyes glistened and she laid her hand on her chest. "A faith Asa now has."

Fiona had seen the difference it made in his life. The way he talked and behaved, and his quick and sincere apologies.

"He's still working through his baggage, dropping weight that holds him back and continues to steal his joy. His peace. His temper. And when he gets there, you'll see that same look of innocence." Her words carried passion and confidence. "Because the stain of what we went through and endured has been washed clean from our soul, not a shadow of shame is left to be spotted." Her eyes closed as if she was feeling a washing this second. When she opened them the smile that spread across her face drew Fiona to whatever it was that had put it there. Bright and full of hope.

Fiona carried her shame like a broken trophy. "I'm sorry I misjudged you, and for whatever happened to you. I surely didn't mean to minimize that."

Amanda nodded her acceptance of Fiona's apology. "I haven't forgotten it. It makes me a better detective. Helps me comfort those who are suffering the same pain. Gives me purpose."

Fiona's purpose had been born out of darkness, too, but she had no real comfort to offer others in pain. She couldn't get past her own.

"I certainly am not thankful for it. But I refuse to let the darkness win," she said with powerful conviction. "Don't let Rhyme win. Learn how to shine, Fiona. Accept that it is possible."

Like fireworks...or, maybe like Asa saw her, a star. Fiona watched as Amanda started to amble down the sidewalk to her unmarked car.

How did one learn to shine? She had so many questions and doubts.

"Amanda!"

She pivoted and shielded her eyes again.

Fiona jogged and caught up with her again. "How do you reconcile the fact that the God you place your faith in let that darkness happen to you? I thought He was good and powerful. He could have prevented it."

"I asked those same things, expecting a detailed answer. Over and again for years. And you know what?"

Fiona shook her head.

"I didn't get one. But I did come to the revelation that my God let His only son—His beloved son—die in my place. Even when He asked if what was about to happen—the darkness He would have to endure—could be passed from Him. He told Him no. The agonizing, torturous death of Jesus in the end was for my benefit. Your benefit. And His glory."

Fiona was well aware of who Jesus was. But she'd never thought about it like that. The thought of someone dying in her place a gruesome death...it jogged something loose inside and moved her.

"What I went through happened because we all have free will—even the bad guys. And bad people do bad things. Our world is dark and broken. God used the evil intended for me in the end for my benefit—to mold me into the woman I am today. And to use it for His glory. The key is letting Him. You always have a choice."

Even the bad guys.

Even Fiona. She'd chosen to go it alone. But she desired that washed soul idea Amanda talked about. Hers was far from clean.

"Thanks," she whispered.

"What are you doing out here?" Asa called from the front stoop. "We got something."

She hugged Amanda. "Truly, thank you." Then she raced to the front lawn. "On the vic?"

"No. The old youth pastor from Abundant Life finally returned our call. We got the name of the girl that Robert Williams might have been grooming or having an inappropriate relationship with. You know her. And that's not all."

Asa pulled into an apartment complex on Kings College Road to see none other than Andi Fleming, the secretary at St. George's. Her maiden name was McMahan and in her teenage years Alexandria had gone by Lexi instead of Andi. Presently divorced. She'd been under their noses this entire time.

"What's going on with you?" he asked. Fiona had been mostly quiet since her talk with Amanda. It couldn't have been a negative conversation; she'd hugged her. Asa itched for the details. She remained silent, gnawing on her thumbnail and staring out the window. "Is it something Amanda said?"

"Yes," she mumbled.

"About me?" He couldn't imagine anything about him would zip her lips for an extended period of time.

"No. How much do you know about her past?"

He parked in a visitor spot and left the SUV running. "Basic things. We haven't been together long enough to start divulging intimate details. Why?"

"Nothing." She unbuckled. "Do you think we have a link to Rhyme that involves Andi Fleming? She's the youth connected to Robert Williams. And now she's at the school where Jenny Miller worked."

"It's possible she's been inadvertently or purposefully giving our killer information. She would have been too young when you were abducted, though, and she didn't attend St. George's. We can't connect her—at least right now—to any of the other victims."

Asa led the way to Andi's apartment. It was after four o'clock. If she'd been at church, she should be home now.

He knocked three times and finally she opened the door. Recognition lit in her eyes. "Agent Kodiak, Agent Kelly. What are you doing here?" She stepped outside. Sure sign she didn't want them to come in. The smell of cinnamon and apples wafted out, along with a musky scent. Like aftershave. Fiona must have caught the whiff. She gave him the eye. He gave a slight nod to agree. A man was inside or had been recently.

Andi was wearing running shorts and a baggy T-shirt. Full makeup and ponytail.

"It's so hot out here," Fiona said, fanning herself. "Could we please come inside?"

Wide eyes, mouth open, as she searched for a response that was polite. Finally, she parted the Red Sea and let them cross. "Sure. The air's on and it felt good out here to me."

"Uh-huh," Fiona said, taking the lead.

Cozy apartment. Lived-in. A red candle burned on the end table. No sign of a man, but two take-out cups sat on the coffee table.

"We'd like to ask you some questions." Asa retrieved his notepad.

"Please, sit down. Can I get you anything to drink?"

They declined a drink and Andi perched on the edge of the couch. Asa sat on the love seat and Fiona remained standing.

"Did you find out any further information about Jenny?" she asked and fidgeted with the edge of her T-shirt.

"This isn't about Jenny Miller. It's about Robert Williams."

Her face blanched and she twisted the bottom of her shirt into a knot. "Oh." Her voice was faint. Childlike.

"You know he was murdered and staged by the Nursery Rhyme Killer, and Jenny as well. It's been all over the news. The past crimes and this new one. Why didn't you tell us you knew more than one victim?"

"Who told you I knew Robert Williams?"

"You, for one," Fiona said. "With the 'oh.' Implies you knew him. But we found out from his widow, Tanya. She couldn't remember your name. Your old youth pastor filled in our blanks now that he's back from a mission trip."

Andi chewed on her bottom lip and glanced down the hall.

"Anyone else in the apartment?" Asa asked and followed her line of sight.

She shook her head, but she was lying. Why would she hide someone? Did she know who the Nursery Rhyme Killer was? Or maybe she was with a married man.

Fiona moved and blocked Andi's view of the hallway, forcing her to focus on either Fiona or Asa. "Look, I get why you didn't want to tell us about Robert. He hurt you. Abused you. Took advantage of and manipulated you."

Andi glued her gaze to the worn beige carpet.

"You don't go by Lexi because you want that part of your life to be over. That girl is gone. You're a new person, Andi. With a new life. A good job. But we need you to verbally confirm if Robert Williams behaved criminally with you. Can you do that? Can Andi help Lexi be strong?"

Asa didn't think she'd talk but finally she trained her sight on Fiona. "My mom and dad divorced when I was young. He walked out on us…" Andi told a story that was tragic and textbook. A young girl who felt abandoned by the man in her life—her father—*needed* a man in her life. Robert Williams preyed on her thirst for approval and love. Her mother spent most hours working to put food on their table.

"Everyone had a crush on him and he was giving me attention." Andi hung her head. "I knew he was married but he said he didn't love her. That he wanted to leave her but the church would make him step down from leadership and he wanted to be near me. So I believed him."

"It started a year before he died. Mrs. Williams caught him rubbing my back at that party. He denied anything inappropriate. Of course. So did I. But it didn't stop. Not until he was murdered." She wiped her eyes. "I feel bad over it every day."

"You shouldn't." Fiona grasped her hand. "He targeted you for specific reasons. And probably other girls, too. He was someone you were supposed to trust. None of this is your fault."

Asa leaned forward. "Did you tell anyone?"

She shook her head too fast. Too much. She'd told someone.

"A friend? Another youth leader? A teacher? No one?"

Andi did another peep over Fiona's shoulder. Either she didn't want the mystery guest to overhear or it could be the very person she'd told. They had no reason to force themselves into the back of the apartment—no probable cause. But they could wait him out.

"Okay," he said. "But if you told someone…they might have passed on the news and the killer got wind. Or you accidentally informed the killer. So think about that." He pulled a Violet—been abrasive, harsh and accusatory.

Andi fisted her hands and rubbed them down her thighs. "I didn't do any of those things. I wish I hadn't done what I did with Robert Williams. It's affected my whole life."

Fiona pointed to herself. "I understand more than you

know, Andi. But today someone shared something profound with me. She said not to let the darkness win. Learn to shine." She paused a beat at the door. "Maybe do that."

They let themselves out.

Asa couldn't be sure what Amanda had shared with Fiona but it had been emotional and spiritual. When Fiona wanted him to know she'd tell him, hopefully along with the secret she'd nearly come clean with this morning. Until then, they'd work the case.

"I want to know who she's hiding. Let's circle back and wait him out. Drop me off at the gate, and I'll stay out of sight in case he makes a quick exit, then come back and we can watch from those bushes."

Fiona agreed. He tossed her the keys and she dropped him off near the mailboxes, where he had a clear view of Andi's apartment but they didn't have a clear view of Asa. He scanned the cars. Nothing familiar.

No one left the apartment.

Fiona parked at the complex adjacent to Andi's apartment and Asa used the parked vehicles as blocks while he hustled to her and to sweet air-conditioning. He hopped inside.

"I hope this works soon. I'm hungry."

Asa's stomach rumbled on cue. "Me, too, but here we are. Nothing to do but wait...and talk." Would she bite? Reveal the secret?

Fiona held his eye. "Do you want me to go with you tonight? To get Kacie's belongings from the roommate?"

That wasn't what he had in mind to talk about. He'd been putting it off. The boxes were left in the little shed behind the house after Kacie's roommate moved out—couldn't live there anymore. "If you want. Ty and Owen are gonna help me do the heavy lifting."

"I do. I'll help you go through things and decide what to do with them."

Might as well call the whole team in. "We can eat at my place. I have so much food I don't even know what to do with it all. Freezer full. We can have a casual meeting, brief for tomorrow."

Fiona tapped her thumbs on the steering wheel for several moments, then sighed. "I know that's not what you wanted to talk about. I was hoping you'd forget. Should have known better." A nervous laugh followed, then she laid her head back against the driver's seat and ran her palms down her thighs. "When the police interviewed me seventeen years ago, I lied. And I've been lying ever since."

A pit formed in his stomach. "About what?"

Fiona let out a heavy breath. "I told them that Rhyme seemed nice one minute and mean the next. I told how he seemed confused and disoriented then fully in charge. Switch. Switch. Switch. The profile we built is solid. And a few things I could have told would have solidified it even stronger."

"But?"

She looked out the window, rubbed her lips together. "I said I escaped." She turned to Asa and her eyes filled with moisture. "But that's not true. Rhyme—the primary personality—let me go. Not once. But twice."

Asa's mind reeled. "He let you go?"

She nodded.

"Fiona, that's key. We need to know why."

"I don't think Rhyme is the killer. His alter ego abducted me and took the girls—I still don't know how. If they came willingly to party—if Rhyme is the older friend, or the alter ego—or if he abducted them one by one. Either way, the secondary personality set everything into motion."

Rhyme had let her go not once but twice. Asa had no clue

what the endgame had been or was now. His insides folded in and he felt the acid burn his throat. Fiona stared into space, allowing herself to go back in time to share this secret she'd carried so long. She was being courageous now and he was thankful.

"I'd put on the old nightgown and waited my fate. But when the door opened, that horrible man in the mask was kind. 'You're not supposed to be here,' he said."

"Why?" Did that mean the other girls were?

"I don't know. I said I escaped out a window. I didn't. Rhyme said I had to leave. I thought he was playing a sick game."

A sick game had been played with her. Was still being played. Asa balled a fist. Fiona laid her head on the steering wheel as if simply remembering exhausted her and forced her to hide her face in shame. She had nothing to feel shame over. "What happened next?"

"He led me from the room, down a little hall. I—I heard them—Colleen, Josie and Sierra. Wailing and begging to leave, beating on the door they were trapped behind." She shivered.

Asa's gut felt like a ton of bricks had landed in it. He laid a hand on her thigh and encouraged her to go on. To get it all out. The good, the bad and the ugly.

She lifted her head and faced him, her hollow eyes haunting him. "I heard their terror, felt it myself. But I never flinched. Never turned back. Never said a word or asked for their release, too." She absently shook her head. "That makes me as much a monster as it does him."

"That's not true, Fi. You were in shock. Terrified. In survival mode."

"Colleen had bruises on the outside of her hands where she'd fisted and banged on the door. And I—I can't unhear the pounding and the pleading. It's there when I go to sleep and when I wake up. Every time someone knocks on a door, I hear it." A tear gathered in the corner of her eye and slipped over the edge.

"But that wasn't the only chance I had to help them. Instead I let him…" She squeezed her eyes closed and a few stray tears pushed out and down her cheeks.

Asa's blood drained from his head and pooled like ice in his gut. He wasn't sure he could bear to hear the rest, but she needed to confide. For his support. For some release—he'd felt that when he'd told her his secret. "You let him what?" he murmured.

"At the edge of the woods, he stopped me, laced his hand in mine and told me that I was special. Pure. Lovely and undiseased." She touched her hair. "He toyed with my hair—it was long back then—caressed my cheek like a lover."

Asa squeezed his fist tighter to refrain from screaming out in anger at the torture he'd laid upon her.

"I never cried. Didn't outwardly flinch, but inside I thought I was going to die, that my heart would burst out of my chest any moment. Fall right onto the forest floor. He told me he'd been watching me and seen my kindness and goodness. I had no clue I'd been stalked or for how long."

Asa pulled her over into his chest and held her. "It's okay, Fi. You're safe. All that is behind you now." He held her that way as minutes ticked by, squeezing her tight and hoping she felt secure in his arms. Asa understood that kind of fear. Finally, she eased from his arms.

"I wish that was all. It's not." A shaky breath released from her lips. "I could have stopped all this long ago."

Asa's blood turned cold. "How?"

Fiona swallowed hard and cast her gaze to the floorboards,

unable to hold eye contact. Asa laced his hands in hers and held firm. "You can tell me."

"You'll hate me," she whispered.

"Never," he said with conviction, then tilted up her chin so she could peer into his eyes. See the truth. "Never."

She searched his eyes then licked her bottom lip. "He asked if we could seal ourselves together."

Asa's stomach dropped.

"I had no idea what that meant, but I said yes. And...he began to slowly slip off his mask, but..."

"But?"

"Before I could see his face, I closed my eyes. Asa, I didn't want to see him. But if I had, then I could have described him to a sketch artist. Recognized if Trent Barton or Daniel Osborn was Rhyme. But I was a coward, afraid he'd kill me for knowing his identity, though he never asked me not to look. Because even deeper down... I knew he wasn't going to kill me either way. I could have stopped this."

Asa raked his hand through his hair. "After he took off his mask..."

Fiona's bottom lip trembled and she touched it and winced. "I remember his breath. Mint and a hint of alcohol. He asked me if I'd ever been kissed." She wiped a tear. "I hadn't. I remember his taste. Sweet and tangy."

Asa couldn't move. Couldn't swallow. This vile monster had violated her, put his lips on his wife's. He'd kill him.

"I kissed him back. I was too afraid not to. I could tell he enjoyed it...a lot. He thought I liked it, too. But I didn't."

"I know you didn't, baby. I know. I'm so sorry."

"You'd think that was the worst part but..." She shook her head. "It was that when it was over, I thanked him for being kind and for letting me go. And I was...thankful. I got to get away and I never asked for him to let the others go. I mean, he liked me, was obsessed with me, so he might have. I'll never know now except part of the reason I want to be the one to catch him is because I want to know if he would have—let them go for me."

What good would that do her now? If he said yes, Fiona would spend the rest of her life broken and sick. He understood that feeling and had only been working through it since he'd become a person of faith. "It'll plague you, either way. Fiona, promise me if we arrest him, you'll never ask him that."

"I don't know if I can make that promise, Asa. I need to know," she insisted.

Asa pawed his face. She wouldn't even give him this one thing. "Okay," he said with resignation.

"I wish I could promise you. I do."

He nodded. "After that kiss what did you do?"

"I stood there with my eyes closed, listening as he slipped his mask back on his face, then I opened my eyes and he said, 'We'll have many firsts. Just you wait and see. But you have to go now. It's not safe and I can't be sure of how much time we'll have.'"

No wonder this monster was so angry. Asa had been Fiona's first for so many things the NRK wanted to be. He had a vendetta against Asa.

"I ran for what felt like forever and I could hear cars in the distance, but then he started calling me. Like he'd let me go with false hope only to have the thrill of hunting me and taking it away. He'd snapped. Changed. He found me in that tree and dragged me back, without saying a word, except I was a naughty kitty and going to get no pie. Then hours later, he let me go again and I was so afraid he'd hunt me down like before, but he didn't."

He pulled a tissue from the glove box and handed it to her. She dabbed her eyes. "This time he led me to the road and told me he'd be watching out for me. To wait for him. He'd come back for me. I flagged down a car, told the police about the others, but it was too late. And it's all my fault for not going back and trying to do something. For not opening my eyes and memorizing his face. For not fighting when he kissed me."

"You did get help. If you'd have gone back, you would have been killed, too. You survived." Asa hadn't tried. Didn't call anyone. Didn't go after Raymond Vect and he wasn't all that much smaller than him. This was different. "Did you know anyone older? A young teacher maybe in his twenties? Anyone?"

"No. Believe me, I've racked my brain."

This presented a much clearer picture of Fiona and her irrational thoughts that the NRK wouldn't kill her, as well as her obsession and drive to find him. Because twice he hadn't. That meant nothing now, though. The alter ego had his sights on her. "Thank you for telling me. I wish you'd have done it years ago."

She balled the tissue in her hand. "I should have. I was just—am—so ashamed."

No one knew shame like Asa. "I don't think any less of you. I couldn't."

If they'd have been this honest with one another in the beginning, would things have turned out differently? It would have helped, but leaning on each other wasn't enough. He'd learned that over the past several months. They needed to lean on God. Asa prayed daily that darkness would be exposed and justice served. Sometimes there seemed to be no justice, but he refused to give up believing a day would come, bringing it. In this life or the next.

"I wish I knew why he fixated on me. What did I do to catch his eye? Why did I get to live?"

Fiona had been tight with her sister, especially after their move. If Rhyme had been stalking her, wanting her, then he'd have been jealous of Colleen like he was jealous of Asa. That could be why he took Colleen. Saw her as a threat and removed her. The other girls might have been collateral damage. He was new to murder back then and hadn't figured out everything. Far from practiced.

Fiona gasped. "Asa!"

"I see him."

The man they'd been waiting on stepped into the sunshine, hugged Andi, then folded himself into his newer model, black Acura. This was an interesting turn. "Why does Andi need to hide Daniel Osborn from us?" The head of school was her boss but that was no reason to duck into the back of the apartment. Neither of them was married and both were consenting adults. What was going on?

"I don't know. But let's find out."

Chapter Fifteen

Fiona stood in Asa's living room staring at several boxes. The back of Asa's truck still held Kacie's bedroom suite, a futon and an oversize chair and ottoman. Owen and Tiberius had helped load it. Violet, Selah and even Cami had arrived about ten minutes ago. Guess it was time to make nice with Cami. Fiona entered the kitchen. Cami had always reminded Fiona of Tinker Bell, especially now with the big bun on top of her head. "Cami."

She held a sheet of aluminum foil in one hand, a poppy chicken casserole in the other. "Hey."

"I'll cut right to it. Can we put the past behind us? We got along once, didn't we?" *Take the olive branch, Cami. Let bygones be bygones.*

She raised perfectly sculpted eyebrows and cocked her head. Any minute she'd toss fairy dust on her. Send her to Neverland, away from Peter Pan. Fiona was Wendy in this story. "Asa gave me a shot at this job. He's been to every one of my art shows. What have you done, Fiona?"

She married Asa. Did Tink hate Amanda, too? Maybe not. She hadn't hurt him like Fiona. "Nothing."

"No, you hurt Asa. You didn't catch him in his office crying. Or falling asleep at his desk because he couldn't stand to be in that house or sleep without you. I helped him find a new place for fear he'd die of exhaustion or spend all his money on a chiropractor. You didn't see the weight loss, the excessive drinking at first. I walked through that with him. Me and Ty. So pardon my loss of love when it comes to you these days."

No one had walked with her through her darkest pain. She'd chosen to move. To deal alone. "I appreciate you and Tiberius doing that. I never wanted that for him. But he divorced me."

"He didn't have a choice."

"I didn't have a choice, either!" Fiona couldn't stop hunting Rhyme. Raymond Vect had been caught. Asa had closure. He wasn't the one being held captive. But maybe they could have fought harder, longer. They'd given up and given in. It was complicated.

Cami shoved the casserole in the oven when the preheat button beeped and closed the door with more force than necessary. "You put a serial killer before the man you claimed to love, Fiona. You had a choice."

If Asa could have stuck it out...no. No, Cami was right. Asa was right. He'd all but said the same thing when he handed her divorce papers.

This marriage hasn't even counted! You can't be married to two men and you've been married to him much longer than you've been married to me! I won't— I can't keep being the other guy. I—I can't, Fiona. I love you. But I'm spent.

Those four words came next: *I want a divorce.*

"I loved him," she whispered.

"Not enough."

"You tell him you're in love with him?"

Cami wadded up the foil. "It's not like that."

Then what was it like?

"I got in a rough relationship about a year ago. It got real bad and I called Asa. He came and arrested my boyfriend, took me to the hospital and didn't leave my side for three days. I love him. Like I really love him. But I'm not *in* love with him. But you can take this to the bank—I'd die for that man." She paused before leaving the kitchen. "Please don't give him false hope or hurt him again."

"I'd die for that man, too," she whispered after Cami left the kitchen. She should have done better by Cami. When Asa was attending art shows, she was locked up in the spare bedroom with Rhyme—all her boards, leads, articles.

"What are you doing staring into space?" Tiberius asked and opened the fridge, frowning. He grabbed a gallon of Milo's Tea. "This'll have to do." He poured a tumbler and saluted Fiona.

Fiona joined everyone in the living room. They were already discussing the case. Owen and Selah were on the love seat eating chocolate cake and sitting closer than necessary. Owen caught her eye and she gave him a knowing look.

He shook his head but grinned. Owen was going to cause a nice fat issue when he broke the analyst's heart in a million pieces. That was how he rolled. Guess he didn't practice what he preached.

Asa stood before the boxes. "Thanks for coming out. Helping me. It means a lot. Though I'm sure it's all in the name of free food," he teased.

Owen raised his plate. "Amen, brother! Preach."

Asa cocked an eyebrow. "And that's why we're gonna do some work tonight, too. Earn that dinner."

Violet sat in the recliner. Legs crossed. Arms folded over her chest. Not reacting. If Fiona had to do a profile on her, she'd be in a pickle. The woman was complex and quiet. Un-approachable, as if an invisible wall had been built around her that made a person feel the need to stay back. Stand down. Retreat. While she'd allowed Fiona to stay at her place, she wouldn't describe her as hospitable, and Fiona had learned little about her.

They had one thing in common, though. Violet had a room in her house she kept locked, like Fiona had. But Fiona hadn't asked Violet about it. She was still keeping her dark-est secret from Violet. Wouldn't be fair to request her to spill the beans on her own.

Asa pointed at Selah. "What do we know about that antique clock we found at Weinstein's?" He got straight to business.

"English lantern clock. Made before 1841 but I don't have an exact date. Haven't been able to track the online or local business that sold it. Our killer may be a collector and had it for ages. The gown, however, came from a store called Back in Time. Several of them located throughout the US. One in Jackson, Mississippi."

"Did you contact them?" Asa asked.

"I did. They said someone came in about three days ago and purchased that exact gown and cap. Paid cash."

Fiona's pulse spiked. "Video cameras?"

"No, and the cashier working was a sixteen-year-old girl who was Snapping with friends at the time, so she didn't have a great description. 'Sorta tall. He had red hair. Beard. Dark eyes. Or maybe blue. Or maybe his hair was blond. Like I don't really remember. Sorry.'"

Asa pinched the bridge of his nose as he updated the team on their recon earlier with Andi Fleming and Daniel Osborn. "See if you can connect him to Robert Williams. He attended Abundant Life. I want a detailed background on him. Boxers-

or-briefs kind of background. Find out what connection he has to Alexandria McMahan Fleming."

Selah used her thumbs like rockets to text notes to herself with her phone. Her perky nose scrunched as she studied the screen.

"What did you get from Ryker's Realty?" Asa asked.

Violet's upper lip curled. "Not a lot. Not everyone was in on a Sunday, but we made phone calls, too. Weinstein is the perfect colleague, friend. He attends Life Church, which is where our backyard neighbors attend. They invited him about seven months ago and he's heavily involved."

"In children's programs?" If he was a pedophile, he'd want to be near children, and with a stellar record, his background check—if the church did them—would show he was A-okay to work in that department.

"No. Homeless Outreach. No one from our team or MPD found anything that would point to pedophilia. His house is clean. Too clean if you ask me. Everything about him was too clean until I talked with the Vanhorns. The neighbors behind him. Thirties. Two kids. Boy and a girl. Both under twelve. Mr. Vanhorn said our vic always fit his runs in at the time when his wife, Chrissy, is out with the kids. Talks to her and helps her out—like moving a picnic table. One night he couldn't sleep and thought he saw him in their backyard. He put the kibosh on Chrissy and the kids being anywhere near him. That was about two days before Weinstein was killed."

Peeping.

Asa rubbed his scruffy chin. "'Wee Willie Winkie' fits... What if he's strategically planning his runs with a false pretense to talk to Chrissy but actually wants to interact and groom her kids?"

Fiona's stomach clenched. Pedophiles had a special way of making her nauseous. "I can see why Rhyme would think

Weinstein was naughty if he was molesting children. But why can't we find anything on the computer in his house? We searched every nook and cranny." He was young enough that he might now be working up to fulfilling his dark fantasies with one of the Vanhorn children, but there should be evidence of his fixation on children. Photos, chat rooms, disgusting videos.

"Decoy computer? Maybe he's a smart pedo," Tiberius offered and helped himself to the remaining cake on Owen's plate. "Where would he hide his stash?"

Violet thrummed her fingers on the arm of the recliner. "I'd hide it in a place no one would look. Like an empty house on the market I'd listed. Then move it from location to location. Keep it all in one place, like my laptop. Easy to migrate. Even child molesters have evolved with the culture and trends."

"Yet my mom still can't figure out how to work the filters on her iPhone," Selah scoffed.

"Your mom a molester?" Violet asked, all joking aside.

"No-o-o-o." Selah drew out the word and raised her eyebrows.

"Then don't worry about how technologically ignorant she is." Her flat expression didn't reveal snark or irritation. Simple facts.

Selah poked her lips out and her eyes widened. "All righty, then." She continued using her phone keyboard. "I'll print his vacant listings in the morning. There will be a lot, I'm sure."

Owen leaned his elbows on his knees. "Try houses that have less chance of selling and are closest to his personal residence. He can get there quickly when he gets an itch, and has to move whatever it is he's hiding less often. Houses overly priced or foreclosed that need an overhaul to repair. Or old homes that need to be updated."

If this turned out to be true, the department was going to

eat crow after commending him publicly for helping with crime prevention.

"Cami," Asa said, "call and get in touch with the Realtor who's taken over those properties so she can get us into the homes."

"Not a problem."

If their suspicions were right they had solid cases that involved adults who hurt children or adolescents and died for it. *What happened to you, Rhyme? Who hurt you to shape you into the man you are today? And why take Colleen, Josie and Sierra? What did they do?*

"Fiona, you and Violet revisit St. George's tomorrow and follow up with Daniel Osborn. I want to know why he didn't want to be seen. If he has anything to say, Violet, get him to say it."

And how was she going to do that? Womanly ways?

"Okay, enough work talk. I need a break from it and so do you." Asa sniffed. "Is something burning?"

Cami jumped up. "The poppy chicken." She raced into the kitchen, then hollered, "Nick of time."

"Good thing," Tiberius called back. "That's my favorite and the only reason I'm here." He winked at Fiona and she grinned.

The team trickled into the kitchen for casserole and more desserts while Fiona stayed in the living room with Asa. "Do you want to go through these boxes with everyone or wait until later and go through them...the two of us?" While everyone loved Asa, no one knew Kacie well. But she'd been family to Fiona. A little sister. Fiona's heart ached for Colleen and for Kacie.

Asa toyed with old packaging tape that had come loose on the box. "I'd rather wait, if you don't mind. I can take you back to Violet's after we're done or we can wait until another day." Going through personal belongings and saying good-bye would be hard. Fiona would want to put it off, too, but she wouldn't be around forever. Chicago would want her back soon.

"I'll stay," she murmured.

He nodded. Laughter flowed from the kitchen. Exactly what Asa needed. "You gonna eat?"

"In a minute. Go ahead."

Asa meandered toward the sounds of friendship and laughter, jesting and ribbing, and passed Violet as she entered the living room with a plate of poppy chicken and salad. "I don't do casseroles, but I'll attempt it this one time."

Fiona sat on one of the sturdy boxes. "I love casseroles." Violet's fridge held a large amount of produce, yogurt and assorted cheeses. She didn't hit the gym or run, but she did have a pull-up bar over her bedroom door. Fiona hadn't been on a run since the morning Asa came by the house. She planned to hit pavement in the morning before they visited St. George's, which reminded her...

"How are you going to get Daniel Osborn to talk? You have special interrogating skills?"

Violet picked at the poppy chicken; she'd yet to take a first taste. "I know how to get under the skin."

"Me, too." Her stomach rumbled and she almost asked Violet to share, but she didn't seem like that kind of person.

"So does our killer. Could the profile be wrong?" She scooted the casserole to the far edge of her plate then dug in to her salad.

"Are you trying to get under my skin now?"

Violet's mouth did the twitchy thing that bordered on a smile. "No, but what if we're not dealing with a man with DID but someone even more diabolical, scarier?"

"Then I most definitely hope the profile is correct." Rhyme was scary enough. "But I'd bank my life on the fact that it is."

Violet lifted one shoulder. "I wouldn't go offering my life on anything. Nothing is that sure, Fiona."

Once she'd have banked on making it the rest of her life with Asa. Violet had a point.

"What if all this time he's simply a demented sicko who has been and continues to mess with your mind?" Violet asked. "Killers do that. I'd have done it. If I were in love with you in an abnormal and obsessed way like Rhyme, I'd find ways to terrify you—like pretend I'm a violent psychopath one minute. Because he is, make no mistake. But then I'd act all sweet and kind and confused—like you stated in your eyewitness account. What if that was just his way of gaining your trust?"

Fiona shook her head. No. No, it wasn't one diabolical man. It was a man with DID, but Violet was right. She'd been giving Rhyme mercy and attaching humanity to him—blaming his alternate personality for everything.

Violet leaned in and held Fiona's gaze. "I'd control you from afar—murder on your wedding night to bring you back to me. And every time you behaved accordingly, I'd call it affection from you. Us connecting."

There was a twisted connection between them.

"I know you're withholding information about that night. It's all over your face."

Fiona opened her mouth but the truth wouldn't come.

"You're his to toy with as long as he wants to toy with you."

Fiona lost her appetite. She'd gone into the police academy and the FBI because of Rhyme. He'd see it as devoting her life to him, and in a nauseating way she had.

"Every time you gave me your attention, I'd get a thrill from it. Do it again. In any way I could. Like trying to kill you at the farmhouse. Force you to fixate on me like I fixate on you. I'd kill Kacie. I'd kill Jenny Miller and Clay Weinstein. Keep you right where I want you. Away from Asa. Close to me." Violet stabbed a cherry tomato onto her fork. "It could even be someone who's inserted himself into your life. Perhaps not heavily but you might know him."

Fiona might and she'd had the chance to see his face. He hadn't requested she not keep her eyes open; he'd trusted her in a sick way to not tell—because he thought they were bonded, sealed forever. By her not looking, he perceived it as Fiona protecting him. She wouldn't lie. She was pure. Not being able to identify Rhyme would keep her from being a liar. Unknowingly, she'd given him a million wrong signals.

"With your DID profile, you wouldn't even think of him as a suspect. But I assure you—because it's what I'd do—he's been in your personal space. Perhaps talked to you—as simple as asking where the deli counter is at the grocery store."

The woman's uncanny ability to think like a killer gave her the shivers. Had Fiona and the BAU analyst gotten the profile wrong? Was this killer she'd been sympathizing with at times actually a warped murderer who'd been playing mind games all these years?

Another chill wrapped around Fiona's spine. "If I didn't know Rhyme was a man, I'd ask if you were the killer."

Violet paused in midbite. "I could be a killer. It's not all that difficult." Her bluish-green eyes held hers.

"If you're suffering from social awkwardness, fine. I can deal with that. But you're going to need to clarify when you are and are not joking."

Violet laid her fork on her plate, eyes somber. "Everyone has the capacity to take life. It's a matter of what triggers you. Asa would kill Rhyme for what he's done to him—to your marriage, to Kacie. Rhyme's pulled the trigger. I wouldn't trust Asa to arrest him, Fiona. If you find him, restrain them both or it'll be a cold-blooded battle. What's your trigger?"

"What's yours?" Fiona wanted to make sure and never pull it.

"I don't know," she breathed.

Between the possibility that the killer had been toying with her all this time and never had DID, to Violet's belief everyone had the capacity to kill... Asa would kill Rhyme.

Would Fiona?

"This blows," Ty huffed as Asa took lead into the crawl space upstairs. The cramped area could be used as attic-like storage space. This was the third home they'd combed for paraphernalia Weinstein had used for a possible child porn addiction.

"Yep." The cobwebs, spiders and ants he could handle. It was the raging inferno that was about to slay him. Like a dragon had breathed fire into the place. Each attic, hot blasts of angry air. "Owen wouldn't send us on this wild-goose chase to punk us, would he?"

Ty laughed. "Yeah, he would. But we're dealing with kids here so...no. And I gotta be honest. If Weinstein is a pedophile, then I kinda want to give our killer a pass on this one. Let's see him hang for Kacie, man. I'm all in and so sorry. Dang, though. Kids. I hate kid cases. Hate them."

They kept Asa up at night, too. "It might not be true. He killed fast this time. I think it's a ploy to keep Fiona concentrated on him. He has a pattern of this. Weinstein may have been an unsuspecting guy who got bit by darkness for no real reason."

It was a stretch, but stretches and leaps were all Asa and the team had. They were hot, irritated and in desperate need of a shower. And Asa was spent. After everyone had finally left last night, Fiona had stayed for two hours helping him comb through Kacie's belongings, filling up bags with clothes for Goodwill. Asa sorted what he wanted to keep, like certain items of jewelry, and what he could throw away. It was all so wrong. Painful. But Fiona had been a huge comfort and help. They'd told dozens of Kacie stories that made them laugh and helped make it bearable.

He'd dropped her off after midnight and been in the office by eight. Cami had beaten him to work, made coffee and called the Realtor. She'd met them at the first house and gotten them inside the last two. They were hitting dead ends. Hopefully, Violet and Fiona would fare better.

"My mama used to say that everything happened for a reason." Ty cursed and batted cobwebs from his hair.

"I don't buy that." All this evil. This darkness. What was the reason for his mother's death? Kacie's? "I think the reason bad things happen is because bad people do bad things."

"Dude, I'm with you. If a leaf blew east, my mama said God must have had a reason for it to go that way." His chuckle held zero humor. "I call that overspiritualizing things."

"Why's your mama watching leaves blow?"

They both laughed. Delirium. From the heat. Had to be. Sweat dripped from his brow, slicked down his back. "Hey, for real, though, I don't think there's always a reason, but I do believe that God uses bad things for good."

"Yeah. What good's coming out of Kacie's death, bro?"

His pulse spiked and his stomach knotted. His sister was gone. A vapor in the wind. Snuffed out before she had a real shot to live. "I don't know. Yet." May never know. But he had to believe something would. He had to.

The crawl space was dimly lit. In the corner he spotted something. Inching closer, he identified what was lying on the floor. He dipped inside his pocket and withdrew a glove and evidence bag, then lifted the candy bar wrapper. "Hey," he said and bagged it, "someone brought this up here. And sat right here in this area to eat it. Why?"

"They were hungry?"

Asa pressed on the exposed insulation near the wrapper. A piece of pink fiberglass material fell away. "Ty!" Nestled in the insulation was a laptop, a few magazines and a digital camcorder. His lungs constricted. The last thing he wanted to do was watch whatever might be on it, but that came with the territory. Asa used his camera phone to take pictures of the scene before they removed the filth hidden in the insulation and called in crime techs. Then they bagged it and headed out of the attic and into the blessed air-conditioning of the car.

"The question now is how did the Nursery Rhyme Killer know this was here?"

"My guess is something was heard or seen by him. He stalked and hunted until he found this evidence. He may have been the one to leave the candy bar wrapper. A clue." The team had narrowed down the possibilities to painters, construction workers and catering. Fiona's guess was good. Made sense. But that wasn't the line of thinking Asa had been going down.

Rathbone.

He'd only discussed this possibility with Violet—her degree in psychology and unusual skill to think like a killer would help him determine if the idea was plausible. There was always a margin for error and that meant even with the working profile they had.

Rathbone would have been in the area when Fiona was abducted and for all the subsequent murders. He fit the age range and was infatuated with her. Violet agreed the idea was plausible. Asa had been running it down after work hours. Alone in his town house. No eggs in the morning. Only loneliness, heartache and grief.

He called the team and had them get the case room ready. They needed to review connections, add what they now had to the profile and rally for a game plan. Hopefully, Fiona was making headway with Daniel Osborn. After going home for a quick shower, he met Ty, Owen and Selah in the major case room to view the recordings on the camera. Fiona and Violet hadn't returned yet.

Now Asa leaned back in his office chair and prayed. After watching those videos and searching the private laptop of Clay Weinstein, he needed that evil tar washed from him. Sometimes they had to wade through the sludge of darkness to break out into light and expose it for what it was. This man had a disturbing fetish. He'd recorded the Vanhorn girl. They knew who his target had been. An hour ago, they'd broken the news to the Vanhorns. It didn't appear that Weinstein had the chance to fulfill his sickness. The Vanhorn girl had been spared. The Nursery Rhyme Killer had killed him first.

Asa was convinced he'd still been in the planning stages of killing Weinstein. Stalking. Watching. Waiting for it. And if that was the case, then the NRK would have let the vic harm the Vanhorn girl. How would that be protecting her? Why not prevent instead of exact vengeance on her behalf? The NRK knew he was targeting the girl.

Was this about vigilantism? He had no compelling desire to be a hero. Fiona was wrong. She tried to make the NRK seem almost heroic...had he not abducted her and killed her sister.

"Knock, knock."

Amanda.

"Hey, come in." He straightened his posture and waved a hand for her to have a seat. Since her call to another case, he hadn't talked to or seen her. She'd made it clear they were done...for now. Until he could convince her he was over Fiona.

He wasn't sure he *was* over her, but he was certain they were over. "It's good to see you."

"It's good to see you, too. I'm actually here about the case I've been working, though."

"The one with the vic clutching a human bone?"

"Yes."

"You need us to consult? Does it have a twisted religious undertone or it is ritualistic?"

"No. I mean. It's something. Asa, the cause of death was manual asphyxiation. She had the same imprint pattern on her neck as Jenny Miller and Clay Weinstein. That in itself was bizarre so I had forensics run a test. The fibers on my missing-persons vic are consistent with the same kind of rope used in the Nursery Rhyme murders."

"Was she staged?"

"Not like a nursery rhyme, but we think it might be staged in another way."

"We?" he asked.

A man poked his head in the door. Tall. Athletic. Mid-to-late thirties. Dress shirt. No jacket. No tie.

"Come in, John," Amanda said. "This is John Orlando from the Missing Persons Unit at the MPD. John, this is the special agent in charge of the SCU division, Asa Kodiak."

Asa shook John's hand. Firm grip.

The clean-cut detective sat beside Amanda. "Amanda shared with me her experience with the Nursery Rhyme Killer case. While my victim wasn't staged like a rhyme, she is telling a story. She's clutching a human femur. They're testing it."

Definitely strange. The killer must have wanted the police to have the bone. To tell them something, show them some-thing. But rope fibers weren't enough to connect this murder with the Nursery Rhyme Killer. "How does this affect me or the SCU?"

Amanda leaned forward. "It's odd, is it not, that the same signature applies to the NRK victims and this girl? How many killers in this region happen to use manila ropes to strangle their victims?"

"I'll give you that. But…" He held his hands out. "I don't know what you want me to do."

John leaned forward, arms braced on his knees. "When I transferred to Memphis three years ago, I got a stack of cases. Missing girls dating back at least sixteen years. All nineteen to twenty-two. Blonde. Blue eyes. All missing from bars or clubs in the Memphis area. Never been found. But this latest girl—meeting the same physical criteria and had been in a bar when she disappeared—was only missing three days before she surfaced in a public park. With a bone that's at least fifteen to twenty years old, according to the ME. Amanda says that the profile for the Nursery Rhyme Killer is DID and he's been killing at least seventeen years."

"Possibly." But that idea was taking a turn. Not ruled out but not as solid as it once was. He still had some low-key investigating to do on Rathbone.

"Is it possible that your killer's alter ego is the Nursery Rhyme Killer and the primary personality is killing girls? Been doing this for as long?"

Where was Violet when he needed an M. Night Shyamalan quip? "I don't think so."

"Weren't the first victims girls?" John asked.

"Yes, but schoolgirls under seventeen. It's not a secret the NRK uses a manila rope. You could have a copycat as far as the signature goes. There's no proof these missing girls were taken and killed by one person—they're still missing."

"But they were all blonde and blue-eyed," Amanda said.

"Except for Fiona. Brunette. Hazel eyes. She got to live. These girls fit the same physical profile and went missing in all the same types of places."

The NRK had told Fiona she didn't belong with the other girls and let her go, but the blue-eyed blonde girls must have because they died. Amanda and John had clearly been discussing theories.

"What if he took those girls in a frenzy?" John asked. "But then once he had them, he physically couldn't do what he'd been fantasizing about? But he does murder them—with manila ropes. They were in gowns, which might be the start to a nursery rhyme. Over time, he develops his style and his signature."

One man with two personalities and both of them murderers using the same instrument to murder, but targeting different women? Seemed more in the land of make-believe. "This is extremely far-fetched." Laughable even. Surely, this seasoned detective heard it as it came out of his mouth. Of course, he had several missing women and families, too, who were grieving and desiring closure. Detective Orlando was grasping at straws, which Asa understood—he was doing some grasping of his own and would be willing to chase down outlandish theories if it meant catching a killer.

"But is it possible?"

Asa had experienced things he'd never dreamed a human being was capable of doing. "Anything is possible. Can't underestimate anyone. Run your investigation and we'll see if our lines intersect. If it is the Nursery Rhyme Killer, I'd be more interested in what he's up to with that old bone. The NRK is calculating and doesn't make mistakes. If he allowed this body to be found with a human femur, then he has a reason and it's key." He pulled his business card from the holder on his desk and handed it to Detective Orlando. "Call me if it points toward our killer. I hope you find whoever did it."

Amanda paused before leaving. "That rope, though. That's odd."

"I admit that's odd. Same fibers. Could have been purchased from the same place, but the exact same rope to kill this close together? I don't get a great gut feeling. Was the woman sexually assaulted?"

"Yes. I know the NRK doesn't do that, but the other personality, he might."

"I'll talk to Violet."

"Okay." As she was closing the door, she paused. "I miss you." She shut it before he had a chance to say he missed her, too. Probably out of fear that he didn't.

But he did.

Needing another jolt of caffeine, he rose and headed for the coffeepot as Violet and Fiona entered the office.

Fiona joined him. No doubt she'd seen Amanda and John at the elevator.

"Who was the detective with Amanda?" she asked.

"John Orlando," Violet said.

Asa tossed her a quizzical look.

"What? I know people. He's with the missing-persons unit."

"How well do you know him? Not personally, I mean, professionally. He has a strange theory—it's comical, actually, but there's a kernel that pops."

"John's a serious guy. He's analytical. Logical. I like him."

"Sounds like the male version of you," Asa said and snorted, then sipped his coffee. Blech. It'd been sitting too long.

"And yet you consistently ask me for counsel on cases. What did he pitch out to you and why? What does he have to do with Strange Crimes?"

Asa proceeded to share John Orlando's idea with Violet and

Fiona, along with John's thoughts on why Fiona's sister and her sister's friends were taken. "Possible?"

Violet frowned. "Highly unlikely, but we can play what-if. That would mean that one personality is killing and staging in rhymes and the other is raping and murdering young women—and burying or disposing of the bodies. Could Rhyme be a vigilante killer and, unbeknownst to him, his alter ego—which he created as a strong protector—is murdering women in a violent way?" She batted her head from side to side. "If the abuser is a woman, it's possible. He'd detest women, want to dominate and control them since he had no control under his own abuser's hand. Unlikely. But possible."

"With this what-if theory, you're saying that Rhyme is fully aware of his nursery rhyme murders but not the murders of the sexually assaulted women. But technically he's committing them all." This was mind-boggling and reaching. But they'd play every angle.

"Yes. He's protecting children or at least exposing evil deeds done to children," Violet said. "He may not know the more dominant, violent alter ego has been murdering women for as long as he's been killing." Violet skipped coffee and plopped an herbal tea bag in a cup of hot water; a flowery scent wafted in the air. "At the end of the day, this one man is the only one who has been abused. He's the only one committing multiple murders with two different signatures. And if this is true, every doctor and criminologist on the planet is going to want to study him. I get dibs."

"It's all conjecture. We have to follow facts and I'd like some facts on Daniel Osborn," Asa said and drank the horrible coffee.

"Osborn said Andi insisted he hide because if we saw her with an older man we'd think she hadn't changed her ways. That was weak," Fiona said. "Upon further conversation, we discovered that he, too, was a youth sponsor at Abundant Life and knew Robert Williams. He said he suspected Robert's inappropriate conduct, but did nothing because it was hard to believe. He gave Andi a job as a way to apologize and help her start over. He's her mentor."

"You buy that?" Asa asked.

"Not particularly. He was all too pleased to admit he can be connected to the Shetlands when he attended their church, to Maria Windell—since he freely admits he worked in the food pantry—as well as attended Abundant Life and knew Robert Williams." Fiona dumped her coffee out. "This is awful."

"Can he be connected to Alan Minton?"

Violet tossed her tea bag in the garbage. "No. He claims not to know Alan Minton or that he ever used his father's construction business, but Clay Weinstein was his Realtor. Sold him a house three months ago. He has narcissistic tendencies and a fascination with Fiona. He's a solid person of interest."

"Major case room," he said and motioned for them to follow. Ty and Owen were already in there talking and munching on chips. Selah was seated at the end of the table, nose in her laptop and chomping gum like a cow chewed cud.

Asa grabbed a marker and went to a fresh board. "We can easily connect Daniel Osborn and Trent Barton to the victims. However, they have solid alibis for Kacie." He paused. It ached like a stabbing wound to voice her name, knowing she was gone. Instead of falling to pieces, he pushed forward. Shutting down wasn't helpful to anyone, including his sister.

"Did you have any hits on the corpse in Alan Minton's hidden pantry?"

"Unfortunately, no." Selah removed her glasses and rubbed her eyes. "No dental records to identify her. She is of Asian descent. About thirteen years old. Most likely sent over under the false pretense of a job and a new life only to be victimized and murdered. Like so many girls, we'll probably never know her identity. But we know who Minton was, and he deserved what he got."

Maybe so, but it wasn't for them to play judge. There was a process.

He'd told Fiona he'd kill Rhyme when he got his hands on him, but that would make him exactly like the Nursery Rhyme Killer, bringing him down to his level. While hunting monsters, it was all too easy to become like them.

"What about Furman?" Ty asked. "I can't find any religious background on him. Dad died of cancer. He lived with his mom. Kept the family home. Violet says nothing looks updated."

"The house, unlike most in this area, has a basement." Owen pointed to the location board. "He's not so far outside the kill areas it couldn't be him."

"He didn't like seeing Violet today," Fiona said and sipped her coffee. "We caught him coming out of the office carrying a ladder and he nearly beheaded a teacher with it when he tried to duck us."

"He had no new information but he's sketchy." Violet added a honey packet to her tea and stirred.

Asa's phone rang and he answered.

"Agent Kodiak? This is Lucy Walcott from the forensic lab. We recovered trace evidence from your sister—so sorry for your loss, Agent."

"Thank you," he mustered. "What kind of evidence?"

The room went silent, everyone hanging on the phone call. He put Lucy on speaker and laid the phone on the table.

"There were traces of silica sand, limestone, soda ash and nepheline."

"Nice. Now to a bunch of morons like us…give it to us elementary-style, please."

"Fiberglass. Insulation. The kind you use in attic spaces, walls, ceilings. The pink stuff."

Okay, that was elementary enough.

"It was transferred to the vic—to your sister's neck and cheeks."

Asa clenched his jaw. He'd had his hands on her neck, his face against hers, meaning he hadn't worn the mask. Kacie had seen the face of her killer. The NRK *had* made a mistake. That might be a sliver of good coming from the evil that had stolen his sister. "Thank you. Anything else?"

"We got a partial print from her neck. We're running it, but no promises. Also, we've been doing some innovative testing using gas chromatography to analyze fragrances. We found some components transferred from suspect to victim. We can't tell you how long they'd been on her—we're working on that to create—"

"What did you find, Lucy?" His brain hurt. How were people this smart?

"Linalool, coumarin, vanilla bean oil, bergamot, tonka bean, musk. So we're looking at perfume. I did a little—"

"Shalimar," Selah said. "It's a handful of the components used in the making of vintage Shalimar." She sheepishly grinned. "I know from the Shalimar bottles at Jenny Miller's crime scene."

"Yeah, exactly." Lucy's tone was flat. Selah had stolen her thunder. He didn't care who got the glory as long as they got the info.

"This guy either collects it or he's in contact with someone who is wearing it."

"Furman's mom lives in a nursing home. He visits her. He's devoted to her. When his father passed he moved back in to care for her needs," Asa said.

"He was using a ladder today, too," Fiona added. "He could

have easily called for maintenance, but he's clearly capable and handy with fixing things. Possibly does side work often. Even if his own home hasn't been updated, we haven't seen all of it. Like the basement."

Furman. Fit the profile. "It's enough to get a warrant."

Ty chuckled. "It's a stretch, but you and I both know you're going to ask Judge Watley and she's going to give it to you because she's sweet on you."

"I plead the Fifth." He smirked. It was true. Plus, Fiona had been harmed and that would help push it through. "I want to see what's in his bedroom and his basement."

"And his medicine cabinet," Violet added. "If he's on antidepressants, antipsychotics, that will help put a nail in his coffin."

"Selah, dig harder on Daniel Osborn. Especially during the time frame he attended Hope Community and Abundant Life. Find pictures with Robert Williams. Owen, you go see Tanya this time and take a photo of Daniel. See what she says about him." He stood. "Ty, go back to All Star painting and take Fiona. Talk to the manager again and any employees who may have been doing a paint job in an attic or where he might have done work to get insulation on his skin within the twenty-four-to-forty-eight-hour period prior to Kacie's death."

Daniel didn't strike him as blue-collar. But looks could be deceiving. He'd have Selah work the Rathbone angle. He didn't trust Owen not to snitch. Later, he'd tell Fiona. When he was more prayed up.

"Violet, you're with me at Furman's." Once they got the warrant.

Chapter Sixteen

Hours had passed since Fiona last ate. Her head ached and her back was well on its way to joining in the achy-breaky party. The sun hinted at dipping below the horizon and the temperature had chosen to remain unbearable.

"Who do you like for it?" Tiberius asked as he turned onto Poplar. "I like the assistant head of school."

"It could be no one we've come in contact with. We looked through the photos at Weinstein's crime scene. No one in the crowd was familiar. No one dumb enough to wear a hoodie or a low-fitting ball cap and large sunglasses. Rhyme's too smart for that." Fiona was still reeling over the fact the initial profile might be wrong. It was one crackbrained killer, or Rhyme did know what he was doing as far as the murders that were staged, but might not know about the others. Except...the bone. What was that all about?

"Why would someone place a bone of a possible previous victim in with a new body? That is if Rhyme is responsible for these single female abductions and murders." She'd been abducted. Girls had been murdered. A wave of nausea smacked her. Had she been looking at this all wrong?

"Showboating? He wants us to know—wants everyone to know—he's been at this a long, long time. Maybe the alter ego is sick of Rhyme getting all the limelight. He's been avoiding the police a long time, too. As long. He deserves recognition." He shrugged. "I've never actually dealt with DID cases before. I don't think many are even real."

"This one may not be, either. He could simply be toying with me." Playing cat and mouse all these years. Her entire life had been pressed on Pause while she spent it married to Rhyme. Cami and Asa were right about putting Rhyme first.

"Maybe." He pulled into the parking lot for All Star painting; only two other cars present. They exited the car and walked toward the small brick building with large tinted glass windows. "It's the door on the right. Nothing fancy."

No one was at the front desk. A half-eaten cheeseburger and some fries rested on wrinkly yellow paper. Someone was in the middle of dinner and the scent of a birthday cake or cupcake made its way to Fiona's nostrils. Her stomach rumbled. Tiberius grinned.

"They need a bell. I love driving people nuts ringing those things. They put them out but they hate when you ding them. Makes zero sense." Tiberius continued to ramble, but Fiona tuned him out and patiently waited.

About two minutes passed and the toilet flushed, then a man who epitomized blue-collar stepped into the hall. Paint splattered his navy work shirt. His name—Joe Pendergrass—was embroidered on the name tag. Late thirties, maybe early forties. Thinning hair. Bushy eyebrows hooded his coffee-colored eyes. His hands were rough and speckled with paint.

"Agent Granger—" his voice held a measure of surprise

"—what can I do you for?" He casually glanced at Fiona, a curious expression in his eyes. "Ma'am."

She acknowledged him but let Tiberius take the lead. He'd already built rapport.

"I need another favor. Can we get a list of employees who were working in areas where they might be near or have to move insulation this past Monday or Tuesday?"

He frowned and rubbed the back of his neck. "Um…yeah. I guess. Can I ask why?"

"Afraid not. We're not at liberty to discuss the case."

"Again, none of the guys here are murderers. No way." He plopped in the office chair and went to work on the computer. For a painter he had excellent typing skills. "We had three jobs going on Monday and finished up one. Tuesday we still worked on the other two and had two more. Dude, all of them could have been around insulation. Four were brand-new homes. One doctor's office—that one we finished Monday. And…a church's children's wing."

"How many men were on each crew?" Fiona asked. It might be easier to go through the guys than pick which establishment would have given them insulation.

"Six. Same six both days."

Six interviews were cake. They'd take the list then cross-reference to see if any of them had been on paint jobs connected with previous nursery rhyme crimes.

"We'll take that list," she said.

"You getting close to catching the guy?" he asked as the printer came to life.

"We hope so." She leaned on the counter. "How long you managed this place?"

"My dad owned it and I worked here in summers since I was seventeen. Took it over when he retired. Guess that makes me the owner, too." He grabbed the sheet. "Hot off the press."

Instead of handing it to Tiberius, he placed it in Fiona's hand, his finger brushing hers.

Subtle flirting. Not her thing. "I imagine you hear a lot of stuff being in people's homes, don't you?" she asked.

"Occasionally. They forget we're there. One time I had to break up a domestic dispute."

"Guy get rough with his lady?" Tiberius asked.

"Nah, she got rough with him. People do crazy stuff." He smiled at Fiona. "I could tell you some stories."

"I imagine you could."

"We could tell some tales, too," Tiberius said and shook his hand. "Thanks for the help."

"Anytime. But, again, no one working for me did this. I'd stake my life on it."

Fiona pushed open the door. "Well, we won't hold you to it, if you're wrong." She grinned and nodded then headed for the SUV.

A man wearing an old army jacket, in this heat, tattered pants and a ball cap approached. His face was grimy and he carried a cardboard sign letting folks know he'd work for food. "Any change to spare?"

Sadly, this was common. So many vets now on the streets. And there were those who pretended to be homeless. It was hard to tell. Tiberius frowned, but Fiona never could pass up someone in need. Her own grandfather had been a Vietnam vet and this guy wore a pin on his hat. She dipped into her purse she wore strapped across her body and fished out twenty dollars.

"Here ya go, man. Try to take of yourself, okay?"

"Yes, ma'am. Thank you, ma'am. You're too kind."

She nodded and headed to the Suburban, closing the door on the terrible heat.

"He's gonna use that to buy booze, you know."

"You don't know that. Everybody thinks that and it's not always true." She frowned and buckled up. "At least I did something." To make up for the time she'd done nothing. Twenty dollars wasn't even close to being enough.

Her phone rang.

Dad.

She'd called him after Kacie died. He'd been at the funeral and they'd briefly talked. And the invite to dinner came. Dread filled her belly. She answered. "Hey, Dad."

"Hey, doll. I was calling about dinner. Tonight?"

"Sorry." As hungry as she might be, work wasn't done. Not by a long shot. "I can't tonight. We're in the middle of an investigation."

"And you don't eat, Fiona Mary Kelly?" he asked, slight irritation in his voice.

"Actually, no. I'm not saying it's healthy, but it's true. I promise I'll get by before I head back to Chicago. Don't cook. We'll order pizza or go out." That way if she ended up having to bail, he wouldn't have cooked for nothing.

"Okay. I miss you. Be careful."

A pang of regret hit her in the gut. She loved Dad, but Colleen's death changed their family and distance had grown between all of them. "I promise, I'll come see you. And I'll be careful. Love you." She hung up.

"Families are whackadoo, huh?" Tiberius said as he adjusted the left vent closest to him. "My parents. Zealots."

That could simply mean Christians where Tiberius was concerned. "Yet you majored in religious studies but you don't like any of them. What's that about?" She wanted the attention off her. It was hard talking about family dynamics.

"Curious why people behave like freaks of nature over gods." The hard tone had her studying him. This wasn't about religion in itself that had him knotted up. It was the behavior behind it that tore up Tiberius in a way that had left him bitter. Someone religious had done a number on him.

"Mmm… You see your parents much?" She scrolled through her emails. One from Luke. She opened it.

Please don't hate me. I acted infantile. I know. Let's have dinner. Casual. No underlying motives. Call me. Reply. Something. I hate we aren't even talking. Watch your back out there. I worry about you.

Luke

Luke had been blowing up her phone and now resorting to emails. Luke was a complete jerk at times, but so was Asa. Asa would hate her seeing Luke, but she didn't want a romantic relationship, and Asa didn't get to dictate whom she had a meal with. Luke had been there when she needed to get space and helped her with a job transfer. He'd been the one to help her find an apartment and get moved in. His behavior had been inexcusable, but so had Asa's. She'd told them both that and received profuse apologies from both.

One dinner wouldn't kill her.

She texted him and let him know she could meet him for a late dinner tonight.

Where? he texted back.

She checked her watch. Asa would want to wrap up soon.

Your call.

Tamales? Blues City Café.

Tamales sounded like a dream. She texted him back she'd meet him around nine.

Good deal. I'll have us a table waiting.

"What's going on over there?" Tiberius asked. "Asa?"

"No."

"Well, I know you're not engaged in girl talk with Violet. How is that going, anyway? Living with her? What's her place like? I haven't been able to sweet-talk myself inside." He grinned and turned on his blinker.

"Why you want in her house?" Violet wasn't Tiberius's type. He dated nonserious, noncommitted women. He probably had a Tinder or Bumble account, or both.

"She's a curious person. I like puzzles."

"Then buy a puzzle of a house."

"That's too easy. Speaking of Violet, did she question you yet about the night you were abducted?"

"No." Having told Asa the truth made it seem lighter. Like she wasn't carrying so much of it. Telling it again might continue to lift that weight she'd been holding hostage. "She has weird techniques. They work, but..." She laid back her head and closed her eyes. "I'm tired."

"We're all tired, Fi Fi McGee. We're the people in documentaries who have shed blood, sweat and tears trying to catch these sickos. We don't get to be on the other end of the screen eating pizza, drinking beer and being entertained by serial killers. I had a girl at St. George's tell me she 'so wished' she could do my job and 'get in a serial killer's mind, it would be freaky cool.' And I thought, girl, you'd pee your pants and cry for mama."

True. Fiona had done both of those things.

"Somebody's got to fight it, though. I figure, maybe we're special somehow. Built to do it. Even if it does wear our bodies down and fill our heads with images we wish we didn't see." He turned into the field office. "I plan to go home and drink my day away."

She half laughed and unbuckled. "What do you think of the manager at All Star?"

"I think he makes bad food choices and is a messy painter." He held out his hand. "Let me see that list of employees."

She handed him the list.

He skimmed it.

"Huh. That's interesting."

"What?"

"Trent Barton worked both of those jobs. I thought he worked at the bar now." He frowned.

"He does. I guess he's still on with the painting crew part-time. But according to his tax records, he hasn't worked for them in a few years. Probably getting paid cash now for part-time work."

"He could have painted during the day. Mollie's doesn't open until five."

"But he was home a little after eleven the night Kacie was killed. You've said yourself he couldn't have done it, Ty."

It didn't make sense. What was she missing? He was popping up like fungus. She couldn't turn a blind eye to it.

Tiberius shifted in his seat and did a double take. "Uh, Fi."

"What?"

"We got another present, I'm afraid."

She snapped her attention to the back seat. Sitting directly behind her was a fresh bouquet of posies. Nausea swept over her. "Did you lock the Suburban when we went in to talk to the All Star owner?"

"No. I could see the vehicle."

But they hadn't been looking.

Her heart hammered against her ribs. "The homeless guy."

Violet's words came back to her about the killer inserting himself into her life even for brief moments.

"You think he was the Nursery Rhyme Killer?"

Blood whooshed in her ears and she clung to the car door to keep from slumping. "I do."

This was most likely not the first time he'd interacted with her.

And wouldn't be the last.

Warrant granted. James Furman was not home but that didn't matter. They'd leave him a notice letting him know they'd been there. Asa forced entry into the house. Spices from an early dinner, hint of cinnamon. Violet studied the chessboard. "No pieces moved since last we were here." She studied the littered mess. The BBQ bag still sat out.

Asa, wearing gloves, picked it up. Tom's—a little joint on Raines Road. The same place Ben said he and Jenny had met for dinner. If Furman liked their food it was possible he saw them together once. He entered the bedroom. Violet had been nosing around in the bathroom. A simple room. Dark colors. Water glass half-empty by the bed. Ibuprofen. A Fitbit. He dug through the nightstand drawers, clothing drawers, riffled through papers and odds and ends on the nightstand. Nothing ringing any warning bells. Nothing in the closet. No hidden compartments.

"He has Zoloft and Xanax in his medicine cabinet but that's not revealing. He could have mild anxiety or panic disorder." She entered the bedroom. "Anything in here?"

"No." He'd checked under the mattress, under the bed. Anywhere a person might hide things.

"Asa," Violet said. Her voice, small.

She held a silver chain with a medallion dangling.

"What's that?" he asked.

"St. Nicholas medal. He's the patron saint of children. Protector of children."

Furman had access to fiberglass material. Worked with children and had access to files and personal information. This medallion wasn't exactly singing his innocence. He missed work for "migraines" but he wasn't religious so he said. Why the religious medallion? "Can we find out if he had any side jobs with All Star or Minton Construction? If they paid him cash off the books they might remember the name Furman or there might be a second set of books."

"I'll get Selah on it and I'm heading down to the basement."

"I'm right behind you." His phone rang. "Hello?"

"Agent Kodiak, it's Detective John Orlando."

"Detective, how can I help you?" He must have something useful.

"We got a DNA match for the bone. Belongs to a Sally Ratcliff. She went missing seventeen years ago—she was fifteen. It might interest you to know that she attended St. George's. That puts her there with Agent Kelly and in the same grade as her sister, Colleen."

Asa's head turned fuzzy. "Blonde and blue-eyed?"

"No. Brunette and hazel-eyed."

Like Fiona. "When did she go missing? Prior to or after Fiona's abduction?"

"Three weeks after. Went camping with her cousins at Arkabutla Lake. She went for a walk in the woods and never came back. Someone wanted that bone found. Wanted us to know it's Sally Ratcliff. The question is why?"

"Does she connect at all with the current vic you have?"

"No. We've done an exhaustive search and there's no connection between the body of Allie Walker and Sally Ratcliff. I don't believe the rope used to kill my vic and your vics is coincidence. Not with the connection between Ratcliff, your agent and her sister. The person who killed Allie Walker, and probably Sally Ratcliff, as well as your nursery rhyme vics, is one and the same."

Asa was becoming a believer himself.

Where did the bone fit in? "I'll get my team looking into Sally Ratcliff. Let me know what you find and I'll do the same."

"Sounds like a plan. And we're keeping the bone from the press for now. I don't think it's smart to have that out there yet. Gut feeling."

"I agree. Have you notified the family?"

"Not yet."

Once the family knew she wasn't missing but dead, the media would, too.

"Do you want me to wait? They'll want to know, but a few more days wouldn't hurt." John waited while Asa debated.

"Could you give me seventy-two hours?" He wanted to talk to the Ratcliff family in connection to the first murders of the teenage girls before that bone was exposed—someone in the family might be their guy.

"Yep, then a family needs some closure." John hung up. Asa wasn't sure what to make of the situation. He made his way to the basement, where Violet was digging around.

"Find anything useful?" he asked.

"No. You?"

He told her about the phone call. "What do you make of it?"

Violet inhaled and closed her eyes. "Depends on the profile. If I'm a psycho killer without DID, then I want Fiona to know about Sally. She's key to something in the past, something to do with the first murders. Is Fiona holding anything back?"

Yes, but that was her story to tell. Asa didn't feel comfortable divulging what had been told in confidence. "I guess you'll have to ask her."

"That's an affirmative yes."

"I don't think it's relevant to Sally Ratcliff."

"No, but Fiona is. Same hair and eye color. And her sister and the other two vics are relevant—classmates."

"And if you had DID?"

"If I'm the primary and I'm a vigilante killer taking lives of those who have hurt or are about to hurt children and I have no idea what my alter ego is up to—which happens to be abducting young women and girls, raping them and strangling them—but I somehow discover what he's doing, maybe through a memory. I see myself killing someone and it scares me. Because I didn't kill anyone that I know of, but I suspect he might be up to nefarious activity. Then I find a decayed body. I'm confused and panicked. I'd want to know who it is. Did I do this? How many times? How many girls? So in a means to an end, I take another life in the same way as what I saw in the memory and include the bone. Who better to find out who it belongs to but forensic experts? Then I'd sit on the news and wait. This bone might be significant to me."

The woman's realm of thinking was terrifying, but he wouldn't tell her that. She hated to hear it. More than likely it scared her, too.

"And if he finds out it's Sally Ratcliff?"

Violet peeled off her gloves. "Well, that depends on who Sally Ratcliff was to him. It could set off grief or rage. Both will produce more victims."

"Let's toss this idea out to the team."

Back at the field office, Fiona informed them of Rhyme and the latest bouquet of posies. He was too cocky. Too close. He'd never left her gifts before Jenny Miller's death that Asa was aware of. Fiona promised there were no more secrets between them. He was trying to trust her.

After laying on the be-more-careful lecture thick, they exchanged case information, everyone trying to absorb what was happening and how this bone might fit into the puzzle.

"Did you know Sally Ratcliff?" Asa asked Fiona.

"If I did, I don't remember."

Selah turned her laptop screen around. "This is her. Nothing to write home about but she has pretty eyes."

Fiona studied the screen, squinting. "She looks familiar… Wait. I did see Colleen and her friends hanging around with her a couple of times now that I remember. She seemed out of place. Cliques and all. But I don't think Colleen ever talked about her."

"I want Sally's old home address," Asa said. "Her parents' current address. Do the full victimology on her. Who did she hang out with? Talk to? Boyfriends? Personality. Talk to teachers, administrators and, heaven help us, churches. Can we connect her to any kind of painting crew, construction crew? What perfume did she wear? I want it all. First thing in the morning, we'll interview the family and friends."

"Have they been notified about the bone? That she's been found after seventeen years?" Fiona asked.

"We have seventy-two hours." He rubbed his temples. "Don't go back to St. George's. We can talk to old administration and get annuals either online or from her family. I don't want Furman, or Daniel Osborn for that matter, getting wind that we're looking into Sally. That her disappearance might connect to the Nursery Rhyme Killer." If either of them was the Nursery Rhyme Killer, he didn't want them to know they had an ID on the bone. They'd lose the upper hand if they had one.

Selah piped up. "I'll take care of annuals, clubs, organizations she might have been involved in as well as any other pictures."

"I'll take the old administration and teachers," Violet added.

"I'll work on locations. Where she resided, hung out, worked, even babysat, and see how many other missing girls there are around the campsite where she went missing. He may have hunted in Mississippi before migrating to the Memphis area." Owen loosened his tie and stretched.

They'd been burning the candle at both ends. The team needed proper rest and downtime to privately process the horrors they'd seen and heard in the last few days. It wasn't healthy to keep going with no stopping point—no quiet time.

"Let's wrap up. Start fresh tomorrow." He gave Fiona a knowing look. "That includes you."

"I am off the clock." She crossed her chest.

"You riding with Violet?" No longer was she under his direct protection, and after everything that happened, he couldn't keep her safe.

"No, my dad asked me to dinner." She flicked her thumb, and her neck flushed.

Liar, liar, pants on fire.

"Fiona, please don't work this case."

"I'm not."

Then what? She was clearly withholding information. Wait. Surely not. Surely, she wasn't going to see Rathbone. If he asked, he'd appear jealous and she'd get defensive. If he tailed her for protection and she caught him, she'd never believe it was the truth. Either way, he looked terrible and he didn't have hard evidence against Rathbone. He let it drop.

The team packed up and called it a night, but the fact she might be meeting Rathbone and he could be the killer drove Asa nuts. He ran to the elevator and raced into the lot, hoping to find her. He caught her at her rental.

"Hey."

She stiffened. "Hey."

"Where you really off to tonight?" So much for letting it drop. "We both know you aren't going to your dad's."

"You going to call and do a fact check on me now?" She didn't hold any anger in her voice—she was too tired. It was in the droopy right eye.

"No." He touched her cheek. "You're tired, Fiona. That means you aren't on your game and I worry. My sister was slaughtered—" he held back the dam of tears that wanted to rush to the surface "—and he's already come after you once. Been close enough to leave you tokens. My heart can't take... if something happened to you, I'd..." He worked the emotion through grinding his teeth and breathing. The loss of Fiona would send him into the abyss. He wouldn't come back from that one.

Her face softened and she tossed her purse in the car, then stepped into him, wrapping her arms around his waist and clinging. Not taking but offering comfort, and it was here he felt the warmth and security. How could such a fragile woman, though strong, make him feel safe? He embraced her, smelling her hair—coconut. He laid his head on hers and breathed her in.

"Don't go wherever it is you're planning to go," he murmured in her hair. "Come back to my place. Stay with me. I'll make you dinner. We'll talk awhile, maybe watch an old Hitchcock movie. Remember when we used to do that?"

She nodded against his chest.

"You'll be safe and I can sleep better knowing you're in the room next to me. Maybe we'll fall asleep on the couch together. Wake up with cricks in our necks." Many nights when they'd been dating that's how they'd fallen asleep. Occasionally, when times had been easier in their marriage, they'd unwind at night. No shoptalk. Only hopes and dreams and laughter. Sleeping in each other's arms as if there wasn't a prowling lion outside their door. Nothing lurked, crouched, or came for them.

It was Asa and Fiona Kodiak. Two people in love. Forever.

"That sounds so tempting," she mumbled into his shirt, her warm breath reaching through the material, heating him up. "But I can't, Asa. I have to go."

"Tell me where. Let me come. Let me in," he pleaded.

She peered into his eyes. "I have. I told you my deepest secret, Asa. I don't have any more. But I do have private things and that's not the same."

Wasn't it? If it wasn't something to be kept secret, why keep it a secret? But she wasn't going to budge. Deep down his gut warned him she was only trying to protect him from the fact she was about to visit Rathbone. Nothing romantic, but Rathbone might be a killer. She was the one who needed protection.

He framed her face, slid his fingers into her thick, short hair. Man, he loved her hair. "Will you call me when you get back to Violet's? Let me know it's safe to go sleep."

Moisture filled her eyes; she closed them and tears slid down her cheeks.

"Why are you crying?" Could he fix it? Make it better? Easier?

"I wish things... I regret... I don't know." She opened her eyes and sniffed, then inched up on her tiptoes and lightly placed a kiss on his lips.

Didn't matter she was keeping a secret or why. Didn't matter that this thing between them was going nowhere. He cupped the back of her neck and kissed her, falling headlong into it with hopes it would bring her back to him—to his place, where he could keep her safe. In the moment of this powerful kiss anything else she may have planned or wanted to do would fall away. For once it would be about him. Not killers. Not anything else. Only him.

A purr rose from her throat, sending a spray of fireworks off in his head. This woman had a hold on him and, God help him, she always would. But did he have a hold on her? Could they try to find their way back to one another? God was a worker of miracles. A reconciler. Anything was possible. She was pliable in his arms. Ardent. There was more than physical release in her kiss. There was heart behind it. Kindness. Generosity. And he felt certain there was hope in it. In this mountain-moving kind of kiss.

They could. Move mountains.

The one separating them.

"Come home with me," he whispered against her lips. No other reason than safety with one another.

She kissed him again and held his cheeks in her hands. "I want to. But I can't." Before he could say another word, she slipped into the car and closed the door. She rolled down the window. "I'll call you and let you know you can sleep. Maybe—maybe things will be different when we catch him."

He wanted them to be different now. He wanted to be enough now. In the middle of the mess. Because a mess would come again. That was life. There would be bumps along the way. What next killer or mountain would she place between them?

"Maybe."

He watched her drive away. He prayed for her safety and that God would stitch up his bleeding heart. He paused on his way to the car. A chill swept up his spine.

The road wasn't silent. It wasn't full with traffic, either.

He surveyed the perimeter. Couldn't see anything, but someone was watching.

The Nursery Rhyme Killer was watching.

And Asa had no clue where Fiona was headed.

Fury swept through Rhyme. He'd watched Asa Kodiak kiss Fiona as if she belonged to him. And Fiona. How disappointing. He'd deal with her in good time. When it was all said and done, she'd come running to him. Thank him for his graciousness over the years. She'd know they were kindred.

Killing Kacie hadn't taught Asa a single thing.

When Fiona had left his place for the lady agent's home, he thought he'd helped her see the truth. Asa was helpless. Powerless. He couldn't even save his own mother. Or sister.

But then this—this blatant act of disrespect for him. He'd punish her before forgiving her.

Naughty Kitten wanted to kill her. He'd tried. But Rhyme would never let that happen. Her life—and even her death—belonged to Rhyme alone. Naughty Kitten said he was protecting him, like he always had. Rhyme beat his fist against his forehead. He wanted Naughty Kitten out of his head. His words. He had to stop him from killing Fiona. Stop him from taking control.

He'd been yelling at Rhyme more often, demanding he relinquish it. Giving Naughty Kitten free rein meant losing Fiona.

But Rhyme was discovering Naughty Kitten's secrets. Naughty secrets. In the end, Rhyme would have the last word. Over Asa. Fiona.

And Naughty Kitten.

He'd silence him.

He had a plan. He only needed to keep his faculties. Stay in charge.

If he couldn't control Naughty Kitten, Fiona would die.

Chapter Seventeen

Fiona sat in her car in an open parking lot a block from the Blues City Café, weeping against the steering wheel. Asa's kiss had moved her with such tender force and surrendering power. Waves of hope—one after another.

Her crying wasn't because she'd kept her meeting with Luke private, but the fact that she couldn't deny the truth that she not only still loved Asa, but had also fallen all over again. The change in him showed her a new man and she wanted to know more. He knew her deepest secret, her greatest shame, and hadn't held it against her. But there was no clear way to move forward in a relationship with him. Rhyme blocked her path. If she'd gone back to Asa's, Rhyme would know. He was watching. And he'd retaliate. Fiona had to protect Asa, but in doing so it meant giving in to every one of Rhyme's whims. She hated that. Hated herself for giving him everything he wanted.

Herself. Her time.

How was she supposed to break free? It consumed her. And

because of it she hurt herself and Asa over and over again. It was unfair to both of them. She wasn't heartless or evil. But she was selfish. She'd tried to extend an olive branch, give him to Amanda. Keep him alive by letting him go. She'd tried to shine. But she had no light on her own or of her own. Instead, she'd kissed him again. Confused him. Confused herself.

Now she had to go in and talk to Luke. She appreciated his care for her over the years, but he had to understand that if she was going to be working alongside Asa, it was best if they had no contact. It disrupted the team. Disrupted her and Asa. He would be irritated, but understanding. She opened the lit mirror on her visor. Red, puffy eyes. Pale cheeks. But a halo of light enveloped her face.

Try to shine.

How?

She pinched her cheeks for color, wiped her eyes, ran her hands through her tousled hair. Asa had always loved her hair—the feel of it in his hands. She did a few seconds of deep breathing then stepped out of her car. The streets were sparse but the parking lot was full. The Redbirds game hadn't let out, nor had the show at the Orpheum. In the distance, she could hear the Carrie Underwood concert in full swing at the FedEx Forum.

By the time she left, there would be enough foot traffic to be safe. She hustled down the sidewalk and entered the Blues City Café. The smell of onions, spices and garlic sent her stomach into a divine spasm. Man, she was starved.

She looked around the joint but didn't see Luke. So much for saving a table. She settled at a table for two by the window to watch for him.

The minutes ticked by.

After about ten, she texted him.

Where are you?

Fender bender. So sorry, Fiona. Rain check. I don't know when I'll be done here.

She sighed and ordered tamales and a sweet tea. Might as well eat. She texted back.

Everyone involved okay?

Yes. My neck is gonna feel it tomorrow, though. I'll call you.

K

Great. She texted Asa and told him to sleep safely. Her tamales came and she dug in to the beefy deliciousness. As nutrients filled her belly, exhaustion sank into every bone. She drank her tea and paid the check. Violet didn't live far. Neither did Asa and the temptation to go back over there was intense, but it wouldn't end well. Or be fair for either of them.

The mugginess blanketed her as she set off up the block to her car. She passed a vagrant sleeping next to a building and bypassed a group of girls barely dressed. Then the area near the parking lot thinned out and goose bumps formed along her arms. Three of the parking lot lights were out. The other flickered. A horn honked in the distance and someone hooted. She paused and scanned the perimeter. Nothing, but the creepy feeling that the bogeyman was lurking persisted. Pressing the fob, she unlocked the car as a presence made itself known, but it was too late to duck and run.

A strong arm shoved her against the car and instantly disarmed her, slinging her gun across the pavement. A male, dressed in black, including a ski mask, wrapped his meaty, gloved hands around her neck and applied an insurmountable force.

"You're mine," he hissed and Fiona felt the sting of a blade nick her neck.

She bent forward to throw him off, but he was compact and yanked her backward toward the furniture store and away from foot traffic; her feet tripped underneath her.

Fiona couldn't breathe; his arm was like a vise around her throat, the knife now at her ribs. "Hold still." He hurled insults. "I'm gonna enjoy this. I been waiting for this. Not exactly my type."

She fought to keep from being thrown under the rusty metal stairs into the darkness.

He slurred another horrible name for her. Her heart raced and adrenaline fueled her flight-or-fight. She tried to scream, but his grip tightened and her call for help died on her lips.

She elbowed his ribs and he loosened his grip.

Inhaling a deep breath, she dropped to the ground and kicked him in the A-frame. He cried out and cursed; she kicked him again, then jumped up and swung for his face. Her fist connected with his nose and a crack sounded.

"You're dead!"

No way to get to her gun. No weapon. She did what she'd been training to do since she was seventeen.

She ran.

Again.

This time she had the muscle. The stamina. The speed.

She shot up Gayosa Avenue to South Main Street, pumping her arms. Not looking back. She ran straight into the Majestic Grille. The hostess's eyes grew to the size of half dollars as she burst into the establishment. Her purse had fallen in the parking lot. No cell phone. "I need a phone. Now." Fiona's creds were hanging around her neck. She flashed them to the hostess. "Federal agent. Phone. Now!"

Asa was going to have a coronary; he'd begged her to stay. "I thought it was safe to sleep," he answered in a half-sleepy, half-joking manner.

"I'm at Majestic Grille. I've been attacked."

"What?" His voice transitioned from sleep to awake in a beat. "I'm on my way. Don't leave." He hung up, and in about six minutes he blew through the doors like a hurricane. His eyes flamed like fire and his nostrils flared. "Are you hurt?"

"No." Not really. He'd nicked her and her neck stung, but she'd live. She didn't bother with an apology. He wouldn't want to hear it.

She followed him outside and into his SUV. "Details."

"I was meeting Luke," she said weakly. This is where it was going to get ugly.

His grip tightened on the wheel, but he said nothing.

"But he didn't show. He was on his way and got into a scrape with his car."

Asa pulled into the outdoor parking lot. They'd parked here often. "A scrape with his car. So you ate and left and were attacked."

"Yes."

"Fiona, I'm going to tell you something and it's going to miff you. I've been investigating Rathbone." He held up a hand. "Before you get defensive, hear me out.

"He's known you a long time. He transferred and secured you a job so you could be with him. He left six months ago and wanted you to come work the private sector, but you refused. So the crimes started again and you came. He hates me and always has. He has prowess, ability, skill to stalk, tail and be smart about not getting caught. He could have easily kept up with the investigation."

Fiona didn't want to believe a word, but Asa made a strong case.

"Tonight someone saw us in the parking lot at work. I felt it. Then Rathbone was late. Then a no-show. He had time to follow you. Let you go in and be here waiting."

"He had a fender bender. That should be easy enough to verify," she said. It couldn't be Luke. She didn't know him when she was seventeen, but he'd been born and raised in Memphis.

Asa called a buddy at the MPD who worked in traffic and asked for the information. "You sure? Okay, thanks, Bill." He hung up. "No report. No call to an accident."

The blood drained from her head. "Maybe they didn't call the police and worked it out between each other. That happens."

"Fiona, it's time to wake up here." He hopped out of the car, his flashlight looming. Fireworks from the end of the Redbirds game shot off, spraying the night with red and white. Asa found her gun and she grabbed her purse. "We'll leave your car here and deal with the tow or ticket later. You're coming back to my place."

She didn't argue.

Luke Rathbone. Rhyme?

"I hurt him. Maybe broke his nose." If Luke was Rhyme, he'd have the marks to prove it. He'd told her he was fine.

"Well, let's go check out his face."

"Okay."

"I assume you know his address." His voice held an edge. She told him. "He's got great security. He'll see us coming."

"Good. I want him to see me coming." He punched the gas

and didn't say another word the whole seven minutes to Harbor Town. Asa slammed the vehicle into Park and bolted from the SUV. Fiona jogged to keep up with his clipped pace. He banged on the front door and didn't let up until Luke ripped it open, a scowl on his face.

His face.

Fiona's knees morphed into jelly.

Bruising had already formed around his eyes; his lip was split and his nose swollen.

"Oh, no," she whispered and then she realized what was about to happen. "No!" she shrieked but Asa had already lunged for Luke and they landed a few feet inside the entryway.

Luke's head hit the tile and he swore, but Asa was relentless, accusing him of killing Kacie and hurling threats of violence.

Fiona yelled for him to stop.

Luke cursed and called him crazy, then punched him in the face. It didn't faze Asa.

Fiona didn't know how to stop Asa's blind fury or Luke's equal retaliation. She didn't have the physical strength. She dug through her purse, fingers fumbling until she found the whistle on her key ring and she blew with all the air in her lungs.

The shrill tone halted them long enough for her to break it up. "Luke, you're under arrest," she said.

"For what?" he growled. "What's he gone and done? Turned you against me?"

"The Nursery Rhyme murders, attacking me twice—"

"And the murder of my sister!"

Luke stood, his mouth agape, and then he had the audacity to laugh.

"So it's come to this, Kodiak. Trumping up murder charges to get me out of Fiona's life. Well done. It's imaginative. I'll give you that." He wiped fresh blood from his already battered nose. "But you, Fiona. I'm disappointed in you."

"Explain your face."

"I told you I was in a fender bender earlier." He rubbed his cheek and winced. "My airbag deployed."

"You said you would be sore and never mentioned abrasions." She didn't know what to believe.

"I didn't want to worry you."

He moved toward her, but Asa blocked him. "Don't you even look at her."

"I want to see your car."

"It's in the garage. I had it towed here instead of a body shop. Go have a look. You'll find the airbag deployed and scratches on the front bumper." He motioned her to go through the living room to the attached garage. "You know the way."

Asa didn't toss out a barb about it. "Go look, Fiona. I'll stay right here."

"Oh, I'm sure. You're loving this, Kodiak. And I'm gonna love it when you have to apologize. You have no proof of anything. This is all a jealous and juvenile ploy."

Fiona hustled through the living room, looking for anything incriminating. She moved into the kitchen and then into the garage, where she found Luke's Lexus in the exact condition he'd described. Scratches but no paint on the bumper. The airbag deployed.

Could he have done this after the punch to his face? Could he be diabolical enough to plan a fake car accident so if his attempt on her life backfired and she fought, he'd have an alibi?

She returned to the entry way. "It's like he said," she whispered. "No police called. Did she give you her name? Insurance information? Anything to back up this story?" What if he had purposefully hit someone to have an alibi? Then did the further damage when the night went south for him? The tamales might come back up.

"It didn't do any damage to her car. I told her it wasn't a big deal—because it's not—and to go on. I don't have any information, but I think her name was... Sandra? Sandy...? Sally? I don't remember. I was ready to call you and come home for some painkillers."

Sally? Was that a low-key but audacious admission?

Asa's cheek twitched, then he interrogated Luke for alibis for the nights of Jenny Miller, Kacie and Clay Weinstein's murders. Luke's answer was working late and he gave him names of colleagues who could verify that. But alibis were easy to fudge if you had loyal buddies willing to lie.

"Anything else you want, you can go through my lawyer. I'm done here. Off my property or I'll have you escorted off by police."

Asa hesitated then thought better of it and backed out of the house. Fiona stood inside the door unable to think straight. "Luke?"

"I didn't do this, Fiona. I would never hurt you. But him?" He pointed to Asa. "That's all he's done. Think about that. You should go," he said softly. "I'll forgive you. Tomorrow. You don't see clearly when he's in the picture."

Asa slung off-color mud.

Luke returned it, then closed the door.

"He did it, Fi. He did it." He spit blood from his mouth and glared at the front door. "We have to prove it."

Fiona directed him to the car. How? "Let's get some ice on that fat lip."

Asa had a lot of repenting to do. Once again, his temper had stolen the best of him and he'd worked so hard to bring that bad habit into submission. But when he'd seen Rathbone's injured face, all Asa saw in his mind was Kacie's throat being slit, the fear she must have felt. He saw Fiona as a girl running from this sick jerk and hiding in a tree, urinating on herself in terror. He'd lost complete control of his faculties and his tongue. His pastor would say to give himself grace, that no one was perfect. But he wanted Fiona to continue seeing the changes she'd admitted to noticing earlier. Now he'd messed it up.

Hopefully, God wouldn't hold it against him or Fiona. No, He wouldn't. That wasn't who God was.

One of the early Scriptures he'd memorized was about vengeance belonging to God. Could he forgive Rathbone for making his life and the lives of those he loved complete and utter torture?

Last night, he'd slept maybe three hours and they were fitful. This morning, he'd made coffee and he and Fiona had drunk a cup in silence. No eggs. No laughing. He'd dropped her at Violet's for a shower and change of clothes. Violet hadn't said a word when he explained everything—just walked into her room muttering about pulling triggers.

Now it was almost lunchtime. They'd chased leads and he'd talked to Amanda about Luke Rathbone and his suspicions. She promised to talk to John Orlando and if Rathbone connected to Allie Walker—his vic—in any way, she would call him. They'd let a little silence filter through the phone. His was loaded with regret. Amanda deserved a better man, who had a whole heart to offer. Asa thought at the time he'd been ready to move forward in a relationship. He'd been wrong.

After talking with her, he and the team had done the victimology on Sally Ratcliff. Violet and Ty had gone out to talk to her family. Parents were now divorced. Dad lived in Collierville. Mom had moved to West Memphis, Arkansas. The sister lived in Southaven, Mississippi. He was waiting for an update from them. Fiona knocked on his office door while peeping her head inside. "I know you have your sights set on

Luke. I'm not fighting you on it, but he's alibiing out and we still have other viable suspects. I want to question Furman."

She was right. They had to track all the leads. "Have him come in. Do it here."

Fiona nodded. "Asa, I'm sorry. I really am. Guess I keep apologizing, too. But I didn't know you suspected him."

"If you had, would you have gone anyway? Questioned him? Used yourself as bait? Been reckless regardless?"

She averted her gaze from him.

"That's what I thought." She would have done all those things. Even after Kacie had been murdered because Rhyme was her main priority. Not Asa or his feelings.

She turned her head at a noise. "Tiberius and Violet are back."

Asa grabbed his coffee and entered the office area. "Conference room."

"You got it, Michael Scott." Ty chuckled at his reference to *The Office* and headed for the major case room.

"He's in full form," Asa muttered.

"Yeah, and you didn't have to ride with him all day hearing it." Violet nudged Fiona. "I found my trigger." A small twitch to the corner of her mouth declared a joke.

Fiona snickered. "That'll definitely do it."

Inside the room, his team took their places around the table. Violet ran point.

"Mr. Ratcliff and Mrs. Ratcliff both said the same thing about Sally. She was a good girl. Quiet. Kept to herself. Didn't have many friends. A loner. They had no idea who might have taken her except they told the police about an older guy they didn't approve of her hanging around with."

Ty interjected, "The thing is, the sister said she was bullied a lot at school by some of the more popular girls. Caught her crying in her bedroom about it and she'd even threatened suicide."

"What girls?" Fiona asked.

Violet didn't miss a beat. "Josie Cramer, Sierra Donovan and Colleen Kelly were at the top of the list. Popular girls."

"But I remember seeing Sally with them a few times at school right before their murders. Why would she hang out with girls who bullied her?"

"Maybe they were using her for something," Ty said. "Maybe to get in with the older guy friend?"

The room was quiet, everyone coming to the same conclusion. Fiona had her bottom lip tucked between her teeth.

"Who was this guy?"

"Yeah, you'll love this. Our one and only Trent Barton," Ty said. "He was several years older than Sally, but he had access to her through his cousin, who the sister says was her only real friend. A kid who worked at the Ridgeway Country Club. Sister says Trent gave her the full-on willies and she told her parents he was hanging around. They forbid Sally from talking to or being anywhere near Trent."

If Luke could fudge an alibi then Trent could have, too.

"This guy keeps showing up on our radar. Go over his alibis again and this time push." Fiona caught Asa's eye. "I'm not dumping on your theory about Luke Rathbone."

"I am," Owen stated. "That's ridiculous. I've known Luke for over ten years. He's a pain in the rump, but he's not a killer. And I'd know if he has DID."

"DID might not fit the profile. One sicko killer might be doing exactly like Violet said. Push her and pull her back. Right?" He waited impatiently for Violet's confirmation.

"It's true."

"Besides we can clear this up easily. Selah, run whatever hoodoo you do to find out if Luke had any connection to the Ratcliff family or the Ridgeway Country Club." Owen crossed his arms, satisfied at his argument.

Asa growled and tossed his hands in the air, then called John to get a copy of Sally Ratcliff's files. A few minutes later he had a digital copy.

"Hmm… Trent Barton was questioned in her disappearance. He has an alibi. Imagine that. The day of Sally's disappearance he was with his grandmother." He paused. "Wait a minute. Trent Barton's grandmother is Ellen Fontaine-Winslow. He lives with her? How did I miss that?"

He'd missed a lot of information that happened over the course of Kacie's murder.

Fiona held up the report. "The Woodruff-Fontaine mansion. Directly across the street from Mollie Fontaine Lounge, where Trent Barton works."

This shed new light. "If he had DID, they'd want to keep him close—maybe he couldn't keep the other jobs so they threw him a bone at the lounge. A high society family like that and Grandma being up in age wouldn't have the same mindset toward mental illness as our more progressive culture." Old-school ways said pull up the bootstraps and snap out of it. They didn't think meds were much needed and saw mental illness as weakness and an embarrassment.

"Fiona, did you ever visit the Ridgeway Country Club as a teenager?" Violet asked.

Fiona slowly nodded. "I went there to pick up Colleen and her friends. Josie, I think had a membership. I had to go in and look for them a few times, but I never hung out or swam in the pool."

"So if Trent Barton was there with his cousin—who I want to talk to—then he might have set sights on Colleen and the other girls."

"And me."

Asa paused a beat. "And you." He scanned the interview notes. "Cousin is Cole Winslow. He was nineteen at the time of Sally's disappearance, but a sweet boy they said, so they allowed her to spend some time with him, but not usually alone. Trent Barton would have been..." He searched. "Twenty-four. Sally meets this older guy and it's exciting—"

"He's a good-looking guy," Selah added. "What? He is. Who says killers have to be ugly or even average?"

Ted Bundy was attractive to women, too. He brushed off Selah's remark. "Cole introduces her and then that's it. Trent's in with his charm. With her and her friends." Asa glanced at Fiona. "Did Colleen ever talk about an older guy?"

"Yeah. It may have been how she got the pot. She wanted to go to a party once but I told her no way because I suspected it was going to be trouble so I ratted on her. She got grounded and never went."

Asa slapped his palm on his forehead. "*That* time. What if the reason you got jumped in the pharmacy parking lot was to shut you up and keep you from telling again? You were taken to ensure the original plan went off without a hitch. You weren't supposed to be there, but fear that you'd keep Colleen and possibly the other girls away again meant having to deal with you, too. You weren't his type—whichever personality was killing blond-haired, blue-eyed girls. But you had to be dealt with."

Sally was the key to getting the girls to the party. "She must have thought they'd include her if she introduced them to an older guy who liked to party. Trent may have given Sally weed to entice them. They thought they were using her for drugs and maybe to get to older guys, but Trent was using Sally to get to them." Sally wasn't at the cabin that night, so why kill her three weeks after the other girls' murders? Maybe Sally knew too much and needed silencing.

They were close but missing a piece.

"Cole Winslow said in his interview that he saw Sally the Friday morning before she left. He stopped by her house—had permission. This is verified by the parents. She said she was going camping for the weekend with cousins and would be back late Sunday night. She never returned. Notes say he seemed genuinely upset." Violet laid down the notes. "We've proven that time changes people's story. After all these years, he might have a new one."

"Find where he lives now, Selah. In the meantime, let's focus on Trent Barton. Trent's mother is Andrea Barton. She's divorced and lives with her mother, Ellen Fontaine-Winslow and another sister, Mary Ann Winslow—I assume Cole Winslow's mother—in the Woodruff-Fontaine mansion," Asa said.

"Grandfather? Father?" Violet asked.

"Grandfather deceased. Suicide. Father moved to South Dakota after the divorce."

"A house full of women. Interesting. I'd like to talk to them." Violet picked up her purse. "Who's with me?"

"Me," Asa and Fiona said in unison.

Chapter Eighteen

Asa parked on the side street in front of Mollie Fontaine Lounge and ignored the paid parking. It was barely ten in the morning, but they wanted the jump. Crossing the street, they stood before the massive French Victorian mansion.

"I read some information last night about this place. It's five stories. Basement to tower at the top," Fiona said.

Asa looked up to the top of the home, a tower with round shiplike windows. Probably had a proper name. Looked like ship windows to him. Or big round eyes watching the street below.

"It's a historical landmark. They've been approached several times to sell to preservationists of the Victorian era. Make the place a museum like some of the mansions on the street, but the widowed owner refuses to leave. Says she'll die in the house like her ancestors before her and walk the halls even in death."

Asa turned his nose up. "She thinks her ancestors still haunt the joint?"

"It's not an uncommon belief." Fiona pushed the black iron gate that led to the walkway up to the house and it screeched open.

Violet continued to silently study the home. It did have amazing architecture and symmetry.

Asa rang the bell and waited. "Five stories. This could take a while. What do three women and one man need with this much house?"

"Who knows. It's gorgeous but it also freaks me out," Fiona said.

The door opened. A woman in her early sixties with sleepy dark eyes and limp hair, and dressed in athletic wear, appeared. "May I help you?"

Asa went through the drill, introducing them. The woman before them was Andrea Barton, Trent Barton's mother.

Asa explained they were revisiting old cases to connect to a new one. "Our earliest victims went to school with a Sally Ratcliff. Did you know her?"

She cocked her head. "No. Should I?"

"She was friends with your son and nephew. We thought maybe she'd visited your house at some point."

"I can't say. I've worked the night shift at St. Jude for over twenty years. I sleep during the day. I doubt she would have been at my house, and after the divorce I moved in here. And in a place this large, I wouldn't know. I'm sorry. Have you talked to Trent or Cole?"

"Andrea, who's at the door?" A stern voice with slight bravado carried through the old house and then a woman appeared. Taller than her daughter. Black hair pulled back in a severe bun. Sharp angles and lines giving her face a cold and calloused appearance. She reminded Asa of an owl. Round, dark eyes a little oversized—like the windows above. A small nose and a slash for lips painted in red.

"Mrs. Ellen Fontaine-Winslow, I presume." Asa stepped forward, threw her a smile but she didn't respond. Those owl eyes homed in on him and for a moment he felt like a mouse about to be swooped upon.

"And who are you?"

Asa went through the introductions again. "May we come in and ask a few questions? It's pretty hot out here."

After a slight pause, she motioned for her daughter to open the large stained-glass doors. They stepped inside, the original scuffed floor creaking under their weight. A winding staircase with red carpeting made an impression. To the right was what appeared to be a parlor and to the left an old ballroom. It didn't seem at all to be updated. Could she still have vintage gowns, an old English lantern, or old bottles of perfume as well? They couldn't get a search warrant yet.

"You can call me Ellen." Mrs. Fontaine-Winslow pointed to the antique sofa and tables. "These are all original to the house. I couldn't bear to throw it out and bring in such inferior quality furniture. They do not make good furniture these days. And I know the late Dr. Taylor would have wanted the ballroom to be preserved. You know he had exploratory surgery right here in the ballroom. His spirit lives on in these halls and especially in this room."

"Is that so?" Asa asked and tried to hide his skepticism.

"Oh, yes, my ancestors walk these halls. Especially at night. You can hear them moving around, shifting things and occasionally hear Mollie Fontaine herself, crying over loss—her first and second husbands and both babies. I've heard it."

Asa eyed Fiona, who was not doing a good job masking her skepticism, while Violet remained stoic, observing everything.

"Ellen, do you own any vintage gowns or Shalimar perfume?" Fiona asked.

"I am a wearer of Shalimar. But I can't say I have old bottles lying around. Who knows what's packed away. Are you here about collectibles?"

"No," Asa said. "Do you remember Sally Ratcliff?" He repeated what he'd said to Andrea Barton. Ellen scowled at him and addressed Fiona.

"I do not remember a young girl coming over. And I would not have approved of one so young spending time with grown boys. I'd question her upbringing."

Her grandson might be a serial killer. What did that say about her or her daughter?

"Come and join me in the parlor," she said, giving Fiona her attention. "Sit." Clearly she wasn't a fan of Asa. He nudged Fiona and she gave a slight nod. She would take over from here. He and Violet took seats on the short couch.

"Ellen, you have a lovely home. Spirits and all." Fiona knew how to butter up the bread. He held in his amusement. "Have you seen the news? The horrible nursery rhyme crimes?"

She stiffened. "Horrid."

"That's why we're so desperate to have any information possible on Sally. Are you sure she never visited? It would have been almost twenty years ago."

Ellen pointed a bony finger at Fiona. "My mind is as sharp as it's ever been. I'd know if a girl was in my home."

"It's a big home."

"I said, I'd know." This woman knew how to put a person in check. Fiona got scolded in a serious way.

"Yes, ma'am." They were getting nowhere.

"When Sally Ratcliff went missing seventeen years ago, Trent was questioned and he said he was with you that weekend. Helping you on a home repair project. Do you recall that?" Asa asked.

"I said my mind was sharp, didn't I? Of course, I recall it."

She shifted in her chair; her hand tremored and she tucked it into a ball.

Fiona leaned forward. "I've always been a fan of the Victorian era and this house has fascinated me since I was a little girl. Would it be possible to get a tour? I'd love to hear the history."

And get a good look at all the rooms, search without searching.

"We have many people who knock on our door and want tours." She stood. "I'm not a business. I'm a homeowner, but I'd be willing to show you around. Maybe we'll hear some of the ancestors milling about. One morning I woke up and found an old wardrobe had been moved across the room. Can you believe it?"

"Oh, yes," Fiona lied and they followed a rather spritely Ellen Fontaine-Winslow to the stairs.

"Keep to the walls. It's the original floating staircase and, well…we wouldn't want an accident." They climbed to the second floor as Ellen shared family history and showed them bedrooms. "This is Trent's room. Now, this room has strange acoustics. Can't hear a peep from in here."

Convenient.

From a light pink room, a woman in her mid-to-late fifties appeared. She wore a soft cotton gown and pale pink robe. Her dark hair reached her waist and her dark eyes darted between each of them. She rubbed her arms and Asa noticed what looked like a peculiar puckered burn on her right wrist. For the first time since they entered the mansion, Violet perked up.

"Ann, we have guests. You are not dressed appropriately." Ellen talked to her as if she was a child.

"My apologies. I thought I heard a noise." Her voice was childlike, a hint above a whisper. She clutched a porcelain doll to her side.

"You did. It was us."

Violet moved closer to Ann, eyeing the odd burn. "Do you remember if a young girl ever visited here? Twenty years ago. Sally Ratcliff."

She froze, her eyes locked on Violet. Suddenly, she burst into screams as she clawed at her hair and wrenched her body as if in pain. "No! No!" She pointed at Violet with a trembling hand and shook her head like a lion with prey in its mouth. "Make it go away! Make it leave!"

Hairs on Asa's neck stood at attention.

Andrea rushed to Ann and Ellen stabbed Violet—who stood unmoved, impassive—with a fiery glare, then she paused and looked closer. Her cheeks blanched and she gasped. "I think it's time you leave," she whispered. Ellen blocked Violet's view of her daughter.

"I'm not moving until I talk to her." Violet's icy tone sent Ellen back one more step, her hand over her chest, as if Violet was somehow giving her a heart attack.

"Violet," Asa warned. "She can't talk like that."

Ann continued her violent fit as Andrea tried to wrangle her out of the hall. Violet didn't budge. Asa gripped her arm and she begrudgingly stomped down the stairs.

"Thank you for your time," Asa said and he and Fiona followed Violet outside.

"What was that?" he asked Violet once they were in the SUV.

"That woman is a sociopath and I'd put money down that she has abused every one of her children and probably her grandchildren. And she smelled like vanilla. It was sickening."

None of that warranted a showdown with an obviously mentally ill woman. What about Violet set her off? "If we do go back, you don't need to be there. You put Ann Winslow in a tailspin. You have any idea why you caused her agitation?" Asa asked. "Why did she call you an 'it'?"

Violet remained silent then finally spoke. "I suppose when she saw me, she didn't see a human being. She saw a thing. A monstrous thing."

"But why?" Asa persisted. "Clinically speaking?"

"She's mentally ill."

"Did you notice the gown on her? Looked an awful lot like the ones we were forced to wear." Fiona shivered. "I got a bad vibe."

"I've had a bad vibe this entire investigation," Asa said and drove them back to the field office. They discussed the case and worked to narrow a profile that seemed to fit. Now that they'd seen mental illness in the family, they could lean toward a DID profile fitting Trent Barton. Either way, he was dangerous. Both personalities were killing for different reasons. One for pleasure and thrill, and the other as vigilantism—but there was a measure of thrill with the staging and means of killing. Both identities used ropes and that meant something. Was significant. The tough part was fitting Trent to all the crimes when he had an alibi. Same with Luke Rathbone. He fit the other profile—a demented killer messing and obsessed with Fiona. But he didn't fit in connection with the abduction of Sally Ratcliff.

"What about the manager from All Star painting? Joe Pendergrass?" Fiona asked. "He gave us a list with Trent's name on it. But what's to say he wasn't on those same jobs? He was as covered in paint as any other crew member. He could have easily removed his name from the list."

Asa hit the intercom button and asked Selah to check with the employees on the list about Pendergrass.

"Can we fit Daniel Osborn at the country club? He would have been midtwenties at that time and he has the country club vibe. He might have 'mentored—'" she made air quotes "—Sally Ratcliff like he mentored Lexi McMahan, Andi Fleming, whoever."

"Agents." Cami entered the conference room. "Mr. Furman is here."

Good. "Put him in the interview room. Fiona's coming." He stood. "I'll be watching."

Fiona grabbed a notebook and headed for the interview room.

The day had stretched out, the hours dragging by. Asa's neck muscles spasmed. When—if—this was ever over, he was making an appointment for a massage. Hope was ripe as they inched closer than they'd ever been before. And he'd been praying this time, which brought a measure of peace he hadn't experienced before. When he did wake from nightmares and images burned in his brain, there was comfort as he prayed and read.

He checked the time. Almost 7:00 p.m. No one had eaten. After this interview he was calling it a day. Tomorrow they'd interview Trent again in connection to Sally, and if his nose was jacked up, they'd know he'd attacked Fiona in the parking lot. Cat would be out of the bag if he had been a naughty kitty.

He checked his phone. Text. From Amanda over an hour ago. He must not have felt the buzzing.

Can you come by tonight @10? Let's talk.

Talk about what? He wasn't sure where he stood. He wasn't over Fiona, but it was over. And while he did have feelings for Amanda he couldn't press Play on him and her until they were sorted through. But they could talk.

10 is fine. Be there.

He walked into the viewing room as Fiona sat across from Furman in the interview room.

Furman's hair was in disarray, his beard bushier and his clothes rumpled. The guy looked almost as frazzled as everyone on their team.

Good. Frazzled meant easily rattled, and they might get some answers. Trent looked good for the murders; didn't mean he'd committed them.

Fiona was getting nowhere with Furman. According to him, the Saint Nicholas medal belonged to his mother. After her third miscarriage, she'd purchased it and then she got pregnant with James. She'd worn it faithfully until she entered the nursing home. He admitted to suffering from anxiety and insomnia but he laughed when they'd asked him if he'd ever been diagnosed with DID; his answer was no and he even offered them access to his medical records. Fine. Just because he'd never been diagnosed didn't mean he didn't suffer from it. His offering medical records meant nothing. Keeping her cool, she said, "James, you have no alibi for the murders."

He twiddled his thumbs. "That doesn't make me a killer."

"The last time we visited, you had a ladder in hand, which means you had access to insulation and could have fibers on your skin even now."

"Me and a million other men in Memphis. Proves I was changing out a ceiling tile."

"You have access to children's files."

"So does everyone in our administration."

If he suffered from anxiety, now was the time to ramp him up from twitchy to full-blown panic and see if he'd reveal anything telling. "You're hiding something. You have a chessboard set up and you don't play chess. You have a Tom's barbeque bag but you don't like barbeque not to mention Ben

Chambers said he and Jenny Miller had eaten there once. You easily could have seen them. Unless you come clean, we're going to keep coming for you. We'll disrupt your professional and personal life. Every time you turn around, we'll be there."

Furman wrung his hands, and a sweat broke out on his brow as he weighed his options. "I didn't kill anyone. But... I admit I knew about Jenny Miller's affair with Ben Chambers."

Ah, finally. Getting somewhere.

"I tried to tell you without actually telling you! I told you she was too personal." His furiously rubbed his temples as if a headache was coming on.

Fiona casually sipped her coffee. "Why didn't you come right out and say it? It was a crime and you knew it. That makes you complicit." A stretch but it might scare him into revealing more truth.

"I was not complicit!" He wiped the sweat slicking down his temples. "Look, I caught them in the library going at it one day. I confronted her—I did—but..."

"But?"

He removed his glasses and rubbed his eyes. "She knows I'm involved with a married woman—a teacher at the school. Jenny said if I breathed a word she would tell the woman's husband. She also said she was ending it with the student. I didn't believe that for a second. So I couldn't tell. The woman I'm seeing eats barbeque. Not me. And she's who I play chess with. I was thrown off the day you came in and I'd had a migraine, which leaves me foggy."

He made sense. "Why don't you take medications for the migraine?"

"Because they interfere with my anxiety meds and I need those more. I didn't want anyone to know I was on the anxiety meds. People might think I have no control over my life and it could affect my job."

"That's a stigma."

"Maybe but it holds true in some places."

Fair enough.

"I need a name. If you turn out to be clean then I don't see any reason her husband needs to know other than it's the moral thing—to tell. Secrets destroy relationships." Keeping back hers, and Asa keeping his, contributed to their downfall, along with a million other things.

All the suspects were keeping secrets. Pretending to be someone in public that they weren't in private. Even Violet held a tsunami of a secret. She looked toward Asa behind the one-way glass as it dawned on her.

All their victims had been pretending, too.

Upstanding property lawyer illegally buying a child bride. Crime prevention activist and real estate agent, pedophile. Grandmother who beat her grandchildren. A teacher and faithful loving churchgoing wife who slept with a student. A pastor who beat his own son. A leader in the youth department at church abusing a young girl.

This wasn't about protecting children or vigilantism at all!

This was about revealing the truth, exposing lies. A tale of two lives. The killer had been abused at the hands of someone who pretended to be light in public but was evil in private—this would motivate his killings. Over and over he was killing liars. Fakes. The irony was Rhyme also wore a mask, but he thought his doctor's plague mask was eradicating the diseased liars—none innocent or pure. Did he not realize his true mask was one of flesh? By day, pretending to be innocent. By night, the mask was his true nature. Evil. Dark. Murderous.

"A name, Mr. Furman," she insisted.

"Angela Patterson. She teaches biology."

Asa would be fact-checking it right now.

Furman might be off the hook, but Luke, Trent Barton,

Daniel Osborn and Joe Pendergrass remained suspects. After the interview Fiona met up with Asa in his office.

"What do you think?" Asa asked her as he gathered his belongings.

"I believe him." She yawned.

"I do, too. What hit you in that interview room? You looked at me."

She told him her reworked profile. "He's revealing true identities—dark ones—through the rhymes." No longer a vigilante, a protector. But a storyteller.

"Good call." He headed for the elevator.

"You want to get some food?" They hadn't eaten in hours.

"I can't." He scuffed his shoe on the floor. "I'm seeing Amanda."

Disappointment punched her gut. "Oh. I thought she put you on hold."

"She did, but she wants to talk." He sighed and lifted her chin. "I can't say I don't love you, Fi. A part of me will always love you, but I can't be on the back burner every time a killer or a difficult situation arises. You said when the NRK is caught things will be different. But that's not fair to me to always wait in the number two spot until things are smooth and then you have time to make me a priority in your life."

"I know. I know that." They were closer to catching Rhyme than ever before and Fiona had expected early signs of freedom and closure. Instead, she continued to feel heavy and burdened. Asa had freedom. Stress, yes. But there was light in his eyes that once wasn't. Yeah, he battled his temper and mouth, but there was something inside him that wasn't in Fiona.

Learn to shine, Fiona.

"Fi? You understand?"

"Yes," she mumbled.

"Are you okay?"

Not in the least. "I want to be." Catching Rhyme had been her equivalent of being okay. Of finally being able to breathe. What if it wasn't? Was it possible that justice didn't equal freedom? "How do you keep standing strong, Asa? I feel underwater, and every time I try to stand, currents sweep me away. But you stand, even with what happened to Kacie. You stand firm in wild waters."

"You know how I stand," he whispered.

His faith.

"Catching Rhyme won't bring you lasting peace. There will be another wave of darkness. In the form of a sadistic killer, a tragedy, a health scare. Your car might break down in this stupid July heat and force you to walk five miles in the noonday sun." He sort of laughed. "It's always going to be something. Life has proven that, Fi. I got justice with my mother's killer going to prison. I didn't get peace or any kind of lasting joy. I had to find that somewhere else. And so do you."

The pastor had spoken that morning she attended church of freedom. In Christ. That He was the only way to be set free. Nothing else she'd ever tried had worked. All she'd gained on her own was loss. "I'll consider it."

He clasped her hand, and rubbed it with his thumb. "Things can't be different without change. You gotta be able to let him go and find peace, whether or not we catch him."

They rode the elevator down and quietly walked to the parking lot.

Change. Asa had.

She hadn't.

Before she stepped out, she met his gaze. "I can't guarantee I can do that." She swallowed the tidal wave of regret and hurt. "You shouldn't have to spin wheels with me. It's my fault things fell apart with Amanda. If I hadn't shown up..." She bit back tears. She'd been selfish but the words she needed to say were like billions of needles tattooing her heart. Sharp, burning pain. But they needed to be said. "Amanda is a good person. Sadly, I like her. But it's hard to tell the only man you've ever loved to move on with someone else. Not telling you to is selfish of me. I'm so sick of being selfish." She lightly brushed his scruffy cheek with her lips. "Move forward, Asa. It's what we're meant to do. Those of us who actually can."

Asa's eyes welled with moisture and his jaw worked. After a slight nod, he got into his car but waited until she was in hers before he left. Instead of going straight to Violet's, she drove around thinking over everything Asa had said. About justice. Freedom. Putting him first regardless of what difficult situation or killer was in the way. She'd never done that. Could she? Would she? It would require change.

It might be time to turn a new direction.

But she was afraid. She was even more afraid not to. It was ruining her, eating away at her like a growing ball of tar covering everything good and her hope for liberty. She was exhausted and needed change. For herself.

She finally made it back to Violet's, exhausted and starving. She parked behind her and collected her purse. Violet wouldn't mind her coming in this late—she was also a night owl. Fiona had often heard her stirring around in the third bedroom. She used the spare key and entered the dimly lit living room. "Hey, honey, I'm home," she mocked, trying to muster some joy, but failing miserably. "Violet?" she called.

The house was too quiet.

A cold finger of fear crawled up her spine. "Violet?"

Maybe she did go to bed early, but Fiona's gut screamed a warning. She drew her gun, inched down the hall, past the room Violet kept locked 24/7 even when she was in there. "I don't do the jumpy-outy-scary thing." Ironic humor. Fear licked up her like flames. She toed open Violet's bedroom door.

The lamp on the nightstand glowed.

Violet was lying on the bed, unmoving.

Fiona rushed to her side, laid her gun on the side table and checked for a pulse. Blood covered Violet's face, plastered her hair to her cheek.

Please let there be a pulse.

A flash of white caught her attention.

The plague doctor's mask.

Fiona grabbed for her gun.

Felt a sting in her neck.

The last thing she saw before darkness was Violet's lifeless body.

Fiona fell limp into Rhyme's arms. "Easy, love. I got you." He caressed her face, ran a thumb over her bottom lip. "So beautiful. So pure. So real." He removed his mask and placed a gentle kiss to her mouth, the electric thrill racing through his blood. This was the only way. Naughty Kitten would kill her otherwise. "You're safe. You'll always be mine." He glanced at the other agent on the bed and studied her facial features. A pity. Without any more thought, he carried Fiona to his car parked down the sidewalk and laid her in the back seat, then stole one more kiss.

Just one. There would be time for more when she woke. He'd set the plan in motion. This time Fiona wouldn't be fooled and she'd see Asa Kodiak for the real man he was. A weak and helpless liar. Then she'd willingly be with Rhyme forever. He'd already packed her bags and put them in his trunk.

"We're almost home, love."

Chapter Nineteen

Fiona's eyes fluttered open. Groggy. She tried to rub the grit from them, but her hands were stuck. Her brain was fuzzy, her mouth like cotton. Why were her hands stuck? She smelled mothballs, must, vanilla. This wasn't Violet's house. Her place smelled like lemon.

Violet!

She was dead.

The memory of what had ensued earlier hit with a sudden force. She'd been abducted. Again. By Rhyme! She forced her eyes to open wide and after a few seconds of blurriness, the room came into clear view. Fiona was in an attic—no, it was narrower and more confined, and cold. Above was an open beam that led to a peaked roof, not flat. An old Victorian chair was propped in the corner. A few old boxes, a headless mannequin, an old doll buggy. There were two round windows mostly covered with yellowed paper. On a small rickety table, an old lantern burned. She was in a tower. Trapped like Rapunzel.

The Woodruff-Fontaine home.

If she screamed would old lady Winslow hear? Andrea worked nights. Ann—the woman in the gown—might hear. She shifted into an upright kneeling position and caught movement near the darkened back corner.

"Hello?" Fiona called. As she strained she noticed long blond hair. Then the wide eyes. Amanda!

"Fiona?" she said through a groggy voice and a wince.

"Yes! It's me. Are you hurt?"

"My head. I feel dizzy and nauseous. I think someone hit me. When I got home from work."

Fiona struggled with what felt like zip ties keeping her bound. "What time was that?" She wasn't sure if she'd been out for minutes or hours.

"Six-ish."

If she'd been knocked out at six, Asa didn't meet up... Asa! "What time did you text Asa to come over and meet you?"

Amanda shifted and winced again. "Text? I never texted Asa."

Cold dread sent a shiver through her. Rhyme had used Amanda's phone to lure him to her house. Where was Asa now? Was he alive? Tears sprung to her eyes. *No time to fall apart imagining the worst. Think!*

"Why do you think I texted Asa? Who has us? The Nursery Rhyme Killer?" She shifted and struggled against her own zip ties. "Fiona, where is Asa?" Amanda's shaky voice mimicked Fiona's own feelings. Fear.

"I don't know. He said you texted him to come over at ten. We left around eight forty-five." That gave Rhyme time to kill Violet, wait on Fiona then bring her here and get to Amanda's and lie in wait for Asa. "We're in the Woodruff-Fontaine mansion—the tower. It's the fifth level of the house. Andrea is at work, and I would imagine that Ellen's bedroom is on the first floor since she's up in her years and Ann would be close to her mother given her situation."

Amanda screamed, "Help! Help us!"

Nothing.

Using her core, Fiona stood and banged her feet on the hardwood, hoping she would be heard in this big old home. Ellen would only think she was an ancestral spirit moving about. If she heard anything at all. "Let's get down the stairs. Can you stand?" Fiona asked.

Amanda worked herself into a kneeling position and then into a standing one. "Yes."

Fiona paused. "The staircase looks narrow and steep. And dark. If you lose your balance, we'll both break our necks."

"Okay."

They slowly eased down the first round of stairs that curved into a second sitting area of the tower. It, too, was littered with antiques, trunks, an old spinning wheel.

"Keep going," Amanda hissed. Thudding sounded.

A door squawked open and hope deflated.

"I hear you, kitty." The same words he'd used all those years ago. Trent Barton wasn't masking his voice anymore and it sent a shiver down her spine. "Are you trying to make a break for it? Don't be a naughty kitty. Up!"

They had no choice.

He approached them with a large silver blade. Trent kept his menacing eyes trained on them and forced them into kneeling positions, then squatted in front of Fiona. "Last we talked, you asked me to do something naughty."

"I see you have," she said and nodded her chin toward his bruised nose, which she'd punched in the parking lot.

"You know what they say about paybacks. You'll get yours soon enough. I should have killed you ages ago."

He must be the alter ego. Rhyme didn't feel hatred toward

her. In a sick way he felt kinship with her. Could she get his alter ego to switch back? "Where's Rhyme? Rhyme doesn't want to hurt me. Let me talk to him," she coaxed.

Trent's sneer was nothing but contempt and disgust for Fiona. "I have better things to do right now. I prefer blonde and blue eyes." He raised up and started toward Amanda.

The missing girls. Blonde. Blue-eyed. Sexually assaulted. Strangled.

Oh, no. No. No!

"Wait! The bone! I have the bone. Let me talk to Rhyme." She was putting her life on Violet's profile—that Rhyme didn't know who the bone belonged to but wanted to find out, so he tucked it in with Allie Walker for the police to discover the identity. Whether or not Rhyme killed Allie was uncertain. "Rhyme wants to know who the bone belongs to. Come out! Come out to me, Rhyme. It's Fiona!" How did one force out a personality? She'd only seen things like this in movies.

He paused and came back to Fiona, squeezing her chin with unadulterated force. "What bone?" Trent didn't know what the other personality had done!

"Let me talk to Rhyme."

He grabbed Fiona by her hair. "What bone?" He cursed her and forced her to look him in the hollow, evil eyes.

"Your grandmother or your aunt is eventually going to wake and hear this, hear us."

Trent laughed. "Ann is too afraid to move or speak without Grandmother's permission. I could kill you right in front of her eyes. And Grandmother? Well...we have an understanding."

She quaked and worked to try and get the stupid zip ties off. Amanda seemed to be doing the same. "What kind of understanding?"

Keep him talking. Avert his attention from Amanda and keep her safe. Keep him from killing her, too. The more he talked with her, the more Rhyme might come out and then she'd have more of a fighting chance. He might even let her go again.

"The kind where I know her dirty little secrets so she lets me have mine."

"What dirty secrets? That she hurt you as a child? She wouldn't want high society knowing that."

"She's a witch!" He held out his hands. "Switched them raw for being bad. 'What have you done now, Trenton? You naughty kitten.' I'd be forced up here in this tower with no dinner. She thought it would scare me—being locked in here for hours on end—but she was wrong. I loved it up here. Loved the darkness. Aloneness." He spit on the floor. "Then she took the one good thing out of this house."

What? "Your grandfather?"

"What do you know about him?" he spat.

"I know he died by suicide. Did your grandfather protect you from her abuse? Did she drive him to it?"

Trent put his nose right against hers; she expected evil, horrid breath, but his was minty. Only a hint of cigarettes. Still she worked not to gag.

"My grandmother took a big fat rope and strung him up herself."

Explained why he used a similar rope—to exact punishment and kill like his grandmother—but he was lying. "How could a frail woman get a grown man up these stairs?"

"He came up here to escape her nagging. She brought him his tea. He drank it and fell out of his chair, asleep. I suspect it was laced with a sleeping sedative. When he fell out, she forced Ann to help her. I was on the second level and sneaked up. Saw it myself."

That's why she alibied him out in the abduction of Sally Ratcliff—and who knows how many other crimes he'd committed here under her nose. She said she'd know if a girl was under her roof—maybe she knew good and well Sally had been here. Trent knew Ellen's secret and held it over her. How sick was this family?

"I'm sorry you had to see that."

He laughed. "I'm not. It was freeing."

"Why did you take my sister? Josie? Sierra?"

He pointed the blade at her. "They came to the country club, flauntin' and tauntin' me. They knew what they were doing—"

"They were fifteen and sixteen!" Bile rose in her throat as she listened to his sick, twisted fantasy about the girls. "Why did you take me?"

That wicked grin spread across his face and he threw back his head and howled, sending a paralyzing fear through her. Like pure wickedness had filled his soul and screamed for blood. A wild, piercing blackness embodied his eyes. "You were a tattletale keeping those girls away. Couldn't have you doing that again and I had plans for you."

A noise drew her attention. Creaking of a door.

A squeak of the floor joist.

Trent frowned.

Asa! Asa could have found them. The stairs squawked and groaned under the weight.

Slow. Like someone not sure what might be up here. She looked at Amanda and she gave a slight nod. They might be rescued.

Trent paused and leaned over the wall into the stairwell. "I hear you. If you're trying to make a grand entrance, it's no use."

No fear. No worry in his voice.

The steps became faster, heavier.

Closer.

She didn't know who was coming, but she needed to get Trent to switch personalities. Now! "Please let me talk to Rhyme."

"Be my guest, Agent Kelly."

A shadow stepped into the light and Fiona gaped.

Blood drained from her head and her muscles pooled like water. This wasn't possible. Couldn't be happening, but it was. Over the years, she'd seen him. At her grandmother's funeral—he'd consoled her, if only for a moment. Her college graduation. He'd placed money in her hand and said she'd dropped it, but she didn't. He'd left her holding it. A gift. Over and again. More recently the older man at her college lecture in Chicago. He'd sat behind the Man Bun guy with shockingly blue eyes. Asked her how it felt to be in the hands of the killer—his hands. And at the Fourth of July event. She'd bumped into him and dropped her funnel cake. He'd told her, "Nobody likes to share." He'd meant he didn't want to share her with Asa.

And the homeless man.

Every time he'd appeared in some kind of high-quality facial disguise, but the smile—the teeth and the cleft in his chin. She should have known those had not changed. The lips that had once kissed her. How had she failed to recognize them? "I—I know you."

The profile had been far off the mark. Not a man suffering DID. Not even one insane man playing mind games with her all these years.

Two men.

Two serial killers working in tandem was less than one percent. Fiona had never once entertained the idea she'd been interacting with more than one person.

Trent Barton was the alter ego who had been attacking

her. Wanted her dead, and raped and murdered blond-haired blue-eyed women.

But Rhyme—the Nursery Rhyme Killer—was Finley Lamm, the maintenance man at St. George's who'd run interference in the locker room, had been changing the ballast in the ceiling and been very helpful. A man who easily had insulation on his skin that had been transferred to Kacie.

Finley slid a stray bang out of her eye. "Of course, you do. We've known each other seventeen years. And now we have forever."

How did he and Trent connect? How long had they been in killing cahoots and why?

"This idiot changed his name for you, Fiona." Trent wielded the knife in the air, his voice heavy with disgust.

Changed his name? Wait.

Finley Lamm was actually Cole Winslow! Trent's cousin. That's how the dots connected.

Cole. Finley—Rhyme. Why would he do that?

"Do you like it?" Cole asked, his eyes glazed with such wicked darkness she couldn't stand to hold eye contact.

Did she like it? Why would it matter? She remained silent, her mind reeling and her heart about to burst from her chest. She flicked a glance to Amanda, who was kneeling with a quiet calm, wary, but there was fear in her eyes. Rightly so. Cole might want Fiona, but Trent wanted Amanda. Cole touched her cheek and she fought not to wince, to anger him.

"Finn is a male form of Fiona. You and me are the same. And Lamm...well, you can figure that out, love."

"Give me a break, you idiot!"

"Stop calling me an idiot." Cole jumped up and faced Trent. "I am sick of you calling me that. I am not an idiot! I told you, if you'd be patient I'd bring you the detective and no one would even suspect you. I've done that. I've proven I'm hardly incapable! I am not weak or stupid." He sniffed the air. "Why doesn't it smell like her up here?" he demanded. "It has to smell like her when I punish!"

The vanilla scent—his grandmother's scent. "Like when she punished you?"

He kneeled in front of her. "Every day, she forced me into this tower. Not a drop of food for the naughty kitten who'd been born bad. But I hadn't been bad. I'd been as sweet as a little lamb, like in the rhyme."

Fiona swallowed. "And what was your excuse? Were you born bad, too?" she asked Trent.

"No." He grinned. "Or maybe. But I did what I got punished for. Cole only begged to come out and pled forgiveness for being born a naughty kitty. I tried to tell him to embrace it—be naughty. Idiot."

Well, he certainly had.

"I said, don't call me that." Cole shoved Trent.

Trent shoved him back. "Watch your step, cuz."

A sweet little lamb. Lamm. Lamm. Nursery Rhyme Killer. Nursery rhymes.

A name to match Fiona... Fiona Mary Kelly. Mary.

Mary had a little...lamb. Lamm.

Vomit hit the back of her throat as she played through the rhyme. Rhyme was her lamb, following her to school one day. The teacher—Asa?—turns the lamb out. But the lamb lingered there until she appeared. The children ask why the lamb loves her so and the teacher replies:

Oh, Mary loves the lamb, you know.

Her obsession. Rhyme had mistaken her thirst to take him down as love for him. So much, he changed his name—and also to hide his identity. Cole was the cunning one. If Cole and Sally had been friends, and she disappeared then it was possible Trent took Sally. Cole probably suspected then found the bone and wondered, so he killed Allie using Trent's MO and left the bone. It would all lead back to Trent. Trent's light bulb moment when they'd interviewed him last now made sense. He must have suspected Cole of setting him up to take the fall for the nursery rhyme killings and the other women if it ever came to it.

He wasn't weak or an idiot. He was diabolical. Calculated. No mercy. No kindness. He was volatile.

Cole was in Trent's face. Amanda sat quietly but alert, waiting for a chance to get free.

Another shove and Trent fell to the floor, his knife tumbling out of his hand. If she could only get it and free herself. She used her foot and worked carefully not to draw attention.

"This is enough. We got work to do." Trent wiped his mouth with his forearm, ignoring that he'd dropped the weapon. "Where's the package?" he asked.

"Your bedroom." Cole grinned.

Trent cursed and stomped downstairs. What package?

Fiona got the knife, and when Cole turned she used her foot to draw it up by her behind. If she shifted she could get it with her hands. Cut herself loose.

"You and me, we're going to be together now. I should have come for you much earlier but I've had to prepare. I packed your bags."

Fiona's stomach quivered.

"How did you do it? How did you know your victims' secrets?" She couldn't allow him to transport her to a secondary location. She needed him talking. Busy. Just a little longer.

"They're nothing but mask wearers and pretenders. Alan Minton—I drove the school bus and one day she was at the window when I made a stop. I remember thinking she should be in school. Then I saw him yank her by the hair and I knew. The voice makes it clear."

"What voice?"

"The one that leads me to my mission. The day I saw Grandfather hanging. Grandmother told me, 'Naughty kittens deserve to die. They shall have no pie.' And she was right. They do deserve to die."

She scooted forward as if interested in the story, gaining ground on the knife. Amanda worked and struggled but remained silent. Smart girl. Don't draw attention to yourself.

"I started watching, studying, following. Bigwig property attorney. Imprisoning a girl. Hiding her and his way of life."

"How did you know he killed her?"

"Concrete in the back of his truck. I slipped inside at night. I saw. And I unmasked him."

"Is that how you found out about Maria Windell? Kids on the bus talking. How did you know about the Shetlands?"

"Worked as a subcontractor for a little company that paid cash. We did an expansion job at Hope Community. I was working late and I heard him yelling at his kid for trying not to wear a mask. Poor kid. It was his father who was the mask wearer. And his wife did nothing."

And Trent Barton also worked for the painting crew that had done the paint job on the expansion. Another one of Cole's setups.

"Robert Williams?"

"Painting crew at Abundant Life. I caught him behind the youth stage—in a back room near the props, making out with that girl."

"Off the books?"

"No. I worked for All Star for a few extra jobs under my given name. I was interviewed. By Agent Granger. And I was careful to avoid him at St. George's when he showed up." His grin showed how proud he was of himself.

Tiberius never mentioned his name because Trent Barton

was lighting up on all sides, connecting to all victims, and one name meant nothing.

"And Clay Weinstein? You didn't have to force entry. Why?"

He playfully popped Fiona's nose as if they were having a big time. "I had an estimate for a painting job and was in the neighborhood. I told him I couldn't stay but a minute." His grin was wild and wicked. "I had my eight-year-old daughter with me. He opened the door right up."

Luring a sick man with a fake child. No, he was no protector of children. Through odd jobs and the jobs within the school system, he'd infiltrated lives and wreaked havoc. "We're together now. You can let Amanda go."

"I promised her to Trent."

Fiona looked at Amanda and she shook her head. She wanted to stay and help them both, but the best-case scenario was to get her out of here while Trent wasn't in the room.

Sally. Cole didn't know they'd identified the bone. And she was going to sit on that a minute, but she could keep him talking. "You killed my sister because of Sally Ratcliff, didn't you?"

"They treated her like garbage every day! She wanted to die from the shame, but she also wanted them to like her to the point she'd have done anything to be one of them. It was pathetic, but Sally was special to me."

Hazel eyes. Brunette.

"But you were kind to her. You picked her books up once at school after Josie knocked them out of her hands. I watched over you like I'd watched over Sally."

Fiona remembered that! She didn't know the girl's name, but she'd given Josie a talking to. Did no good.

"I'm sorry about what happened to Sally."

"Me, too." Sorrow pulsed in his eyes and then he kneeled

and cupped her face. "See, we're alike. We both liked Sally and you have the same eyes."

No, they didn't but she said nothing. If he cared for this girl like he cared for Fiona then Violet's theory was correct. When the time was right she'd use it to her advantage. When Cole learned of his cousin's actions it would cause a serious commotion.

"I know why you killed Kacie. And Clay. But why Violet Rainwater, the agent who I was staying with?" Her death was Fiona's fault and she'd live with that forever.

He bent down and pressed his mouth to her ear. "I couldn't kill family. Or maybe I can."

Fiona sat stunned. Family? "What does that mean?" She studied him. The smile. The lips, the square chin with identical clefts and high cheekbones. The hair and eye shape. Only the color was different. Rhyme had dark eyes and Violet had blue-green.

It was there. Similar traits. Had Violet known all along? How were they related?

"How is she…?" The door to the tower squeaked and footsteps sounded, slower, heavier. Trent cursed several times then he appeared.

Fiona's heart lurched into her throat. He dropped the package on the floor.

Asa.

The jarring brought Asa back to consciousness. His head ached where he'd been whacked. Amanda hadn't answered her door, but a text told him to come around back to the porch. He'd rounded the corner only to be ambushed from behind. His hands had been zip-tied behind his back, his ankles as well.

Muffled voices forced his eyes open.

"Asa Kodiak. It's nice to see you where you belong. On

the floor like the snake you are." A man with dark hair and eyes smiled. He seemed vaguely familiar. "Let me introduce myself." He gave a mock bow. "Rhyme. Or you can call me Cole Winslow. Or Finley Lamm."

How many personalities did this guy have? Wait. Finley. Lamm. That name registered. The maintenance worker at St. George's? As Asa's eyes adjusted, his whole world tilted. In one corner Fiona was kneeling, hands behind her back, and in the far corner Amanda was tied up in the same way. "Let them go. This is between us. You and I both know that."

Cole's fist connected with the side of his head. "You don't make the rules, here, Agent Kodiak. I do. Welcome to my kingdom."

Cole crossed the room and kneeled by Fiona, kissed her cheek. Asa's blood went hot and he worked his wrists to free himself, the plastic cutting into his flesh.

"I'm sorry it's going to happen like this, but you need to see the truth, Fiona." He motioned, and for the first time Asa saw Trent Barton.

What was happening?

Not one killer. Two. It all clicked into place.

Trent hauled Amanda across the room and beside Fiona. Both women on their knees facing him. Trent whispered in her ear and she shuddered but remained silent. She was his type of victim.

"Don't you touch her."

"Aw, that's so heroic of you." Trent wrapped his hand around her neck and squeezed.

Asa fought to break free.

"Make him stop," Fiona pleaded with Cole.

"Stop it. Enough. I told you what the plan was. Follow it." His tone was authoritative. Strong. He was in full control.

"Now—" he came around behind Fiona and Amanda "—I'm gonna give you a choice." Evil delight danced in his eyes.

Asa went back to age fourteen. Raymond Vect had said the same thing. No. No. He couldn't do this again. God wouldn't allow this again. His insides quivered and quaked. Sweat broke out on his forehead and his hands shook with adrenaline.

"Oh, I know all about you, boy wonder. The boy who had to choose. What was that like? Picking your sister over your mother and watching Raymond Vect slice her open right in front of you. Kacie knows what that feels like now."

"Don't you talk about my sister!"

Cole only laughed. "News media called you brave. I think we both know better. A better man could have done something about it. You were helpless. You've always been helpless."

Fiona shook her head. "No, don't you do this to him."

Amanda looked confused. Her mouth moved, but no voice. Prayer! But that wouldn't help them now. Or at all.

"You wear a mask of control. Power. But you're no different than Grandmother or anyone else I've exposed." He put the knife to Amanda's throat. "The new girlfriend. She's cute." He caressed Fiona's hair. "Or the woman you couldn't even stay married to. Because of me. How's it feel knowing that she chooses me over you? Even on your wedding night. She came back to me. I knew she would."

Asa wasn't in control. He'd never had control. "It felt horrible. It crushed me. It wrecked our marriage. You're right." Agree with him. Be compliant. Keep him calm and figure out a way to save them all.

Fiona held Asa's gaze.

"Pick."

Asa couldn't do it. He ground his teeth, worked on the zip ties.

"It's okay," Amanda said. "It's okay whatever you do, Asa. I know where I'm going."

Fiona remained silent.

What he hadn't asked with Raymond he'd ask with Cole. Hope for a shot. God, help him. "Would you...would spare them both? Please. I'm humbly asking you to spare them both."

Cole sneered. "While I appreciate your humility, the answer remains no. One of these women is going to die."

Trent snorted. "You always had a flair for the dramatic."

"Shut. Up!"

There was a rift between the two men. Could he play off that?

"Look, agent man, it really doesn't matter what you decide," Trent said, "I'm taking this little honey and he's taking her. Either way, you lose. He's toying with you." He shot a scowl to Cole. "I'm ready to get this done."

Cole's nostrils flared and he made tight fists.

The truth smacked Asa upside the heart. Fiona was right. Raymond Vect would have never let his mother live. He was toying with him like Cole right now. Asa had no control then or now. Amanda would be with Jesus and Fiona wouldn't. Even still, he could not sentence this woman who was special and sweet and kind to death. And he could not offer up Fiona. Not in any way. He'd be killing himself.

And that was real power. Real strength. Laying a life down. Christ's death wasn't a moment of weakness or powerlessness. At any moment during that bloody torture, He could have taken Himself down. But in dying... He gained victory. He showed His power and His strength.

And His love.

For all.

Asa had been trying to be powerful by protecting ones he

loved and failing. But to sacrifice, to lay it all out there…that was a true act of love.

The only answer was to sacrifice himself. He was the only choice. The NRK wanted him dead, anyway. Maybe in his death it would give Fiona and Amanda a chance to live—even now he could see Fiona had something behind her back, possibly a knife, and Amanda was still wriggling.

This was going to be it. He was ready.

"Amanda, I'm so sorry that all this has happened to you. You didn't deserve it." A mountain lodged in his throat as tears fell down her cheeks. She probably thought he was choosing Fiona since he'd done it twice since being with her. "I wanted to move on and I wanted to do it with you. I thought I was ready. I wasn't. Please forgive me. And I'm so sorry for what you're about to hear. I don't mean to add salt to the wound." But if he was leaving this world, Fiona needed to know the truth.

Fiona's face was a mask of calm and composure.

"Fi, God, help me, I love you. The moment you walked into that first class at Quantico, I thought I could marry that woman. All swagger and smart mouth." He laughed and choked back tears. "Marrying you was my greatest accomplishment. And leaving you was one of my greatest failures and heartbreaks. I want you to find—"

"We know who the bone belongs to, Cole," Fiona said, cutting off Asa's parting words.

"What bone is she talking about? She said that before," Trent boomed. "Have you been messing with my museum?"

"I told you to stay away from Fiona. But you don't listen. So I had to take matters into my own hands." Cole lifted the knife from Amanda. "You think I don't know what you've been doing all these years? Grandmother can call that banging and clanging ghosts, but I know what you've been doing with those girls after you kill them." He turned to Fiona. "They're all buried in the secret passage on the first floor. It leads to the old servant quarters. I could show you."

Trent moved a step. "I said shut up."

"They all have their driver's licenses hanging around their necks. But not the oldest one. So I had to wonder. If you'd go after Fiona...who else would you go after?"

"You were right, Cole," Fiona said. "Trent stole Sally from the campground and he had his way with her then he strangled her. Your Sally. And he'd have done the same to me!"

"It's not Sally," Trent insisted.

"It is," Fiona said. "We have DNA evidence. You can call John Orlando in Missing Persons and ask him. He's been holding off on releasing the information so we could finish our investigation. It's true. Trent betrayed you. You killed my sister and her friends for bullying and harassing her. You cared about Sally and wanted Trent to leave her alone. Like you wanted him to leave me alone."

Cole beat at his forehead. "You swore you didn't know about her disappearance."

"Every day she's been under your nose. You're a big, dumb idiot to him," Fiona continued. "But you're not. You're the smartest of the two." He perked up at that and smiled. "Yes, you've been clever and careful."

"I have. Oh, I have." His maniacal laugh sent a shiver down Asa's spine. Fiona was about to set off an explosion. It was there in Cole's red face and protruding veins, his short bursts of breath and tight fists.

"Trent, how do you think we found you? You're connected to all the murders. Rhyme killed Allie Walker—your type—in the same way you kill and he tucked Sally's bone in with it. That connects you to not only the nursery rhyme murders, but Allie Walker and Sally and the other bodies they'd be bound to find when they searched this house. You're the fall guy. You always have been. He planned it that way. Who's the real idiot?"

Oh, well played, Fi. If only Asa could get these zip ties off.

"I knew it!" Trent glared at Cole.

"You killed Sally!"

"Maybe I did." Trent's voice held entirely too much arrogance, proving he had no real brains and control. "I tried to get you to take her—to take this kitty—" He poked a finger at Fiona. "Why do you think I brought her to the cabin after the other girls? You needed pushed to embrace it—the darkness."

Looked like he'd embraced it just fine on his own.

Trent snarled. "But you were weak! Letting her go. Twice!"

"I wasn't weak. I strangled those little diseases who'd faked being so sweet and weren't at all."

"After I pushed you to." Trent looked at Fiona. "I tried to tell him you'd never stop hunting him. And then you really got close. I had to silence you."

He attacked her at her house. In the parking lot downtown.

He pointed to Cole. "He thinks you've made your life a tribute to him. That you're only trying to catch him to be with him. You approve of his unmasking liars—do it yourself. As if you are both in the same line of work. It's laughable."

Cole let out a wild, bloodcurdling cry and lunged for Trent.

Time to make a move.

Chapter Twenty

Fiona finally got the knife behind her; it had been grueling work to secure it without them noticing. Cole and Trent were in a murderous fight; the knife in Cole's hand fell to the floor.

Asa worked to break free. Amanda grasped for anything to help cut her loose.

"I'm almost out," Fiona hissed.

Trent had Cole in a headlock. Cole punched him in the gut and shoved him. He fell into Fiona and she almost lost the grip on Trent's knife. Cole grabbed his knife and when Trent reared up, he plunged it into his chest. Trent fell to the floor, gasping for breath, a trickle of blood running down the side of his lip. Cole snatched Amanda by the hair. "I said choose!" His voice was frantic, enraged.

Earlier Asa was going to offer up himself like a sacrifice, but that would have enraged Cole. His entire display tonight was to show that Asa was a helpless, powerless man who was fooling Fiona. He would have immediately killed him for any heroic behavior, and Fiona couldn't bear to see that. Pitting the two cousins against one another had helped give her time and cut their opponents in half.

She couldn't watch it now. "He can't!" she cried. "He can't because he's weak. I see it now. He can't even make a choice and it should be an easy one. Who would you choose, Cole?"

Cole tilted his head and frowned. "Fiona, you should know that I would always choose you."

"Because you sincerely love me. It's pure. But Asa, he says he loves me but won't choose. He's weak. I see it. I finally see it." She almost had the knife in a position to cut.

Cole raised his hands in a victory pump. "You hear that, Kodiak? She sees it. You've been unmasked. And now it's time to die." He grabbed a rope in the corner and hauled it toward Asa. Fiona worked frantically to get the stupid zip ties off, but she had to be careful so Cole wouldn't notice. Cole wound the rope, which was connected to the open beam at the top of the tower, around Asa's neck. No. No. "Up," he commanded as he grabbed a chair. Asa didn't move. "You get up here or I kill the girlfriend."

Asa obeyed and climbed onto the chair.

God, if You're listening and caring, then let him live. Let him live! Help me out of these ties. Help us all live.

Cole pulled the rope tighter.

"Tell him you love me, Fiona."

There was nothing she wouldn't do to spare Asa. "I love you, Cole. Since that day we met and you kissed me. I kept my eyes closed to protect your identity so no one could force it out of me. I never wanted you to get caught." It was all she could do not to throw up, but she couldn't get to Asa. She needed to stand up to cut free. Sitting kept her hands at an odd angle.

"You're going to die. Fiona and I are going to be together." He glanced at Amanda. "I told Trent he could have you but Trent's dead."

"No!" Fiona and Asa screamed but it was too late.

He raised the knife and plunged it into Amanda. Her eyes went wide and she gasped and fell to her side.

Fear blanketed Fiona. Sent her into paralysis. Like time moved in slow-mo, Cole kicked the chair out from under Asa. He had no hands to grab the rope. He was truly helpless.

Cole cocked his head. "Hmm… I thought I'd hear his neck break. Well, this will do, too." He clutched Fiona's upper arms and helped her stand. "It's fascinating, isn't it?" Asa's red face would soon turn blue. If his neck didn't break he'd die of asphyxiation. She had to move quickly. Occupy Cole to keep him from hearing or seeing the plastic break loose. The knife was in position. Right here, right now. In this moment all she wanted was Asa. Difficult situation. Death on the line. Nothing would or could ever come between them again. She'd already made the commitment to change. Whatever it took. Not for Asa, but herself.

"Let's show him as he dies," she said, biting back a sob, "how much we love each other. Cole…kiss me again." Nausea swept over her. Asa was dying, swinging from the rafter. Amanda was dead or near dead.

But she was almost free.

God, please! I can't… I need You. I need You!

Nothing was truer. All she could do was call on Him and hope for rescue.

"Fi—Fi," Asa gurgled, "Don— Don't!"

But she had to. No more scared girl in the woods. She was a survivor. A gush of strength and courage pushed into her body and a calm that made no sense. She placed her lips on Cole's and closed her eyes to restrain tears. This vile monster was kissing her. Enjoying it. She put pressure on her zip ties and they split. She shoved the knife straight into his gut, then raced for Asa.

Cole screamed a hair-raising cry and lunged on her back, cursing and threatening her. Above her, Asa had gone quiet. No more thrashing. She reached out for the chair, to pull it toward her, get it under Asa's feet, but Cole ripped her off the ground.

"You've been a naughty kitty."

"Well, so have you!" she hollered and charged him. A swift jab to his throat brought him to his knees. Fiona raced back to Asa and lifted him up as she drew the chair toward her with her foot. *Come on, Asa! Breathe! Oh, God. He stands firm in faith! Help him stand! Give him faith to firmly plant his feet on this chair and for me to get it under him!*

Cole was up, knife in hand, blood staining his entire shirt. She got the chair and haphazardly placed it under Asa's feet so he could stand, but he was slumped. Slack in the rope said he could breathe…if he'd keep standing.

God, let him stand and breathe!

Fiona dodged Cole's attack, but he came at her swinging. She grabbed a lamp and threw it at him. It connected with his head and the knife dropped. He rounded on her but she slid across the tiny floor and flew down the stairs, slipping and nearly falling all the way down. She had to lead him away from Asa. Cole was right behind her as she threw open the door to the third floor. She had two more floors to get down. Cole was on her tail, but hopefully slowing with his wounded condition.

One flight.

Cole hurled curses and threats.

Two flights.

She tripped and fell down the last set of stairs and landed on the hardwood at the first floor. Looking up, Cole was coming, clutching the banister, murderous intent in his eyes. Where were the women in this house? Did they not hear this commotion? Forcing herself off the floor, she scrambled to the front door and fumbled with the locks, then swung it wide open and shrieked.

Violet stood on the stoop, gun pointed right on her face.

She wasn't dead! But she was holding a gun. How did she know Fiona was here?

She was family.

No. She was in on this? She'd pretended to be dead so Cole could get the jump on Fiona?

Violet shoved her away and fired.

Cole dropped to the floor just before reaching Fiona.

Violet stalked inside and towered over him, her face expressionless, her gun aimed at his head.

"But we're—we're family," he panted.

He'd killed Trent and Trent was family, too.

"We... We talked about...this...tonight. We...are...family." The horror of what was happening showed on his pasty face.

"Then you know how easy that was for me." Calm. Quiet. Collected.

His eyes grew wide, fear distorted his once attractive facial features. Then his eyes went lifeless.

"Call an ambulance. Now!" Fiona raced up the stairs, Violet behind her on the phone. When she made it to the tower, Asa kneeled over Amanda, who had free hands and feet, and applied pressure to her stab wound. "Ambulance is on the way."

"Stay with us," Asa pleaded with Amanda.

"How did you get free?" Fiona asked.

"Amanda made it to the knife and cut me loose. Where's Cole Winslow?"

"I killed him." Violet didn't even have one tremor in her hand. "I'm going to check on the rest of the house. They're either dead or deaf." Was she truly checking or did she now finally feel she had the chance to talk with Mary Ann Winslow—Cole's mother? Was he her lamb, too?

Amanda faded in and out of consciousness.

"I think God heard me." She'd broken free in time. They were all alive and Violet had shown up in the nick of time. Fiona couldn't have orchestrated that kind of success.

"He's always heard you, Fiona. You didn't believe it when He didn't answer in the way you thought He ought to. But He's always heard and been with you. And me."

An ambulance squealed in the distance.

Asa held pressure on Amanda and prayed out loud.

Fiona joined in.

Three days had passed since Cole Winslow had taken Fiona hostage. He was no longer Rhyme. She'd made him too personal and he'd come between her and Asa and her family. The pain she'd expected to dissipate after catching him hadn't. Justice had been served. But Asa was right. Freedom from Cole had to come from somewhere else.

The last three hours she'd spent at New Hope Church, Asa's church, talking to his pastor about freedom. About being rescued. Saved. About what true peace meant and how to have joy in all circumstances. Her grandmother would be proud that she was taking some new steps toward faith. Whether or not Asa had lived Tuesday night didn't change whether God was good or faithful. She couldn't determine that by circumstances. Circumstances didn't always change.

That came through faith.

Once again the church had rallied and brought so much food to Asa's he didn't know what to do. Owen and Tiberius had put a hurtin' on an apple crisp by Vickie Carroll. They'd mentioned wanting to meet her and kiss her on the mouth for

how good it was. The last thing church people needed was
Tiberius and Owen kissing them on the mouths.

She'd scrubbed her own lips for an hour after she'd kissed
Cole. But the dirty act had turned out for Asa's good. For all
of their good. Finally, Fiona had closure. The freedom and
healing would come in time. And after today's counseling
session she'd learned it was okay to not be okay. But she was
going to be.

Amanda was stable. Asa had been by her side often over
the last few days and many church members had come to pray
and offer support and comfort.

While darkness lurked in the halls of God's house and hy-
pocrisy abounded, light also shined in people who were trying to live their faith the best they could. The bad had put
such a sour taste in Fiona's mouth, but seeing people rally together and love on her when they didn't even know her...
that gave her hope. Because it turned out hope wasn't out of
reach for those who had the courage to reach for it. It was an
anchor for the soul.

Fiona had reached out and grabbed on.

She was in uncharted waters.

But she wasn't alone. And she was going to learn to shine.
Not like fireworks, but a star.

The new question was what she would do next. The case
was wrapped up. Daniel Osborn had given several press con-
ferences with poise. Turned out he *was* trying to do right by
a girl he felt responsible for and knowing he would be connected to the victims and be a suspect is what kept him, at
Andi's urge, in the back bedroom. He'd had the moxie to
invite Fiona to dinner again. She'd declined. Someone else
held her heart. But she had no clue where that was going to
go, if anywhere.

Mr. Furman resigned from his position as assistant head of

school due to his immoral behavior in having an affair with
Angela. She, too, had resigned. Fiona had no idea if she'd
stay with her husband or end up with James Furman. Sometimes reconciliation was possible. Sometimes it wasn't. That
didn't mean a good future wasn't ahead if a person welcomed
it and changed.

Joe Pendergrass took their advice and was going to put all
employees on the books. Or so he said.

Luke really had been in a wreck and when he heard what
happened to Asa and Fiona, he'd come to the hospital. Shook
Asa's hand. Looked like he'd conceded. Asa apologized for his
behavior and while they wouldn't ever be golfing buddies,
they'd come to a civil closure.

She'd received a text from Asa about thirty minutes ago
telling her to come to the old house. It probably finally sold.
And that thought hit her with force. But then it would truly
be final. Nothing left to hold on to. Not their marriage, the
past, Cole Winslow. Fiona would collect her things at the
office—she'd left her bags that Cole had packed behind. He'd
touched them. She didn't want them. Tomorrow she had an
early flight back to Chicago.

Cole may have been her reason to go into law enforcement,
but he wasn't the reason she planned to stay. Fiona's love for
justice and to fight against evil gave her purpose, and it turned
out she was pretty good at it. Good had come out of all this
tragedy. Families would have closure. They'd found seventeen
bodies in the walls of the Woodruff-Fontaine house with the
driver's licenses hanging around their necks exactly like Cole
said, all wearing creepy white gowns that apparently belonged
to Cole and Trent's grandmother.

Trent Barton had taken Fiona's sister and friends, and Cole
Winslow had been in on it. Both had different reasons for
wanting to kill them. It had been a sick game. And they'd been

playing games with one another in a sick siblinglike rivalry all this time. Were they born or made? Maybe one of each? Fiona wasn't sure. It didn't matter. No one would be hurt by either of them again. As for Ellen Fontaine-Winslow, there was zero proof that she'd abused Trent and Cole now that they were both dead, managed to hang her own husband or that she had any knowledge of the bodies buried in the home—but she'd been adamant about her sharp mind and knowing who was under the roof. While she insisted to the police that the stirrings she heard were ghosts, Fiona suspected Ellen knew exactly what was taking place under her roof and that included the night they all almost died.

Ghosts didn't haunt the Woodruff-Fontaine mansion.

Pure evil claimed territory over that home—at least from the moment the Winslow family inhabited it. And when the crime scene was released, Ellen Fontaine-Winslow would move back inside and no doubt die there. As far as Ann Winslow, she'd rocked a doll in her arms and remained silent. At least that's how Fiona had found her. Violet hadn't mentioned finding her first.

Fiona pulled into the driveway behind Asa's truck. He must be inside. The Realtor lock was missing on the front door and disappointment leached into her bones. She loved this house. She entered and called out to Asa.

"In the kitchen."

Inside the kitchen he stood by the table in jeans and a T-shirt. "How'd it go with Pastor?"

"Good. Really good. How's Amanda?"

"Better. She has color back and her family is with her. She'll be back on the job in a few months."

Good. "Did the house sell?"

"It's officially off the market. Are you relieved?" He tilted his head, studied her eyes.

Was she? No. But she couldn't keep up payments. "I guess. I mean we're throwing money away. I can't stay here. I have a job in Chicago and a SAC who'd like me back."

Didn't matter that they loved one another. Too much damage had been done and telling Asa she'd put him first forever wouldn't hold water. She'd done that at their wedding. He wouldn't believe her and she didn't blame him. She'd messed things up too badly.

He closed the distance between them and held her hands. "What if an SAC here would also like you back?" His smile sent a loop-de-loo through her middle.

"At work or...?"

"I meant what I said in that house. Our relationship has been wobbly. Rickety from day one. It's caused some spills. Some cussin', but I don't think it's so far gone it can't be fixed." He released her hands and put his hands on the table and wiggled.

Nothing.

He pounded with his fists.

Solid.

"You fixed the table." Emotion clogged her throat and she covered her mouth with her hands.

"I fixed the table. And I want to fix us."

He wanted to trust her. Be with her. The house. It wasn't sold. It was off the market. He'd taken it off the market. A leap of faith that she'd come home. To this house. To him.

"I love you, Fi. I want to start over. Let's date. Let's get to know the new us."

"See if we still like each other?" she teased.

"I know you'll like me," he joked back. "Jury's still out on you."

She wrapped her arms around his waist and he embraced her. "Is that right?"

"Time will tell."

"And what about my job?"

"You always have a job here. If you can work for me. I'm the boss. The shot-caller. The Bear." He kissed the top of her head. "Besides, we're understaffed, anyway."

Her heart took flight. It could work this time. Things would be different. Dating her ex-husband. Sounded silly and a whole lot of fun. "I'm sorry for putting him first. Cole Winslow. For the secrets. No more of them. Not ever. I'm sorry for all the hurt." She peered into his lovely stone-gray eyes. "I love you. I've only loved you. It wasn't enough. I know I need something, someone—" she pointed upward and grinned "—to help me. Help us."

That was all he seemed to need to hear. His lips met hers. Nothing but a wave of love and hope and the taste of a future with a man who was devoted to her—to them.

He broke the kiss. "I figured you can live here alone. For now."

"We're going to make it this time." She'd bank her life on it.

"Oh, you better believe it."

★ ★ ★ ★ ★

Read on for a sneak peek at Violet's book, A Cry in the Dark, *coming soon!*

Chapter One

Ever the dutiful daughter, Violet Rainwater climbed the cracked steps of the sagging apartment complex, wishing someone would put her out of her misery.

Inside, the putrid scent whacked her upside the head—like the smell of assisted living centers, where residents were far from assisted. She entered the elevator and punched the grimy button for the second floor. She stepped out and curled her nose. Someone had attempted to cook, and the smell of burned toast and bitter turnip greens mingled with the stale air.

Fluorescent lights flickered overhead and hummed, signaling a ballast was about to go kaput. Her chunky boot heels clicked along the phlegm-yellow tile with dark flecks. Behind the faux wooden apartment doors, daytime TV and talk shows blared. An apartment on the left opened and an ancient woman with crags deeper than the Grand Canyon glared, cigarette hanging from her lips, the ash longer than what was left to smoke. Her housedress hung off her bag of bones and her white hair stuck out in random tuffs.

"Morning," Violet said, ignoring the burn in her eyes from the curling smoke as she strode past the woman.

"Yeah, what's so great about it?" she snarled and snatched her newspaper off a welcome mat with a sunflower.

Violet paused, turned and studied her. Nothing flowery about her. A woman hardened by life. By disappointment. Failures. Same face Violet would peer into three doors down. "You're breathing, aren't you?" she asked. Why was she even engaging with the woman?

"Barely." She huffed and pointed to her face. "I remember when I was young and pretty."

Violet had heard that one before. But surface-lookers didn't stick around long enough to go past skin-deep, or they'd see what she did when gazing long enough in the mirror. None of it would be defined as pretty.

Pushing thirty-six, she'd seen and experienced more than any person should in a lifetime and that was before becoming a criminologist and forensic psychologist then an FBI agent with the strange crimes unit.

Strange crimes were in her DNA.

"We're all worm food eventually," she quipped and carried on down the hall for the Monday-morning ritual she'd been enduring for the past two years; ever since she'd transferred into the SCU from the violent crimes unit out of Jackson, Mississippi, or unless a case had them out of town. The SCU south division covered the entire southern states and there were more bizarre crimes, many with strange religious undertones, than one might imagine.

And that kept their specialized task force traveling often. It had only been three months since they'd finally closed the Nursery Rhyme Killer case—a local Memphis case—and they hadn't been called anywhere since. Didn't mean there wasn't work to do, like review open cases and do mountains of god-awful paperwork.

Violet shuddered as she remembered that hot July night. The Nursery Rhyme Killer had gotten the jump on her. Her colleague, Fiona Kelly, had been staying at her home, cramping her style, and she'd assumed the noise had been Fiona. Otherwise, she wouldn't have been ambushed.

As he'd trained a gun on her, staring her down, he'd seen the same thing Violet had quickly recognized.

Familial traits.

He'd shown her mercy—let her live.

She hadn't returned the favor.

Violet reached apartment 12 at the end of the hall; her chest constricted and the ball in her gut tightened. Why did she do this to herself? Why did she keep coming back knowing it would never change? She'd lost hope before she'd ever reached double digits.

Grandmother made it crystal clear that she only tolerated Violet, and most days Mom wouldn't even speak or look at her. She rapped on the golden knocker hidden underneath the rag wreath with a welcome sign hanging in the middle.

Violet had never been welcomed here. Not in the apartment or in the lives behind the door.

But they kept letting her in, knowing she'd have money to give them like she did each and every month. Penance for being born and a strain on their lives. She swallowed hard and touched the hollow of her neck as her skin flushed hot. This feeling never changed either.

Grandmother opened the door, her hair recently set and her nails painted light pink. Neither Grandmother nor Mom made it past five feet. Violet towered over them at five foot nine. Got her height from dear old dad, too.

"Hello, Violet," she said, her voice identical to the late Olympia Dukakis.

"Grandmother." She entered the too warm, cramped apartment and set the Gibson's old-fashioned donuts on the counter. Mom's favorite. Plucking a white envelope from her purse, she laid the money on top of the breakfast box.

Mom sat by the window in her recliner. Petite and frail, her sandy brown hair hung in a loose braid down her back and needed a shampoo. Mom had never taken care of herself. Had gone weeks without bathing and days in the same old sweatpants and T-shirt.

Growing up, Violet hadn't understood what depression meant and all that it entailed.

"Hello, Mama," Violet said softly and sat on the burnt orange sofa across from her. "You having a good week?" She cocked her head and studied her. Nails gnawed to the quick. Pale cheeks sunken like craters and dark half-moons under her silver eyes. Sleep had been eluding her for some time. Violet remembered the screams emanating from Mom's room and Grandmother's calm and steadying voice to help her chase the nightmares away.

A nightmare named Adam, who had abducted Mom at only fifteen. Held her captive for eighteen months until she'd produced him a daughter.

Then he'd set her free. But Mom reminded her for years after Violet hit puberty and began to look like the monster who created her that she had been let go but had never been free.

Mom finally responded to her voice.

"It's Monday, Violet. Not much of a week yet." She kept her gaze focused outside, at the traffic leaving exhaust in its wake.

"I mean since last Monday. I brought you old-fashioned donuts from Gibson's. You could stand to eat."

Mom whipped her head around and glinted. "Don't tell me what to do. No one tells me what to do. And stop calling me Mama. I hate that."

Violet's insides shriveled and her lungs compressed. "Right," she whispered. All her clinical education and head knowledge about victims of trauma did no good. Not on her heart. Not when it was her own flesh and blood rejecting her. Funny thing about rejection: no matter how often it came it never got easier to handle.

Grandmother entered the room and eased into the recliner next to Mom's. Sandwiched between the plush chairs was a small table with southern-cuisine magazines in a tall stack and a half-empty cup of coffee. "Saw the news about a nasty killer the SCU caught in Oregon."

Violet nodded. Four divisions of the strange crimes unit covered the country, working with local law enforcement and other agencies. Oregon was in the northwest division. "Yep."

The silence choked her.

"You help with that?" she asked.

"No. Not my division and they didn't ask for assistance." She rubbed her clammy palms on her thighs. "You need anything? I brought you some money, but if you need anything..."

"We do alright. Always have." She arched an eyebrow. "When you weren't making trouble, of course."

Violet's insides flushed hot. She couldn't deny that truth. The fires she'd started, the items she'd stolen. The morbid fascination with death.

She supposed she was her father's daughter. Mom had made sure she knew that well. And it had become her motivation to enter law enforcement.

She would find him—Adam. She'd been searching for years. She needed to come face-to-face with him and see if it was true. Because she felt like it might be.

Violet might be just like him.

That one incident. That one girl.

But she'd had it coming.

"Of course." She stood and straightened her blazer. Mom was no help in the search. Grandmother forbade Violet to speak of that time. Mom never talked about him unless she was angry or coming out of a nightmare. She had very little to go on.

"I'll see you next Monday unless I'm traveling." She waited a beat. No one had anything to say to her. She nodded once. "Grandmother. Reeva."

Mom didn't wave or say goodbye. She never did.

Out in the hallway, she picked up her pace to remove her from the awful place she regretted visiting before she ever reached the parking lot. She punched the elevator button and when it opened, a blonde curly-haired kid bounded out with a grin, her mother already calling for her to slow down.

She ran right into Violet, her sticky hand leaving residue on her pant leg.

Lovely.

"Hewoo," she said, and her sparkling blue eyes peered into Violet's. Innocence. Goodness.

"Hello," Violet said, uncomfortable and irritated at the stain on her pants. But it had no comparison to the stain inside her soul.

"You're pretty."

The preschooler wrapped her arms around Violet's leg like a leech.

"Mommy says I'm pretty, too."

Must be nice, and it was true. The kid was cute. The mom, with an exasperated expression, threw her hands in the air. "Charlee!" Her smile was apologetic. "Sorry, she never meets a stranger."

Violet awkwardly lifted her leg, the kid attached, and motioned for the mother to peel her off so she could get going. "Might want to teach her stranger danger. Or she's going to end up in parts in someone's freezer."

The woman gaped and her face blanched. She scrambled to untether her daughter's tiny arms from Violet's leg. "Come on, honey." She gripped her hand and turned back to Violet. "Why would you say something like that?"

"Why not?" She stepped into the elevator and shrugged. "It's possible." Violet might have done the woman a favor, waking her up from a fairy-tale kingdom. There was entirely too much of a false sense of security in the world. No one thought anything bad could happen to them.

Until it did.

The doors closed and her phone rang.

Asa Kodiak. Special agent in charge of their SCU division and one of the very few people Violet would consider a friend. She answered. "What?"

"And a good Monday morning to you, too," he said through his grit-and-gravel voice.

The elevator opened and she hurried outside, escaping into the fresh October air. Third week in the month and it was only now starting to feel like fall in Memphis. "I don't have time for pleasantries." She frowned at her sticky pants. "I've had enough of that for one morning."

Asa grunted. "We have a case. We leave in an hour."

And that was why she and her entire team kept bags packed. Quick exits. "Where?"

"East Kentucky. A little place called Night Hollow. Though the sheriff pronounced it *holler*." He sighed. "Found three bodies. Female. In a cave. The latest victim is only a couple days deceased."

"Why us?" Where was the strange and bizarre? The cuckoo-cachoo that rang the SCU alarm?

"The victims' eyes have been taken, then sutured shut."

"So?" It was grotesque but it would fall under Violet Crimes.

"And a series of numbers have been carved across the forehead of the most recent body. From what I'm told it appears the other two vics likely had the same numbers applied. There were some nicks on the bones of the forehead and the coroner can see some remains on what's left of the second victim."

Ah. Now it was getting strange. "They have any idea what the numbers mean?"

"Not a clue. It gets worse, but I'll brief everyone when we meet."

"We flying or driving?"

"Flying. Meet at the airport in an hour. Not sure how long we'll be there. I told the Louisville field office that we'd consult and then go from there."

"Crime scene been released to FBI?" she asked.

"Yes. Louisville sent the ERT to process the scene and collect evidence. Bodies have been taken to the county coroner but the evidence will go to the Quantico lab."

Good. The emergency response team would be better equipped than a small hollow in backwoods Kentucky.

Asa huffed. "Media is already swarming. Dubbed him the Blind Eye Killer."

"Lovely. See you in an hour."

The back door into the kitchen stuck and he put some grit into it. He'd have to fix it. The fact Mama hadn't already ridden him about it must be a fluke. Nag. Nag. Nag. All the time. Every day.

"Sonny! That you?" Mama called in her high-pitched squawk, the tone like vermin scratches down his back.

"Yeah," he returned then muttered, "but I hate being called that and you know it, you hag." He entered the tiny kitchen, the linoleum fading and peeling back at the edge of the yellowed and dingy cabinets.

He laid a plastic bag with two foam boxes of food from The Cabin on the table. Mama's house slippers swished against the old hardwoods as she shuffled into the kitchen. "What'd you get?" she asked.

"Beans, greens and cornbread." He removed a box and placed it at her seat at the head of the four-chair table. But it had only been him and Mama sitting at it for more than twenty years.

After situating their food, he poured two sweet teas. She grunted and wrapped her bony fingers around it, her long yellowed nails clinked against the smooth glass. Her hair had been pulled back in a severe bun at the nape of her neck. She'd never worn it any other way.

Once he'd seen it spilling down her back. When he'd been spying on her and Mr. Franks who had lived next door. His daughter had been pretty. And Sonny had wondered what her hair would look like spilling down her back like Mama's.

Sonny sat across from her and she held out her hand. He instinctively clasped it and she blessed the food.

"Amen," he muttered and splashed hot sauce on his greens. Bitter like Mama. They ate in silence, the TV as background noise from the living room.

"What's troubling you, Sonny?" Mama asked, holding her fork in midair as if the good Lord himself had whispered Sonny's sins into her ear. "What have you done that needs forgiveness?"

"Nothing, Mama." Sonny's insides jittered and his pulse pounded. He couldn't meet her eyes.

She stood to her feet.

His stomach knotted, but underneath the fear and humiliation of a grown man about to be inspected, rage simmered. Mama slowly rounded the table, circling him and sniffing. Then her glint pierced his very soul.

"I smell her on you. The perfume lingers." With every syllable, spittle from her disgust dotted his lips and nose. "You've given in to temptation." She poked him in the chest.

Invisible ants crawled under his skin and his bones rumbled as he pictured picking up the vase of silk lilies on the table and bashing in her skull, watching her bleed out like a pig on the faded floor. A thrill zinged through his middle until the slap across his cheek snapped him back into the present with a sting.

"How many times have I told you? How many times is it going to take to teach you the lesson of morality? You rotten boy. You shall be judged."

"Don't," he whispered. He knew what came next. After his sins were found out. After she pronounced him guilty. "I haven't been bad, Mama." But he had. He'd been very bad.

But it wasn't his fault. He couldn't help himself. Couldn't stop himself.

Until it was over.

Then the shame and the overwhelming guilt flooded his system until the rumbling started. The rumble in his bones and the ants crawling under his skin.

It was their fault. Like sirens singing him to shore and ensnaring him.

"Get in the bedroom. Right this minute."

No. He hated this part. He slammed his fist on the kitchen

table, the glasses sloshing tea and the vase teetering. "You don't tell me what to do anymore! You can't make me."

She stepped into his personal space, her dark eyes boring into his, and he cowered.

Like he always had. Like he always did.

"You. Will. Take. Your. Punishment. Or you'll burn in the pit for eternity. Do you want to burn for eternity, Sonny?"

Tears burned his eyes and wet his cheeks. "No, Mama. Don't let me burn." Paralyzing fear overcame him, but he forced one foot in front of the other until he reached Mama's bedroom.

He knew the drill. Been here many times before.

It was time to face the wall covered in crosses, reminding him of his sins. Slowly, he unbuttoned his shirt.

"There, that's a good boy," Mama cooed. Her cool hand ran down his bare, scarred back. "This is for your own good."

"Yes, ma'am."

He braced himself as the dresser drawer slowly opened.

"Say it," she demanded.

He balled his fists. "Forgive me, for I have sinned," he whispered. "'Do not lust after her beauty in your heart, nor let her allure you with her eyelids.'"

And the first lash of forty to come lit his back up like fire. "Again! Say it."

Don't miss A Cry in the Dark, *Jessica R. Patch's next psychological thriller from Love Inspired Trade!*

Acknowledgments

It's true that it takes a village to raise a child and a book baby is no different. First and foremost, thank you to the late and "Great" Dorothy Ellen Smith for teaching me nursery rhymes, in particular "Wee Willie Winkie." I get the point now: Quit chattering and go to sleep!

My agent, Rachel Kent, who has believed in my work from day one and has worked tirelessly to make sure it gets into the hands of readers. I thank you for taking a chance on me and for the friendship we've developed over these many years.

My editor, Shana Asaro. It is a pure joy and pleasure to work with you. You have a keen eye and have made not only this book but all my others better than they began. Thank you.

The team at Harlequin for great cover art and publicity; I appreciate your hard work.

Susan L. Tuttle for your many years of friendship, brainstorming, and your incredible feedback on this story. You are invaluable to me as a friend and craft partner.

"Mr. Anonymous," thank you for tirelessly answering my

many questions about the FBI and helping me to make this fictional task force plausible. Anything I have stretched or missed is solely on me.

Thank you to the lovely crew at the Woodruff-Fontaine mansion for giving me a tour, answering many questions and giving me fun ideas!

All the readers who continually buy my books and share them with friends. You are why I write. I thank you for your support. Though I may not know you personally, I do feel like we're old friends.

My husband—you have made so many things possible for me and always supported my dream to write. You have eaten your weight in takeout and chauffeured me on research trips. Those memories and laughs, I treasure. Thank you. I love you. And to my children, who never mind the takeout!